Catherine Jones was in  her husband for twen adjusting to life in civv three children. Catherin ous novels for Piatkus, which was shortlisted f *Award*. She has also wr an army wife under the name Annie Jones, *Gumboots & Pearls*.

Also by Catherine Jones

Sisters in Arms
Army Wives
Gumboots and Pearls

Going Solo

Catherine Jones

PIATKUS

For more information on other books
published by Piatkus, visit our website
at www.piatkus.co.uk

Copyright © 2000 by Catherine Jones

First published in Great Britain in 2000 by
Judy Piatkus (Publishers) Ltd of
5 Windmill Street, London W1T 2JA
email:info@piatkus.co.uk

The moral right of the author has been asserted

A catalogue record for this book is available from the British Library

ISBN 0 7499 3199 X

Set in Times by
Action Publishing Technology Ltd, Gloucester

Printed and bound in Great Britain by
Mackays of Chatham plc, Chatham, Kent

This book is for Ian.
He encouraged me to fly.

Acknowledgements

Many people helped me with this book, some by supplying useful facts and figures, some by introducing me to those who could, but they all played an equal part in allowing me to gather the information I needed. First and foremost I need to thank the Commandant, Staff and members of the School of Army Aviation at Middle Wallop, who gave me endless help and time. In particular I would like to thank Sqn Ldr PL Miller RAF (Retd), who arranged my visits and who was unfailingly cheerful when I had to ring him up later to check my hastily scribbled notes. I must also thank Col NDD Thursby, Lt Col CS Wilson BEM AAC, WO2 J Ferraro, Mr DS Mallock and lastly Lt GJ Cheong Leen R Sigs and Cpl JC McLeary RLC (Cat). I must also thank the CO and members of 5 Regt ACC, in particular Lt Col Neil Moss AAC, Capt Julian Facer AAC, Capt Roo Pennell AGC, Cpl Julie Wiles QARANC, as well as Maj Mike Allardice RA for his time and information. I didn't just need help with information about helicopters, and in particular I am indebted to Dave Witton, a Citation pilot who was endlessly patient, good-humoured and helpful. As usual, the team at Piatkus have been tremendously helpful and in particular Gillian Green for helping me over a couple of false starts.

There were others along the way who fielded my phone calls and odd questions. They asked not to be acknowledged by name, but I thank them too.

Chapter One

It came as no surprise to any of the other potential helicopter pilots that Kate Hayleigh was the first person on her course at the School of Army Aviation to be sent solo – after all, she had been flying aircraft of one sort or another since the age of eight. As she watched her instructor walk away from the aircraft, she felt faintly smug about her achievement but had none of the elation she had experienced on her very first solo when the Chief Flying Instructor at her gliding club had told her to push off in the K21 glider and bring it back when she'd had enough. That day – her sixteenth birthday, which meant she had achieved the legal minimum age to fly a plane – she was on her own in the air for the first time in her life, although never in the past four years had the instructor in the rear seat needed to touch the controls. She remembered how she had found thermal after thermal, how she had climbed to four thousand feet, and how, to celebrate her freedom, she had looped the loop, not once but twice. She also remembered the CFI's reaction when she landed: he'd been livid that she had indulged in the unauthorised aerobatics and had grounded her for a fortnight after publicly bawling her out.

She brought herself back to the present and reminded herself that today she was being trusted with an elderly but nonetheless expensive piece of military hardware and not a wood and canvas glider, and that this was not a moment to show off but to restrict herself to a textbook take-off, circuit and landing. She waited for her instructor to walk clear of the prop before she wound up the power, checked the instrument panel and then commenced her circuit. As always, she got a rush of pleasure at the suddenly expanding horizon as the little Chipmunk soared into the air, revealing acres upon acres of Hampshire and Wiltshire countryside. There's simply nothing, she thought happily, nothing to beat flying. Her control of the plane, as she flew her circuit, was instinctive, leaving her free to concentrate on her radio procedure as she informed the tower of her position, kept a sharp lookout for other aircraft in the area and went through the pre-landing checks. She brought the machine smoothly round from the cross wind leg, brought her speed down to around seventy knots and then aimed at one of the fluorescent spots on the grass airfield that denoted the runway and brought her plane down on a perfectly judged and even glide path. At the critical moment she pulled fractionally back on the stick, holding the plane off the ground until it sank, feather light, on to the grass. She looked across at her instructor, standing at the edge of the big airfield, who gestured for her to go round again. Kate grinned and thought, brilliant – more time in the air. Given the chance, she would fly all day and not tire of it. She repeated all her previous actions and flew a second flawless solo circuit of the airfield, but this time, when she landed, her instructor indicated that she should taxi back to the hangar. A minute or so later, she reached her objective, where she shut down the plane's engine. She flicked the switches and listened as the engine sputtered and fell silent, then undid the buckles of her harness and climbed carefully out of the aircraft. She removed her helmet and ran her fingers through the short blond curls that bubbled round her face, and stretched like a cat. A fellow student, walking out towards her for his own flight, waved at her as he neared her.

'Hi, Matthew,' Kate said.

Matthew stopped beside her. 'Congratulations.'

'What for?'

'Going solo, stupid.'

'Oh, that.'

Matthew gave her a wry smile. 'One small achievement for Kate Hayleigh, one giant step for Matthew Grant.' It was said without malice.

'You'll crack it.'

'Maybe.' He shrugged disconsolately. 'Still, can't gossip

all day. See you later.' As Matt resumed his walk towards his plane to continue his flying instruction, Kate watched him go, acutely aware that he was on the brink of being chopped. The instructors gave the students ratings for each phase of the course: blue, green, brown or red. One red or too many browns meant going on review and then almost certain curtains. So far Kate had been sailing along on a series of greens and a couple of blues – the latter only given for excellence – but Matt had already got several browns on his record, and unless his performance improved considerably they all knew he was the most likely candidate to be put on review. Kate felt sorry for him, but they'd all known that, given the high failure rate for the course, some of them wouldn't make it. She was fairly confident that she'd pass, partly because of her previous flying experience and partly because she'd never failed in anything she'd attempted.

She watched him begin his pre-flight checks and then turned and made her way to the crew room.

'Congratulations,' applauded the other members of her course when she entered. There were half a dozen of them there, lounging comfortably on the armchairs round the walls, some studying charts, some reading manuals and some just drinking tea and discussing aspects of flying.

'Thanks,' she acknowledged. She added jokingly, 'Of course, they only allowed me to go solo because I'm a woman. Otherwise, what explanation could there possibly be for me to have been sent off on my own when the rest of you losers are still having to prove yourselves to the instructors?'

A ribald selection of mostly good-natured remarks filled the air as Kate left to put her flying helmet in her locker. As the senior officer, albeit only a lieutenant, and the only woman on the course, she was aware that she had a very high profile – a fact that was resented by one or two of the other trainee pilots, but which she rather enjoyed. In some respects it was cheering to know that pretty well everyone on the base, from the Commandant downwards, knew who she was. But then it also meant that she could afford to make fewer mistakes because every single one was noticed and commented on. Not that she did make many mistakes, she thought. And being the first on the course to go solo had precious little to do with being a woman and everything to do with being the most competent pilot. She slammed her locker shut and went off to find a telephone and share her happiness with her best friend, also an army officer.

'Hi, Maria. Is this a convenient moment?'

Maria recognised her voice instantly. 'Kate! Good to hear from you. I can chat if it's quick. We've got a VIP arriving in half an hour and I've got to meet him at the helipad.'

'Well, I'm just ringing to say that in a few months it may be me ferrying in your visitors. They've just sent me solo. I've a bit to do before they let me loose on helicopters, but I'm on my way.'

'That's terrific. I am so pleased for you. It's what you wanted, isn't it? Have you phoned your mother to tell her you're following in Daddy's footsteps?' A silence ensued. 'I'll take that as a no.' Maria sighed sadly. Kate knew that Maria disapproved of her ongoing row, but today wasn't going to change anything. As Kate obviously wasn't going to comment on the subject of her relationship with her mother, Maria went on, 'Look, I've got to dash shortly but I'll come over this evening.' Maria was based at the headquarters at Wilton, only a few miles away from Kate, who was at the School of Army Aviation at Middle Wallop, in the heart of Salisbury Plain. 'Will you be in the mess or are you planning to go out celebrating?'

'No celebrating proper till I've passed completely. I still need my wits about me all the time. There's plenty of time to get chopped.'

'But you won't,' said Maria confidently. 'If there was ever anyone born to be a pilot it's you.'

'Thanks for the vote of confidence.'

'No more than you deserve. And Kate . . .'

'Yes?'

'Think about telling your mother. I know you have your reasons for feeling bitter, but isn't it time to put it all behind you? It's been a long time, and she is your mother, despite what you feel. Doesn't she deserve better than this?'

Kate remained silent.

'All right,' said Maria. 'But please think about it.'

As Kate rang off she knew that she ought to do as Maria

4

had asked – to think about getting in touch with her mother – but could she really consider forgiving the woman who had been so selfish as to almost succeed in wrecking her daughter's life?

At lunchtime Kate returned to the mess, grabbed a bag of crisps and a pint of orange juice from the bar and went to the peace and quiet of her room. She propped her pillows against the headboard and settled comfortably on her bed with her feet up to mull things over. As she dipped into her crisps and sipped her juice, Maria's comments echoed and re-echoed in her head. Was her friend right? Maria knew her as well as anyone: they had been through army training together; they had shared secrets, experiences and even boyfriends. It had been a long time since Kate had joined the army and effectively cut herself adrift from her family. Perhaps it had been long enough.

Chapter Two

Kate and Maria had met as officer cadets at Sandhurst, where they had quickly discovered that they each had qualities and strengths that the other lacked. Kate, the product of an élite girls' boarding school and the only daughter of a high-ranking officer, was at ease with the discipline and much of the jargon, while Maria, who came from a large and boisterous family with a preponderance of brothers, settled quickly into the male-dominated environment and was able to act as protector to Kate while she taught her about holding her own in a macho world. Kate had been quick to learn about handling men, just as Maria had watched Kate at a number of social functions and had gleaned a multitude of social skills in return.

'So how come you are so good at all this small talk and social claptrap?' asked Maria after a drinks party at which Kate had once again proved her prowess at being able to talk to anyone and everyone and to appear interested in even the most boring of conversations.

'Oh, my parents were heavily into that sort of thing. As a kid I often had to hand round the nibbles at their interminable parties, and I suppose I picked up the knack of surviving the endless chit-chat by osmosis.'

'Any reason for all the entertaining?'

'My father was in the forces and was hell-bent on getting promoted – as was my mother.'

'What? In the forces?'

'No, silly. Promotion for my father. She was a professional wife.'

'Ah,' said Maria. It seemed to make sense.

Their days at Sandhurst continued and their friendship deepened as the challenges became harder, the workload heavier and the demands on their time near impossible. They cracked drill and running several miles without stopping; they passed kit inspections and room inspections; they began to understand army ranks and jargon; and they learned how to minimise their sleep requirements and to maximise their efficiency.

Then came the night of their first formal dinner, held by one of the male training companies and to which both girls had been invited. The dress for the female cadets was what they referred to as their 'penguin kit' – a long plain black skirt with a white blouse – and they both assumed that most of the others attending would be dressed in the male equivalent: dinner jacket. However, the peacock array of uniforms sported by the male officers who taught the cadets took their breath away. Maria was surprised at Kate's reaction, as she assumed that Kate was *au fait* with almost all aspects of the armed forces, their traditions and uniforms.

'But your dad is in the army,' she said, still bemused.

'No he isn't,' said Kate.

'But you said . . .'

'I don't think I was specific. I said he was in the forces.'

Maria's brow creased. 'I don't understand.'

'It's not difficult. My dad is in the air force.' Kate explained that although she had seen her father's mess kit, it was the same as all the other RAF officers': smart enough air-force-blue bum-freezer jacket and trousers, waistcoat, bow tie and gold trim. She had thought that the army would have its own version. But nothing had prepared her for the multiplicity of different outfits that adorned the commissioned officers, for each regiment and corps had developed its own variation on a theme. There were red jackets with high collars, green jackets with frogging, and black jackets with red facings, while the female officers wore elegant gold gowns with green sashes over one shoulder. Kate thought that it was quite the most wonderfully romantic and glamorous backdrop for a dinner she had ever seen.

Maria was too busy ogling the fit young officers to give

much thought as to why Kate should have joined the army when her father was in a rival service. 'Don't they all look sexy, or what?' she whispered with a lascivious leer, gazing at the neat rear-view of a man wearing the tightest pair of trousers either had seen in a long time.

'Don't stare,' said Kate demurely, almost unable to take her eyes off the delicious bottom herself.

What with the wonderful uniforms, the candles and the regimental silver, Kate felt as though she had been whisked back to an era of long ago; a scene that might have been described by Thackeray or Austen or Tolstoy. Later, as she sat at the wide dining table, polite conversation taking place around her, a military band playing selections from a popular musical, she decided contentedly that despite her motivation for joining the army being more than a little bit suspect she had undoubtedly made the right decision. And anyway, it had scored a point against her parents and had allowed her to leave home and get away from them as soon as she had become eighteen.

Although Kate was happy with her choice of service in the armed forces, both she and Maria knew that they had to decide on the corps or regiment they were going to join when they got their commissions and left Sandhurst. Until a few years previously the decision had been easy – then the options had been the WRAC, the Education Corps if you had been trained as a teacher, or the QAs if you wanted to nurse. The lot of most female officers was to provide nothing more than admin fodder. But now there was a myriad of opportunities: they could join the Royal Signals or the Ordnance Corps, the Catering Corps or the Pay Corps – to name but a few. Had either of the girls had a degree, she would have had an even bigger choice, but as Maria and Kate considered their possible options they were glad that the decision was only as hard as it was. In the end the pair of them decided that they would be hard pressed to find a niche that seemed to offer as much, in both career prospects and travel, as the Royal Signals. For both of them, travel had been part of the incentive to join up, and the one thing the army needed, wherever it was based around the world, was communications.

'Although it's a shame I can't join the Air Corps,' Kate said to Maria one day with undisguised envy, having heard a male cadet boasting about passing the selection process for flying helicopters.

'No chance,' said Maria, looking up from the pair of shoes she was bulling: an evening ritual, and one that was easier carried out in the company of a friend and over a cup of coffee. 'I don't seem to remember the army saying it was an equal opportunities employer when we signed on the dotted line.'

'But flying is only like driving a car. It's not something that requires particular strength or large amounts of testosterone.'

'Ah, but it's a boys'-toys thing, isn't it? Let a woman fly a helicopter and the world as men know it will cease to exist. This may be the twentieth century, but you've got to remember some of the army still lives in the nineteenth.'

Kate laughed, in spite of her frustration at being denied the one career move she really wanted.

'One day women will be allowed to fly for the armed forces. They are going to have to give way eventually.'

'So if you believe that, why on earth did you join the army? Surely with your background you'd have been better off with the air force.'

Kate shrugged. 'You don't really want to know.'

'Yes I do. I wouldn't be asking if I didn't.'

'It's a long story.'

'Am I in a hurry to go anywhere?' Maria indicated the rest of her kit waiting to be cleaned ready for inspection the next day.

'I had a row with my parents.'

'I gathered that.'

Kate looked up sharply from making meticulous circles with polish on an already gleaming toecap. 'Do you want to hear this story or don't you?'

'Sorry,' mumbled Maria. 'I won't interrupt again.'

'When I was about eight my dad took me gliding for the first time and I got a crush on the Chief Flying Instructor. He was a man called Mike, and I don't suppose anyone noticed when I was that age. I don't suppose even he noticed. He used to pull my pigtails and give me piggybacks and I thought he was the most wonderful person in the world. Then, when I was about fifteen my folks got posted out to Germany. By this time Daddy was an air vice marshal, and Mummy was far too busy entertaining to try and get him even further up the ladder to notice anything that I got up to. I went out to Germany for the main holidays but made my own arrangements for half-terms and exeats. They knew I was crazy about flying and that I spent most of my time at the gliding club, and beyond the occasional letter or phone call to check I was still alive, they pretty much ignored me. I had a friend at the club called Martha – I suppose she's about thirty, and she has a caravan parked on the airfield and does all the catering there for the hungry pilots. She promised to look after me, so as far as my parents were concerned, if I wanted to stay with her rather than fly out to Germany it was fine by them.'

Maria looked horrified. 'But you're their only daughter. Didn't they want to see you?'

'Daddy was working every hour in the day, and it has always been obvious to me that my mother had more important things to do at weekends; like endless entertaining of the right people to try and achieve her ambitions, ambitions that have nothing to do with anything I could offer.' Maria looked bewildered, so Kate explained. 'If Daddy gets high enough he'll get a knighthood, and Mummy just longs to be Lady Hayleigh-Ffoulkes more than anything in the world.'

'You're joking.'

'Sadly, I'm not.'

'So this is why you hate your parents? Because your mother uses all her energies to get your dad promoted?'

'Good heavens, no. The reason we had the final bust-up was over Mike, the CFI. Because I was spending so much time at the airfield, because I was there in the evenings too, I saw increasing amounts of Mike and we began to have a relationship. Over the next couple of years it got quite serious, and then my mother and father found out. Mike was a flight sergeant in the RAF and I suppose Mummy was terrified of what people would think if word got out that an AVM's daughter was seeing an other rank. She made sure that it all came to an abrupt halt by giving my school strict instructions that I wasn't to be allowed out at all and I never saw him again. I couldn't forgive my parents for that; they took away

Mike *and* my gliding – the only things that made life worth living as far as I was concerned. They were no better than bullies.'

'But you were just a teenager. They were only doing what they thought was in your best interests. And they could hardly let you keep on gliding if it meant you would still see Mike.'

Kate glowered at Maria. She didn't want her friend to be on the side of her parents, however reasonable her viewpoint was.

'It wasn't only that.' Kate put down her duster and the polish. 'I realise now that it probably was just a schoolgirl crush and that nothing serious would have come of it. But it wasn't what was done, it was the *way* in which it was done. I expect, under the same circumstances your mother would have take you to one side and explained things to you: about the unsuitability of falling for an older man: that the fact that I was the daughter of an air vice marshal and he was a flight sergeant made it even more unwise. But they didn't even discuss it with me. It was just a series of orders and directives down a telephone line to other people. They never considered my feelings; my mother didn't talk to me about it. It was as if they were conducting some sort of military operation.'

'Oh, Kate.' Maria could see now why Kate had been so devastated by the whole business. 'You must have been so hurt.'

'What made it worse was that when I finally rang my mother to have the whole business out with her, she told me that if that was my attitude she would rather I didn't go out to visit them for the summer holidays, because having a sulky teenager slamming doors around the house would be inconvenient as they were hosting some very important VIP.'

'You're joking!' Maria was aghast.

'I wish I wasn't.'

'So what did you do?'

'Got a job for the summer at a hotel in Devon and set about planning how to be completely independent. I'd been supposed to be going to university but that would have kept me financially dependent on my parents and I wasn't having that. Joining the forces seemed the obvious thing to do although wild horses wouldn't have dragged me into the air force.

There was no way I was going to go anywhere where I might run into them again.'

'You poor kid,' said Maria with feeling.

Kate shrugged. 'Water under the bridge now,' she said, trying to sound casual and pragmatic but not really succeeding. 'But the whole episode is pretty sordid, so keep it to yourself. It's not the sort of thing I want the world to know.'

Maria nodded. 'Do you think you'll ever make it up with your parents?'

'Would you? Although it's Mummy who I really blame. I'm certain she was the main mover behind all this, but I don't think he'll ever stand up to her so that's that.' Kate didn't add that she had always felt that when they did spend time together, she had had a special relationship with her father, that he had been on her side, that they had sometimes giggled and exchanged winks over her mother's snobbery and social aspirations. She had thought that at least her father might have tried to temper her mother's actions over Mike and her flying, but he hadn't. It wasn't just hurt that she had felt, but betrayal too.

'God, what a mess. I can't imagine falling out with mine. How dreadful.'

'Take my advice, don't try it. It's every bit as awful as you think it is.'

Despite assurances from commissioned officers and the senior NCOs at Sandhurst that the army had made giant strides in its attitude to sexual equality, Kate continued to mutter about the unfairness of not being considered for the Army Air Corps on grounds of her gender. The female cadets were told, on more than one occasion, that since the mid-seventies they had made huge strides forward in the way they were treated and employed by the army, but Kate still felt that there was a long way to go. One of the platoon commanders had even made them laugh by telling them that when she'd been a cadet – not at Sandhurst, but at a very separate establishment on the other side of Camberley – her course had even been taught to arrange flowers.

'And what's more,' Captain Endicott had continued, 'it wasn't considered ladylike that we should march as a squad between lectures. We were told to walk with a purpose. We only wore flat shoes for drill; for everything else we were required to wear high heels.'

'What, even on exercise, ma'am?' one of the cadets had asked.

'Exercise? We weren't expected to go off on exercise. We were expected to be in charge of the rear party back in the barracks.'

The platoon had laughed, but it did emphasise that the role of women in the army had moved from the dark ages to the modern day in a remarkably short time. That they would progress further in the near future was not in doubt, but it was not considered politic for junior female officers to rock the boat by trying to move things too far and too fast. There were a good number of senior male officers who had very fixed views about women anywhere near the front line, or even in the army at all, and who would sooner contemplate the prospect of being on the receiving end of a direct hit by a nuclear missile than consider sharing a trench or an armoured personnel carrier with a girl. All Kate could hope for was that attitudes would change while she was still serving.

Kate was still contemplating using some of her hard-earned savings to learn to fly powered aircraft when she was summoned to Captain Endicott's office.

'What have you done?' asked Maria.

'I can't think of anything,' said Kate with a worried frown. It was a little like being summoned to the headmistress's office, when even those with a clear conscience would automatically assume they had committed some transgression or other. She sighed and squared her shoulders. 'I won't find out standing here discussing it with you.' She marched off to her platoon commander's office as quickly as she could and was relieved when, on entering, she was offered a seat. If it were going to be a ticking-off, she wouldn't have been allowed to sit down.

'I see from your records that you are a solo glider pilot,' said Captain Endicott.

'Yes, I've been flying gliders almost as long as I can remember, ma'am,' replied Kate.

'Would you like to graduate to something with a bit more power?'

13

'Yes, ma'am. And I've been thinking of taking some lessons down at Blackbushe. I'm not sure how much they cost but I could probably afford half a dozen.'

'Would that be enough to get you a licence?'

'Good heavens, no. I think you need about forty-five hours for that and there's no way I could run to that amount.'

'Supposing there was some help available. Would that make it easier?'

'Yes, but . . .' Kate didn't understand.

'The RMA offers about ten flying scholarships each intake. They are only available to cadets who are not going to join the Army Air Corps. As we both know, this means that you are eligible – providing of course you can pass a fairly basic medical. I would just like to know if you would be interested. And are you?'

Kate barely had to reply; her face said it all.

'I can't promise that you will be successful. There are usually twice as many applicants as places available, but I will be happy to put your name forward.'

Kate was so keen to race back to tell Maria the good news that she almost forgot to salute as she left the platoon commander's office.

'Gosh, lucky you,' said Maria.

'Do you want to have a go? I'm sure you could apply too if you wanted.'

'Me? Good Lord, no. I get airsick if I look at a plane ticket,' said Maria. 'No, I'm just really pleased for you. Let's hope it pans out.'

A week later Captain Endicott was able to pass on the good news to Kate.

'Well done,' she said. 'You've got to go for a briefing with the OiC Flying to get all the details.' She handed Kate a memo with the details of when and where to attend.

'There's just one problem, ma'am,' said Kate, a little hesitantly.

'Yes?'

'I haven't got any transport.' Blackbushe was a fair hike away.

'Don't worry. This is an official part of your army training now. We'll get you there and back.'

Kate just couldn't believe it. Lucky, lucky her.

The next evening she reported to the OiC Flying's office in Old College. Waiting outside the door were a group of male cadets, obviously there for the same reason.

One of them looked at Kate and said, 'You must have the wrong place. This is for the flying scholarship briefing.'

'Yes, I know,' said Kate. 'I've been awarded one too.'

Nine pairs of eyes swivelled in her direction. Most just out of curiosity, but in a couple Kate detected undisguised resentment. So much for women now being treated as equals in the army by its more junior members. Chauvinism obviously wasn't just the prerogative of the old and bold officers, as she'd thought.

Major Reece opened the door of his office, did a quick head count to ascertain that all were present and ushered them into his spacious room.

'Find a pew,' he said. There were several wooden chairs, a leather armchair and a table. The cadets perched or sat on all of them. 'Glad to see you here,' he began. 'And in particular you, Kate. Good to see a girl interested in aviation.' Kate didn't think that everyone present shared his sentiment but didn't say so.

'Thank you, sir,' she mumbled.

'Right, who has flown before? And I don't mean on a charter to the Costa del Sol,' added Major Reece. Three hands, including Kate's, went up. 'Who are you and what have you flown then?' he said, pointing to the nearest cadet.

'I'm Cadet Brigsby, sir, and I've flown a few hours in a Beagle Pup.'

'P1 or P2?' asked Major Reece. Brigsby looked blank. 'Did you pilot it or were you under instruction?' he explained.

'Oh, I had a go with the controls, sir, but I wasn't under instruction. It was more of a joyride really.'

'OK. That's fine. And did you enjoy it, that's the main thing?'

'It was brilliant, sir.'

The other cadet had been given a one-hour flying lesson as an eighteenth birthday present

'And what about you, young lady?'

'I've got about three hundred hours P2 on gliders and thirty P1, sir.'

Major Reece whistled. 'I'm impressed. Well, there's no point in me asking you if you enjoy flying, is there? You boys are going to have to look to your laurels with Miss Hayleigh around, aren't you? She sounds like a better-qualified pilot than I am.' As he sported a pair of wings on his uniform from his days as an Air Corps pilot, Kate felt she could have done without that comment. There was enough of a feeling of simmering resentment in the room without him holding her up as something special.

Chapter Three

'Wow, a whole weekend with nothing to do! What a luxury,' said Maria. 'I'm going to Oxford to meet a friend. What are you going to do?'

Kate stared out at the low clouds and the trees bending under the force of the gusty wind, the last of the leaves being ripped forcibly from the boughs to join the soggy piles and drifts on the ground.

'I was planning to go flying, but . . .' She shrugged. Flying was possible but it would not be enjoyable. It would be better to wait for an improvement in the weather, and one had not been forecast until the middle of the following week.

'Why don't you come with me?'

'But if you're meeting someone you won't want me hanging around.'

'It's a girlfriend, and anyway you could go and do some shopping then meet up with us for lunch.'

'Well . . .'

'Oh, come on. Please?' wheedled Maria. 'I'll buy lunch.'

'OK, then.'

Kate was standing in the Covered Market eyeing up some leather belts and trying to decide whether she really wanted one, and if she did, which one to buy.

'Kate?' said a hesitant voice behind her. 'It is you Kate!'

Kate looked round. 'Martha! What on earth are you doing here?'

'I was about to ask you the same thing. I haven't seen you for months and months.'

Kate shuffled her feet uneasily. She felt rather ashamed of the way she had treated her old friend. She hadn't spoken to or seen Martha since her last visit to the gliding club – the week before her parents had found out about her and Mike.

Martha sensed her discomfort. 'Let's go and find somewhere for a coffee and you can fill me in on all your news.' She took Kate by the arm and steered her out of the market and around the corner to a small café. Over cappuccinos and large hunks of sticky date and walnut cake, Kate regaled her with her tale. Martha, amply built, sensible, thirty-ish, had been Kate's mentor and confidante for over ten years. She had been the big sister that Kate had never had and had probably heard more of Kate's secrets, hopes and fears than her mother ever had. She listened now in silence as Kate recounted how she had broken her links with her parents.

'Well, I gathered something like that had happened when you stopped coming,' Martha said when Kate finally fell silent. 'I thought at first that you and Mike had had a bust-up. But when I asked him about it he said that your dad had got really heavy with him and had threatened all sorts of stuff – the worst of which was a life ban from the gliding club.'

'Daddy threatened what?' asked Kate, her mouth gaping open with incredulity.

'Well, that was what Mike said. I don't think he had any reason to lie. After all, your father was in a perfect position to pull strings and it was pretty obvious to everyone that you were spending far more time with Mike than was strictly necessary.'

'And I thought the reason why I didn't get a reply to any of the letters I sent him was that my school was censoring my mail, but I never thought that Daddy . . .' She stopped, her voice cracking as she got dangerously close to tears. She gulped and pulled herself together. It had never crossed her mind that her father had been directly involved. 'I assumed it had been all my mother's doing, that she had given all the orders and my father had just gone along with it because he always does.'

'Don't blame your father for all of this. You've got to realise that if Mike was going to have to make a choice between seeing you and gliding, then you never had a chance. He always was a bastard like that.'

'You can't know that,' said Kate, leaping to his defence.

'I can,' said Martha with a chuckle. 'Do you remember me warning you about getting sweet on him?'

'Yes,' said Kate faintly sulkily. 'I think you said that he had a couple of failed marriages behind him and I should steer clear of him.'

'Well, what I didn't tell you was that I was one of those marriages.'

Kate's coffee cup clattered in its saucer. 'What?'

'Look,' said Martha. 'It's not something I make a big thing about. It hardly lasted any time at all.'

'But you still like him,' said Kate, still stunned.

'Of course I do. I lost him to flying, not another woman. There was no bitterness when we split up. And I know him well enough to know that anything that might come between Mike and gliding was always doomed. I'm afraid if your dad told Mike that if he contacted you or saw you again he would get posted right away from the gliding club, then you were history as far as he was concerned. That's probably why he didn't reply to your letters.'

Kate stared at her coffee cup in disbelief. Who was the bigger bastard: her father or Mike?

It was towards the end of her first term at Sandhurst that she received a letter from her father. She recognised his spiky writing as soon as she picked it out of her pigeon hole, and stood staring at it for a few moments before pushing it into her handbag. Why was he writing? she wondered. Did he want to bury the hatchet or did he have to communicate with her because of some pressing news? She had not heard a word from her parents since her terse letter telling them that she was about to join the army and wouldn't be coming out to Germany to see them either that summer or any other. She got to her room and removed the letter from her bag with an unaccountable feeling of trepidation. For a second or two she thought about throwing it in the bin unopened, but with a sudden resolve she ripped open the flap. She scanned the letter quickly for any sign that it contained bad news, which it didn't, and then read it a second time more carefully. He had obviously been in contact with the staff at Sandhurst, because

19

he knew how she was doing and that she had been awarded a flying scholarship.

'So he's got his bloody spies watching me,' Kate muttered angrily, refusing to acknowledge that her father might have genuine reasons for taking an interest in his daughter's career. He continued by saying that as long as she was happy with her decision, however hasty and ill-considered, to join the army and not the air force, then so was he.

'Your mother and I have decided to forgive the shabby way you treated us,' he wrote, 'and we thought you would like to know that we are being posted back to England shortly after Christmas and will be moving into a house we have bought near Windsor. If you wish to come and visit we will be happy to see you.'

The letter shook her resolve. It had been easy to ignore them and pretend they didn't exist once she was self-sufficient and with a roof over her head that went with the job. But now what? Could she really ignore this? As an attempt at reconciliation it left a lot to be desired, but she supposed that it had cost her father a certain amount of loss of face to come even this far to meet her. Should she accept the olive branch he was holding out? She wondered if her mother knew her father had written to her – probably not. Perhaps Kate had behaved as badly towards them as she felt they had done towards her. Could she spend the rest of her life pretending they didn't exist? They were her parents, after all, and she was their only child. And perhaps, although this was particularly difficult to admit, they had been right to stop her seeing Mike. If he valued his hobby above his relationship with her, then she was probably better off without him. Not that she would ever admit that to them. She hadn't even admitted it to Maria. Kate thought she would have accepted that she took second place to his livelihood, if her father had threatened his promotion prospects or even his continued employment by the RAF – but his hobby! That had really stung.

And now a letter had arrived from her father, bang on cue, as if he had known that she had found out that their actions, harsh though they were, might have been justified. Was it time to bury the hatchet? She needed some advice on this one, so she went to Maria, who knew far more about family life and close relationships than Kate ever would.

'This is really down to you, Kate,' Maria said. 'I know you feel your parents are the absolute limit, but I'm sure they only did what they did because they love you.'

Kate felt she knew better. 'Mummy is a raging snob and made Daddy do what he did because she couldn't bear the thought of me going out with someone who was socially inferior.'

'Because she thought you could do better,' insisted Maria gently. 'And the longer you take to bury the hatchet, the harder it will be when you do want to do it.'

'You may be right, although not so long ago, the only place I wanted to bury it was in between their shoulder blades.'

'Go on, write back to him. Ask if you can go out to Germany and stay with them over Christmas and help with the packing up. It isn't as if you've got anywhere else in particular to go for the holidays.'

'I'll think about it,' was all that Kate would promise. This wasn't a decision to be taken lightly.

Kate hadn't really expected to be welcomed back like the prodigal daughter, but she had hoped that the atmosphere over the festive season might have been a little less strained. Her father, apparently, was prepared to try and make a fresh start, but her mother was of a different opinion. There were times when Kate wondered why she was bothering to make the effort. She believed they were fond of her, but love? Her father, except for rare glimpses of a softer side that she had only seen when they went gliding together, always seemed so remote and austere and preoccupied with work, and as for her mother – well, Kate was positive that she'd only produced a child because it was the socially acceptable thing to do and not because of any burning maternal instinct. Her mother had certainly bundled her off to school as soon as she could and had never demonstrated sadness at their partings or any joy at their reunions. But Kate reasoned to herself that if her parents were prepared to do their duty by her, then she ought to be capable of doing hers by them. It was hardly an attitude that was going to be conducive to peace and tranquillity. Frankly, thought Kate, it was more like a cold war. Things were made faintly easier by the fact that for quite a lot of the time they seemed to be spared seeing too much of each other, as her parents had a number of functions to attend, none of which apparently included Kate. Her mother, overtly chilly and distant, came out with such excuses as: 'We didn't arrange for you to attend because we thought you would find our way of doing things difficult to adapt to now.' Or: 'I'm sure the RAF way isn't as smart as the army way, so we didn't think you'd want to come along.' After each tight-lipped statement, Kate took a deep breath and avoided rising to the bait. Perhaps, she thought, her social exclusion was part of the process of re-acceptance into the Hayleigh-Ffoulkes family circle. So on the evenings when she was left to her own devices she heated up the leftovers from lunch in the microwave, and settled down with a glass of white wine and BFBS television. And as she remembered the excruciatingly ghastly parties she'd had to attend the previous year, chock-a-block with pompous officers, their dreary wives and their spotty, gangly offspring, she couldn't make up her mind if she was glad of the excuse to stay at home or hurt at being left out.

By the time Sovereign's Parade came round in the following April, relations between Kate and her parents had thawed out a few more degrees. Kate had managed to ingratiate herself a little more by helping as much as she could when they moved into their house in Windsor, and nearly completed her rehabilitation by winning the Queen's Medal, which was awarded to the best student academically, as well as the flying prize. Her father even said that he thought that Sovereign's Parade, with its glorious backdrop of the Grand Entrance of Old College, was one of the most impressive things he'd ever seen. Whether or not he was proud of his daughter's part in the proceedings wasn't mentioned.

The morning after Sovereign's Parade and the subsequent ball, Kate and Maria had left Sandhurst and been sent off on attachments to different signals regiments prior to joining their special-to-arm training course in Dorset. They had both had a wonderful time, finding the work interesting and their social lives hectic. They had been reunited at Blandford for their troop commanders' course, where they further developed their skills at burning the candle at both ends. Kate, temporarily, gave up flying in favour of learning to drive and Maria had got her love life in such a tangle that she, also temporarily, gave up men. Now that they were commissioned officers and not just cadets, they became less encumbered by rules and regulations and treated more like responsible adults – even if a lot of the time they didn't behave as if they were. Blandford had certainly been fun, recalled Kate. The months there had been busy yet carefree. She had virtually no responsibilities, beyond passing various tests and exams; her monthly mess bill was always considerably smaller than her salary, leaving her sufficient to save towards a car; and all she had to worry about was where her final posting would be at the end of the course.

'I'd like to go to Cyprus,' said Kate once when they had been discussing possible options.

'Yes,' agreed Maria. 'Just think of all that wonderful sun and sea.'

'I was thinking of the gliding,' said Kate. 'The thermals in a climate like that must be fantastic.'

Maria had given her a withering look. But neither of them really considered Cyprus as a realistic option, and on their dream-sheets they had both requested Germany.

As the course drew to a close, Kate found, to her delight, that she had been posted back to the divisional signals regiment in Germany where she'd spent her earlier attachment.

'You jammy thing,' said Maria enviously as they compared notes. 'Trust me to get the comcen at York.'

'But York's a lovely place.'

'It's hardly overseas, though, is it? And it's about as far from you as I can get.'

As the final few days at Blandford sped by, Kate looked forward with increasing delight to her new posting. Her boxes had been packed and dispatched, her letter to the CO had been written and mailed, and the ferry crossing for herself and her little car had been booked. All that now stood between her and her posting was some last-minute admin, the final few days of lectures and the end-of-course party.

On the afternoon of the knees-up, she was sitting at her dressing table drying her hair and scrunching her curls to make them even more bouncy, at the same time as wondering if she ought to wear her outrageously décolleté black dress or her figure-hugging blue one, when Maria charged through the door without knocking.

'Kate,' she gasped over the noise of the hairdrier, 'urgent message for you.' She'd run all the way to Kate's room. Kate switched off her drier and turned towards Maria. 'The Commander wants to see you in his office straight away. It's urgent.'

Kate frowned, not quite understanding what Maria was saying, although there was nothing complicated about the message.

'The Commander? Wants to see me? Now? But it's Saturday.'

'Yes.'

'What about?'

'How the hell should I know? You can't have done anything wrong – you never do.'

Kate had already come to the same conclusion.

'Should I finish drying my hair?'

'No. I don't think so. I don't know. Does it matter?'

Kate stood up, bemused, gave her damp curls a perfunctory brush and slipped into a sweatshirt and a denim skirt. 'I hope this is OK,' she said, smoothing the front of the skirt. 'I wasn't planning any more interviews with the brass and most of my stuff is packed ready for the off.'

'I'm sure it is. You'd better hurry. Tell me what it's all about when you get back. Perhaps,' she added as Kate exited the room, 'perhaps they've discovered that you've got the wrong posting. That you're supposed to be going to York and not me.'

'Dream on,' said Kate as she turned into the corridor and walked briskly towards the front door. She left the mess and turned right, towards the administrative buildings. It didn't take her long to cover the short distance although the closer she got towards her objective the more worried and nervous she became. What could she have done? What on earth could be the problem if the Commander had to come in on a weekend to talk to her about it? She entered the building and made her way to his office. The door was open. She knocked.

'Come in.'

Kate entered. The Commander was sitting behind his desk looking as though he had been dragged away from a game of tennis. His forehead was glistening slightly and he was wearing a rumpled white aertex shirt.

'Ah, Kate. Take a seat.'

'I'm sorry about my clothes, sir,' began Kate.

The Commander shrugged to indicate that it was of no import. 'Look, Kate, there's no easy way to do this.' He paused and pressed the tips of his fingers together. In the little silence Kate wondered if there was a problem with her posting. 'It's your father.' The shock of those words made Kate feel suddenly sick. 'I'm afraid there's been a terrible accident. In a glider.' The Commander lowered his eyes from Kate's face and began to examine his fingertips. 'I'm afraid he's been killed.'

Kate didn't know what to say. What was there to say? Surely this was some sort of joke. But the Commander wouldn't joke. She looked away from him and out of the window.

She cleared her throat. 'When did it happen?'

'About lunchtime today.'

Kate thought back to lunchtime. She and Maria had gone to a favourite pub of theirs, the one in the village with the ford running across the road, and had horsed around with a group of the lads off the course.

'Does my mother know, sir?'

'Yes. In fact she phoned the duty officer here and asked him if we could let you know. Before it got on the television or anything. I can't say how sorry I am to have to break this news to you.'

'Yes, thank you.' Kate felt she ought to be crying but she felt oddly calm and detached, almost if she was hearing about someone else's parent who had been killed. 'Um, what should I do now?' She felt she ought to know the answer to this herself, but her brain didn't seem to want to function. In fact most of her senses appeared to have gone quite numb.

'I've asked the duty officer to arrange some transport home for you today. I gather you've got a couple of weeks' leave before you're due to report to your new unit.' Kate nodded. 'Is there someone here who could hand back in any kit you've still got on your signature?' Kate nodded again. Maria would

25

do that for her. 'Well, in which case, I don't think there will be any need for you to return here.'

Kate wanted to know some details. Surely a man of her father's experience hadn't just ploughed into the ground. 'How did it happen, sir?'

'I'm afraid I haven't got many details. Only that he was having to land out in a field, away from the club, and he crashed.' Kate nodded. That was how a lot of accidents happened, she knew that, but surely not to her father. He had thousands of flying hours. Perhaps something had been wrong with the glider. At least from the sound of it there hadn't been anyone else involved. It would have been awful if it had been a mid-air collision; if another pilot had been killed too.

'Are you OK?' the Commander asked, worried by her silence and her calm.

'Yes. Um, it's just come as a bit of a shock, that's all, sir.' Kate was suddenly aware that the expected tears were about to make an appearance. 'If you'll excuse me, sir, I think I'll go and pack.'

'OK, Kate.' There was the sound of movement outside the door. 'Ah, good. Here's James. Come in, would you?' An officer dressed in impeccable number two dress entered the Commander's office and saluted. Captain James Bryant was obviously the duty officer.

'Have you sorted out some way of getting Kate back home?' the Commander asked him.

'Yes, sir. It's all fixed. The MT sergeant has some stores to pick up from Aldershot, so they will give you a lift. Can you be ready by three thirty?'

Kate shook her head. 'But I've got my car.'

'It really isn't wise for you to drive all that way on your own. We'll get your car up to Windsor for you in the next day or two. Best you get home now as safely and as quickly as you can.' They were probably right. She glanced at her watch. She had forty minutes.

'OK.' The Commander stood and walked round his desk. He held out his hand to Kate. 'I really am terribly sorry.' Kate shook his hand and nodded, but didn't trust herself to speak.

'Do you want me to come with you?' asked James. Kate shook her head and left the Commander's office as quickly as politeness would allow. Blinded by tears at last, she turned away and retraced her steps to her room.

'My God, Kate. What's the matter?' Maria was sitting on Kate's bed, anxiously awaiting her return and the reason for this unusual interview, and was shocked by her friend's tear-streaked face.

'Oh, Maria,' sobbed Kate, and flung herself on to her bed. In the privacy of her room she let the sobs she had held back rack her as she cried, with huge gulps, into her pillow.

Chapter Four

The awfulness of her father's death would have been bad enough, but it was compounded by her mother's slide into depression. From being from an organised and organising virago, Honour Hayleigh-Ffoulkes degenerated into a suddenly old, gaunt and tired woman. Only a week earlier she wouldn't have dreamed of leaving her bedroom without powder, lipstick and eye shadow all carefully applied, and now she sat around with unkempt hair, a stain on her blouse and her shoes scuffed and unpolished. She seemed incapable of doing anything for herself. She couldn't run a bath, let alone a house. Kate called in the family doctor, who prescribed antidepressants but was unable to help with practical details. The care of Kate's mother was something she was going to have to sort out herself. Kate suggested that they should try hiring some sort of home help, but all this did was reduce her mother to hysterical screams and accusations that Kate didn't care. For Kate this was the last straw of unreasonableness, coming as it did from the woman who had handed her over into the care of a nanny almost from the day she was born, then bundled her off to boarding school as soon as she could; who had never once actively encouraged her only child to come home for a holiday . . . And she now had the audacity to accuse Kate of not caring.

'And why should I?' Kate muttered angrily as she slumped dejectedly on the sofa. But even as she said this she knew she really didn't have a choice. She had a duty. A duty to her father, a duty to her mother. So Kate, emotionally battered by the death of her father, exhausted by coping with her mother and the funeral and with no relations to speak of, caved in under the pressure and abandoned her dreams of serving in Germany. She asked if her posting could be changed so she could be close to Windsor.

For months, most free evenings and every free weekend, she flogged up the M3 to Windsor to look after her mother, to cook for her, to dust and tidy, to wash and iron, for a scant reward of the occasional muttered thank you. Honour developed asthma – stress-related, according to the doctor – which forced Kate to spend yet more time at home. Her flying became almost nonexistent, her social life ceased entirely and she devoted every scrap of energy to getting her mother back to full health both mentally and physically. Then finally, over two years later, when Maria and the signals regiment returned triumphant from the Gulf War, Maria was offered a posting to Cyprus. Kate tried to sound pleased for her friend, and consoled herself with the thought that, although it was only a poor relation of an option, she would be able to fly out there for a holiday.

Once Maria had got herself thoroughly settled in her new job, Kate began to make arrangements to go and see her friend. Tentatively she broached the subject of her plans for the summer holidays with her mother. It was received in a stony silence.

'I'll be flying out on a weekday, so I'll come and visit you for a weekend just before I go and as soon as I get back,' said Kate hoping to placate her mother. It wasn't as if Honour couldn't cope for short times on her own. She wasn't an invalid, when all was said and done.

Silence.

'It's a great opportunity. And Maria knows all the best places to go on the island so I'm bound to have a great time.' More silence. 'I won't get a chance like this again.' Her mother got up and walked out of the room. Kate slumped in her chair. Why shouldn't she go to Cyprus? she thought. Why was her mother being so unreasonable? Couldn't she see what she was doing to Kate's life? Kate wanted to scream and rant at her but she knew it would do no good. It would only make her even more intractable and, God only knew, she was bad enough already.

Kate picked up the remote and began to flick through the TV channels. She wasn't really interested in watching anything but she was damned if she was going to run after her mother with more explanations and apologies. She was going to Cyprus and if her mother didn't like it she could lump it. After twenty minutes of desultory viewing, Kate was forced to conclude that there was nothing at all on the box. She switched it off and went into the kitchen to make herself a coffee. Her mother was sitting at the big pine table, her forehead glistening with sweat, her shoulders heaving, gasping for breath. It was immediately apparent that she was in the throes of another asthma attack. She was making no attempt to try and help herself and there was no sign of her inhaler. What was she playing at? Was she trying to make herself seriously ill? Kate's mind produced a nasty, suspicious little thought.

'Where's your puffer?' she asked. Her mother gave her a glassy, almost insolent stare and didn't answer. Kate ran back into the sitting room to grab Honour's handbag. She raced back to the kitchen, where she tipped the contents on to the table. No puffer.

'Is it in your bedroom?' Honour narrowed her eyes but didn't reply. Kate wanted to shake her but now wasn't the moment. She raced out of the kitchen into the hall and took the wide, shallow stairs two at a time, skidded on the parquet floor of the landing and hurtled into her mother's room. Rapidly her eyes scanned all the likely places. Nothing on the dressing table, nor the bedside table nor her chest of drawers. What about the bathroom? Nothing by the basin. The medicine cabinet? Zilch. What had the bloody woman done with it? Kate ran back to the bedroom and pulled open a couple of drawers, but still drew a blank. Where could it be? Her mother always had it near her. She carried it with her like a sort of talisman. Kate suddenly had an idea and, skidding out of the bedroom again, hurtled down the stairs and back to the kitchen. She pulled her mother's chair away from the table and delved into the deep pockets of her cardigan. Yes. She felt so angry she had to back away immediately.

'Use it,' she commanded, shaking with rage and proffering the inhaler at arm's length. Honour looked up sharply, shocked by Kate's tone of voice. She flinched as if she'd been slapped in the face but reached out a hand and took the puffer. Obediently she held it upright, put it to her lips and inhaled sharply as she squeezed the dispenser. She repeated it a couple of times and almost instantly her breathing began to improve perceptibly.

Kate perched on the table, well away from her mother but watching her intently as her breathing became less laboured until it was little worse than a wheeze.

She waited until Honour was obviously over the worst of her attack before she spoke. 'That's it. That's the last time you ever pull a stunt like that on me. If you're well enough to behave like this, you're well enough to look after yourself. I've given up just about everything for you and I don't expect to be repaid with yet another display of complete selfishness. If I wasn't around you'd bloody well *have* to fend for yourself.'

Honour sagged slightly, but Kate had more to say. 'One way and another you've been blackmailing me emotionally to keep me traipsing back and forth, to be at your beck and call, to be on hand any time you feel a bit lonely and a bit down, and I've had enough.' Honour shook her head as if to deny Kate's accusation. 'Don't pretend it isn't so, because it is. If I'd had that first posting to Germany, two years ago, it's possible I'd be living in Cyprus now, not just planning a holiday. I've given up a lot for you, I may even have jeopardised my career, and you repay me like this. How could you? How could you deliberately try and deny me my first decent holiday in years?'

Honour didn't answer. She looked down at her hands. She suddenly looked rather old and frail, but Kate was feeling too angry to be moved.

'Go on, tell me how you could have done this to me? I'm your daughter, for God's sake, not a paid servant.' Honour shrugged. Kate wasn't sure if it was an apology or because she didn't know the answer herself. Having said her piece, Kate felt calmer. Her outburst had had the same effect as lifting a lid on a saucepan about to boil over – now the pressure had gone, the seething resentment had subsided.

She took a deep breath and said quietly, 'I am going now. You know my contact number at work and in the mess. But I'm not coming home again until I get a proper apology.'

Honour spoke at last. 'I didn't mean ... I just wanted to ...' She looked pathetic. 'I've been so lonely,' she said finally.

'Well, get out and make some friends.' Kate's exasperation was tinged with pity. 'Go and do some work for the local Conservative Party, or the WRVS, or SSAFA. There must be dozens of things you could do to fill your time and meet people, and I'm sure they'd be only too happy to have a willing volunteer. But stop relying on me. I've got my own life to lead and I'm bloody well going to do it now. And I meant what I said about the apology.'

Chapter Five

Over two years on, Kate was still waiting for her apology and she still felt anger about her mother's behaviour, her refusal to cope and her blindness to the damage she had done to her daughter's career through her actions. If Kate hadn't asked for her posting to be changed to one in the UK, it would have been her, not Maria, who had gone out to the Gulf War. And it might have been her, not Maria, who had subsequently been offered the plum posting to Cyprus. Kate had since had a tour out in Germany, cut short because of her being accepted for helicopter training, but somehow she had never felt that she had completely fitted in with the regiment. It was something to do with those who had been out to the Gulf and those who hadn't. Kate felt a constant niggle of self-pity that she had had to stay in England when all the action had been happening. It was hard to forgive her mother for the effect of her selfishness, and unless Honour showed at least some signs of contrition Kate wasn't inclined to. And Maria could nag her about it all she liked; Kate could be very stubborn.

When Maria arrived in Kate's room in the Army Air Corps mess at Middle Wallop ready to help her celebrate going solo on the fixed-wing phase of the helicopter course, Kate was wading through an exercise in equipment recognition.

'Give me ten minutes and then we can go down to the bar to get a drink,' said Kate. 'I'd hoped to have this squared away before you arrived.'

'Don't mind me. I'm sure it's more important that you know what the enemy's kit looks like than it is for me to have my thirst slaked,' said Maria with a grin. 'I don't want you taking me out on the range because you can't tell the difference between my nice NATO four-three-two and the enemy's armoured vehicle.' Kate threw a rubber at her and returned to her photographs of armoured personnel carriers spread out over her desk, while Maria browsed along her bookshelf to see if there was anything more interesting to read than flight manuals. Finally she found an old edition of *Cosmo*, settled down comfortably in the armchair and idly began to flick through the pages.

An article caught her eye and she delved into it. 'Have you read this?' she asked after a few minutes.

'Hmm, what?' asked Kate, still engrossed in her work.

'This article about family rows.'

'I have.'

'And . . .?'

'And what?'

'You ought to make up with your mother.'

'Not that old chestnut again,' said Kate mildly, still studying pictures of Russian armour.

'But . . .'

'No. I tried, remember.' There was a dangerous edge to Kate's voice.

Maria took the hint and dropped the subject, and went back to looking at the dog-eared magazine while Kate worked quietly on at her exercise. Five minutes later Kate pushed the papers and pictures into a pile and stood up.

'Come on, I'll buy you a drink.' Her annoyance over Maria's mention of her relationship with her mother was forgotten.

'And introduce me to some aviators?' asked Maria hopefully.

'If you play your cards right, although there may not be many who come in. The rule is twelve hours bottle to throttle, so no one drinks much till Friday.'

'They make up for it then, do they?'

'I should cocoa.'

When they arrived, the solitary figure of Matthew Grant, morosely nursing a pint of bitter, was the only person in the bar.

'Hi, Matt,' said Kate. 'Let me introduce you to a friend of

mine. Matt, this is Maria Denver; Maria, Matthew Grant.'
The two shook hands and Kate offered to buy Matt another
pint.

'No thanks, and I'd better be going in a minute. I'm not
much company tonight anyway. I'm on review tomorrow.' He
drained his beer and was gone. Maria looked disappointed.

'He doesn't think he's going to pass the course,' explained
Kate once he was out of earshot. 'He's got a couple more
hours in which to go solo in the Chipmunk and then it's
curtains.'

'It obviously matters very much to him.'

'I don't think it makes it any easier that a woman is doing
better than him either.'

Kate ordered their drinks, and they sat down in a corner.
Slowly, the bar began to fill up with a variety of permanent
staff, trainee pilots, qualified pilots, wives, girlfriends and
hangers-on, until by the time Maria was ready to leave and
drive back to Wilton, it was quite busy. Reluctantly Maria
bade the young men gathered about her farewell.

'Thanks for coming over,' said Kate. 'It was good to see
you again.'

'It was nice to meet some of these hunks,' replied Maria.
'And Kate, I know it's a taboo subject, but I really think your
mother has a right to know that you've soloed. Think about it.
Especially considering what happened to your dad.'

Kate's face hardened. 'I really don't want to discuss this.'

'I know,' said Maria sadly, 'although I wish you would.
But I promise I won't mention the subject again.'

'Good,' said Kate with feeling. Then, with a smile, 'Now
bugger off so I can go and get some beauty sleep.'

But when she returned to her room, the last thing she felt
like doing was sleeping. If she wasn't flying the next morning
she would have returned to the bar and ordered herself a
massive Scotch, but it was out of the question. Damn Maria,
and damn her mother.

She went through the motions of undressing and getting
ready for bed, although she knew it was unlikely that she would
get much sleep. The mention of her mother had wound her up.
And what made matters worse was the knowledge that really
she was just as much to blame for the state of affairs that existed

between them as her mother was. They were as bad as each other: both quick-tempered, proud and unforgiving.

She lay in bed and flicked though the magazine Maria had been reading earlier. She saw the article about family rows and shut the magazine in annoyance and dropped it on the floor. But it had been a long time. Was it time to let bygones be bygones? And if her mother hadn't apologised after this length of time, was she likely to now? Somehow Kate doubted it. Damn and blast Maria. She'd gone and stirred up the whole can of worms again and left Kate feeling that this state of affairs was all *her* fault and nothing to do with her mother.

Angrily Kate plumped up her pillow and tried to get comfortable. She switched the light off, but as she did so she wondered why she was bothering. She didn't expect to get much sleep. She must have drifted off, because a helicopter on a night-flying exercise clattered in overhead and woke her up. Kate looked at her watch. Three o'clock in the morning. I give up, she thought. She switched on the bedside lamp and pulled her dressing gown on as she swung her feet out of bed. Perhaps if she had a cup of tea she might find sleep easier to come by. She shivered slightly as she filled her kettle and plugged it in. She needed a sleepless night like a hole in the head. Tomorrow was a heavy day – a long cross-country navigation exercise, then ground school on avionics, meteorology and the principles of flight – and she knew she would need to be able to call on all her powers of concentration in order to get through it. The kettle boiled and Kate slopped the water over a tea bag in a none-too-clean mug. Clasping her hot drink, she sat on the stool in front of her dressing table. She shut her eyes and wondered what things would have been like if she had ignored her mother's pleas and organised some sort of professional help. Her career would have taken such a different course if she'd gone to Germany. She couldn't forgive her mother. Perhaps if just once she had been grateful for what Kate had given up, if just once she had said thank you, if she had just tried to make an effort to help herself . . . but no. Thinking such thoughts wasn't making it any easier for Kate to find it in her heart to forgive her mother, but she knew guiltily that she was wrong. She was going to have to give in. But not just yet. She'd think about it a bit longer. She didn't need extra hassle while she was so busy on this course. And there was always the possibility that Honour wouldn't have anything to do with her. Well, thought Kate, if she made the effort, at least her conscience would be clear. As she finally drifted off into a restless sleep, she wondered if she was ever going to have any sort of proper family life. Frankly, in the bleak, cold small hours it seemed an unlikely prospect.

Chapter Six

Next morning the alarm dragged Kate unwillingly from her restless night. As she lay in bed, listening to the seven o'clock news, there was a discreet knock at the door and a member of the mess staff appeared with her early morning tea.

'Open the curtains, would you, please?' Kate asked as the steward placed the cup by her bed. She wanted to see what the weather was doing. It didn't look too bad. Cloudy, but there were a few breaks showing patches of blue sky. It would be a pleasant day for flying. She swung her feet out of bed and looked at herself in the mirror on the wall opposite. She looked grim: pale, with big shadows under her eyes. She would have to conceal those, otherwise she knew that she'd be the butt of endless jokes in the crew room about too much bed and not enough sleep.

She slapped on some make-up and did her best to disguise the evidence of her rotten night, finished her tea and then went downstairs to breakfast. She poured herself some orange juice and stuck a couple of slices of bread in the toaster. Waiting for it pop up, she picked up one of the papers and perused it. Her toast flipped up and she carried it, the paper and her juice across to an empty place at one of the tables. Matthew was opposite, tucking into a plate of bacon and eggs.

'The condemned man ate a hearty breakfast,' said Kate without thinking.

'Precisely,' said Matthew.

'Oh, God. I'm sorry. I didn't think.' Kate felt awful. If she had been more on the ball she'd never have made such a crass remark. Apologising wasn't going to make it any better now. What was said was said.

Silence descended as they both munched their way through their breakfasts and read the morning papers.

'Do you want a lift over?' asked Matthew as he pushed his plate away. The mess was about a mile away from the hangar that was their base during the day.

'Love one,' said Kate. She didn't really – she would have preferred to make her own way over – but she didn't want to hurt Matt's feelings. He needed all the support he could get over the next couple of days if he was going to get off review and progress to the rotary-wing phase. Out of the eight personnel on their particular course, she and Matthew were the only officers; the others were either senior NCOs or junior ranks. It was natural that they should support each other – a cause of some speculation and the occasional bawdy remark from the others. Matthew knew more about tactics and the combat role of helicopters than Kate did, but obviously Kate was streets ahead of him when it came to the practicalities of flying and subjects like navigation, instruments and the theory of flight.

Kate and Matthew returned to their rooms to gather together all the kit they would need for the day and then drove over to the huge hangar where their crew room was situated.

'Good luck,' said Kate when they parked. Matthew was due to fly straight away and Kate wouldn't see him again till lunchtime. He had a further five hours of flying in which to go solo, in which to conquer his problem in landing the Chipmunk without kangarooing all along the airstrip, and it was crucial that he stopped making mistakes.

'Thanks,' said Matt with a wry smile. 'I just wish I could rely on skill, like you do, and not luck.'

Kate watched him walk over to meet his instructor for his pre-flight briefing, then turned and made her way over to the crew room.

'Christ, you look rough,' said Sergeant McGuiver as Kate walked in. 'Busy night?'

'Yup,' said Kate refusing to rise to the bait. 'There were punters queuing up around the block wanting to pay for my services.'

Sergeant McGuiver was caught off balance by her sassy remark and subsided into silence. Kate went to the kitchen area of the room and made herself a cup of tea. She pointedly didn't ask McGuiver if he wanted one. Then she got out her charts and began planning for her cross-country flight. After twenty minutes or so she wandered across to the air traffic control tower to get the latest met and the notices to airmen – or NOTAMS. These were an essential part of her planning which would tell her if any particularly dreadful weather was forecast, and if any airspace had been put out of bounds or there were areas of heavy activity, like a gliding competition taking place. As she walked across to the tower she watched a Chipmunk make its final approach to the airfield. This had to be Matthew. The descent looked fine – surely he had to get it right this time – but just as he should have come in for a textbook landing, the plane suddenly ballooned back up into the air. Kate groaned and wondered fleetingly how on earth he had managed to get on the course in the first place.

Matthew's struggle to solo continued, and it was against the odds that he managed to complete his first one just before his last chance finally disappeared.

'Talk about scraping in under the wire,' he announced with evident relief, as everyone in the crew room cheered his success.

'Well done, Matthew,' said Kate. 'I knew you could do it.'

'I'm glad one of us did. Personally, I wasn't so sure.'

But then they graduated to instrument flying, and Matt's problems came roaring back.

'They don't lie,' Kate told him one evening as they stood in the bar for a pre-dinner drink.

'I know that, but I constantly feel that I'm banking or climbing and it's terribly difficult to ignore it.' Kate didn't know how to help him. If he couldn't get himself to ignore his imagined sensations, he was never going to completely trust his instruments, and if he didn't do that he wouldn't pass the phase. 'Anyway, it's different for you.'

'How so?' asked Kate, already expecting the answer that her high ranking on the course was down to all her previous flying experience.

'Well, the instructors are bound to give you an easier ride, just because you're a woman.'

Kate couldn't believe she was hearing this. Especially not from Matthew, whom she had helped and encouraged and supported from the instant it had become obvious that he was really struggling. She opened and shut her mouth but no words came out. Then, finally: 'You don't really believe that crap, do you?'

'It stands to reason, doesn't it? They're all frightened of bawling you out if you go wrong in case you burst into tears.'

'I don't burst into tears. How can you say that? You really can't think they're going to let me pass this course and send me off in a million-pound helicopter if I can't fly it properly? Besides which,' Kate was getting into her stride now, 'besides which, we're talking lives here. If I'm not safe, I'll kill someone. Can you honestly see it at the Board of Inquiry? "Oh yes, we let her fly even though we knew she was dangerous because we didn't want her to get upset." Get real, Matthew.' Kate subsided and Matthew looked suitably chastened.

'Well, no,' he admitted sheepishly.

'Good,' said Kate. But she wondered how many others held that view. In all probability, most of the rest of the men in the army, she thought. So much for sexual equality.

Matthew finally managed to scrape through the instrument phase, but now everyone, including himself, was beginning to wonder if, despite his undoubted motivation and ethusiasm, he had the ability to make it through to the end.

They took a break from flying for a week as they all had to learn survival skills, in the event of ditching in the sea, and how to cope with a lack of oxygen at high altitude. Matt, a strong and capable swimmer, did really well on this section, one that Kate found fairly tough, as she was no great shakes in the water. It was good to see Matt full of confidence for once, but Kate could only hope that this confidence would help see him through the next few weeks.

With this new-found sense of self-worth, a return of his old assurance, and the difficulties of landing Chipmunks behind him, things seemed to improve for Matt once they got back from the brief sojourn with the Royal Navy and their survival training unit. They were finally allowed to get their hands on Gazelle helicopters. Kate found now that any earlier advantage had utterly disappeared, as flying helicopters was a completely different skill to anything else she'd ever done. She quickly discovered that the smallest of movements using the cyclic control – the helicopter's equivalent of a control column – had a violent effect on the direction the helicopter took. In fact, during her first flight, when the instructor had invited her to rest her hand lightly on the controls and follow him through some basic manoeuvres, she had found herself confused, as she hadn't detected any movement of the controls at all despite the fact that they had turned, quite definitely, to the right. When he swung the helicopter over to the left, she had noticed a minute twitch of the cyclic and had felt relieved that she wouldn't have to own up to not knowing how he'd achieved the turns.

'Now you do it,' her instructor had said. He'd told her that he would keep control of the collective and the rudder so all Kate had to do was to ape his delicacy with the stick, but her first three attempts had resulted in the aircraft lurching wildly over the sky.

'This is impossible,' she'd said.

'You've got to be more gentle.'

And she'd tried, but again without success. Eventually, she had managed to get the Gazelle to do what she wanted, without gaining or losing height, and maintaining a steady bearing.

'Brilliant,' her instructor had enthused. 'Now, I'd like you to do it using the rudder pedals as well.

When they had landed at the end of her first flight, despite the fact that the weather hadn't been particularly hot, Kate found she was drenched with sweat.

'You wait till we start to teach you how to hover,' her instructor had said. 'You'll be wringing your flying suit out then.' Whoopee, Kate thought.

Back in the crew room, Kate had swapped notes with the other students and they'd all agreed that their co-ordination skills were sadly lacking. Matt's morale took another visible up-turn, as the playing field seemed to have levelled out again. As they progressed still further, and everyone began to complain about the impossibility of hovering, he became almost chipper. But it wasn't to last.

'Hovering is like balancing on a beach ball,' Kate had complained.

'It's like balancing on two beach balls,' one of the other students had interjected. 'And they're on top of each other and the whole shebang is balancing on top of a jet of water.' Everyone had laughed but had inwardly thought what an appropriate description this was.

'I thought *flying* helicopters would be tricky,' said Matt, 'but actually that bit seems to be quite easy. It's when you stop flying them and try to hover, so you can land the buggers, that it all goes to rat-shit.' It was rapidly becoming apparent that Matt's confidence was losing the battle against his doubtful flying ability. Kate tried to cheer him up.

'And yet when the instructor does it, it looks so bloody easy,' she moaned. 'He keeps telling me to relax, not to fight it, but I just can't seem to make myself. You know what it's like, as soon as it starts to wobble it's instinctive to grip the stick to try to regain control and it only makes things worse. And then it's those dreaded words, "OK, Kate, I have control", and I've blown it again.'

But despite having the same problems as the rest of the students, Kate overcame them first and was sent solo before any of the men. 'The instructor only let you go on your own because he was too scared of your flying to go with you,' someone wisecracked when she got back into the crew room.

Kate, yet again, kept her cool. Another sexist joke, she thought wearily. 'More than likely,' she replied as she put her heavy flying helmet down on a chair. She eased her neck. The weight of the helmet was the only thing she had found she disliked about military flying.

'It hasn't done much for Matt's confidence to see you go off on your own,' said one of the students from across the room.

'He'd have felt the same if it had been any of you,' said Kate but without conviction. There was little doubt that he was suffering from a renewed crisis of confidence, but she also knew that most men would resent being beaten by a woman, and military men were even more inclined towards this attitude than their civilian counterparts. She didn't think that, nice as he usually was, Matt would be any different, although he might just try and conceal it from her. She wondered how he would react if he didn't make it through this phase and progress to advanced rotary. Personally, she thought that if she were struggling as much as he seemed to be, she would be relieved to be chopped, but then she wasn't a bloke. She wasn't hampered by this macho thing that they all had, that it was a *failure* not to be able to do it. She knew the men all thought that flying helicopters was like driving cars – it was something they should be able to do, and do well, simply because they were men. The fact that some men were crap drivers didn't register with them because, without exception, they were all of the opinion that only women were crap drivers. Kate had once tried to explain that it was really all to do with co-ordination, judgement and concentration but had got shouted down for her pains. Now she was aware of a faint atmosphere of simmering resentment in the crew room.

'Look,' she said, 'it's not my fault that the instructors think I'm ready to go off on my own and they don't think that Matt is.'

'Well, he can't offer them blow-jobs.'

So that was what they thought, was it? Bloody men. She was hurt that this had even crossed their minds, let alone that they had voiced it out loud. She decided to drop the subject of flying and going solo. 'I'm going to make myself a cup of tea. Would anyone else like one?'

'Good idea, Kate,' said Sergeant McGuiver. 'Get back in the kitchen where you belong.'

'Since you've taken that attitude you can make your own bloody tea,' she snarled. She had had enough of their gibes and jokes at her expense.

'Ooh,' he said in a camp voice, 'get her! It must be that time of the month again.' The other students fell about.

Wankers, she thought, but she couldn't be bothered to say it. She banged the kettle about crossly. This had been such a good day to start with, and going solo had left her feeling really up-beat, but these stupid remarks from grown men who should know better had really pissed her off. She was also furious at having risen to the bait. It was exactly the response that made them have even more digs at her. She knew from

44

past experience that if she ignored their imbecilic comments they soon got bored and turned their attention on someone else. She crashed the kettle on to the work surface, plugged it in and turned to look out of the window as she waited for it to boil. In the middle distance she could see Matt's helicopter wobbling about, a few feet above the ground, in a desperate struggle to maintain a hover. The wobbling got worse and worse until he swung the machine sideways off the invisible bubble of air that formed at this height between the rotors and the ground and which it was supposed to be balancing on, flew around and then returned for another attempt. She felt incredibly sorry for him, but however much she willed him to succeed she could see that his chances of success were so slim as to be anorexic. Behind her the kettle spouted steam. She tore her attention away from Matt and sloshed boiling water into a mug. Topping up her tea with milk, she returned to the window in time to see Matt smack his Gazelle on to the ground in an unacceptably heavy landing. Kate winced. That was dreadful. She couldn't bear to watch any more; besides which, she had to go and prepare some maps for her next flying exercise.

'They can't blame favouritism this time, can they?' Maria had said when Kate phoned her with the good news.

'I wouldn't bank on it,' said Kate, recalling the comments of just a few hours ago. 'I was talking to the wife of one of the instructors at a curry lunch last Sunday. She said how she was pleased to meet me at long last, and did I know that her husband is my instructor because of a bet.'

'You're joking? What sort of bet?'

'He's on for a case of champagne if I get through, because he's the most chauvinist officer in the Air Corps and is looking for any excuse to fail me.'

Maria whistled. 'What are you going to do?'

'Pass, of course.'

Over the next few days, all the other students, with the exception of Matt, went solo. Time for Matt was running out. If he didn't succeed soon he'd be chopped.

'Try not to think about it,' Kate said to him at the bar that evening.

'Easy to say,' replied Matt morosely. 'I mean, look around you.' He gestured to the walls of the bar, which, over the years, had been decorated by the various courses with items of flying memorabilia, photographs of helicopters, cartoons about flying and regimental plaques from various Army Air Corps squadrons. 'Everywhere you go in this place there's something to remind you that others have made it through the course. So why can't I do it? What have they all got, what have *you* got, that I haven't?'

'I don't know.' Kate toyed with her glass of tomato juice as she tried to think of a suitable and sympathetic answer. 'It's no good me telling you to relax, because you know that that is what is required. And I also know how impossible it must be for you to do exactly that when you feel that the slightest mistake will send you back to your regiment.'

'I know they can't send me solo until I've proved that I'm safe, but the trouble is, I'm sure that if they just gave me the chance and stopped breathing down my neck, I could fly a textbook circuit, hover the wretched thing perfectly and then land like a feather.'

'But they won't, will they?'

'I've only got three more hours before they pull the plug on me, Kate. If I don't get through, I think I'll resign my commission.'

Kate was horrified. 'You want to fly that much?'

'Absolutely.'

Kate certainly wanted to fly with all her heart, but she had a much more philosophical approach. As far as she was concerned, every day spent at Middle Wallop was a bonus; every day spent in the air was like being on holiday. The fact that she was getting paid for it, that she had the army's blessing to indulge in her hobby morning, noon and night, was her idea of heaven on earth. And if, for some awful reason, she got chopped – well, it had been brilliant fun while it lasted. For her, the achievement had been in getting selected; for Matt the achievement was only to be found in having wings sewn on to his uniform. It was obviously this macho thing again. Kate was glad, for once, that she was a girl.

Two days later the inevitable happened and Matt was called in to see the Commandant. Later, when he returned to the crew room, he tried to make light of his interview, but it was obvious to all that he was dangerously close to tears.

'And they've put a recommendation on my file that I shouldn't be considered for the course again at a later date.' His eyes glistened damply.

'So what do you do now?' asked Sergeant McGuiver.

'I've been given some leave while they sort out a posting for me.'

'Where will you go?' asked Kate, anxious that he shouldn't break down just yet.

Matt gave a hollow laugh. 'Anywhere that I can get to without having to fly.' The other students laughed dutifully at his brave attempt at humour.

Matt's departure made the remaining students quite subdued for a week or so. The workload was still stiff – the theory was being piled on in their lessons in ground school, and each flying exercise built on the knowledge gained from the previous one, so there was no room for any slacking. They covered instrument flying, night flying, low flying, flying in confined areas, tactical flying, navigating at different heights, map-reading and anything else which would make them competent and confident military pilots. They flew over mountains and they flew over water. They learned how to assist the artillery by spotting targets and directing fire. And as these new skills were covered, other members of the course failed to come up to snuff. Sergeant McGuiver couldn't hack flying helicopters on instruments, and a corporal got totally stressed out when it came to tactical flying to the extent that he completely froze and the mission had to be abandoned. Each time a member of the course was axed, those left wondered who would be next. Surely, as the months passed and they got closer to the end, it was getting too late; there was too much time and money already invested in them for those left to fail. But they were assured by their instructors that this was not so.

At weekends, Kate got away from Wallop. She would jump in her car and more often than not pick up Maria, and then spend the weekend partying, either in some of the livelier messes around Salisbury Plain or, if things looked as if they were going to be a bit dead, up in London, where they would stay with one of Maria's brothers and check out the scene there. By the end of the weekend, however, Maria invariably had the same complaint, that all Kate could talk about was flying and that she was so preoccupied with it as to be verging on boring.

'But it's my life,' Kate countered.

'But not mine. Why don't you want to talk about men or fashion or music?'

'Because it's so trivial.' They were sitting in a bar off Leicester Square having a couple of drinks before deciding where they were going on to next.

'Men, trivial?' said Maria in disbelief, having to raise her voice to be heard over the hubbub that filled the packed bar. 'You're not still funny about sex are you?'

'No, I'm not,' said Kate indignantly. 'Anyway, what's this "still" business?'

'Oh, come on. You must have been the only woman in history to spend six months at Sandhurst surrounded by men on a ratio of almost one hundred to one and still remain a virgin.'

Kate shrugged and gave an embarrassed little smile. 'But it wasn't a conscious decision. I just wanted more than a roll in the hay. And anyway, it was more lack of opportunity.'

Maria raised her eyebrows. She had found opportunity aplenty. 'And what about this relationship you had with Mike? When you first told me about it and said how it had got serious, I assumed that at the very least the two of you had bonked.'

'But I was only sixteen?'

'So what, it's even legal at that age!' Kate remained silent. 'You're hopeless,' said Maria, laughing. 'And no boyfriend at the moment either, I suppose?'

'It's tricky.'

'Don't give me that. There are loads of blokes at Wallop to choose from. I had hopes of you and Matt till he got chopped.

'Matt?'

'Why not? He was nice enough and had two arms, two legs and a head. And then there was Andy, wasn't there?'

Kate smiled at the memory. That had been good, but it had been well over a year previously and she had known at the time that it wasn't going to develop into a long-term relationship. 'Yes,' she said, 'there *was* Andy.'

'You and Andy made a wonderful couple, you know. But nothing now?' persisted Maria.

Kate shook her head. It wasn't as if she hadn't had the odd fling but they rarely came to anything much. And to be honest she really didn't care.

'Look, my priority at the moment is flying helicopters and there really isn't room in my life for—'

'Two sorts of chopper,' said Maria before she could finish her sentence. Kate couldn't help smiling.

'So, still waiting for Mr Right to come along, like the hopeless romantic that you are?'

'Not really. I'm just not like you.'

'Nympho you mean.'

Kate couldn't help grinning at Maria's description of herself. It wasn't that Maria was a good-time girl but she did have a different set of morals from Kate and assessed all men that she met, however fleetingly, on their potential in bed. And, as even Maria herself would admit, given the chance, she liked to find out whether or not her assessment was right.

'So, to change the subject, how long is it now before you get your wings?'

'About a month, if all goes well.'

'And am I invited to the parade?'

'Of course.'

'Good. But I shall only come if you invite your mother too.'

'Oh, God. It's difficult.'

'Kate, you can't go on pretending she doesn't exist. I know she's a pain in the backside, but she is your mother. She deserves better. You've got to make it up with her, and this is the ideal opportunity. You can't turn your back on her forever. It isn't as if you have so many relations you can afford to ditch them willy-nilly. Go and see her. Sort it out.'

'Maybe.'

Maria dropped the subject. *Maybe* was a big step forward from a flat no.

Chapter Seven

Kate paced up and down outside the public telephone booth in the mess, plucking up courage to phone her mother. She been thinking about what Maria had said for a couple of days and had come to the inevitable conclusion that her friend was right: she had to make contact again. She might not love her mother, she might not even like her particularly, but when all was said and done, she *was* her mother. But she hadn't spoken to her for nearly three years, and what on earth was she going to say to her now? How are you? Done anything interesting recently? That was so trite. Should she apologise for the silence? But it hadn't been entirely her fault. Her mother had been completely unreasonable.

The trouble was, Kate hated the fact that Maria disapproved of her continuing vendetta more than she disliked the idea of being reunited with her mother. And to make matters more uncomfortable, she knew that Maria was right. Not that Maria had actually said, 'Make up with your mother or don't count me as a friend any more', but she had left Kate in no doubt as to her views. Kate had too much respect for Maria, for her sensible, down-to-earth approach to life, her common sense, her happy-go-lucky relationship with her family, to wish to court further criticism. There was nothing for it but to swallow her pride and make that call.

Resolutely Kate entered the phone booth and put a pile of coins on the shelf. Taking a deep breath, she dialled her mother's number. The phone rang three times and then was picked up. The hiss of an answering machine kicking in was unmistakable.

'I'm sorry,' said the recording, 'Honour Hayleigh-Ffoulkes can't come to the phone at the moment. Please leave a message and I'll get back to you.' Kate was nonplussed. An answering machine? Since when had her mother had one of those? And what was she doing out at this time of night? Honour never went out in the evening. Irrationally, Kate felt annoyed that her mother was doing these things without consulting her daughter. Caught off guard by the lack of personal response, she replaced the receiver, and phoned Maria instead.

'So have you rung your mother yet?' asked Maria accusingly as soon as she heard Kate's voice.

Kate was absolutely sure that her friend would give her a rifting if she admitted she hadn't actually spoken to Honour. She hedged. 'Well . . .'

'I take it that's a no,' said Maria.

'No, I did, only . . .'

'Only what?'

'I phoned a minute ago but I got an answering machine.'

'So?'

'I didn't like to leave a message.'

'Coward.'

'But I've promised myself that I'll try again tomorrow night.'

'Just make sure you do, or I won't come to your wings parade.'

Kate knew that Maria was perfectly capable of carrying out her threat, and she wanted someone to be there for her. Apart from a rather ga-ga aunt in Scotland, she didn't have any relatives to invite, and her only friend based close enough to come for the day was Maria.

The following evening she steeled herself to make the call, and was annoyed to find that, yet again, she was faced with a machine to communicate with. Damn, she thought, but she knew that if she didn't leave a message, it would be even harder to make contact the next time she tried.

'Mum,' she said. 'Mum, it's me. I thought it might be possible for us to get together again. Perhaps I could come up to Windsor to see you. Would that be OK? Next weekend, perhaps? Give me a ring sometime.' She gave the phone number of the mess clearly to the tape machine and then slowly replaced the receiver. She wondered how long it would be before her mother got back to her – if she did at all.

It was a week before Honour called. Kate had all but given up and was assuming that her mother was using the machine to screen her calls and was deliberately snubbing her with her refusal to pick up the phone.

'But I was away, darling,' her mother said. 'How could I possibly know that after all this time you would suddenly take it into your head to apologise for the way you treated me?'

Kate seethed inwardly. The way she had treated her mother! God, what an interpretation of the facts! She was on the brink of either putting her straight or slamming down the receiver when she remembered Maria's disapproval of her continuing dispute.

'Away? How nice.' She tried not to sound too tight-lipped.

'Yes, darling. I've been on a cruise in the Med. I can't tell you how relaxing it was.'

'I'm so glad. So you're feeling fit and well then?'

'Couldn't be better.'

'And your asthma?'

'Oh, the occasional attack, but nothing too serious. Nothing that stops me from getting around or doing what I want to do.'

'Obviously,' muttered Kate between gritted teeth.

'I'm sorry, I missed that.'

'I said, I'm so glad,' she lied.

'So,' said her mother brightly, as if they had only spoken the previous week, 'what have you been doing with yourself? I suppose you still fly in your spare time?'

'So how was it?' asked Maria when Kate phoned her to tell her that she had done the deed.

'Much as I expected. She blamed me for the rift. Couldn't see anything unreasonable in the way she had behaved. She's been gallivanting around recently, cruises and the like. I think we can safely assume from that that she is over Daddy's death.'

'Sounds like it. But it's only to be expected. After all, it's been over three years now, hasn't it?'

'Nearer to four.'

'So it's inevitable she's managed to pick up the threads. She was probably coming out of all the grief and depression when you two had that row. You pushing off was possibly for the best. It made her take control of her life again. Anyway, aren't you pleased that she is completely independent? Surely that's what you wanted?'

Kate knew in her heart that Maria was right, but irrationally she was annoyed that her mother was coping so well without her. She wanted to have been missed, she wanted her mother to have appreciated what Kate had done for her in the months after her father's death, to have been relieved and grateful that she had made contact again. And none of that had been forthcoming. She sighed. Her mother's reaction had been better than the alternative; Maria was right about that. There was no way she wanted to return to the time when Honour hadn't even been capable of making toast without Kate to help her. So why was she so irritated by the situation now? Perhaps she didn't really know what she did want.

Over a year after being passed as a suitable candidate for helicopter training, and a month after she spoke to her mother, Kate passed her final handling test and was awarded her wings. Her mother came to Middle Wallop for the day to see her daughter presented with them.

'I think your father would have liked to have seen this day,' she said as all the successful students sipped champagne at the reception that followed.

'I know. I'm so sorry he's not here,' said Kate.

'But I'm not sure he would approve of your posting. Northern Ireland! What on earth are they doing sending a girl out to a place like that?'

Kate tried to explain that there were any number of girls already stationed out there, not necessarily doing office jobs, but some of them actually on the streets acting as searchers. She pointed out that Maria had been in the Gulf, but her mother refused to listen.

'As if you haven't spent enough time already out of the country.'

'But I joined the army because I wanted to travel. One tour in Germany is hardly a lifetime's banishment, and anyway,

Northern Ireland is still part of the UK, in case you hadn't noticed.'

Honour Hayleigh-Ffoulkes snorted. 'And why aren't you using your proper name?'

'How do you mean?'

'Your birth certificate states quite clearly that you're called Hayleigh-Ffoulkes.'

'I know. But do *you* know that Dad was known in the RAF as "old Holy Fuck"?'

'Don't be so ridiculous.'

'He was, I can promise you, and I'm not going to be called the same, so I quietly dropped the Ffoulkes when I joined up. I didn't tell you because I knew what your reaction would be.' Honour snorted again and looked thunderous. Tough, thought Kate. She had to make her own way in the world, and it was up to her how she was going to do it, how she earned a living and what she called herself. Unlike Maria, she didn't think that parental support was ever going to be an option. The best she and her mother seemed to be able to hope for was luke-warm affection brought about by a rather inconvenient blood-tie. Hardly the traditional mother/daughter relationship but, Kate supposed, a better deal than poor old Cinderella or Snow White had had. At least she and her mother were communicating again. Perhaps things would improve with time although Kate wasn't going to hold her breath.

Unfortunately, but, as she was to learn later, predictably, and despite the fact that it was August, it was raining when Kate arrived at Belfast International Airport. The cloud cover had been ten tenths from just after they left the coast south of Liverpool, all the way across the Irish Sea, and Kate was only able to get the barest glimpse of the ground as the aircraft prepared to land. She had been looking forward to this early afternoon flight as it would be a novelty to be a passenger in a plane and be able to sit back and enjoy the view with no responsibilities whatsoever. However, after forty minutes, there was precious little view to enjoy. It was so different from flying into Akrotiri, she thought, as at last they broke through the thick clouds and she watched trees and hedges dividing bright green fields grow bigger and closer until they seemed to be skimming over their tops. The fields in England had been shades of brown and gold, from teddy-bear fur to toffee as the harvest was being gathered and some fields had even been ploughed. But here there were hardly any fields of grain as far as she could see; only grass, dairy herds and hay – truly the Emerald Isle, she thought.

The pilot smacked the 737 hard on to the runway, and as the smart glass and stainless-steel buildings of the civilian airport – with *Welcome to Belfast* in large letters on the roof – flashed past to Kate's right, she could also see the drabber, more utilitarian buildings and hangars that comprised RAF Aldergrove to her left. Aldergrove, her home for the next two, or possibly three, years. Then the pilot applied the reverse thrust and the brakes simultaneously, and Kate had to brace herself against the seat in front as she was thrown forward. By the time she had regained her composure they were taxiing off the main runway and about to link with the umbilical that was being directed towards the aircraft door.

Kate gathered her belongings, wishing she had a coat, and shuffled off the aircraft with the other passengers. She followed the signs that directed her along the grey and red corridors to the baggage hall to wait for her kit to arrive. As she waited by the conveyor belt for the luggage to be unloaded, she was acutely aware of all the Northern Irish accents around her. Suddenly she began to understand how members of the SOE would have felt when they had been parachuted into France during the Second World War. She shook herself. Brace up, she commanded herself sternly. Don't be so bloody melodramatic. But it didn't help. She still felt as though she stuck out like a sore thumb. She had been warned not to travel showing any outward signs of being anything but a civilian – no items of military kit to be displayed, worn or carried at all – and it had given her a vague sense of unease, a feeling of mild paranoia, but now that she had arrived in the Province . . . Oh God, all she had to do was open her mouth and everyone would know she was English and so probably something to do with the security forces. She'd worked herself up into such a state that she couldn't see that thousands of people, totally unconnected with the military, moved to and from Northern Ireland all the time.

She looked at the faces around her anxiously, wondering if there were any members of the IRA amongst them, and half expecting to see the spokesmen from various organisations whose faces were so familiar but whose voices had to be dubbed because they weren't allowed to speak directly on the television.

'Mind your back,' a heavily Irish-accented man's voice said.

'Sorry,' mumbled Kate. She turned sideways to allow a youngish, bearded man to pass, pushing an unwieldy luggage trolley. He parked his trolley beside her.

'Doesn't it always take an age, though?' he said conversationally.

'Does it?' said Kate, acutely aware of her own English accent.

'You'se over here for a holiday?'

'Yes.' Kate was hardly going to tell him the real reason for her arrival. She felt increasingly apprehensive and really didn't want to talk. Who was this man? Why had he picked on her to chat to? Did he have a hidden agenda? Had he targeted her on purpose?

'That's nice. Where are you staying?'

'With friends.' Please would the baggage handlers get their act together and take the luggage off the plane so she could escape?

'That's grand. Where do they live?'

'Belfast.'

'Oh, really. That's where I live. Whereabouts?'

Kate's stomach lurched. God, this was a minefield. Which side of the sectarian divide did he live, and what the hell was a safe area, a neutral area, that she could mention? She wished she'd read more about the whole business of the euphemistically titled Troubles before she'd arrived. She felt fearful that she would say the wrong thing, make some dreadful but basic mistake, get identified as a liar and consequently, because she was obviously hiding something, a member of the army.

The conveyor belt jerked into life. Thank God! The relief was almost overwhelming.

'Oh, look,' said Kate. 'Our luggage will be here in a moment. Excuse me.' She lunged forward to get closer to the bright blue rubber band and away from her interrogator. Unless he abandoned his trolley, he wouldn't be able to follow her, due to the crush of passengers jostling to spot their own cases, and she didn't think he would risk that. As the conveyor belt filled with luggage, she saw a familiar-looking green and brown case, half wedged under a holdall, approaching her along the belt. Good. Slowly it crept towards her. Kate leaned forward, checked the label and grabbed it. Yes, now she could get out of here. She flashed a nervous smile at the Irishman and followed the signs to the exit. She walked down a sloping corridor towards the door – and the rain. Bugger, why *hadn't* she thought to bring a coat? Because it's August, stupid, and no one wears a coat in August – but they do in Northern Ireland.

'Kate,' shouted a familiar voice as she walked out of the door and into the drizzle.

Good heavens! She knew that voice. She looked around her so as to locate its owner. For a second she was so stunned she hardly knew what to say. 'Andy! Good God, what are you doing here?'

'Waiting for you. I didn't imagine that there are two people with this name and your qualifications.'

She overcame her initial shock and faint flutter of excitement mixed with a dose of embarrassment, and leaned forward and gave him a kiss on the cheek.

'It's good to see you.' The last time had been in Cyprus on that wonderful holiday with Maria.

Andy took her case. 'Come on, let's go to the car. We can talk more easily there.'

They ran across the road, dodging heavy raindrops, and headed for the short-stay car park. Kate was glad of the pause in the conversation, as it gave her a chance to gather her thoughts. She should have realised that she might run into Andy again. After all, it was his connection with the Army Air Corps that had been part of his attraction in the first place. But even so, this was a shock. She wondered if he wanted to pick up where they had left off. And did she? They reached the car before she had a chance to address this particular question.

Andy got his keys out and began to unlock the car. 'One

good thing about working locally is that I didn't have to leave to come and get you till I saw the plane land.' He opened the boot and threw her case in.

'Handy.' She shivered as chill rain trickled down her neck. The boot was slammed shut and Andy dodged round to the passenger door and opened it for Kate, who scrambled thankfully into the shelter offered by the car.

'I wasn't sure how you'd feel about seeing me again. I've often wondered what I did to upset you,' said Andy mopping rain off his face with a yellow hanky. All right for him, thought Kate. At least he had had time to prepare himself for this moment. He had known they were going to meet again ever since her posting order had been published. But it had come as a complete shock to her.

'It's nice to be welcomed by a familiar face.' Kate was aware that this didn't really answer Andy's enquiry. As a bolt from the blue this one was a prize-winner and she needed time to get used to the situation before she could even think about commenting, and possibly a couple of days before she felt she would know how to handle it. For a second she wished she were more like Maria, with dozens of discarded boyfriends and broken hearts in her past. Maria would know the protocol for this scenario.

Andy was looking at her curiously, obviously expecting a fuller and better answer. As a distraction, she launched into an account of meeting the unknown Irishman at the baggage reclaim, while Andy extricated his car from its space and drove to the exit.

'He was probably only being friendly. The huge majority of the people here are perfectly ordinary and law-abiding. It's a lovely country in many respects. It's a crying shame it's been completely buggered about by a few people for so long.'

'You're probably right, but I was incredibly conscious of my accent. I almost felt as though I had a flashing neon sign strapped to me saying "this is a target".' Andy laughed obligingly.

They drove away from the airport complex, the windscreen wipers slapping rhythmically but ineffectually against the heavy rain, down the long straight road that led past the permanent RUC security checkpoint and the line of cars waiting to pass through it. Andy slowed down to negotiate a roundabout and Kate felt another frisson of apprehension as she saw names emblazoned on it that had, until now, been only headlines on the evening news: Lisburn, Belfast, Craigavon. It was then a matter of minutes before they arrived at the military base of RAF Aldergrove on the other side of the runway.

At the gate, Kate gazed at the wet and dispiriting married quarters that she could see peeping at her over the high security fence. The guard checked both her and Andy's ID cards carefully, saluted, and the barrier opened to allow them to drive through.

'Welcome to Aldergrove,' said Andy cheerfully. Kate, used to the more relaxed security of mainland bases or those in Germany, felt a fresh wave of apprehension at the thought of the sort of threat that merited these types of measures. Sure, bases in UK and overseas had been attacked, as had off-duty soldiers, their wives and families, but it had been a rarity. Here, anyone connected with the armed forces was considered a legitimate target. Proxy bombs, snipers, car bombs, booby traps had all been used, and had often killed or maimed unwary, careless or simply unlucky members of the security forces and the general public. The security at Aldergrove demonstrated that only too clearly. Kate felt, perhaps unfairly, that a huge iron door had just clanged shut behind her. Was this what it was like to be banged up in prison?

Andy drew the car up outside the front of the mess and ran round to open Kate's door and extract her luggage. He dumped her suitcase and her shoulder bag by the front door and then excused himself to go and park the car where it wouldn't obstruct access to the building. Kate stood by her case and stared at her future home. It wasn't the ugliest building she'd ever seen in her life, but it might merit a place as the most unremarkable. It looked suspiciously like a pre-fab. She picked up her bags and stood waiting until Andy arrived.

'It looks better on the inside,' he said encouragingly, as if he'd read her thoughts.

Kate felt a new wave of despondency. What with being a little tired, the lousy weather, this drab mess, and her feeling of embarrassment at re-encountering Andy, she wondered if things could get any grimmer. It must have showed on her face.

'I promise you'll like it here,' said Andy firmly as he took her luggage and propelled her towards the door.

The mess steward approached her, introduced himself and offered to show her to her room. He took the bags off Andy and strode ahead of her along a ground-floor corridor

'Here you are, ma'am.' He put the case and her shoulder bag on the floor at the foot of the bed. 'I hope this is OK.'

Kate looked round the room. It was a clone of almost any bedroom in any of the messes she'd stayed in: the size, the furniture, the soft furnishings, even the wash basin in the corner.

'It's fine, thanks.' As she said this she was aware of a high-pitched whine that was rapidly increasing in its decibel level. An aircraft was about to take off. Kate took a couple of steps across to her window and was in time to see a British Midland jet hurtle down the runway, not three hundred yards from her room, and launch itself into the leaden sky.

'You'll get used to it,' said Andy from the doorway.

'There's no double glazing,' said Kate in horror, aware that she was stating the obvious.

'Just wait until one lands and you get the pilots applying reverse thrust right outside the mess,' said Andy cheerfully. Kate remembered her very recent landing, when the pilot had made the jet stop within yards.

'Great,' she said, without enthusiasm.

'I'll let you unpack,' said Andy. He left, shutting the door quietly behind him. Kate barely noticed; she was mesmerised by yet another shuttle plane taking off just behind the barbed-wire security fence, which was there either to keep people off the runway or to stop undesirables from attacking the base. But which was it?

Chapter Eight

Kate sat on her bed, surrounded by half-unpacked belongings, and wished for the umpteenth time that Maria was in the next room, like she had been at Sandhurst, so she could go to her for advice.

'Now what do I do?' Kate asked herself. She looked across the room at her reflection in the mirror and smiled ruefully. 'Of all the messes on all the bases in all the world, you have to walk into mine,' she said out loud in an appalling parody of *Casablanca*. She sighed heavily. It wasn't as if she had even finished her affair with Andy properly. She had just caught the plane at Akrotiri and flown out of his life. She had never been in touch with him again. 'What with him and Mother, this is becoming a bit of a habit,' she muttered at her reflection.

Her MFO boxes, sent from the mess at Middle Wallop a couple of weeks earlier, stood in the corner of the room. Someone had obligingly unscrewed their lids for her. Kate wandered across to them and lifted the lid of the first. Out of her carefully packed belongings she extracted a kettle and a jar of coffee. No milk, but what the heck, she could drink it black now and get some from the mess kitchen later. She filled the kettle at her wash basin and plugged it in, then returned to the tea chest to find a mug. As she delved into the depths she found a photo album. Forgetting her mission to make herself a cup of coffee, she sat down on the bed and began to turn the pages. Across the room the kettle, ignored, boiled and clicked off. As Kate gazed at the pages of her album, each picture brought back a flood of memories. A snapshot of a meadow of brilliant spring flowers with an improbably blue sea in the

61

background caught her eye. Cyprus! She could still remember the smell of the orange groves as she and Maria had driven away from Akrotiri airport. Orange groves and hot tarmac and aviation fuel. And somehow the unlikely combination had merged into a wonderfully exotic scent, so different from anything she had come across before. And it had been a wonderfully exotic holiday. Never before had she spent days of such hedonistic pleasure enjoying the sun, sand and sea and evenings of fun and laughter in the company of Maria and the other army officers. And then, of course, there had been Andy.

Kate clasped the photo album to her chest and flopped back on to the bed, a slow smile spreading across her lips as she remembered her holiday on Cyprus and her brief affair with Andy. In her mind she went back to the very beginning of her stay there. The details of her visit had been etched on to her mind, partly because it had been such a fabulous break, but also because it had been where she had finally lost her virginity.

Cyprus had been everything that Kate had imagined it would be, and more. Before her trip she'd been to the library in the education centre and mugged up on its history, geography, climate, flora and fauna, and had already decided which of Cyprus's renowned beauty spots she wanted to visit. She'd never had a Mediterranean holiday before – her parents had always taken her to culturally rich places like Paris, Salzburg and Vienna so she could spend two weeks each summer appreciating a succession of Old Masters, Baroque buildings and sites of historical interest – and the thought of two weeks of indulgence and indolence had been almost as enticing as the travel books' descriptions of the sun, sand, sea and scenery she could expect to find.

Kate remembered her first glimpse of the island from the oval portholes of an RAF VC10 as it began its approach. Beneath the wing of the plane Kate had seen a sea of ultramarine and turquoise and beaches of shimmering sand. Inland were dusty grey-green olive groves and brighter, more verdant areas that she had judged to be orange orchards. She had seen little villages of shining white houses and a larger town with what had looked like a fort. Then the plane had banked in the opposite direction, and instead of the ground, all that was visible was the sky. The 'Fasten seat belts' sign was lit, and a few minutes later Kate had felt the judder of the flaps and then the undercarriage being lowered. As she lay on the bed, rain lashing at the window, she grinned as she recalled the contrast to the approach to Belfast International earlier that day.

It had been the weather that had made the first impact on Kate's senses as she stepped off the VC10 at RAF Akrotiri. The heat was intense. Even in May the concrete runway was shimmering with mirages in the midday sun. As she walked across to the terminal, she could see Maria waving at her frantically from one of the windows. Once inside, she had to wait impatiently for her bags to be unloaded, then there was customs and immigration to negotiate before, finally, she could go through the doors on to the concourse.

'Kate!' shrieked Maria from thirty yards away. Maria looked stunning, with a fabulous tan and a ridiculously skimpy sundress that showed off her endless legs to perfection. The sun had lightened her hair slightly and now her dark curls had a slightly auburn tint, which looked glorious against her bronzed skin. She ran towards Kate, and almost every male head in the building turned to watch her and her gazelle-like elegance.

The two girls hugged, delighted to see each other again. 'Gosh!' Kate couldn't disguise her admiration. 'You look gorgeous. It must really suit you being here.'

'It does. It's wonderful. It was bloody cold when I arrived, and I didn't have a coat, which was grim, but what the heck when the summers are like this?'

Kate held her bare arm against Maria's. 'I've got a lot of catching-up to do as far as the old suntan is concerned. I feel I look like something out of a laboratory specimen jar.'

'A whitey from Blighty,' said Maria with a grin. 'Don't worry, a few days on the beach and you won't stand out so much.' She eyed Kate's luggage. 'Give me the holdall and the carrier bag and you take the case. I'm afraid it's a bit of a trek to the car and then it's a quite a drive to Ayios Nikolaios, but we can stop halfway for a drink if we get too hot.'

Between them they lugged the bags to the car and piled in. The car was baking, so they waited for a few minutes with the windows down before setting off on the long journey. By the time they arrived at the Eastern Sovereign Base Area on the other side of Larnaca, Kate was dripping with sweat and was hot and thirsty, but Maria assured her, as they tooled up the hill behind Dhekelia, that they only had another twenty minutes or so to go before they arrived at the signals regiment. 'And that's the gliding club, by the way,' said Maria, apropos of nothing in particular. Kate, sweltering, tried to look enthusiastic and then glanced enviously at Maria, who seemed unaffected by the climate.

'You get used to it,' she said when Kate remarked on it, but Kate found this hard to believe. It was blistering.

The road was bordered on one side by the Green Line – the dividing line between Turkish Cyprus and its Greek counterpart – and Maria waved cheerfully to some of the UN troops who were manning an observation post. Shortly afterwards they reached the little village of Ayios Nikolaios and Maria pointed out her favourite bars and tavernas. It brought to life all the descriptions in her letters that Kate had read avidly and enviously over the past months. Ahead of them, on the top of a hill, Kate could see the array of antennae and aerials that marked the position of the signals regiment. In a couple of minutes they were drawing up outside the officers' mess.

The mess consisted of a number of bungalows built round a central patio. If it hadn't been for the wide verandas draped in bougainvillaea and hibiscus in vivid shades of fuchsia, lobster and vermilion, it would have looked faintly scruffy. Maria explained that this wasn't the proper officers' mess but a stopgap while a new purpose-built one was erected. Apparently the old officers' mess had been burnt to the ground – history didn't relate how – some twenty years previously, and since then the officers had been housed in a converted junior ranks' club till something better could be provided. The female quarters had been made from a converted blanket store and the men's accommodation hadn't been much more sumptuous. Now at last something more appropriate was being provided, but as the new mess was being built on the site of the old makeshift one, the officers were once again homeless. These buildings, known by their occupants as The Swamp, were functional and without frills. However, they were saved from being completely austere by the flowers, which were the prettiest and most exotic that Kate had ever seen outside Kew Gardens. They brought to mind thoughts of Pacific Ocean atolls, desert islands and hula-hula dancers. This was exactly the sort of faraway posting she'd envisaged in her mind's eye when she'd joined up. Perhaps one day . . .

'I've booked you into the mess for a few days. Then I've got some leave too so I thought we could go and stay in the leave centre up in the Troodos mountains for a while, and then you can spend the last half of your stay in one of the resorts. I've got one of the hotels to give you a whacking great discount so it won't cost too much.' Kate thought this sounded marvellous, and she didn't mind that Maria hadn't been able to take leave for the whole duration of her visit. Maria had already explained that if she took leave every time someone visited her she would never have any left for herself.

Maria had been busy on Kate's behalf before her arrival. She'd organised Kate's accommodation for her stay, made enquiries at the gliding club, fixed up a hire car for her, made sure that any party invitations included the two of them, and had even managed to find the time to pick and arrange some flowers on Kate's dressing table.

By late that evening Kate felt she was almost a part of the regiment too. Maria was obviously very popular, and after dinner, as they sat around the bar drinking brandy sours, they were joined by most of the other single officers. Kate was automatically included in the conversation and the banter, and made to feel completely welcome and at ease. Someone put some music on the battered mess stereo, while another officer found a set of poker dice and suggested they should play for matches. The hours passed in convivial drinking, laughter and silly games. The evening air, now the temperature of a warm bath, was stirred lazily by the ceiling fan, and through the windows came the sound of a myriad of insects that chirped and chirred and buzzed. This, together with the deferential mess staff, the chintz-covered armchairs and the mess silver, made Kate feel as if she was in some sort of time warp that had thrown her back into the days of Empire and the Raj. All it needed, she thought, was for someone to walk in wearing a solar topi for the illusion to be complete.

The following day, a Wednesday, Maria had to work, but she had given Kate directions to the regimental swimming pool, the NAAFI, the saddle club and the library and told her to go and amuse herself until her day's work finished at two o'clock. Kate, aware that her tan was woeful compared to everyone else's, opted for a morning by the pool armed with lashings of suntan lotion and a good book. She actually longed to go to the beach, but wasn't due to pick up her hire car until after lunch.

Lazing by the pool palled after a couple of hours, and despite being very careful, Kate was aware that her shoulders were on the brink of burning. It was time to go back into the shade. She decided to return to the mess via the NAAFI to get yet more suntan lotion and was walking back to her room after her errand when a helicopter clattered overhead and landed on the helipad quite close by. From where she was standing, Kate could see a couple of shiny black staff cars lined up ready to meet the visitor and his – or her – entourage, and a group of officers standing stiffly to attention all sporting their best tropical dress uniforms. Maria had written and told Kate that because the regiment did interesting work and was situated in a fabulous location, they got more than their fair share of visitors – in fact there was a constant stream of VIPs who could find an excuse, however spurious, for a trip to the Mediterranean. Kate realised she was witnessing the arrival of another bigwig who had managed to wangle a few days in the sun. There was a flurry of saluting and handshakes as the VIP appeared, and then the little cavalcade drove off towards the heavily protected and guarded block where the main work of the regiment took place.

As Kate watched, the pilot of the helicopter left the cockpit, did some checks around the outside of the aircraft and then began to walk in the direction of the mess. His path converged with Kate's after about twenty yards and they walked on opposite sides of the road towards their destination. As they walked she was able to study him covertly and decided that even dressed in unflattering flying overalls he was quite tasty. His hair was sun-bleached to the palest gold that set off his dark tan to its best advantage. And even from a distance of twenty feet, Kate could see that he had dark eyelashes, thus avoiding the startled-rabbit look of so many pale blonds. Kate crossed the road as they neared the mess and they arrived almost simultaneously at the front door. The pilot held the door open, giving Kate an appraising look as she passed. She could see from under her eyelashes that he didn't seem to be too disappointed with what he saw despite her lack of suntan.

'You must be new here,' he said.

'Sort of, I'm a visitor.' She noticed the crown on the shoulder of his flying overalls and added, for good measure, 'Sir.' Then, rather wistfully, 'But I wish I was posted here.' She looked at the pilot in his badly fitting flying suit and thought that, with his beautiful bronzed skin and dazzling smile, he had the same Greek-god look that Maria had.

'I'm going to have a coffee. Can I order one for you?' he said. He smiled at her and Kate felt her heart do a flip. Wow!

'I think I'd rather have some tea, thanks, sir. Would you please excuse me for a second while I drop my swimming kit off in my room? I'll join you in a moment.' Kate sped through the mess to her room across the patio, hung up her towel and costume, ran a comb through her hair and touched up her lipstick. She wondered just why she was titivating herself. Good heavens, since he was a major, even though obviously a young one, he might be married with four children – but on the other hand he might not ... Since she'd joined the army, she'd always been vastly outnumbered by members of the opposite sex, but so far she'd never been quite so instantly attracted to any of them. She wondered if it was just the tan, or the fact that he was a pilot; or perhaps it was because she was here on holiday. Weren't all single girls expected to have a holiday romance if they went away on their own? She smiled at her foolishness and blew herself a kiss in the mirror. She was back in the anteroom before the mess waiter had delivered their order.

'Sorry about that, but if I'm going to go to the beach this afternoon I'd prefer not to have to scramble into wet swimming things,' she said. 'By the way, sir, I should introduce myself. I'm Kate Hayleigh.'

'For God's sake, drop the "sir". I'm Andy McMaster.' They shook hands. 'So being a visitor yourself, you've got nothing to do with this VIP visit today?'

'Nothing at all. I didn't even know it was taking place. I only arrived yesterday, and as I said, I'm nothing to do with this regiment.'

'So you're here for the sun, the sand and the sea?'

And perhaps sex, added Kate mentally, hopefully. 'Well, yes. And a spot of gliding too, I hope.' She said it deliberately, knowing that it might just attract his interest in her. Scheming little minx, she thought, but what the heck?

Bingo! Andy's eyes lit up. 'A glider pilot? How many hours?'

Kate gave him a résumé of her gliding credentials and Andy looked suitably impressed.

'That's great. As a pilot myself, I got the jammy job of looking after the gliding club, so I'll be able to show you around if you come down. Would you like to come along this afternoon? It's Wednesday, so I'll be there myself and I could make sure you get a flight.' Wednesday afternoon was traditionally set aside, throughout the army, for sporting activities.

'Oh. I hadn't thought.' She hadn't expected this fast a reaction and she didn't want to let Maria down. Damn. Perhaps he would change his plans if he was that keen. 'I was planning on going swimming.'

Andy looked disappointed. 'Well, supposing you came down after lunch for a couple of hours. You'd still have time for a trip to the beach after that. If you don't come along today you won't get another chance until the weekend.' Kate was torn. How often did a girl get an offer like that from such a hunk?

'Well, it's up to you.' He sounded so indifferent Kate felt annoyed with herself. She'd blown it.

Andy checked his watch. 'Better get back to my helicopter. The general is only stopping here for about forty-five minutes so I mustn't keep him waiting. If I don't see you today, come along on Saturday. I'll be there then too. The gliding here is fantastic by the way – eight-knot thermals come as standard.'

After Andy had left, Kate made up her mind that she would go to the gliding club that afternoon. Maria was taking her to the local car hire company straight after lunch so once she was mobile she could drive there easily. She knew where the gliding club was, and it would be pointless to waste the opportunity. Besides which, she'd probably done enough sunbathing for one day and she was sure Maria wouldn't mind; they could always go to the beach together tomorrow.

When Maria arrived back in the mess at lunchtime they had a quick bite to eat before she took Kate to pick up her vehicle.

'Now you can do your own thing without having to wait for me to be around to chauffeur you,' she said.

'I was going to talk to you about that,' said Kate. 'Would you mind frantically if I were to go gliding this afternoon? It's just that I met the chap in charge, Andy McMaster—'

'Not Randy Andy already? Good God! You haven't been on this island twenty-four hours and already he's sniffed out the newest bit of skirt. How does he do it?'

Kate felt irrationally disappointed. Probably the only man on the island with a reputation like that, and she'd fallen for his charms. How stupid of her. Crossly she thought that he more than likely had a chart to keep a tally of all the gullible girls he'd bowled over, and a score card for marking off how quickly he'd done it. She felt she would be off the scale, she'd been such a pushover.

Masking her feelings, she said brightly, 'Randy Andy? You must tell me more. And,' she added, 'in his defence, he didn't sniff me out. We ran into each other because we were both heading in the same direction at the same time. He'd just landed his helicopter with some high-powered visitor on board as I went past and we ended up at the front door of the mess at the same time.'

'Yeah, yeah, yeah. I believe you, millions wouldn't. He's the nearest thing we have to Casanova here. Wait till he asks you if you want to see his chopper.' Despite her annoyance at herself for falling for the local stud, Kate couldn't suppress a giggle. 'Or play with his joystick,' added Maria with a lascivious leer.

'He can't be that bad, surely?'

'No. I'm exaggerating slightly. He's just a little bit too conscious of his looks for his own good, and that, coupled with the fact that he's our resident helicopter pilot, means that he tends to think he's got the monopoly on being Mr Desirable. He chatted me up for a bit when I first arrived, but then he dropped me for the Garrison Commander's daughter – longer legs and a bigger bank balance.'

'Well, forewarned is forearmed, as they say. I'll bear what you said in mind when I see him.'

Chapter Nine

Kate arrived at the gliding club shortly after three o'clock and drove to the launch point, keeping a careful eye open for any planes that might be in the circuit and preparing to land. The line of vehicles there was surprisingly small, but then there seemed to be very few gliders – obviously this was a much smaller operation than the club she had belonged to in Oxfordshire. She stepped out of her car and immediately spotted Andy waving at her. She suppressed a smile as she remembered what Maria had told her about him, but in spite of her private resolution to be indifferent to his well-rehearsed technique – if everything Maria had said was to be believed – she found herself oddly pleased that he should look so glad that she had turned up.

'Hi,' he said when she reached him. 'I see you changed your mind then.'

'Couldn't resist the lure of some gliding. The sea will still be there tomorrow, and I don't think I have to worry about the heat wave coming to an end.'

Andy laughed. 'You certainly don't. The two-seater will be back in a little while, so I can give you a check flight if you like.'

'Great. Do you want to have a look at my logbook?'

'I suppose I better had – just to make sure you've got fewer hours in gliders than I have.' Andy laughed as he said this. He had a lovely laugh, Kate thought; somewhere between a chuckle and a guffaw. And judging by the crinkles round his eyes and the way his mouth turned up at the corners, rather like a cat's, he obviously spent a lot of time seeing the funny side to life. If he had a sense of humour he couldn't be all bad. Kate smiled and couldn't help herself warming to him.

'Of course I've got fewer hours, you nit. I've done my five hours' endurance flight but I haven't managed the cross country yet, so I haven't even got my silver award.'

'I'm surprised.'

'I suppose with all those hours I should have by now, but it's just the way my luck panned out. Either the weather was wrong, or there was no one to crew for me if I landed out, or the glider I felt most at home with was having its annual CAA check. Anyway, I'll be incredibly rusty. I haven't flown a glider for ages.'

'Never mind. You don't need to worry about any of that to do some local soaring here.'

As Andy spoke Kate could see a glider enter the circuit and prepare to land. Hurriedly Kate and Andy kitted themselves out with parachutes, calculating the amount of ballast Kate would need. By the time the glider was hooked up and ready to go, so were Kate and Andy.

Their first flight was a quick familiarisation for Kate of the local area as seen from the air. She was so busy admiring the stunning view of the coastline, from Cape Greco – just visible through the shimmering heat haze – to the lagoon behind Larnaca, that she found it difficult to concentrate on the more important nitty-gritty about the border between the Turks and the Greeks.

'If you're ever in doubt about your position, just turn towards the coast to the south,' said Andy eventually.

'Right, got that,' said Kate.

Predictably their second launch resulted in a practice cable break. Unpredictably Kate found that the bang of the cable, released under tension, and then the subsequent urgency of making rapid assessments and decisions made her more apprehensive than she'd ever been before. She'd never thought of gliding as a dangerous sport, but suddenly this practice emergency brought home to her the horror of getting it wrong – as wrong as her father had. As she did her final check of the instruments just before they landed, she could barely concentrate for the mounting panic she felt. She was very pale and shaking slightly when she climbed out of the cockpit a few minutes later.

'Are you OK?' asked Andy, noting her pallor. Kate didn't answer but slumped to the ground and leaned against the side of the glider.

'What is it, airsickness?'

'No,' Kate mumbled. 'I'll be OK. Just give me a minute.' Her heart was still thumping and her forehead was damp with an unpleasant cold sweat. She thought she might be sick or faint if she tried to do anything that involved any movement. She leant against the side of the glider and waited for the feeling to subside.

Andy was perturbed. He couldn't understand it. She'd handled the cable break like a pro, but now here she was sweating and trembling and looking as if she might pass out. Patting hands and muttering sympathetic words weren't the sort of things which came easily to Andy – or indeed most male officers – so he wandered off a yard or two and studied one of the few cloud formations. After about five minutes Kate stood up shakily and apologised.

'But I don't understand,' said Andy. 'You must have done dozens of cable breaks since you began flying.'

'Yes, but not since my father was killed in a gliding accident.'

Andy's jaw dropped. He shut his mouth and then opened it again, like a fish. 'God, I'm sorry, I didn't know.'

'There's no reason why you should. It happened a couple of years ago now. He got too low doing a cross-country flight, tried to land out in a field and got it wrong. He broke his neck. I've flown since but not in a glider.'

'Was your dad a senior RAF officer?' Kate nodded. 'I remember reading the air accident investigation report about it,' said Andy. There were relatively few fatalities from gliding accidents, so the ones that did occur tended to stick in the memories of other glider pilots. 'You poor kid. I'm so sorry.'

'You weren't to know.' Kate sniffed and fought back some unexpected tears brought on by memories, Andy's genuine sympathy and the recent shock. She turned away and quickly swept the traces of emotion from her face with the back of her hand. 'I feel a fool,' she said sheepishly, turning back. 'There was no reason to react to a cable break like that. It's just I haven't . . .' The tears threatened to resurface. She stopped, regained control and said, 'I've done powered flight, but not gliding. I didn't realise how powerful some memories might be.'

The noise of an approaching engine reached them; the vehicle, sent to tow them back, was just yards away and they hadn't turned the glider round, got out of their parachutes or done anything to prepare for the dusty walk back to the top end of the airfield. Quickly they got their act together and then conversation stopped as they trudged across the stony, scrubby ground escorting the aircraft to their destination. When they reached it, Kate walked over to Andy, who had been holding the wingtip off the ground.

'Would you think me a frightful wimp if I didn't fly again today? I still feel a bit shaky.'

'No, no. Of course not. It's my fault anyway. If I'd known about the other business, I wouldn't have done the cable break. I'd have given you more time to get used to being back in a glider again.'

'But you weren't to know. I didn't tell you.'

'All the same . . .' Irrationally, Andy wanted to make up for upsetting Kate, albeit unintentionally. 'Look, what are you doing on Friday evening?' he asked.

'I've got no idea. Maria has all sorts of plans for me and I'm not sure what all of them are. Why do you ask?'

'Because 16 Flight, my Army Air Corps flight, has got a beach barbecue planned and I'd like it if you came along as my guest.'

Unexpectedly Kate felt a quick thrill of pleasure at the prospect. She dampened it down and reasoned that it was only because she was the newest bit of skirt, as Maria had so tastefully put it. Still, it could be a nice evening and she'd never been to a beach party before. 'That sounds fun. Tell you what, supposing I give you a ring this evening and let you know?'

'Maria could come too if she'd like.'

'I'll tell her.'

'No, you go on your own. I'd only be a gooseberry.'

'No you wouldn't. Anyway, I'd like some support.'

'Honestly, I really don't fancy it. You go if you want to but count me out.'

Kate was torn. She really fancied the prospect of this party: a velvety Mediterranean night, good food, pleasant company, wine, swimming; it sounded like heaven on earth. But on the other hand, the only person she would know at the party would be Andy, and she was concerned that, should she go she'd be labelled as his latest floozy, another notch on his bedpost.

'What are you going to do then, on Friday night?' She hoped that Maria might come up with a better option, give her a good excuse to turn this offer down.

'Nothing much. I'd planned on a quiet night because we're going up to Troodos on Saturday and I thought we might set out early to miss the worst of the heat, but it doesn't matter if we don't.'

Kate vacillated visibly. The party wasn't getting much competition from that prospect.

'Go on, go to the party on your own. Andy'll make sure you have a good time, and if he doesn't, you can always make an excuse to leave early.'

'It's an idea. It's just I'm not sure about the drive back in the dark. You said that it was a bit tricky to get to some of these beaches. I was planning on getting a lift from Andy or you if I went. But if I have to go with Andy, I'm stuck there for the duration. As it's his party I can't expect him to drive me home early, can I?' She smiled wistfully at Maria. 'So, how about a lift? Please?'

Maria gave in. 'OK, OK, I'll come but I'm not going to stay all night. We'll leave at ten thirty at the latest.

By the time the two girls arrived at the beach, the sun had already set and the party was in full swing. Maria parked her car on the scrub beside the rough and rutted track which they'd bounced along for at least five hundred yards after leaving the main road, which itself had been little better than a lane. Kate was thankful she'd got Maria to drive, as she realised she would never have found this place on her own in the dark. They grabbed their towels and scrambled down a steep bank on to the still-hot sand. Along the beach, close to the water's edge, was a circle of light, as though a heavenly spotlight was shining down from the stars to illuminate the party. They could hear the distant noise of merriment, but above the sound of voices and music the rhythmic, sibilant splash of small waves breaking could be heard, and the aroma of barbecuing meat competed with the tangy scent of the sea and the warm, damp smell of recently irrigated soil. Maria and Kate headed through the darkness towards the pool of light cast by a dozen gas lanterns and the glow from the barbecue. As they emerged from the blackness, Andy spotted them and waved. Kate was quite surprised at how pleased she felt at seeing him again. But then again, she thought, there was no reason not to feel pleased; after all, he was good-looking and friendly, and they shared a love of flying.

'Hi, Kate, hi, Maria. You're just in time. The food is about ready.'

'Great, I'm famished. It seems a long time since lunch,' said Maria, exchanging air kisses with Andy.

'Good. There's plenty here, so I expect you to tuck in. And how are you, Kate? Recovered from the scare I gave you?' He sounded genuinely concerned and kissed her on the cheek as a greeting. Maria shot Kate a questioning look. What had she and Andy got up to at the gliding club? Kate certainly hadn't mentioned anything.

'I'm fine thanks, but hungry. And then as soon as I've had a bite to eat, I fancy a swim. I've never swum in the sea at night.'

'Best to let your food go down for a while, as Granny would say,' laughed Andy. 'But I can recommend night swimming. If you're lucky there may be phosphorescence, and then it's like swimming in cold fire.'

'Wow, that sounds beautiful.'

Maria tugged Kate's sleeve. 'Are you going to natter all night, or are we going to get something to eat?'

'OK, OK.' Kate threw Andy an apologetic glance and followed Maria to the tables piled with meat, salads, plates, glasses, beer and wine.

'What was all that about?' asked Maria.

'What?'

'About being "recovered"?'

Kate explained about her stupid reaction to the cable break.

'So Randy Andy played the knight in shining armour and rescued you from the imagined horrors.'

'Something like that.'

Maria smirked. 'Falling for his charms, are you?'

'Don't be daft,' said Kate, but she was glad of the dim light all the same, as she knew it would hide her sudden flush. Maria's remark had been a bit too close to the truth for comfort.

She busied herself with piling her plate with food, in the hope of avoiding further probing from Maria. Then the two girls collected a cold beer each and took themselves off to a clear spot on the sand to enjoy their meal. They were both hungry so they were too busy eating to particularly want to talk. They had almost finished when Andy came over to join them.

'May I?' he asked.

'Be our guest,' replied Kate, swallowing her last mouthful. Goodness, she felt full. She flopped back on the sand, replete.

'Wow,' she breathed as, for the first time, she really looked at the star-strewn sky.

'Why wow?' asked Maria, too busy nibbling the last delicious morsels from a chicken drumstick to really pay attention to Kate's actions. Kate explained.

'If you go along the beach a bit, get away from the light, you'll be able to see them properly,' said Andy. 'There's not a lot of ambient light around this end of the island, so all the stars really stand out.'

'I'm too full to move for a bit,' replied Kate. She leaned up on one elbow and looked at Andy. 'I'll go for a stroll to admire them in a little while.'

'I shall be going for a swim in about half an hour,' said Andy. 'Just as soon as I've let my digestion have a chance.'

'Me too,' said Maria. She too flopped back on to the sand and groaned. 'God, I'm stuffed,' she complained. 'If I go now I'll sink.'

Silence descended; Kate and Maria both soporific from over-indulgence, and Andy too busy chewing to talk. Surrounding them was a steady hubbub of conversation; occasionally there came a burst of laughter, sometimes a shout or a clatter of cutlery, but the general noise level was steady and Kate found she was able to ignore it and float away on her thoughts. This place was idyllic, utopian, and wouldn't it be wonderful to be here for a couple of years, like Maria and Andy were, instead of a couple of weeks' holiday? She looked at Andy through half-closed eyes. He had to have the best job in the whole world – flying helicopters in Cyprus, with a great social life thrown in for good measure. If only she was a bloke, thought Kate, and was allowed to fly. Just fancy the bliss of earning your living doing something like that. A nasty little bubble of envy began to ferment inside her and threatened to spoil things. She gave herself a shake and leapt to her feet.

'I'm going for that walk,' she announced. 'I want to get a proper look at those stars, and besides which, I need the exercise after all that food. Do you want to come?'

The question was actually directed at Maria, but it was Andy who answered.

'Great idea. Tell you what, I'll point out some of the constellations.' He stopped and put his plate on the sand beside him, then added, 'That is, if you would like me to and I'm not teaching my grandmother to suck eggs.' He stood up, and behind him Kate could see Maria smirking more than ever.

'Won't you join us?' Kate asked her.

'No, no,' she replied, barely suppressing her laughter. 'I'm perfectly happy here.' Behind Andy's back but where Kate could see it, she drew a heart pierced by an arrow in the sand. Kate shot her a filthy look.

'Right then,' said Andy. He failed to notice Maria's snigger. 'Let's go this way,' he suggested. Kate, with no option, followed. They left the encircling pool of light and headed along the beach and into pitch darkness.

The sand was dry and warm and because it was so soft Kate found it tricky to walk. She kept sinking into it up to her ankles, and because she couldn't see properly it made her stumble. And every time she stumbled, she found herself lurching dangerously close to Andy. Goodness knows what anyone who might be able to see through the gloom might think. She headed towards where the waves were lapping gently in the hope that it would be easier to make progress on wet sand. Andy followed, keeping close beside her.

'We're lucky there's no moon,' he said.

'Why?'

'Because it makes the stars even brighter. Look.'

Kate stopped and looked at the heavens. Away from the light of the party, the stars were brilliant and infinite. Right above her was the Milky Way, so thick with them that it looked more like a cloud than individual points of distant light.

The darkness and stillness was such that it seemed sacrilege to disturb it. 'You know,' she murmured, 'I have often tried to get my head round the idea of infinity, and I just can't do it. I can't grasp the notion that the sky goes on for ever, that it isn't encased in some sort of gigantic bubble.'

'I know what you mean,' said Andy, almost whispering too. 'And don't you find it incredibly humbling to think what minute specks we really are in this huge great concept?'

Kate turned towards him and lowered her gaze from the sky to look at his face. 'Like we're single atoms in some giant structure,' she said in a voice that was barely audible. They were standing little more than a foot apart and Kate was suddenly aware that she wanted him to kiss her. She felt a frisson of raw desire ripple through her, a feeling she hadn't experienced since Mike, a feeling which faintly surprised her yet one which she welcomed. She was aware that her knees were suddenly quite wobbly and that her heart was thudding remarkably fast. Taken together, it was such a wonderful sensation that she smiled. She wondered for a second whether his reputation as a Lothario was because he had this effect on any woman who got this close. But his reputation apart, wasn't this just the perfect moment and place to fall in love: the stars, the sea and a handsome man? Involuntarily the angle of her gaze fell a further few degrees so she was looking at his mouth. She couldn't tell if she leaned towards him or if it was Andy who moved towards her, but suddenly they were in each other's arms, devouring each other. She could feel his tongue probing gently and his fingers massaging her scalp through her luxuriant hair. She moved her arms until they encircled his neck, then pressed against him till she could feel the warmth of his body along the length of hers. She shut her eyes. She didn't want anything to distract her from the warm security of being in his arms, nor did she want this moment to stop.

Infinity, eternity, she wanted to be a part of it, but suspended within this moment. Andy dropped his arms slightly so they were around her waist, and drew her upwards and even closer towards him. She could smell the scent of his skin; clean, and with a faint tinge of suntan lotion. She inhaled as her lips left his mouth and she began to kiss his cheek and his ear. He hugged her closer still and Kate felt herself sigh with pleasure. Eventually, panting slightly, they drew away from each other.

'I want you,' said Andy in a throaty whisper.

Kate, feeling herself tumbling towards an emotional cliff edge that she wasn't sure she was equipped to cope with, said, 'I bet you say that to all the girls,' but she said it with a smile.

'Not *all* the girls.'

'Just some of them.'

'I couldn't lie to you, sweet Kate, but it doesn't make me want you any the less.'

She remembered how Mike used to call her that, *Sweet Kate*. And now, so was Andy. What was it with that phrase that made her weak at the knees? Kate lowered her eyes. Was this *it*? Was this more than lust? Was it love, the moment that she'd often wondered about? Was she ready for it? Would the moment come again, and if it did, could it come at a better or more romantic moment? And Andy, how did she feel about him? Attraction – undoubtedly; she couldn't deny all the sensations she'd felt earlier, and, if she was honest, was still feeling.

A shout of laughter from along the beach interrupted her thoughts and reminded her of the party not far away.

'Perhaps not here,' she said shyly. 'Supposing someone else decides to go star-gazing.'

'They won't,' said Andy amused by her inhibitions.

'All the same . . .'

'Come back with me to the mess then,' he suggested. Kate didn't know how to answer. She longed to say yes, but what would Maria's reaction be? No doubt she would rib her mercilessly when Kate told her to go home without her. She'd be full of cracks about conquests and fulfilling quotas. She'd hesitated too long. 'You don't want to,' said Andy, sounding downcast.

'It's not that . . .' Oh God, why wasn't there a manual to

teach you what to do in this situation? thought Kate despairingly. 'It's Maria. I've promised to go back with her.'

'Ah. I see.' Andy smiled. 'It'll mean owning up to being seduced by my charms if you send her back to Ay Nik on her own.'

Kate was glad it was so dark, because she felt her face burning. 'Yes,' she mumbled.

'Well, I'm glad about something.'

'What's that?'

'It's the *where* and *when* that's the problem, not the *with whom.*'

Kate smiled shyly and said, 'Yes, exactly.'

'So all we need to do now is work out what *where* and which *when.*'

Kate began to giggle, partly because Andy was being so daft, partly because he was so understanding, and partly with relief that the awkward tension she had felt at refusing his offer had evaporated.

'Well, as the idea of going to bed with me doesn't completely repel you, shall I pick you up from the mess tomorrow then?' he suggested.

'No,' said Kate sadly. 'We're going to Troodos for a few days and we're setting out first thing. We'll be back by Wednesday though,' she finished hopefully.

'I'll just have to be patient then, won't I?' He caressed the back of her neck and Kate felt goose pimples spring up along her arms. Wednesday was an age away, could she really expect him to wait that long?

Kate hung her head, feeling as if she'd blown her chances and let him down.

'Come here, gorgeous, and give me another kiss,' said Andy. 'You look as if it's the end of the world.'

He took her in his arms, and again Kate was enveloped in a feeling of warmth and security and love. Mike had made her feel good, had made her feel sophisticated, desired and desirable. But now, with something to compare with that past experience, she could see that it had been remarkably two-dimensional, based on the need to be wanted rather than on any real emotion. How could she have mistaken her crush on Mike for real, aching desire, which was what she felt now? Too

81

young to know any better, she decided. But if she'd been so wrong before, how could she know if she was right now? Was this feeling she now felt only another step up on the ladder to real love? And if it was, how many steps were there? All she knew was that this, right now, felt right. She wished she wasn't going to Troodos, wished she was going to be spending Saturday with Andy, but she could wait. She wondered for a second time if he would. Oh God, she hoped so.

'Did you see many stars?' asked Maria archly when Kate and Andy rejoined the party.

'Heaps,' said Kate quickly.

'How nice,' said Maria in a tone dripping with sarcasm and disbelief. Andy offered to get them all another beer – an offer which was eagerly accepted. 'By the way,' added Maria, 'your lipstick is smudged.' She raised her eyebrows and smirked again.

The Troodos Mountains were beautiful, and deliciously cool after the heat of the coast. Kate tried to concentrate and look enthusiastic at the many sights Maria took her to: the hillside villages, Makarios's tomb, Mount Olympus. On the Monday of their visit, they crossed the checkpoint in Nicosia and drove to the northern, Turkish half of the island and the picture book harbour at Kyrenia. They drove into the hills behind and explored Bellapaix, vowing to read Lawrence Durrell's book, and ate in a taverna whose owner was so taken by the two girls that he refused any money for the wine they drank and charged them a ridiculously small amount for their food. They drove up the panhandle to the longest, emptiest beach Kate had ever seen and swam in limpid, turquoise water that was such an extraordinary colour she half expected to find it had dyed her skin. But all the time Kate was counting the minutes and longing for the day to be over so she would be one day nearer to seeing Andy again. Simultaneously she suffered huge pangs of guilt brought on by this ungratefulness.

'That was a lovely day,' announced Kate, wanting to assuage her conscience, as they drove up the winding road back to the leave centre in the mountains at the end of the day.

'Hmm,' said Maria. 'You seemed to be somewhere else most of the time.'

'Oh, no. I really enjoyed it. Honestly.'

Maria took her eyes off the road for a second to look at her friend. Kate had never been a convincing liar.

'Is there something the matter? You know you can tell me if there is.'

'No. There's nothing wrong. I'm having a great time. You've been endlessly kind and you've made so much effort on my behalf.'

'That's what friends are for.' They drove on in silence for a mile or two. Kate admired the view while Maria concentrated on negotiating a string of hairpin bends. 'So when are you seeing Andy again?' she said suddenly.

Kate was caught off guard. 'Wednesday,' she replied without thinking.

'Aha! I knew it.'

'Knew what?' asked Kate, huffy at being taken in by the ploy.

'Oh, come on, Kate, you came back from your stroll with him along the beach last Friday looking as though you'd won first prize on the premium bonds and with lipstick smeared all over your face. Since then you've been mooning about, but strangely you haven't mentioned Andy once. You don't have to be in the Intelligence Corps to work it out, you know.'

'I didn't mention anything because I knew you'd laugh at me.'

'Not really. Andy's a nice guy . . .'

'But. There's a *but* at the end of that sentence.'

'*But* he's a terrible ladies' man.'

'So?' said Kate defiantly.

'So, I don't want to see my best friend get hurt.'

'You won't.' Kate paused and fiddled with the strap of her handbag for a second or two. 'Look, I would be lying if I didn't own up to thinking he's absolutely gorgeous—'

'You and the rest of the island.'

'Exactly. And I'm terribly flattered that he seems to like me when he can obviously pick and choose.' Maria didn't say that Kate plainly had a flawed mirror, because she was quite the prettiest girl in the Eastern Sovereign Base Area, tan or no tan. 'But I've decided to treat this like a holiday romance. I've been mooning about, as you put it, because I've been thinking about where this relationship – if there even is one – might possibly go once I get back home. I've been thinking about it a lot over the last couple of days and I'm happy to have a fling with him while I'm here and kiss him goodbye forever at Akrotiri. If he's the ladies' man you say he is, I can't expect anything to last when I've gone, but while I'm here . . .'

'Well . . .' Maria sounded dubious. 'You're old enough and ugly enough—'

'Hey, less of the ugly!'

'As I was saying before I was so rudely interrupted, *ugly* enough to know what you're doing, but he is a heart breaker.'

'I've gathered that. Hence my decision.'

'But you're still going to lose your virginity to him.'

'I might.'

Maria jammed the brakes on. The driver of the car following them, which had been tailgating them since Nicosia, hooted and swerved past. Maria ignored it and swivelled sideways in her seat to look at Kate.

'Good God Almighty – alleluia. Finally. I never thought I was going to live to see it. You must be the only living virgin older than twenty in existence outside a convent.'

Kate blushed. 'It's not a decision I've made consciously. It's just the way things have turned out. Besides which, I'm a bit picky,' she added in her own defence.

'You must be to have gone that long since you were legal at sixteen. You're just a hopeless romantic at heart, aren't you?' Kate nodded a little bashfully. Maria whistled. 'God, it's hard to believe. Never mind, lucky old Andy. That's a treat in store for him on Wednesday.'

'You're wicked.'

'I know. But then that's why I've bonked for Britain and you're still a virgin.'

'If I'm such a rarity, perhaps I should be stuffed and put in a glass case.'

'Andy'll stuff you all right. Just don't expect a glass case as well.'

Chapter Ten

Looking back, what Kate really remembered about losing her virginity wasn't the event itself but learning, during the subsequent pillow talk, that the Army Air Corps had started to accept women as potential pilots. As she lay beside Andy, sated, drowsy and still intertwined, Kate had murmured that, in her opinion, sex was better than flying. Andy had agreed, and then had casually mentioned that a certain woman doctor in the army might not agree with her as she had recently qualified as a pilot.

Kate, nuzzled against Andy's left ear, said softly, 'So what? I've got a PPL.'

'No, silly. She's qualified as a helicopter pilot.'

'Still, so what? All it proves is she's got the money for the lessons.'

'She's an Army Air Corps helicopter pilot.'

Kate, her drowsiness instantly banished, shifted so she could extract her arm from under Andy's neck and prop her head up on it to look at him harder. 'She can't be, it's against the rules.'

'So perhaps they've changed the rules.'

'Wouldn't it be wonderful if they have? I could apply.' Kate flopped back on to the pillows. 'Just think, I could fly.'

'I thought you just said that sex is better than flying,' said Andy, idly toying with one of her nipples and making it harden. Kate shivered with the rush of raw sexual desire this roused and felt her skin tingle with goose pimples.

'It is, but ...' She didn't have a chance to finish her sentence, because Andy's mouth closed hers and his hands slid along her body, making her quiver and shiver with excitement and desire. Instinctively, she arched her body towards him.

'You're not sore, are you?' he asked gently. He'd been stunned and then quite touched when he'd discovered that Kate was still a virgin. He didn't think he'd ever made love to someone completely inexperienced before, and found it quite arousing. Even so, he consciously decided that her pleasure must come before his.

'Are you sure about this?' he'd asked.

'I've never been more sure of anything in my life.'

And Andy had used all his experience to ensure that she climaxed before allowing himself to.

Now she didn't answer, but gently took hold of his penis and guided him towards her again. She felt herself shiver with excitement as he entered her and wondered for the nth time why she had waited so long to discover the wonders of sex. This time it was quicker but equally satisfying, and afterwards, as they lay panting from their efforts, Kate couldn't resist returning to the subject of flying.

'So what tips can you give me about getting my application accepted?'

'Hmm? What did you say?'

Kate repeated her enquiry.

'I thought virgins were supposed to be romantic,' said Andy sleepily.

'They may be, but I'm not one any more, am I?'

'OK, I give in.' Andy turned his head sideways on the pillow and smiled at her. 'Look, if you give me a chance to recover, I'll take you down to the flight in Dhekelia and get you some copies of the forms.'

For the rest of her stay on the island, Kate visited 16 Flight every morning, until she became a semi-permanent fixture. Impressed by her keenness, Andy and his flight sergeant explained to her the theory of flight for rotary-wing aircraft, showed her how the cyclic and the collective controls worked and introduced her to the subject of low-level flight and helicopter tactics on a battlefield. They taught her the function of each instrument and warning light in the cockpit of a Gazelle, they checked out what she knew about navigation, corrected some bad habits she'd got into and gave her a book about the history of the Army Air Corps, 'because it looks enthusiastic if you know all about the outfit you'd like to join,' explained Andy when she'd complained it looked dull. They gave her some past entrance exam papers and told her what she could expect to be asked at the selection board, and Kate made notes, listened intelligently and knew that if she didn't get accepted for training it wouldn't be the fault of the flight in Dhekelia. And in the evening Andy completed her education in the other field where he also felt himself to be her personal tutor.

'I've hardly seen you,' complained Maria when they met up for a meal in the little resort where Kate was staying.

'I've been busy,' said Kate.

'Oh yes? Making up for lost time with Andy?'

'Don't be so nosy.' She laughed, and added, 'I have been, as a matter of fact, but I've also been learning all about helicopters.'

'I told you he'd want you to play with his joystick!' shrieked Maria triumphantly. Several other diners, British holidaymakers, turned to stare, and Kate went bright red.

'Shut up,' she hissed, deeply embarrassed.

'Don't be such a prude.' Maria wasn't the least bit contrite.

'Anyway, it's not called a joystick, it's the cyclic.'

'"A rose by any other name . . ." So why this sudden and deep interest in army aviation?'

'Because I've discovered that I may be allowed to join the Army Air Corps, and Andy and his flight have been helping me bone up on things to do with helicopters to help my chances of selection.'

'Kate, that's wonderful. It'd be a dream come true for you, wouldn't it?'

'Kate. Kate!'

Kate was aware that Andy was calling her name.

'What . . .? Where . . .?' she mumbled. She could hear someone hammering on a door.

'Kate! *Kate.*'

'Yeah, what?' She opened her eyes. Where the hell was she? This wasn't Cyprus. She tried to sit up but her back and limbs, stiff from the uncomfortable position she had flopped into, sent a spasm of pain to her brain in protest. God, she was stiff. She rolled on to her side and looked about her properly. Beside her, on the floor, lay her photo album where it had fallen off the bed. Around her was the detritus of half-unpacked boxes and suitcases.

'Kate, are you there?' More hammering.

'Yes. Yes. Come in.' Kate shook her head and rubbed her eyes in an attempt to bring herself back to the present and pull herself together.

Andy popped his head round the door and saw Kate sitting on her bed, her hair tousled and a bemused look on her face. 'I'm sorry, did I wake you?'

'I must have fallen asleep.' Kate rubbed her eyes again. 'I'm sorry. I lay on my bed for a moment and the next thing . . .'

'You must have been out for the count for hours.'

Kate looked at her watch. 'Half past six! Good God.'

'I came along to see if you wanted to come and have a drink in the bar before dinner and meet some of the lads.'

'I'd love to. Give me fifteen minutes and I'll be there.'

'OK. I'll meet you in the bar. When you leave your room, turn left and walk down the corridor, straight across the entrance hall and then follow the sound of raucous laughter.'

'No worries. Remember, I passed the navigation phase.'

When Andy had left, Kate scrabbled round in a case for something clean and relatively uncreased to wear. She found a skirt and blouse that filled the bill and changed quickly. Then she located her make-up bag and comb and did a few running repairs to her appearance. She checked her watch; it was only twenty to seven. She wasn't going to rush along to the bar just yet. That would look too keen. It might send out the wrong signal to Andy and she didn't want to do that. Their affair in Cyprus had been wonderful but Kate had kept to her determination to treat it as just a holiday romance and to forget about him when she left the island. It wasn't that she hadn't wanted to see him again, but she couldn't see a future for them, given his reputation and her own commitment to her job in the forces. She had no reason to doubt Maria's assessment of his character and she was certain that as soon as she was out of sight he would be off hunting for a new conquest. Much better, she had told herself at the time, to make a clean break; to leave on a high and not to look back. It would be humiliating to send letters and make phone calls and then to discover that he had moved on and regarded her as a pest.

Now she thought that perhaps she should have warned him that she was going to ride off into the sunset at the end of the holiday. She'd assumed, though, that that was how he would have wanted her to play it, so she had flown off without leaving him an address or number where he could reach her, and that had been that.

Kate glanced at her watch again. Still too early to go to the bar if she didn't want to seem eager. She picked up her number two dress uniform out of her case and put it carefully on a hanger, but she still puzzled over the present situation. Of course, if Andy had been that keen on continuing their relationship he could easily have got hold of her via Maria. And he hadn't. There, Kate told herself triumphantly, that proved she had done the right thing. But from his greeting at the airport he'd almost sounded as though her disappearance and her silence had hurt him. Had she treated him badly? And now what? Ignore the issue? Apologise? Hope that things could be picked up where they had left off? No. No, that definitely wasn't an option. Oh, bugger, why did life have to be so bloody complicated?

She picked up a blouse and was about to put that in the wardrobe too when there was a knock on her door.

'Come in,' she called.

'Hi.' It was Andy again. 'I suddenly thought it was a bit churlish to let you make an entrance all by yourself. The lads can be a bit boisterous and it seemed like throwing a Christian to the lions. If you're ready I could take you along.'

'Thanks. That's kind. I was just about to potter down there.'

'Good.'

Kate suddenly felt extremely awkward and gauche. Silence descended, and she busied herself by hanging up the blouse.

Andy broke it first. 'How was the helicopter course?'

'Tough, but it had some good times too.'

'Many get chopped?'

'A few. I don't think some of the men thought I ought to be allowed to pass.'

'Why? Did you go on review?'

'Oh, no. It was because I was a woman.'

'Ah.'

Silence again.

Kate picked up a jersey from her case and refolded it. It was something to do.

'Andy?' she said diffidently.

'Yes.'

'Look, I . . . We're not . . . I mean . . . Oh God, this is more difficult than I thought. You're not thinking of picking up again where we left off, are you?' She clutched the jersey. It was now a shapeless ball.

'Why? Do you want me to?'

'No.' She said it too quickly and it sounded rude. 'I didn't mean it like that. It's just I don't want any complications at the moment. I really want to concentrate on flying, doing well. Maybe get selected for Lynx conversion in a while.'

'Don't worry. I don't think my fiancée would be too happy if I—'

'Your fiancée! God, I feel such a fool.' Kate could feel her face burning with embarrassment.

'That was mean of me. I should have told you earlier, but . . . Well, I have to admit to feeling a little put out when you didn't even drop me a line after Cyprus. I thought we were good together. I thought we might have got something going.'

Kate put the crumpled jersey on the bed and sat down next to it. She picked a feather off the counterpane – it gave her an excuse not to look at him.

'I'm sorry. You must have thought that I was a real cow.'

Andy spread the fingers of one hand and rocked it to and fro. 'Well . . .' he said.

'I don't blame you. I just didn't think that what we had going had a snowball's chance in hell of surviving, what with you being in Cyprus and me being a couple of thousand miles away.' She didn't mention that she had also thought that the instant she left the island he would have been looking for fresh entertainment. 'I thought it was better to make a clean break. To walk away from it.'

'I see.'

'And I didn't tell you what I planned because Maria had told me you didn't seem too keen to get serious, that you loved 'em and left 'em. I thought that if I said anything, you'd think that I was getting heavy and . . .'

'I see. And what if you read me wrong? What if Maria gave you duff information? What if it was me who got hurt?'

'I'm sorry, I didn't consider that.' She felt even more of a heel. She had been horribly selfish.

'I see.'

'Will you stop saying *I see*?' Kate's voice was shrill, partly with annoyance at his reasonableness and partly with utter embarrassment that she'd made a balls-up of a relationship and had been so inconsiderate as to cause misery to someone who hadn't deserved it.

'Sorry.' There was a brief, difficult silence.

Kate broke it. She had to try and make some sort of amends. 'Anyway, you're engaged now. What's she like? I bet she's lovely.'

Andy smiled; was it forgiveness? 'She is actually. She's a nurse.'

'Is she here?'

'No, she works at Queen Charlotte's in London. I go back to see her when I can.'

'Good.' Kate felt relief that, despite everything, Andy's life was on an even keel, he was planning to settle down and, whatever he'd implied, her influence on his life had obviously not been lasting. 'Does that mean we can be friends and no hard feelings?'

'Of course. I'm sorry I gave you a hard time just now. It wasn't fair of me. When you pushed off like that I was a bit angry, but I understood your reasons. It wouldn't have worked if we had tried to carry on – not at that distance anyway.' Andy leant forward and gave her a peck on the cheek. 'All forgiven.'

'Thanks.' Kate still felt a little awkward but was reassured that the whole matter was now officially consigned to the past. She smiled back at him.

'Right, well, if you're ready . . .'

'Yeah.' Kate looked at the jersey, decided that it was now a total mess and threw it in her laundry basket. 'Let's go.'

Andy escorted her along the main corridor of the living accommodation, back through the foyer and into the ante-room. She glanced about her, taking in her surroundings, and decided that Andy hadn't been lying: things were, very definitely, better on the inside. The anteroom was spacious, with deep, dark green button-backed leather armchairs and walls covered with watercolours and oils of helicopters performing feats of derring-do in various theatres of operations around the world. The room, despite its size, looked quite cosy with its dark red carpet and heavy velvet curtains. Perhaps, what with Andy's forgiveness and now this pleasant room, things were looking up.

'See, I told you so,' said Andy as if he had read her thoughts. 'The bar is just through that door. Are you ready to face the mob?' A rumble of noise emanated through it.

Kate walked across to the door and stepped through it. She barely noticed the gang of men at the bar or their appreciative glances.

'But this is wonderful,' she said. She gazed around her at the panelled walls, at the post in the centre of the room that looked uncannily like a ship's mast, at the red plush-covered stools and chairs and at the plethora of cartoons, pictures, mementoes, plaques and bric-à-brac which almost hid the panelling.

'It's good, isn't it?' said Andy, obviously pleased at her reaction.

'Did you have a hand in its décor?' said Kate, feeling she ought to ask.

'No. This regiment took the mess over from an infantry outfit who had some sort of connection with the navy – hence the ship's mast. But as you can imagine, it's a popular place. Now then, let me introduce you to these reprobates who are longing to meet you; and, more importantly, what would you like to drink?'

Later that evening Kate phoned Maria.

'Andy! You mean he's out there with you?'

'Can you believe it? I nearly died when I walked out of the airport and there he was.'

'He came to meet you? So he still fancies you.'

'For heaven's sake. He's engaged.'

'That doesn't mean anything, does it?'

'Of course it does. And anyway, I don't fancy him any more.'

'Oh, you fibber! You know he's the most gorgeous thing on two legs.'

'Yes, but it doesn't mean that I want to have another fling with him.'

'You mean you're still waiting for Mr Right to come along. You're still waiting for the knight on a white charger to come and sweep you off your feet. Believe me, it's not like that.'

'You should know,' said Kate drily.

'It's called market research,' countered Maria primly.

'Is it now? And there was I thinking you were just bonking for Britain.'

'It's about time you got yourself fixed up with a steady man,' said Maria, rather obviously changing the subject.

'I keep telling you, I want to concentrate on my career first. There's plenty of time for all of that in due course.'

'But you've been saying that since you were at Sandhurst. For heaven's sake, that was the best part of five years ago. It is possible to fit both a career and a man into your life. Lots of women do it.'

'I will, when the right man comes along.'

'But that's what I keep telling you. There's no such person as Mr Right.'

Chapter Eleven

Despite the weather, despite the rather drab nature of the base, despite her initial embarrassment at the presence of Andy, Kate felt after her first evening in the mess that things might have been a lot worse. The boost to her morale increased the next day when she was taken on her first helicopter flight around the Province and fell almost instantly in love with the place.

'Right,' the Qualified Helicopter Instructor had said to her, having briefed her on take-off procedure, 'we'll fly south to Strangford Loch, then west across South Armagh, north to Londonderry, east to the Giant's Causeway and then south back to base.'

Kate knew this was the plan because she'd already carefully marked everything on her map, but it was reassuring to have it confirmed that they were both working to the same scheme.

She took off as directed and took a southerly bearing. Again the weather was dull, although the cloud base was sufficient to allow them to climb to two and a half thousand feet. They flew over Belfast and the QHI pointed out the imposing edifice of Stormont, and then Scrabo Tower, which marked the head of Strangford Loch.

Beyond Scrabo was a fairy-tale lake of still water, surrounded by green fields, and within the lake were dozens of minute picture-book islands, some barely bigger than a field; there were boats tacking and gybing, villages on the shore, beaches, fishing communities – everything which could possibly conspire to make the observer think of the phrase *rural idyll*. It was simply the most beautiful view Kate had ever seen.

'Look to your left,' commanded the QHI via the helicopter's intercom system. 'That's Mount Stewart. Great place for a picnic.'

Kate looked in the direction she'd been bidden and saw a low, large grey-stone house, surrounded by beautiful colourful gardens within which was a lake and hundreds of mature trees that had obviously been chosen for their foliage. It was certainly glorious but privately she couldn't imagine any reason for her to visit such a place, solitary sightseeing not being her thing. Mentally, though, she logged the beauty spot all the same.

The object of this flight was not to point out places to go on her days off, but to show her where to find fuel when out on operational flights. She also needed to know the whereabouts of hospitals, army bases and any number of hot spots. Kate, happy to be flying, enjoyed her bird's-eye tour of the Six Counties and welcomed the opportunity to learn the layout of this particular theatre of operations.

A couple of days later, Kate and the QHI did the same flight but with the direction of travel reversed and taking off after dark. Kate felt a fresh wave of apprehension at the thought of being over some notoriously dangerous places with only one other person on her side if something went wrong and they were forced to land. Hurriedly she put the thought from her mind and reminded herself that the REME workshop took pride in their maintenance record, so they were unlikely to have a mechanical failure, and anyway, she also had a gun with her. All the same, she was aware of a sense of relief when they landed safely back at base.

It took a couple of weeks before she had completed all the bits and pieces of admin and training which she had to cover before she was deemed ready to help out with the operational role of the regiment. By this time she had got more used to the idea of living in a place where bombing and sectarian acts of violence seemed routine. She was shocked by the relentless number of terrorist attacks from both sides of the divide, but found it even more depressing that only about a tenth of these events made it on to the national news. The vast majority of these ghastly stories were confined to local bulletins. She wondered if the mainland population might not have more sympathy for the ordinary people of Northern Ireland if they knew the true scale of terrorist attacks.

By the time summer – such as it was – was well and truly over, Kate was confident in her role as a Gazelle pilot. Basically her job was to act as a glorified taxi driver for the aircraft commander, a much more experienced pilot who sat in the left-hand seat and operated the sights and surveillance equipment. Kate, as the pilot, was there to ensure he was in the right place at the right time and with a stable and steady base from which to carry out his allotted tasks with precision. She had settled into a routine and actually looked forward to being sent to one of the three outstations in the Province from where most of their operational flying took place. Frankly she found it more interesting to be somewhere like Bessbrook, on standby, than carrying out mundane routine stuff like ferrying round liaison officers or VIPs. The routine days had some advantages, because they allowed her the time to attack her correspondence course for the ground school part of a commercial pilot's licence, but operational flying was what gave her a buzz.

It seemed like a perfectly ordinary day in October when she attended the two o'clock squadron briefing in the ops room. She was due to take over at Bessbrook for a twenty-four-hour duty later that afternoon and before she took off she needed to know the met, the latest intelligence and the tasks planned for her to carry out once she'd arrived. Frequently, once there, something would happen and Bessbrook would retask her to respond to the new circumstances, but it was always nice to know what the basic plan had been to start with. The Paras had recently moved in to 3 Brigade's area, the one that covered South Armagh, and were helping to control the notorious region around Crossmaglen and Newry. Her last few visits to Bessbrook had involved her flying the officers around on familiarisation flights and recces, and judging by the briefing she'd just attended, it seemed that this next trip was to be a continuation of the same.

She collected her personal weapon and secure radio and her bag of washing things and civvy clothes. The clothes were in case the weather was too bad to return by air and they had to do the transfer the next day by road – and the rule was that you never went anywhere on the ground looking like a soldier unless you were actively on patrol. As she swung her bag of personal possessions over her shoulder, her toothbrush fell out. Cursing it, she picked it up off the floor and shoved it back into the bag. She didn't notice the small hole in the side that had allowed it to escape in the first place. Then she picked up her helmet from the store and went across to her Gazelle on the dispersal area and began to check it over. As she was doing this, her aircraft commander joined her.

'Hi, Sergeant Field,' said Kate. Kate had no problem that her commander was several ranks below her. What mattered here was that he had thousands of hours – and therefore experience – more than her in the air.

'Hi, ma'am.' He climbed into the left-hand seat and began sorting out his maps and notes and stowing a few personal items in the mesh door pocket.

Kate finished her inspection of the helicopter's exterior, climbed in and turned her attention to the instrument panel. She switched on the avionics and tuned the radio into the air traffic information system – a continuous broadcast, updated occasionally throughout the day, which gave her the latest met, which runway was in use, the altimeter setting and a code letter. Kate noted the information carefully, then changed the frequency to talk to the control tower.

'Hello, tower, this is Hawk Four Four Zero.' The tower would recognise her call sign as a military one. 'Request engine and rotor start with information Echo. QNH one zero zero two.' The last bit told the tower that she'd listened to the current ATIS message, because she'd used the most recent information code letter, and that she'd set her altimeter to the correct barometric pressure. She continued, 'I am looking for high VFR departure to the south-west.'

'Roger, Hawk Four Four Zero. Clear to start. Call for taxi.'

Kate adjusted her straps slightly, made sure she was comfortable and began the start-up routine. When the temperature of the engine exhaust reached the required level, she let the rotors start to turn. As they gathered speed above her head she checked the control panel, then made sure all the warning lights were out, that temperatures and pressures were correct and that as far as she could see everything was hunky-dory. Above her the rotors were now a blur and the helicopter seemed to be itching to be airborne. Right, then, she thought, time to go.

'Tower, this is Hawk Four Four Zero. Request taxi to heli west.'

'Hawk Four Four Zero, clear to taxi.'

Kate altered her controls a fraction and the helicopter gently unstuck from the ground. Keeping a careful eye out for anything that might get in her way, she taxied the machine to the point on the airfield designated as heli west. Time to call the tower again.

'Tower, this is Hawk Four Four Zero, ready for departure.'

'Hawk Four Four Zero, you are clear to take off south-west, high VFR.'

'Tower, Hawk Four Four Zero, clear take-off.' As she said this, she twisted the collective and zoomed skywards. She didn't need any further help now from Belfast control tower because she was going to fly on visual flight rules – or VFR – but she did need to tell them when she left their control zone, because when she was out of their way it was one piece of metal fewer in the sky for them to worry about. As she gained height, the tower instructed her to change her radio frequency so she could tell the air traffic controller who looked after the approaches to the airport when she was finally out of their hair.

'Hello, Hawk Four Four Zero, change to Approach on one zero two decimal nine.'

Kate acknowledged and altered her radio frequency accordingly. Now she had to tell Approach where she was going.

'Hello Approach, this is Hawk Four Four Zero, outbound to south-west, high level.'

'Roger. Call zone boundary.' A few minutes later Kate and her Gazelle flew over the line on the map that marked the limit of the international airport's controlled air space.

'This is Hawk Four Four Zero. Zone boundary. Changing to operational.'

'Roger.'

Now that Kate was nothing to do with civilian air traffic

control, she had to assume a different call sign, her operational one. She called up the local brigade headquarters to let them know she was about. If she had a problem, she wanted them to know where she was so they could come to her rescue; equally, she might be able to perform a similar favour for someone on the ground in a tight spot.

Kate enjoyed the flying that day. The weather was reasonable, although cloudy, but the clouds were high enough and thin enough for the visibility to be good. In the distance she could see a couple of heavy showers, but they weren't going to bother her. Beneath her the bright green fields, each separated from its neighbour by a hedge or a low stone wall, looked like a jigsaw. South of Banbridge she changed to the air liaison net at Bessbrook Mill.

'Hello, Buzzard, this is Alpha Charlie One Zero Whisky. Your location, five minutes to land.' On the radio, a form of communication that could be monitored by anyone, no one gave away anything like exactly where *your location* was. But Bessbrook Mill would know who she was and when she was arriving, and that was the important bit.

As she crossed the main line railway that joined Ulster to Eire, she could see Newry just to the south. Ahead of her was Bessbrook town, and in front of it, in a small fold in the ground, was the security base. Beside it, on its south-eastern side, there was a small hill covered in trees. On a bright day like this, the place looked almost attractive; almost, but not quite. Despite being sited on low ground, the mill – dank, battleship grey, imposing and forbidding – dominated the scene. Kate stopped looking at the grim building and began to concentrate on her landing – this was, after all, Europe's busiest heliport, as everything – stores, troops, engine spares – arrived and left by air. It was not the place to admire the view. She began her descent towards the perimeter of the security forces fortress. Time for the safety call to warn everyone else in the air that she was about to land.

Prefixing her transmission with the landing site's own code so all and sundry would know it was Bessbrook she was aiming for she called, 'Gazelle, from north to land.'

She crossed over the boundary of the base, an immense corrugated iron fence with watchtowers and sangars at strategic points. 'Gazelle, finals from north,' she radioed, indicating that landing was imminent. She could see a vacant spot on the narrow and confined dispersal and headed for it. Less than a minute later she was shutting everything down. Her transfer from Aldergrove was complete.

She unbuckled her straps and exited the helicopter carefully, hanging on to the leather strap as she swung out of the door and using the upturned end of the landing skid to support her weight as she manoeuvred her other leg over the cyclic. She then retrieved her small bag of kit from the rear of the Gazelle and shut the perspex door of the cockpit securely.

'OK, ma'am?' said Sergeant Field.

'Fine. It'll be good if the weather holds like the met promised.'

They had left the dispersal area and were walking towards the old mill. It was large and slab-sided, and its appearance had not been improved by the bricking-up of its windows.

'But what the heck, it's home,' said Kate under her breath, recalling some ironic lines from a song she'd once heard.

'What's that?' said Sergeant Field.

'Nothing.

When they reached the building, they went into its brightly lit interior and headed towards their accommodation. They handed over to the REME fitter a couple of engine components that they had been asked to ferry down, dumped their bags on their beds and then found the crew they were relieving.

'Much going on?' asked Kate.

'Not a sausage. Just routine taskings, supporting patrols, that sort of thing. It's been quiet for days.'

'OK,' said Kate. She knew the situation could change but was quite happy with what appeared to be on offer. It was nerve-racking enough to be flying over bandit territory, as this bit of Ulster was invariably called, without getting involved in hairy operations. Still, if something came up she'd have no choice but to get involved. She thought about the couple of incidents she'd learned about which had culminated in the IRA shooting down a military helicopter. And there had been other incidents that might have involved terrorist action but the evidence in the wreckage had been inconclusive. She brushed these gloomy thoughts out of her mind – better not to dwell on that sort of thing.

'Right, best I get along to see Zero Charlie.' Zero Charlie, the air liaison officer, would brief all newly arrived pilots on the latest intelligence and information on what was happening in the area. More importantly, he would confirm or change the taskings that they had been briefed on prior to departure from Aldergrove.

Kate took her maps and charts and strode down the corridor to see Zero Charlie. He had a real name and rank but no one used it – he was Zero Charlie to everyone, with the possible exception of his wife and children.

'So what's the plan for today?' asked Kate after they had exchanged greetings.

Zero Charlie confirmed that Kate would be providing top cover for a ground operation the Paras would be carrying out, starting at two in the morning, to clear a car abandoned after a shooting incident. After that they were to give an officer, newly arrived in the brigade area, a familiarisation flight.

'So, no change from the tasking plan I've got?' checked Kate.

'Not unless something else comes up,' said Zero Charlie.

Kate and Sergeant Field checked their maps, marked where they were to be flying when they got airborne again and returned to their accommodation. Kate lay on her bed with a book – she wanted to get as much rest in as possible, as she obviously wasn't going to get a lot of sleep later on. She and Sergeant Field ate as soon as they could and then Kate made up her bed, took off her boots, set her alarm for one o'clock and rummaged around in her bag for her toothbrush.

'Bugger,' she murmured. She remembered that she had put it back after it had fallen out in the hangar, so it had to be somewhere. She rummaged again, but it wasn't there. She spotted the hole; it must have fallen out again and be in the helicopter. Cursing, she put on her boots and returned to her Gazelle. She didn't have a torch with her but there was sufficient light in the compound for her to be able to see clearly. She opened the door of the aircraft and scrabbled around on the back seat. As she did so, another helicopter landed on the pad next door. She watched the landing with interest and mentally gave the pilot marks out of ten. Nine – a bit flash but pretty good. She returned to her search but could find nothing. She got in and sat on the rear seat, crouching forward to check the floor. As she did so, the three occupants of the next-door Gazelle walked towards her aircraft on their way to the mill, their voices carrying on the still evening air. The passenger was a Para, an officer. Kate noticed he had epaulettes but couldn't see his rank. He was young, so probably no loftier than a captain. She noticed he had a sort of swagger in his walk and grinned to herself. He thinks he's Action Man, she thought as she watched him approach. It was obvious the little group hadn't seen her in the back of her helicopter.

'So will you be supporting the clearance operation tomorrow?' Action Man asked.

'No, that'll be Kate Hayleigh,' said the pilot with him.

'Kate? That some sort of nickname?'

'No. It's her real name.'

Action Man stopped dead in his tracks. 'A fucking girlie! Flying helicopters? You've got to be joking.'

'No joke,' said the pilot. 'Actually, she's quite good.'

Thanks for the vote of confidence, thought Kate. Talk about damning with faint praise.

'Is that *quite good*, or *quite good for a girlie*?' asked Action Man.

Kate didn't hear the reply as they'd moved out of earshot. Bastard, she thought. Typical bloody macho type who thinks women shouldn't be allowed out of the kitchen.

She was still simmering with rage when she had found her toothbrush and returned to the main building. As she walked past an open door, she heard Action Man's voice – deep, with a hint of a North Country accent. She stopped to listen.

'You'll never believe it, lads, but the army has finally taken leave of its senses. They're allowing women to fly fucking helicopters now.' In the gales of laughter that followed, Kate could make out a series of ribald and sexist remarks from Action Man's soldiers.

You shit, she thought, you absolute grade-A, sexist, chauvinist bloody bastard. It would serve you right, Action Man, if this clearance operation is a bloody come-on. In fact, she thought with a final burst of vindictiveness, I hope it bloody is! Getting ambushed by the opposition was exactly what he deserved. Kate stormed off to her room and flounced around to try and disperse her anger before settling down for the night. When Sergeant Field asked her what the matter was, he got a lecture on outdated attitudes and sexism for his pains. Finally Kate had calmed down enough to take her boots off and climb into bed – fully clothed, in case they got crashed out earlier than expected. Her last thoughts before she fell asleep involved unnatural and horrid deaths for the hated Para officer.

She was awake the instant the alarm went off and felt surprisingly alert despite the hour and lack of sleep. Sergeant Field grunted and groaned.

'I'll make a brew, shall I?' asked Kate, switching on the kettle.

'Yeah, if you want, whatever.'

'Shake a leg, then.'

Sergeant Field swung his feet off the bed, rubbed the sleep from his face with both hands and absent-mindedly scratched an armpit. By the time he had laced up his boots, Kate was pouring boiling water into two mugs.

'It'll have to be milky or it'll be too hot to drink,' she said.

'That's OK.'

They swigged their tea, grabbed their weapons and night-vision goggles and headed for the Gazelle. Kate did the checks while Sergeant Field got on the net and made sure of the location they were required at. Once airborne they swiftly reached their destination, and all Kate then had to do was hold the Gazelle in a steady hover while Sergeant Field observed what was happening below, using the aircraft's surveillance equipment, and radioed the bird's-eye view of events to the good guys on the ground. Even so it was tiring, the more so because the weight of the NVGs attached to her helmet made her neck ache. The still, early evening air they had enjoyed for their flight to Bessbrook had been swept away by a front coming through, and now they were being buffeted by quite violent gusts which made things even more draining. By the time they got back to Bessbrook, some three hours after Kate's alarm clock had gone off, she felt shattered. She reset her clock and flopped back into bed. Only two hours' kip till she had to get up again. Good God, there had to be an easier way of earning a living, she thought, as she slid into unconsciousness.

The next flight was purely routine. Action Man, whom she now knew was called Captain Thomas, and his troops were being inserted into an area north of Forkhill to cordon the area around the abandoned car. It was Kate's job to give them a bit of high-level cover as the Lynxes carrying them went in. This was an operation which had been a couple of days in the planning, as it was quite likely that the abandoned car might be fitted with some sort of booby-trap or a come-on designed to lure the security forces into an ambush. Once the Paras had the area surrounded, others would approach the car to clear it and then remove it. The Lynxes set the Paras down, and from her lofty vantage point, Kate could see them scuttling across the fields, looking for cover and fanning out from the LZ to make their cordon.

'And now, breakfast here we come,' said Kate as the operations officer informed them on the secure net that they could return to base. 'I'm famished. How about you, Sergeant Field?'

They were discussing their imminent breakfast as they approached Bessbrook once again and began their descent into the compound. Kate was just about to call finals when they heard on the battalion net: 'Zero, this is Charlie Three Alpha. Contact, explosion, wait out.' The voice was spiced with adrenalin.

'Shit. That's Action Man's lot,' said Kate into her intercom.

'Who's Action Man?' asked Sergeant Field. Kate didn't reply; another message was being broadcast.

'Zero, Charlie Three Alpha, explosion my location. Send QRF and a medic. We've got injuries.' Even with static and the crackle of the radio, Kate could hear the rising note of panic.

'Christ, it's a come-on, there was a booby-trap there,' said Sergeant Field.

Kate called finals and dropped her Gazelle on to the pan. In front of them the Lynx crews were racing towards their helicopters. The Airborne Reaction Force had been ordered to deploy to the incident to provide reinforcements.

'Alpha Charlie One Zero Whisky, this is Zero Charlie. Have you sufficient fuel to return to that location?'

Kate looked at her fuel gauge. 'Alpha Charlie One Zero Whisky, roger.'

'Zero Charlie. Don't shut down. They need the MO. He's on his way.'

'Alpha Charlie One Zero Whisky, roger. Out.' She turned to Sergeant Field. 'Wasn't hungry anyway.'

Across the dispersal area they could see the MO and an assistant running towards them with a couple of medi-packs. Sergeant Field opened his door to climb out and let their two passengers get into the back. They ducked under the rotors, chucked the packs on to the rear seats and scrambled in after them. Sergeant Field handed them each a headset, plugged them in, checked they could hear him and then returned to his seat. He had barely finished fixing his straps before they were airborne once more, swinging round to clear the perimeter and gaining height rapidly.

Piling on the power, Kate zoomed back to where the operation had gone wrong. She hovered over the incident. Beneath her the Lynx crews had their engines started ready to move in the ARF. Each Lynx could carry up to nine soldiers. They listened in to the exchanges on the net as the details of the emergency were revealed. There had been a large explosion as the cordon had moved into place; there were three casualties, two very serious. The site of the explosion was obvious – a nasty splat of dark earth radiating across the bright green grass like an inkblot on coloured paper. There was a knot of soldiers grouped near it, presumably tending to the casualties. Kate put the Gazelle down in the next field, picked at random from the ones around, and hoped that there were no nasty surprises dug into this one. In seconds the MO and the medical orderly were out of the back seat and hurtling, heads low, towards the injured. Kate didn't take off. If there were walking wounded, she could take them to the nearest hospital. Stretcher cases would have to go in a Lynx. She waited to find out was required of her. Her stomach rumbled loudly. Tough, she thought; her hunger pangs were nothing compared to the plight of the casualties.

Two more Lynxes arrived and landed in the next field, and

above her a further Lynx circled with the ARF on board in case more support on the ground was necessary. A soldier, helped by a comrade, was walking slowly towards her. With the aid of Sergeant Field they got him into the back seat and strapped in. His face was a mask of blood and he had a nasty deep cut on his cheek, but Kate could see that the majority of the gore was coming from just under the rim of his combat helmet. Something, a bit of shrapnel perhaps, had obviously caught him on his forehead too.

'OK?' asked Kate.

If he was surprised to see a woman pilot, he didn't show it. 'Not too bad,' he replied. The cuts were nasty and probably hurt like hell, but he was a Para and she was a woman and Kate knew his pride wouldn't allow him to admit to feeling pain or discomfort. Kate gave him an encouraging smile over her shoulder and a thumbs-up, then she increased the revs and took off. If her passenger had been very seriously wounded she'd have taken him to the nearest hospital, but as it was he would be better off in Musgrave Park in Belfast because it had a military wing. Twenty minutes there and twenty back – no breakfast for ages. Her stomach rumbled again.

'Are the other two very bad?' Kate asked the soldier over the intercom.

'It looks touch-and-go for Corporal Jukes; he took the force of it. I don't know about Captain Thomas but he looked pretty bad.'

Kate felt a rush of guilt. She remembered how, in her anger the night before, she'd hoped that this operation would be a come-on and had visualised a sticky end for the officer. How could she have done it? How could she have actively wished harm to come to a fellow human being who, apart from having views on the role of women that she didn't share, had done nothing to deserve getting injured. She felt the blood drain from her face, and a cold surge of guilt gripped her stomach. She'd wished for this, she'd wanted some sort of retribution for making her so angry, and it had happened. A mixture of remorse and horror overwhelmed her, and unexpectedly her vision blurred as tears sprang into her eyes. The helicopter lurched as she searched for a hanky.

'Are you all right, ma'am?' came Sergeant Field's voice over her headset.

Kate pretended it was just her nose that needed blowing, blinked rapidly a couple of times and cleared her throat. 'Fine, thanks.' She was aware that he was staring at her, so she flashed him a quick smile. 'Really.'

'If you say so, ma'am.'

Kate concentrated on working out her heading for Musgrave Park. She did some rapid calculations on the wipe-clean plastic pad on her leg.

'Tell them we'll be there in seventeen minutes.'

Sergeant Field radioed the information ahead. Kate was glad that this had diverted his attention from her.

'How are you feeling?' she asked the soldier in the rear passenger seat.

'I've felt better,' he replied gamely. 'I'm dripping blood on your helicopter.'

'It'll clean up,' said Kate. 'We'll soon have you there.'

They swept out of the sky and on to the helipad at the hospital. A couple of medics with a trolley were waiting for them. Despite his protestations, the Para was made to lie on the stretcher and was wheeled away. As they took off again, Kate wondered about calling up on the net to get a progress report about the other two wounded, but she knew it would be unprofessional. She'd only be cluttering up the airwaves, and anyway, it really wasn't anything to do with her. Except that it was.

Back at Bessbrook, all thoughts of breakfast gone, Kate went to the ops room to find out the situation. The atmosphere inside was grim. Kate didn't have an excuse to be there and felt diffident about entering. She hovered while she thought up an excuse to go in and pester for information. She heard a movement behind her and saw the commanding officer of the parachute battalion striding along the corridor. She moved out of the way.

'I was at a briefing at HQNI,' he announced as he entered the room. 'I came back as soon as I heard the news. What can you tell me?'

Kate listened as he was updated. The suspicion was that a gap in one of the hedges had been booby-trapped. The soldiers were taught not to use obvious exits and entrances to fields – stiles, gates and the like – but this gap had been just big enough to encourage them to pass through it, while not big enough to look like an obvious route to take. The bomb had been buried beside it and triggered by a command wire.

'Bastards,' muttered the CO. 'So how are the casualties?'

'Private Williams just has superficial wounds,' said the brigade major. 'He's in Musgrave Park and they'll probably let him out tomorrow. Corporal Jukes is more serious. It's almost certain that he'll lose a foot.'

The CO groaned and sat down on the corner of the BM's desk. 'God, what a bloody waste of a good soldier,' he muttered, his face tense with anger. 'And Captain Thomas?'

'We're still waiting to hear from the hospital. All we know is that he's unconscious and has multiple blast injuries. His flak jacket and helmet saved him from the worst, but they want to do a brain scan. He's in ITU. They'll let us know as soon as they've got anything concrete to tell us.'

'You know his parents live in Spain, don't you?' the CO asked the BM.

'Yes. We're waiting to hear back from the British Consulate. They should be coming back to us' – there was a pause as the BM looked at his watch – 'any minute now.'

The CO passed a hand across his face as if to wipe away his anger and sadness. 'Is there any chance of seeing either Jukes or Thomas?'

'I'm afraid not today, sir. The hospital said no one till tomorrow at the absolute earliest.'

From where Kate stood by the door she could see that the CO looked almost relieved that this difficult duty had to be postponed. The phone on the BM's desk rang shrilly.

'Excuse me a second, sir.' He picked it up and spoke briefly. His voice was grave but nothing was to be gleaned as to the subject of the call. 'That was Spain, sir. The consul has told Captain Thomas's parents about the accident but it seems it is impossible for them to travel. Mr Thomas is a very sick man who needs constant nursing and Mrs Thomas won't leave him.'

The CO sighed deeply again. 'I knew his father wasn't well but I didn't know he was that bad. His poor mother, having this news on top of everything else. We must find out if there are any other relatives who might be able to come. I'll get my adjutant on to it. OK, thanks for that. Let me know if you get any more news.' The CO left the office.

Kate had heard all the available information and turned to go.

'I'm sorry,' the BM called after her. 'Was there something you wanted?'

Kate shook her head. The only thing that she wanted – the chance to rerun the previous evening and take back all her vindictive thoughts – wasn't in his gift.

Chapter Twelve

'For God's sake, what the hell is the matter with you?' asked Andy about a week later. 'You've been mooning about like it's the end of the world for days now.'

'Nothing,' replied Kate and turned to look out of her bedroom window.

Andy stamped angrily across her room and pulled her round so she had to face him. 'Don't give me that. You haven't been to the bar, you don't appear in the anteroom, you don't even watch TV with the rest of us. You don't laugh, you don't talk to anyone; it's like you've suddenly decided that we're not good enough for you any more.'

'No, it's not that. Honestly.'

'Then what the hell is it? Has someone done something to upset you, is that it? Tell me and I'll get it sorted out.'

Why did men always think that if a girl was miserable it was because she couldn't sort out her own relationships? How could she tell him that she still felt as guilty as sin about the incident at Bessbrook? She knew, in her heart, that the only people responsible were the bombers. She knew that she didn't have some dreadful power to make nasty things happen to her detractors. She knew it was nothing to do with her. And yet she couldn't get it out of her head that somehow it wouldn't have happened if she hadn't *wished* it to happen. And with that load of baggage to carry around, she didn't need the others in the mess taking the piss out of her – as they surely would – if she told anyone why she felt so miserable. No, best to stay out of everyone's way until she'd got her head sorted out.

'Honestly, it's nothing to do with anyone here.' She tried to sound convincing.

Andy knew she'd been involved, on the periphery, of the ambush at Bessbrook but she hadn't done more than ferry a bloke with a few cuts and bruises to hospital. Surely that wasn't what had got to her? Surely she wasn't suffering from post-traumatic stress from that little incident? God, if that was all it took to upset females near the front line . . .

'It wasn't having to take Private Williams to Musgrave Park that got to you was it?'

Kate shook her head wearily. For heaven's sake, why couldn't he leave her alone?

'But it's something to do with Bessbrook,' he persisted.

Kate couldn't meet his eye. 'No.'

Andy wasn't convinced. 'Are you worried about how they're getting on? Why don't you ring the adjutant of the battalion to find out how they all are, if that's what's bugging you? He won't mind. After all, you were involved in the operation, so why shouldn't you take an interest?'

Kate shook her head. She didn't want him to know that he was getting dangerously close to the problem.

Andy gave up. 'How about a drink?' he said hopefully.

'Maybe later.'

'Suit yourself then,' said Andy. He left feeling he'd done his bit; he'd shown an interest and if she didn't want a shoulder to cry on, then that was her look-out. He just hoped she'd snap out of it soon. She was being a bloody pain in the arse at the moment.

Kate watched him leave and breathed a sigh of relief. She paced around her room like a caged tiger. She felt restless and needed to do something but she didn't feel like any of the obvious activities that beckoned. She didn't want to go for a drink and she couldn't concentrate on her commercial flying course, she'd run out of books from the library and even her ironing pile was under control. She decided that as it wasn't actually raining she ought to go for a run. Andy's comment about phoning the adjutant to get a progress report on the casualties niggled in her mind. If she ran down to the squadron office at the other end of the base she could get the number. She made her mind up and changed into trainers and a tracksuit.

'I was just wondering how the casualties from the incident last week were getting on?' she asked tentatively when she got through. 'I took Private Williams to hospital—'

'*You* did?' the adjutant interrupted. 'But he went by helicopter!'

Kate resisted the urge to use an expletive. '*I* did,' she said as calmly and as coolly as she could. 'I'm a Gazelle pilot.' There was a gratifying second of stunned silence from the adjutant. So smoke that, thought Kate. 'Anyway, he told me that the other two injured were in quite a bad way. I know it's nothing to do with me really, but . . .' Her voice trailed off. Her burst of confidence, fuelled by the adjutant's attitude, had evaporated.

The adjutant quickly recovered some of his bluster. 'Right, young lady, well, what can I tell you? Poor old Corporal Jukes has lost a foot, but apart from that he's well on the road to recovery. He'll be transferred back to the mainland soon. Unfortunately Eddie Thomas is still under sedation. He's pretty poorly. He hasn't regained consciousness yet.'

'I am so sorry to hear that. Has his mother managed to get over from Spain?'

If the adjutant was surprised that she knew that piece of intelligence, he didn't show it. 'No, his father is still very ill. Poor Eddie hasn't much in the way of visitors, but the nurses sit with him when they have a moment.'

'I'm glad.' God, that could be taken the wrong way. 'I mean, I'm glad the nurses sit with him.'

'Look, you seem to know Eddie. If you could find the time to visit him . . .'

Kate could hardly say that she'd never even spoken to the man and that she only knew about his parents because she'd been eavesdropping.

'It would do us a huge favour if we thought that someone could give him a bit of attention. Especially when he comes round. Frankly, now that we're an officer short, we just don't have the slack in the system to send someone over.'

Kate was in a corner but it was of her own making. She'd let him think that she knew the man. 'OK. I'll do my best to visit a couple of times.'

'That would be brilliant. Give him all our best wishes, won't you?'

Kate had returned to the mainland a few weeks earlier to bring her car over. After a month and a half in Ulster her paranoia had largely subsided and had been replaced by feelings of claustrophobia at being trapped in the RAF base. Having seen any number of beauty spots from the air, she had decided that if she was going to investigate them at closer quarters the only solution was to get mobile on the ground. All the same, it was one thing to desire to visit the Glens of Antrim or the Giant's Causeway and quite another to consider driving into Belfast. Still, she reasoned, thousands of people did it every day. She drove to the squadron office and got out a large-scale map of the city. The last thing she wanted to do was to wind up driving along the Falls Road. No one connected with the armed forces would ever forget the lynching, five years previously, of two servicemen who had done precisely that.

It was with trepidation that Kate set out the next day to drive to Musgrave Park hospital. The route was simple: into Belfast on the M2 and out on the M1. Musgrave Park was on the left – well away from the Falls Road or any other hot spots. Even so, Kate felt relief once she'd gained her destination and was heading for the reception area. The security that surrounded the military hospital was reassuringly tight, and it was a few minutes before Kate was escorted to the intensive care unit and introduced to the staff there.

She'd watched enough hospital dramas on the television to know what to expect, but she still found the plethora of machines, drips, monitors, wires, tubes and technology disturbing. She looked about her in horrified fascination. And the noise! She had always thought that seriously ill people were kept in quiet, dark rooms while they recuperated, but in this ward the lights were brilliantly harsh, and there was a whirr of fans cooling the air and the equipment and a manic bleeping emanating from almost every machine – and there were dozens of them. As she gazed around, one of the instruments suddenly began to go into some sort of overdrive, squawking frantically in alarm that something it was measuring wasn't right. It sounded desperate, but no one rushed or ran despite the seeming urgency. A nurse, summoned by the noise, walked purposefully along the ward, looking unconcerned as she approached the bed, checked the equipment and the patient and then pressed a button to stop the racket. Obviously this was a routine event.

Another nurse escorted Kate to a bed at the far end of the ward and told her that this was Eddie Thomas. For a second, Kate's attention was fixed on the equipment surrounding him. She heard the nurse say, 'I've got a visitor for you, Eddie. It's Kate. She's come from Aldergrove specially to see you.' She turned to Kate. 'He's quite heavily sedated still. He's got some damage to his lungs from the blast and we're still concerned about some swelling to his brain.' Kate took her eyes off all the monitoring equipment and focused on Eddie. Her eyes widened in dismay. She'd heard about his injuries and had formed a notion that as the worst were internal there would be no outward manifestation. She'd been wrong. His face was, frankly, a mess. He looked as though he'd gone the full fifteen rounds with Mike Tyson. Both his hands were bandaged and his forearms were covered with cuts and bruises. From one side of his mouth trailed a thick tube, while saliva trickled from the other, and his torso was covered with little white sensors with wires attached. Kate sat down abruptly on the chair by the bed, her gasp of horror masked by the whoosh and click of the ventilator.

'You've never been to a unit like this before, have you?' said the nurse sympathetically. Kate shook her head. 'It's always a bit of a shock. But once you get used to it, it doesn't seem so bad. We're reducing the level of sedation slowly, as he recovers, and it would be a help if you would sit and talk to him. Talk about anything you like: the weather, the news, what's in the charts. We do our best but we're quite busy so we can't devote as much time as we'd like to our patients.' Kate nodded dumbly. 'Right, I'll leave you two in private. If you need anything, I'll be just over there.' She indicated the nurses' station in the middle of the room and bustled off.

Kate let out a deep breath and stared at Eddie. God, she wondered, what do you talk about to a man who is unconscious, naked but for a bed sheet, and who you have never been introduced to? 'Um,' she faltered. 'Um, everyone at

114

Bessbrook sends their best wishes. Oh, perhaps I'd better introduce myself. I'm Kate.' She stopped. Now what could she say? She looked out of the window. The light rain which she'd driven through had stopped and the sun was trying to break through the cloud. 'The weather has taken a turn for the better,' she said. 'It's not bad now. It might be quite nice this evening. Tonight the lads in the mess over at Aldergrove are going to . . .'

By the time nearly an hour had passed, Kate had informed the unconscious Eddie Thomas about her plans for the rest of the week, the award of the Nobel Peace Prize to Mandela and de Klerk, the battle over the Russian White House, and her views about the IRA. 'I'll try and come back and see you tomorrow,' she promised, 'but I must go now. I want to get out of Belfast before it gets too dark.' As she left, the nurses thanked her for spending time with him, and Kate drove away from the hospital feeling much happier than when she'd arrived.

She couldn't visit the next day, or the next. She rang the hospital and apologised, but, as she explained, she did have a full-time job to do. By the time she did return, she was pleasantly surprised by the improvement in Eddie's appearance. The ventilator tube had been removed and some of the bruises on his face had subsided and faded, although a nasty jagged cut under one eye still looked dire.

'His sedation has been reduced considerably,' she was told by the duty nurse. 'We're rather hoping that he'll regain consciousness in the near future, but you never know with brain injuries. Would you like a cup of tea? I was just about to make one for myself.'

'Tea would be lovely, thanks.' She waited for the welcome cup to arrive and then sat down by Eddie and began to talk to him as before. She'd covered almost everything she could think of that might be of interest on her previous visit, so this time she launched into a description of a flight that she'd completed the day before along the North Antrim coast.

'And I flew over a place called Dunluce Castle. It was just like a fairy-tale castle. So pretty! And the weather was superb.' She turned to look out of the window as she recalled the conditions of the day before, which were in such contrast to what was happening now. 'It's hard to believe how nice it was yesterday when you see what it's doing today,' she continued. 'Just look at the rain,' as the wind threw another squall against the glass. She turned back to the bed. Eddie was staring at her. His eyes were of the deepest shade of blue she had ever seen in her life. Her heart lurched. She allowed the saucer she was still carrying to tip and her cup came perilously close to slipping on to the floor. She caught it just in time and recovered herself.

'Hello,' she said brightly. 'I'm Kate.'

'Kate?' Eddie mouthed. His brow furrowed slightly then his eyes shut again.

'Sister,' called Kate. 'Sister! I think Eddie's coming round.'

The next day part of Kate wanted to go and see how Eddie was getting on, while the other part was stricken with a bout of cowardice as she was assailed once again with feelings of guilt. Now he was conscious she didn't think she could face him. She couldn't look him in those devastatingly blue eyes while knowing that not so long before she had actively wished he would die. She tussled with her conscience between a sense of duty and out-and-out cowardice. Cowardice won. How could she face him now? He was bound to ask why a complete stranger wanted to visit him. She hadn't even been instrumental in his evacuation from the scene of the booby-trap. What could she say if he asked why she was there? She couldn't tell him it was to assuage her guilty conscience, and nothing else she could say would sound remotely like the truth. He might be a Para, but it didn't make him stupid. Not having anything better to do, and not being rostered to fly, she skulked about in the squadron offices, killing time by making up her logbook and doing a few mundane admin tasks.

'Phone call for you,' said Andy, putting his head round the crew room door. 'It's Musgrave Park. What do they want?'

'I can't imagine,' said Kate, reddening with the lie and a fresh wave of guilt. She went to the office and took the call.

'Eddie's asking for you,' the ward sister informed her. 'He's still drifting in and out of consciousness but in his lucid moments he says he'd like to talk to you.'

'Oh,' said Kate, noncommittally.

'Will you be able to get over here today or tomorrow?'

'Well . . .'

'He's being transferred to a hospital on the mainland soon – so his aunt can go and see him on a regular basis. And it'll be easier for his mother to make a flying visit there if she can get away from Spain for a day.'

'I see.'

'So will you? Come and see him, that is.'

Kate could hardly refuse and she knew it. Her sense of duty told her that, having taken on a commitment, she couldn't just drop it. But what would she say to him now he could talk back? Oh, God! She wished she'd never let the adjutant talk her into this. But she still had to give the sister an answer.

'I'll try.' There was a suggestion of a sigh down the phone line. Obviously this answer wasn't really good enough. 'I promise.'

'Good, I'll tell him. It'll cheer him up.'

Yippee, thought Kate sarcastically, I'm glad one of us is pleased by the idea. But she knew she was being incredibly selfish. Now she really would have to try and dream up some convincing reason for her interest in this man.

He was sitting up in bed with a striped pyjama top on when Kate plucked up the courage to visit the hospital the next day. Feeling extremely nervous, she walked the length of the ward. She had come up with a form of words to explain her presence but she wasn't sure it would hold water. And she was certainly unsure as to how it would stand up to any sort of examination. She kept her fingers crossed that Eddie wouldn't feel inclined to be too curious. As she neared the bed she could see that his eyes were shut. Thank God! He must have lapsed into one of his moments of unconsciousness and she could yammer away to his comatose form, as before, and escape without the need for embarrassing explanations.

Feeling happier, she approached the bed and drew up a chair. Now that he was largely free of the electrodes, sensors and other wires and tubes, she was more inclined to look at him. Before, she'd found his injuries and all the medical equipment that surrounded him rather frightening, and as there had been no need for eye contact as she'd chatted to him, she had looked at almost anything but Eddie himself. This time, as she began to natter away, she allowed herself to study his face. Now that most of the cuts had healed and the bruising had faded to almost nothing, she decided that he was rather good-looking in a rugged sort of way. His jaw was too square and his chin too determined to call him handsome, but his skin, attractively smooth, had the vestiges of a tan, despite his days in a hospital bed, and his dark hair was thick and wavy. And then there were those eyes; shut now, but she had the colour imprinted on her memory. It was unfair that a man should be blessed with them. Completely wasted, she thought. So blue as to be verging on indigo, and surrounded by luxuriant lashes. Any self-respecting girl would kill to have eyes like that. She prattled on, telling Eddie about events in the news, some gossip involving a society heiress, and another operation his battalion had been involved with which had culminated in several arrests and the capture of a good-sized arms dump.

'Good result,' said Eddie, barely audibly. His eyes flickered and opened. Kate was, once again, swept away by them. God, he was a hunk. Shame about his stupid sexist attitude towards women. 'Are you Kate?'

'Yes.'

'So it wasn't a fit of delirium that conjured you up.'

'No.'

His eyes closed again as though those few sentences had exhausted him. Kate sat still, and after a few seconds he opened his eyes once more.

'Who *exactly* are you?' he asked.

'Kate Hayleigh.'

'No, I mean . . .'

'A concerned bystander.' She smiled sheepishly. She had her lines ready; she would brush with the truth but leave out the details. 'I played a minor part in the op when you got hurt. When I rang your adjutant to find out how you and the other two casualties were, he said it would be nice if I could visit you because your . . .' She stopped in confusion. Supposing he didn't know how ill his father was?

'Because Mum's tied up with Dad.' Kate nodded. 'So what

were you doing down in South Armagh? Watch-keeping?'

Kate wasn't surprised at the role he'd assumed she'd been playing. Watch-keeping was a good safe job; up in an ops room somewhere, in the warm and dry and out of harm's way. 'Not exactly.' Eddie smiled encouragingly. 'I was flying the Gazelle.'

Eddie nodded as he recognised the name. 'You're *that* Kate.' Kate nodded. What else was there to say? Eddie suddenly looked drawn. It was obvious he was still far from well. A nurse appeared at the end of his bed. 'I think that's enough talking for one day, Captain Thomas. I don't want you overdoing it and having a relapse. I'm sure Miss Hayleigh will come and see you again tomorrow if you'd like her to.' The nurse looked at Eddie expectantly, and then at Kate.

'It's fine with me,' said Eddie, sounding incredibly weary. Kate felt a wave of sympathy. It must be dreadful to feel so unwell.

'I won't be able to get here until the evening, but I promise I'll come.' It hadn't been such an ordeal after all, and close to, he seemed quite nice. If he wasn't such a bigoted chauvinist, she could almost fancy him.

Kate, as good as her word, made the thirty-minute journey to Musgrave Park hospital the following evening. Eddie was sitting up in bed looking far less groggy than the day before. He seemed pleased to see her, although Kate wondered if it was due to the fact that, apart from her, he received precious few visitors.

'Tell me,' he asked after they had exchanged initial greetings, 'what on earth made you want to become a helicopter pilot?'

So Kate told him about her childhood spent at the gliding club, her fighter-pilot father, her rebellion against her mother and her social snobbery, and her decision to annoy both her parents by not going to university and joining the army instead. She omitted the fact that it was her infatuation with Mike that had been the catalyst for her latter actions. She thought that if she included it, Eddie would laugh at her naïvety and for some unaccountable reason she only wanted him to think well of her.

'Quite a rebel,' said Eddie, smiling.

'Hardly. I wasn't exactly chaining myself to the railings and refusing food.' Eddie laughed and agreed with her. The laughter died away and there was a lull in the conversation. Eddie had taken an interest in her past, so it would be only courteous to take an interest in his. Kate broke the silence. 'So tell me why you joined the Paras.'

'I was born just outside Liverpool, my dad was in the petrochemical industry and I think he had hopes that I would end up running ICI or Shell but I wasn't too bright at school. I didn't get into the local grammar, so I was sent to a secondary mod. My mother was so disappointed she cried for a week. I didn't care, though – well, you don't at that age, do you?' Kate shook her head in agreement. 'I must be honest, it was a crap school. It hardly taught me anything because all its resources went into keeping control. At sixteen, with a couple of CSEs and two O levels, I decided I'd be better off earning a living. I drifted in and out of a few jobs; all of them manual labour. There wasn't much going on the job front just then. Then one day I went home and my parents announced that they were selling our house and moving to Spain. They'd always wanted to. Dad had been offered early retirement so they were going to take the plunge.'

'What about you, though?'

'Exactly. I had to find a job where I'd get a room thrown in as well. We'd just had that Falklands War and I had watched every minute of it on the TV. I'd watched the ships sailing from Portsmouth, I'd watched the Harriers being counted out and counted back, I'd watched the *Sir Galahad* going down, and although I hadn't thought about it till then, the army was the obvious choice. I decided that if I was going to join up I would have to be in the infantry. Eight weeks later I was in Aldershot, at the Para Depot, getting kitted out.'

'So you joined as a soldier?'

'Yeah. And once I was in I found I loved it. I was good at it. It wasn't like being at school. I was fit enough to cope with the physical side, and stuff like stripping a gun down and putting it back together was a cinch. I soon found that as long as I did exactly what I was told to do, I couldn't go wrong. By the time I was nineteen I was a full-screw and my company commander said he thought I ought to try for a commission.'

'So you did.'

'And the rest, as they say—'

'Is history,' finished Kate. She found herself liking Eddie more and more, but she needed to clear something up in her mind. 'So being macho and chauvinist is all part of the Para image, is it?'

'How do you mean? It wasn't very macho walking into a booby-trap, now was it, and I don't think I'm that much of a chauvinist.'

'But you don't think women should be allowed to fly helicopters.'

'I've never said that.'

'You fibber,' said Kate.

'When?'

'At Bessbrook, the night before the operation. I heard you.'

Eddie looked deeply embarrassed. 'You heard me talking to the troops.'

'And I heard what you said when you first heard my name. I think your exact words were "A fucking girlie! Flying helicopters? You've got to be joking."'

Eddie turned an even deeper shade of red. He couldn't meet Kate's eyes. 'Sorry,' he mumbled. 'I don't really believe that, though. You know what it's like when blokes get together,' he added sheepishly. 'We all have to outdo each other in the macho stakes. I expect you're a bloody good pilot.'

'For a girlie,' added Kate, trying not to grin.

'No, no . . .' His discomfort was almost tangible.

Kate couldn't suppress her laughter any longer. 'I'm sorry. I'm just getting my own back.'

'Rat,' said Eddie with relief.

Kate looked at her watch. 'Goodness, I must be going. I'll miss dinner if I stay here any longer.'

Eddie looked miserable. 'I'm being transferred tomorrow. I won't see you again.'

Inexplicably, Kate suddenly felt completely dejected. Bloody typical. She had just found a man she could actually fancy, who now appeared not to be a raving chauvinist, and he got sent miles away. She sighed. 'So soon?'

'I'm fit enough to travel, and they want me back on the mainland to make sure everything is in proper working order.

121

Apparently they're still a bit worried about my lungs.'

'Well, I'd better say goodbye then,' said Kate. 'And wish you all the best.' She spoke with a lightness in her voice that was in marked contrast to the heaviness she felt in her heart. On impulse she leaned forward and kissed him on the cheek. As she did so, Eddie took her hand.

'I'll miss you, Kate,' he said, stroking the back of her hand with his thumb. An electric tingle ran up her arm and swept through her body. For a second she felt almost giddy – that feeling she always got doing aerobatics or on the more extreme fairground rides – and she didn't trust herself to speak. Then she gently disengaged her hand, turned and left the ward.

Chapter Thirteen

Autumn degenerated into a winter that was unremittingly miserable: cold, wet, windy, with only a few brief hours of daylight before darkness fell again. Often the Gazelles were grounded because the cloud base was too low for them to be any use operationally. Kate used the periods of enforced idleness to get to grips with her correspondence course for her commercial pilot's licence. As far as the military were concerned, she didn't need it, but it was a useful qualification to have. Who knew when it might come in handy?

Life in the mess was as boisterous as ever, and what with work and play Kate found that she didn't have time to brood seriously on what might have been between her and Eddie, although she often wondered how he was. Sometimes, when she was speaking to Maria on the phone, she would even admit out loud how much she had liked him and how much she would like to know how he was progressing in his recovery.

'So why don't you make more of an effort to track him down?' said Maria with undisguised impatience. 'God, if I found a bloke who was that much of a hunk, I would make sure he didn't get away.'

'But don't most men run a mile if they think they're being chased?'

'Don't be so ridiculous. Who told you that?'

Kate didn't answer. Perhaps she should have known that her mother would feed her duff information.

'Anyway,' continued Maria, 'there's an old adage that goes, "Girls that play at hard to get aren't got".'

'I'm not playing hard to get,' protested Kate.

'But you're not exactly giving him a helping hand. Why don't you write to him care of his battalion? They'll forward the letter.'

But Kate wouldn't be drawn.

'What is it with you and men?' said Maria in exasperation. 'I just don't get it. It's like you don't want to have a man take an interest in you. Just because you have a relationship, go to bed with a bloke, go out a few times, doesn't automatically condemn you to a life-long commitment. Surely you must realise that?'

'I do, but it's difficult to find the time, and there's no one I fancy here.'

'You're weird,' was Maria's pronouncement.

When Kate replaced the receiver she wondered if she was as out of the ordinary as Maria thought. Perhaps she took after her mother, who could never be described as a sex kitten. Kate found that thought faintly depressing. She sighed. Now she'd thought about her mother, perhaps she had better ring her too. She hadn't spoken to the old bag for a fortnight and it was about time she reassured her that her only child was alive and well. Although, thought Kate morosely, Honour seemed so preoccupied with herself, her clubs, societies, holidays and social life, that there seemed to be little space left for her one and only daughter. She dialled the number, but as always, she got the answering machine. She left a message and replaced the receiver. She had vaguely thought of going home for Christmas but she wasn't sure she could be bothered. Her mother was bound to have a load of plans that wouldn't include her, and although they tolerated each other these days, it was impossible to describe their relationship as anything more than that.

As Christmas drew near, Kate finally made up her mind to brave her mother's hospitality for a few days.

'I shall look forward to seeing you,' Honour said, although Kate couldn't detect the least vestige of enthusiasm in her mother's voice.

In the last week before the holiday there was the inevitable round of riotous and sometimes drunken parties, and Kate climbed on to the shuttle to Heathrow feeling decidedly jaded and settled herself into her seat wondering whether the journey was going to be worth the effort.

However, she was to be pleasantly surprised. Christmas with her mother was a jollier affair than it had been for a number of years and Kate found herself actually enjoying the festival, although she wondered cynically if this was perhaps because Honour had got involved socially with a number of groups and clubs in Windsor so that on both Christmas Eve and Boxing Day they were invited out for drinks. Her mother was always easier to tolerate when diluted by the presence of other people. Kate was amused to hear Honour referring to her as 'my daughter the helicopter pilot' as she mingled with the other guests, although Kate wasn't entirely sure that her mother wasn't implying that Kate's skills were due to Honour's parenthood rather than her own dedication and hard work. Still, if Honour wanted to bolster her ego by taking credit for her daughter's achievements, Kate didn't mind too much, especially if it meant that their relationship was thawing out a little.

This time, when Kate had to leave, her mother accompanied her to the airport. Kate took this display of maternal affection as a further indication of the improved relationship, but she didn't want to stretch things too far by expecting her mother to actually accompany her into the terminal.

'Just drop me outside,' said Kate. 'I've only got the one bag and it's not heavy.'

'Nonsense. I've come to see you off, so that's what I am going to do.'

'Suit yourself,' said Kate. 'I didn't want to put you to too much trouble.'

'That doesn't sound very grateful,' her mother shot accusingly as she parked her BMW in the short-stay car park.

I'll never be able to win, thought Kate. Perhaps her mother's bonhomie had only been for the benefit of the festive season – good will to all men and possibly her daughter, providing she didn't take any liberties. But wisely Kate kept these thoughts to herself. She grabbed her bag from the back of the car as her mother locked it up.

'Shall I get you a trolley?' Honour asked solicitously.

'I think I can manage,' Kate replied, and swung it over her shoulder.

'Now then, have you got your tickets?' Kate nodded. 'And your passport?'

This time Kate couldn't restrain herself and she burst into a fit of giggles.

'Mother, I'm only going to Northern Ireland. It's like going to Scotland.'

Honour looked miffed but she didn't say anything, just sailed through the doors of the terminal and headed towards the British Airways domestic check-in desks.

Kate handed over her ticket, assured the clerk she'd packed her luggage herself, and was allocated a window seat.

'Time to go then, Mother. Thanks for a lovely stay. I really enjoyed it.' Kate didn't have to fib over this. It had been a pleasant break and it had been nice to get away from Northern Ireland for a bit – the constant outbreaks of violence could get depressing and wearing.

'Did you? I am glad. You need a decent break now and again. I'm sure you haven't been looking after yourself at all well. Now promise me you'll eat three proper meals a day when you get back to Ireland.'

'Yes, Mother.' Kate knew this was Honour's idea of discharging her maternal duty, and it was easier to be compliant than to point out that if she appeared for every meal in the mess she would be the size of a house in a couple of months.

'And you'll phone to tell me you're back safely?'

'Yes, Mother.'

'Give me a kiss then, and go and catch your plane.'

Dutifully Kate kissed her mother and walked through security. She turned to give a final wave, but Honour had already gone.

Back in Ireland, Kate settled into the old routine as though slipping into a pair of favourite slippers. She had stopped being the rookie pilot and was now a trusted member of the team. Life in the mess continued to be fun, she was popular, and her social life, as far as it went, was good. The only apparent fly in the ointment was the complete lack of any sort of boyfriend, though the last thing she really wanted was to have a relationship with someone on her own doorstep. In her opinion it nearly always ended up causing more problems than it was worth. The chance to meet new friends from other units, however, always seemed to pass her by. Andy acted as her unofficial chaperon and escort, which suited them both. They had agreed there was absolutely nothing between them any more, and it was handy to have a man willing to escort her if she wanted to go out for a quiet drink or a meal, especially as Kate knew he was happily engaged to Emma. As platonic relationships went, this one was extremely satisfactory.

Maria flew out for a long weekend, 'to check out the talent'.

'It's pretty thin on the ground,' Kate warned. 'Most of the men are already spoken for. Anyway, they're probably not your type.'

'How can you say that when Randy Andy is there?'

'But he's engaged.'

'So?'

'Maria! I shan't let you come if you don't promise me that you won't try anything on there.'

Maria agreed, reluctantly. That weekend she proved to be the star attraction in the officers' mess. Her ready wit, her outrageous flirting, her looks and her good humour ensured that the men gathered round her like bees round the proverbial honeypot.

'So how come you two are such good friends?' asked Andy as they sat drinking in the bar before Sunday lunch. 'You're like chalk and cheese.'

'But that's exactly why we *do* get on,' countered Maria. 'Kate's all organised and hard-working and makes me get a grip on myself every now and again; and I'm quite scatty and keen to have a good time and I make her loosen up.'

'Is this true?' Andy asked Kate, wanting confirmation.

'Completely. And I love Maria's family. They're all basket cases – her mum is amazing. If you knew what my mother was like you would understand.'

'And what *is* your mother like?' said Andy.

Maria and Kate exchanged glances. 'Do you think Andy is ready for the unexpurgated version?' said Kate with a grin.

'Well . . .' said Maria dubiously.

Andy looked puzzled. 'She can't be that bad, surely?'

Kate and Maria let out a peal of laughter. 'Better give it to him straight,' said Maria.

'You've heard of Lucretia Borgia?' said Kate

'And Lady McBeth?' added Maria.

'And Mrs Danvers?'

'And Medusa?'

Andy threw his hands in the air. 'Enough, enough. I don't believe you. The pair of you are exaggerating.'

Maria turned her most wide-eyed and innocent stare in his direction. 'As if . . .'

'Well, maybe just a smidgen,' said Kate. 'But she is pretty dire. She's not exactly the cuddly type. I dread ever taking anyone home to meet her.'

'It sounds about as daunting as going to meet a black widow spider,' said Andy.

'Aren't you just so glad you're spared that thrill now you're engaged to someone else?' said Maria without stopping to think. There was an awkward silence. 'Oh God! Me and my big mouth.'

'No, honestly,' said Andy and Kate, almost simultaneously. 'We're just friends,' added Andy.

'We were never that serious, were we?' said Kate.

'Just a fling,' agreed Andy, nodding vigorously to reinforce his point.

'He still fancies you, you know,' Maria told Kate later when they were back in the privacy of Kate's room.

'He doesn't.'

'He does, and you know it too. Otherwise why the big embarrassed silence when I made that goof about the two of you being engaged?'

'Don't be silly.'

'I'm not. If you gave him the slightest come-on he would get rid of Emma.'

Kate shook her head. 'But he adores Emma.'

'It's perfectly possible to be in love with more than one person at once. And frankly, it's absolutely obvious to anyone with half an eye that he's crazy about you. Otherwise why would he always be the man who goes with you to parties, who makes sure you've got a lift, who buys you drinks when you go out?'

'That's just good manners.'

'Kate, I've been around the block a few more times than you and I can tell you that that sort of chivalry has died a death. He does it because he cares about you. It's probably the fact that you're not throwing yourself at him that makes you so fascinating. He's not used to that.'

'Look, I don't want to fall out with you over this, but I can tell you, quite categorically, that you're barking up the wrong tree.'

'You're the one who's barking,' muttered Maria, refusing to admit defeat. Kate looked daggers. Maria decided to change the subject. 'I can't think why you say there's hardly any talent here. I know you think I'm not the least bit discriminating when it comes to men but there really are some quite nice ones here. It strikes me that your problem is that you're too much in love with flying to allow a man to get a look in.'

'Nah,' said Kate. 'My problem stems from the thought of taking anyone home to meet the black widow.' But judging by the snort, Maria didn't believe her.

Kate, deciding that her love life would just have to be put on ice until she returned to her career with the Royal Signals, joined her fellow mess members on forays to pubs in safe areas, took part in the horseplay on dinner nights, became an active member of the mess committee and used her spare time to carry on with her studies for her commercial pilot's licence. She tried to ensure that she and Andy never ended up on their own together, as Maria's comments, however much she tried to ignore them, had stuck in her mind. But despite her best efforts they seemed to be thrown together more often than she would have liked. Was Maria right? Could it be that Andy still fancied her? She liked Andy very much – she would even go as far as to admit that she was fond of him – but he was engaged to Emma and surely that had to have some significance. Not that Kate had met Emma, but from what she'd heard, the girl was quite delightful, and completely besotted with Andy. The last thing Kate wanted to be accused of was coming between Andy and his fiancée. Part of her envied Andy; envied him for having found someone. Sometimes she felt she would like there to be more in her life than work and play. Perhaps it would be nice to think of settling down. The thought of having a place of her own, rather than just a room in a mess, had a definite appeal, although without someone to share it with it would be lonely. So while Kate mostly enjoyed what life had to offer, there was a little part of her that dreamed, rather wistfully, of being swept off her feet and taken away to a world of love, contentment, security and companionship. But she didn't think that her dream world included Andy.

During the dark, cold, dreary days of February, RAF Aldergrove decided to hold an inter-unit quiz competition, and notices advertising the fact were sent to all major and minor units in the Province.

'Come on, everyone,' said Andy one day in the crew room. 'I reckon we should put in a team and try and prove once and for all that the Air Corps is better than the RAF.'

'Yeah, but what if we lose?' said Sergeant Field.

'We won't. Think positive. I think we ought to have heats here to decide the teams. We can organise some games of Trivial Pursuit and those who win can form our team.' The lack of response was unanimous. Nothing more was said about the quiz until it was discovered that their sister squadron in the regiment, the Lynx squadron, had a team entered. Instantly several volunteers came forward, but Andy was adamant that his method was to be used to decide the team. In the end Kate, Andy, a REME fitter called Archie Archbold and one of the clerks proved to have the most extensive general knowledge.

The quiz was scheduled to take place the following week in the RAF Aldergrove gymnasium, as this was the most suitable venue for an all-ranks social event. Eight teams from various units around the Six Counties had been entered, and the format was that all teams would answer, on paper, fifty questions, divided up into rounds of ten questions on a variety of subjects. The four highest scoring teams would then play in the semi-finals using the same rules as *University Challenge*. A grand final would be held at the end of the evening with the promise of large prizes for the winning team.

On the evening of the quiz the gymnasium was packed. Each team was allocated a table, separated by screens from their rivals, and facing the audience. After every round of ten questions the papers were gathered in to be marked as the next round commenced. The teams each had a joker they could play on one of the rounds, which would then score them double points for every correct answer. After the fifty questions had been asked there was a break as the scores were collated and checked, which also allowed the participants and the audience to buy more refreshments from the bar. Andy, as the holder of the most senior rank on their team, insisted that he should buy the round. By the time he returned to their table the compère was about to announce the scores. He read them out in reverse order: the qualifiers for the next round were HQ Northern Ireland, RAF Aldergrove, 321 Squadron Royal Logistic Corps and Kate's team, 665 Squadron Army Air Corps.

They were drawn first against HQ Northern Ireland. While the tables were rearranged so that the two teams flanked the quizmaster, Kate pleaded the need for a trip to the loo, brought on by a hastily downed half-pint of cider, and slipped out of the hall. The screens, now not needed, were in the process of being removed, and Kate was concentrating on avoiding these rather than taking note of the opposition as she hurried to the Ladies'. When she returned, her team was positioned nearest to the entrance to the gym, so she took her seat without the need to pass the side from HQNI.

'Are we all set, then?' asked the quizmaster. Both teams acknowledged that they were. The buzzers were tested, the rules explained and the first of the semi-finals got underway.

'And welcome to you all to this first Unit-versity Challenge Competition,' boomed the quizmaster through the PA. The entire audience groaned at this appalling play on words. 'Now it's my pleasure to introduce the teams. On my left we have 665 Squadron Army Air Corps: Craftsman Archie Archbold, Major Andy McMaster, Lance Corporal Steve James and, last but not least, Lieutenant Kate Hayleigh.' Each of the team acknowledged their own name and the audience applauded loudly once the introductions were complete. 'And on my right, the team from HQNI: Bombardier Graham Young, Major Johnny Johnson, Captain Eddie Thomas—'

Kate didn't hear the last of the introductions, she was too busy leaning right across the table so she could look sideways across the compère to check that this Eddie Thomas wasn't just someone with the same name. Eddie was leaning forward too, and waggled his fingers at Kate in happy greeting. Involuntarily her heart leapt and her mind was filled with thoughts and memories that consisted only of him.

'What happened to you?' stormed Andy after they had been trounced by HQNI. 'You didn't answer a single question.'

'I did,' said Kate, colouring with guilt.

'All right, you answered one. Big deal. I was relying on you to field anything on history or geography.'

'I'm sorry, my mind just kept going blank. Nerves,' she lied. She could hardly admit that her thoughts had been so preoccupied with Eddie that she'd barely heard the questions, let alone been able to concentrate enough to come up with any answers.

'Hi there, Kate.'

Kate spun round at the sound of the familiar voice. She felt her colour heighten still further. She must look like a beetroot, she thought despairingly. 'Eddie! Why didn't you tell me you were back here? And you look so much better!' Although she noticed that he had a scar under his left eye. She was so delighted to see him, she couldn't mask her pleasure. She introduced him to Andy, and explained how they had met.

'So you are the reason why Kate spent all that time at Musgrave Park,' Andy observed. He sounded cross. Obviously he hadn't got over his annoyance at Kate's pathetic contribution to the quiz team. 'Does this explain why you weren't concentrating just now?'

Kate was mortified that Andy should have drawn attention to the fact that Eddie's presence had flummoxed her completely. How was she supposed to play it cool now?

Eddie was obviously amused by her discomfort. He grinned at her broadly. 'I'm sorry I haven't been in touch yet. I only arrived two days ago and I instantly discovered that I'd been "volunteered" to make up the numbers for this shenanigan.'

'I'll forgive you then.' Kate wanted to wriggle like a puppy, completely bowled over with pleasure and excitement. 'So what are you doing here?'

'You mean at HQNI?' Kate nodded. 'I'm posted here as an SO3.'

'For two years?'

'Unless I get sacked, that's the plan.'

'But that's great.'

The compère was asking everyone to return to their seats, ready for the second semi-final.

'Let's go outside so we can talk,' suggested Kate, not wanting their reunion to be interrupted. Their exit did not go unnoticed by their friends and acquaintances, especially Andy, who looked thunderous as he watched them go.

'So what have you been up to?' asked Eddie once they were in the relative peace of the entrance lobby.

Kate felt like saying, *Waiting for a letter from you*, but she didn't. She didn't want to frighten him away now that she had found him again. Maria might not believe in Mr Right, but Kate had proof positive that, for her at least, he existed. She longed to tell Eddie how much she had missed him, how she had dreamed of this moment, but she couldn't find a form of words that didn't sound gushing and cheesy. She was aware that he was staring at her curiously. He'd asked her a question and she was staring at him like a complete idiot.

'I'm sorry,' she stammered.

Eddie shook his head. 'It was nothing important. Look, I feel I owe you for all the times you visited me when I was laid up. Could you bear to come and have dinner with me some time?'

He wanted to take her out! Kate thought she would expire with happiness.

'Is that OK?' asked Eddie tentatively.

'Of course, of course.'

'When?'

'I'm off the rest of this week.'

'You're not working or anything.'

'Not till Monday morning.'

'So how about tomorrow?'

'That's fine.' What Kate really would have liked to have said was *That's wonderful, it's perfect, I can't think of anything I'd rather do*, but knew she must play it cool. Their conversation, stilted and awkward, finally dried up, Eddie made an excuse and returned to the company of his team, and Kate was left wondering if his offer to take her out was made because he felt it his duty, or because he genuinely wanted her company. Oh God, she thought, I've played it too cool and he doesn't think I'm interested at all. She sighed and, not for the first time, wished she had Maria's skill in handling men.

The following evening, when Kate entered the bar in the regimental mess, the ribald remarks and catcalls drowned out the music playing loudly on the hi-fi. News of her reunion with Eddie was the current topic of mess gossip.

'Piss off,' she yelled at them good-naturedly. Her morale was far too high to be affected by this sort of banter.

'So what's he got that we haven't?' asked one of the junior captains.

'Just about anything you care to name,' said Kate, not the least intimidated by the variety of semi-pornographic comments a remark like this was bound to elicit, and which, predictably, were thrown back at her in a raucous torrent. 'You've all got sick minds,' she said as she collected her orange juice and prepared to leave.

'What, going? Aren't you dining with us tonight?'

'Not a chance. I've got a far better offer.' She didn't stop to hear the riposte to this, but judging by the burst of laughter that bellowed across the width of the anteroom, it was probably just as well.

Despite Eddie's protestations, Kate had insisted that she would drive over to Lisburn to collect him.

'It's only sensible,' she had said. 'I rarely drink because of flying. Besides which, I'm told there's a nice little restaurant in Hillsborough and it would be daft for you to flog all the way over here only to go back the way you came.' Eddie couldn't dispute her logic and had given way.

It only took Kate twenty minutes to get to Lisburn. She was stopped at a checkpoint as she came down the hill that led to the town. She turned down her stereo and wound down her window.

The RUC policeman asked for some identification as a soldier gave her car a cursory check. She showed him her ID card.

'You look very cheerful, in spite of the weather, if I may say so, miss,' he said conversationally.

'I'm going to meet an old friend,' she replied.

The constable took in her sparkling eyes and her radiant happiness. 'He's a lucky man. Drive carefully now miss.'

'Thanks, and it's me who's the lucky one,' said Kate as she drove away.

Eddie was waiting for her by the entrance to the mess.

'Are you sure you wouldn't like a drink before we set out?'

'No. There's only so much orange juice I can stomach.' Eddie laughed sympathetically and climbed into the passenger seat.

'Right then, chocks away.'

The restaurant lived up to its reputation: it was intimate, friendly, inexpensive and it served delicious food. Eddie congratulated Kate on her choice, and once they had made their selection from the menu – not an easy task – they turned their attention to each other. Eddie wanted to hear about Kate's flying and Kate wanted to hear about his rehabilitation. She told him about her mother –'You don't really call her the black widow, do you?' he asked – and he told her about his father's illness and his mother's devoted nursing.

'Which doesn't leave much space in her life for me.'

'You have my sympathy there,' said Kate wryly. 'At one stage my mother went into a decline if she thought I was going to go away, even if it was just a few days; now she's so busy I only communicate with her via her answering machine.'

'So you're a virtual orphan, just like me.'

'Except that she still treats me like I'm about ten and tries to tell me what I should and shouldn't do.'

'I can't imagine you pay much attention.'

'It's easy when I'm away from her, but you have no idea how formidable she can be close to.'

'I can't wait to meet her.'

'Don't even think . . .' Kate was about to add that Honour was bound to hate him on sight, but stopped herself. She knew that her mother, snob that she was, would find fault with Eddie's background, social standing, accent, even his regiment. And the thing that irritated Kate more than anything was the knowledge that Honour's own background wasn't anything to write home about. It wasn't as if her family had had masses of property and vaults full of heirlooms. As far as Kate could gather, Honour, the daughter of a businessman, had been raised in an unremarkable house near the air base where her father had first been stationed. But the way she carried on, anyone would think she'd been brought up rubbing shoulders with the nobility and living in baronial splendour.

'I'm sure if I ever do get to meet her I'll find that she's really a dear little white-haired old lady who makes knitted squares for Oxfam and jam for the WI and who is just misunderstood by her daughter.'

For some reason, Eddie's complete misconception of her mother amused her enormously and she began to giggle helplessly. Her amusement was infectious and Eddie started to laugh too.

'Oh, Kate,' he said as they finally pulled themselves together, 'I'd forgotten what wonderful company you are. You know, I always wondered, when I was in hospital, why it was that you used to make me feel so much better when you were around. I sometimes thought that perhaps it was because you took my mind off how rotten I felt. But I can see now that it's the way you are, that it's a gift you have.'

Kate smiled bashfully, not knowing how to respond to such a beautiful compliment.

By the time they were shown to their table in the window of the first-floor restaurant, they had no eyes for anything but each other. Had they been less self-absorbed, they might have admired the pretty pastel-painted cottages, the elegant façades of some of the larger houses and the atmosphere of affluent gentility. But as it was, they might have been dining in a burger bar for all the attention they paid to their surroundings and their food, despite the time they had spent in making their choice.

It was well past eleven o'clock when a discreet cough from their waiter alerted them to the fact that they were the only people left in the restaurant.

'Good God! Is that the time?' said Kate, glancing at her watch. The bill appeared that instant and was quickly settled. Eddie left a generous tip, helped Kate into her coat and then took her hand to escort her down the stairs. As before, when he'd held her hand in the hospital, Kate felt an electric thrill zing through her. What was it with this man that he could produce such a reaction? On the way back to Lisburn she found that her driving, usually extremely good, had degenerated to a standard that was verging on being dangerous. All she could think about was the man sitting beside her and what it might be like to be kissed by him.

'Are you all right?' asked Eddie as, for the second time, she switched on her windscreen wipers instead of dipping her lights.

'Fine,' said Kate, wondering what excuse she could possibly use for her ineptitude. 'I just don't drive that much and not at night.'

'Well, as long as you know what you're doing when you're in the air.'

'I don't have to worry about headlights or wipers when I'm flying.'

'That could explain a lot!'

Kate tried to drive more carefully for the rest of the journey.

'Would you like to come in for a coffee?' asked Eddie hopefully.

'I'd love to, but I really do have to get back. But perhaps another time . . .?' She left the question hanging hopefully in the air.

'I can't make it tomorrow. I'm on duty.'

Kate was pleased to note that he sounded really disappointed. 'Sunday then?'

'Wonderful. What time?'

'How about making a day of it?'

'Brilliant. I'll see if I can't get the staff here to fix me up a picnic,' said Eddie.

'I'll pick you up at about ten thirty.'

'No, I'll pick *you* up this time.'

Kate didn't argue. Eddie shifted in his seat so he was looking directly at her, and Kate found herself leaning sideways across the gearshift towards him. Eddie put his hand around the back of her neck and pulled her mouth on to his. Their lips parted and Kate felt a wonderful, sensuous languor sweep across her whole being. She felt his tongue flicker gently across her lips and responded by allowing the tip of hers to run lightly across his teeth. His fingers on the back of her neck stroked her hairline, making her want to stretch and purr like a cat. She opened her eyes a fraction and noticed that Eddie had his eyes closed. His thick dark lashes lay on his cheek like those of a sleeping child, veiling his scar. Kate suddenly wanted to hold him and protect him, to keep him safe from further harm. She moved her hands from where they had been resting on the steering wheel and encircled his neck. She wanted to hug him but her ribs were beginning to ache from bending sideways. She shifted slightly to ease them and the kiss finished. She sighed. Eddie opened his eyes.

'I've got to go,' whispered Kate.

'I wish you didn't.'

'Me too.'

'I don't think I can wait for Sunday.'

'No.' The conversation fizzled out but they remained gazing at each other

'Stay the night. Please.'

'I can't. It's not that I don't want to, but I ought to get back.' She was fibbing; she didn't have to, but she was frightened of things going too fast. She wanted time to gather her wits.

Eddie nodded sadly. 'I understand.' He opened the car door and got out. Kate leaned across until she had to support her weight by leaning her arm on the passenger seat. She gazed up at him. Gently he brushed her cheek with his forefinger. 'Goodnight,' he said. 'And drive carefully.'

Kate could barely trust herself to answer. Eddie shut the door and walked into the mess, and Kate drove back to Aldergrove with her heart telling her that she was in love and her head telling her not to be so ridiculous.

'You're becoming boring,' Andy complained to Kate one evening in the bar. 'You used to be lots of fun. You used to join in, but now you're either out with your man or swotting for your CPL.'

'So what is it to you?' He sounded irritable and a little like a jealous boyfriend. Kate remembered what Maria had said. She fleetingly thought about confronting him, but by tacit mutual consent, they rarely spoke of their previous, and now distant, relationship.

138

'It's nothing to me. Nothing at all,' Andy countered. 'I just wonder where the old Kate has got to.'

'She's busy, that's what. If I want to spend time with Eddie then I have to get everything done in what little other free time that I have.'

'I hope he's worth it.'

'He is.' And Kate said it with such conviction that Andy was quite taken aback.

'Well, I just hope it doesn't end in tears.'

'Why on earth should it?'

Andy just shrugged by way of an answer, and Kate had an uncomfortable feeling that that was exactly what he wanted to happen. Perhaps he wasn't the good friend she had thought he was.

Chapter Fourteen

As the cold, dark months of winter gave way to spring, Kate and Eddie used their free days to explore Ireland. At last Kate had the excuse and the desire, since it meant long, tranquil walks with Eddie's undivided attention, to ramble through the Glens of Antrim, scramble over the ruins of Dunluce Castle, and picnic in the vast and wondrous gardens of Mount Stewart. But although they visited these beauty spots, they were so self-absorbed that they barely noticed the wonderful views of the emerald-green glens as they opened to a turquoise sea. Nor did they fully appreciate the stunning location or the romanticism of the castle set high on the cliffs above the North Antrim coast. And although they enjoyed the deep peace and beauty of Mount Stewart, they only noticed that the beautiful walled formal gardens offered them shelter from a chill breeze, and they were oblivious to the glories of the magnificent rhododendrons and the foliage of the trees.

If Eddie was duty officer at the headquarters, then Kate would drive over to keep him company; if Kate's mess threw a party, then Eddie was one of the first to arrive; if Kate was invited out, she would ask if Eddie could accompany her. When Kate was in Eddie's company she sparkled with a glow of absolute contentment and joy and when she was apart from him her mind constantly seemed to be elsewhere; which, indeed it was. She was too professional to let it affect her flying, but when she was trying to undertake routine admin tasks, more often than not she found herself staring out the window and day-dreaming about Eddie.

*

'Eddie?' shrilled her mother down the phone. 'Eddie! That's not an officer's name. For heaven's sake, what can you be thinking of getting involved with someone called Eddie?'

'Wait till you meet him.' Kate, used to her mother, refused to be daunted by her predictable reaction.

'And when will that be, may I ask?'

'Well, I was rather hoping we could come over to stay next weekend.'

'I'm not sure it's convenient.'

'Oh, please, Mummy. I'd really like you both to meet.'

Her mother relented a fraction. 'Let me check my diary.'

Kate held her breath while her mother rummaged around on the desk to find it, then rustled the pages as she turned them with deliberate and agonising slowness.

'I have a meeting with the WRVS on Friday and I'm committed to attending a sale of work on Saturday morning . . .'

'We won't mind. We can go shopping in Windsor while you do that.'

'Well . . .' Kate could feel her mother starting to relent. She held her breath. 'I suppose I could manage that weekend.'

'Thanks, Mummy. We'll be with you on the Friday evening. We'll get a taxi from the airport. Please don't make any special arrangements for us.' Kate wondered about suggesting that her mother save some effort by only making up one bed, but decided that it wouldn't be wise.

On the plane over, she tried to tell Eddie, yet again, what to expect, but as always he was convinced she was grossly exaggerating.

'No one's mother can be that bad.'

'But she is. And for God's sake don't call her the black widow to her face.'

'What's it worth?'

Kate shook her head in exasperation. Eddie was refusing to take her seriously. 'You'll see. Just remember, I take after my father, not my mother.'

'And which school did you go to . . . Eddie? The pause before Honour spoke his name and the hint of a sneer in her voice, was only obvious if, like Kate, one had been attuned through the years to notice such things. Her mother had already checked out his career prospects and his family background, and Kate knew that she had instantly taken on board his physical appearance, taste in clothes and accent. So far, Kate judged from past experience, Eddie seemed to have scraped through most of these assessments, but this question might just prove his undoing. As far as her mother was concerned, anything other than attendance at a major public school condemned a man to the very bottom of the social scale, and Kate didn't think that Honour even knew that there were schools that were rated below grammars. Behind her back Kate crossed her fingers and hoped Eddie would realise the significance of the question.

He looked Honour in the eye and, keeping his expression completely deadpan, said, 'Actually I went to an extremely well-known school.' Kate relaxed. 'It's called Liverpool Road Secondary Mod in Birkenhead. You've probably heard of it; it's always in the papers – arson attacks, juvenile delinquency, drug-taking, striking teachers, that sort of thing.' Kate stiffened in alarm, then, catching sight of her mother's face, her horror turned into an uncontrollable urge to laugh. Honour had been caught completely off guard and her smile – prepared for the acceptable answer of Eton, Harrow or Rugby – had frozen into a rictus grin while her eyes flickered in panic. As Kate fought to conquer her giggles, Honour also managed to regain control. Her ghastly smile relaxed and relief replaced the look of fear. She laughed politely to cover up her moment of anxiety.

'Ah, your little joke. How droll you are. Liverpool Road Secondary Modern indeed. Kate always likes people with a sense of humour. Well, you must excuse me, but I have things to see to in the kitchen. Kate, Eddie's glass is nearly empty. Please get him another beer.'

As soon as the sitting room door had shut Kate burst out laughing.

'I don't believe her. She excelled herself this time. *Ah, your little joke. How droll you are.*' She mimicked her mother perfectly. 'But what on earth do you think you're playing at? Why on earth didn't you tell an enormous fib? She'll never be any the wiser. Remember, she only knows about the school I went to. Boys' schools – apart from their names – are a completely mystery to her.'

'She is priceless,' said Eddie. 'I almost expected her to get out the Anglepoise lamp and shine it in my face. Third degree or what!'

'Now do you believe me? I told you she was awful, but you thought I was exaggerating.' Kate went to the sideboard and collected another can of beer for Eddie. He took it gratefully.

'I just don't understand how a mother like that can produce a daughter like you.'

'I grew up in spite of her, not because of her. And I keep telling you, I take after my father.'

'And is she as snobby about everything as you say she is? Truthfully now?'

'Seriously, she doesn't live in the same world as the rest of us. She just doesn't understand why everyone doesn't shop in Harrods and Harvey Nicks.'

'I bet she only lives in Windsor because of the neighbours in the big house on the hill.'

Kate laughed again. Eddie had got her mother summed up to a T.

'So when are we going to tell your mother that we're engaged?'

'But we're not.' Kate's laughter died. 'I mean . . .'

'Don't you want us to be?'

What sort of a question was that? More than anything in the world, more than flying Lynxes even, Kate wanted to be Mrs Eddie Thomas.

Eddie mistook her hesitation. 'I'm sorry. I shouldn't have mentioned it. I just thought . . .'

'No! I mean yes! I mean, I do want us to be.'

When Honour returned to the sitting room to let them know that dinner was served she found them locked in a quite unseemly embrace. Really!

On the morning of Kate's wedding, Honour took her daughter to one side.

'It's not too late, my dear.'

Kate stopped applying eyeliner and turned away from the mirror to stare at her mother. 'What on earth do you mean?'

'We could call it all off; send the presents back.'

Kate could hardly believe her ears. 'But I don't want to. I've never in my life been more sure that I'm about to do the right thing.'

'But it isn't as if you have to get married. I mean, you're not pregnant or anything, are you?'

'That has nothing to do with it. I love Eddie. I love him more than I've ever loved anyone in my life. I want to spend the rest of my life with him.'

'But what can someone of your age know about love?'

Kate didn't want a confrontation and was trying her best to keep calm. 'Mother, I'm twenty-five. I'm as old as you were when you married Daddy. I know what I'm doing. Please believe me and try to be happy for me.'

Honour just sighed and looked far from convinced.

'Look, Mummy, I am happier than I can ever remember being. Can't you just set aside whatever objections you have and at least, if only for today, try to look as though you are happy too? This is my wedding day and I really don't want it spoilt by having you wandering round like a wet weekend.'

'Really . . .' Honour began.

'I mean it, Mother.' Kate was spared any further argument as Maria, carrying a fabulous bouquet of flowers, pushed the door of her bedroom open.

'Here you go,' said Maria. 'These are for you. My little posy is downstairs.'

'That's wonderful,' said Kate, thankful for the interruption. 'Would you be a love, Maria, and give me a hand with my hair?' Then, quite icily to her mother, 'Don't feel you have to hang around, Mother. I'm sure you want to get yourself ready.'

'As you wish,' said Honour, getting the more-than-obvious hint and sweeping out of the room.

'What was all that about?' asked Maria when Honour had gone.

Kate explained. Maria gave a long whistle. 'She is the limit, she really is. I know she's your mother, but honestly . . .'

Kate shrugged. 'I've been related to her all these years and I still can't fathom her out. Does she do this sort of thing

144

deliberately to upset me, or does she do it because, in some perverse way, she thinks she's helping me?'

'I'm sure she can't be doing it deliberately. Surely not?' Maria sounded none too convinced.

'God knows. Just promise me one thing. Don't tell Eddie about what Mummy has just said. Having her as a mother-in-law is enough of a cross to bear without knowing quite how much she disapproves of him.'

Despite the fact that she cried throughout the service, even Honour couldn't complain about the cachet the military presence gave to an otherwise perfectly normal wedding ceremony. Through her tears she noted with smug satisfaction how impressed her friends and acquaintances were with the glamour that the male officers, all in their best dark blue number one dress uniforms, lent to the occasion, although a part of her wished that the uniforms could have been the scarlet tunics of the Guards. Still, it was unlikely that her cronies from the bridge club would be able to boast of anything more impressive than morning dress when their offspring got married.

Kate, given away by Eddie's previous commanding officer and attended by Maria, looked radiant. No one in the congregation, with the possible exception of her mother, could doubt that Kate, dignified, completely confident and simply exuding joy could be making anything other than the right decision.

Eddie's father was too ill to travel, so his mother stayed away too, but the newly-weds compensated by honeymooning in Spain so Kate could meet his family. Despite Eddie's father's ill health they had a wonderful, relaxing fortnight in the hills of Andalucia and returned to Ireland just as the IRA announced a ceasefire.

'This has got to be propitious,' said Kate as they unpacked their belongings and arranged them around their new quarter.

'Are you using long words just to confuse me?' asked Eddie, leaving his task of stacking books on a shelf and moving across the room to give his new bride a hug.

'What other reason could I possibly have other than to prove my education was vastly superior to yours?'

'Bollocks.'

'Umm,' said Kate nuzzling his ear. 'I just love it when you talk dirty.'

145

Outside the rain was hammering down. They had lit a fire, despite it being early September, and the flickering flames threw huge shadows on the wall behind them. Slowly, however, the giant shadows disappeared as the pair of them sank to the floor on the hearthrug and hungrily began to tug off each other's clothes.

Chapter Fifteen

'Are you OK, Kate?' asked Andy. She was sitting on the edge of a chair in the crew room looking as white as paper, her forehead glistening damply with a sheen of sweat.

'No. I feel bloody dreadful. I can't think what it is.'

'You weren't on the pop last night, were you?'

'Good God, no. I've more sense than that when I'm flying.'

'But you went to Sergeant Field's farewell.'

'Yes, but I was on orange juice.' Even this amount of talk seemed exhausting. She shut her eyes and willed the feeling of sickness to go away. 'Perhaps I ate something that was off. I wonder if anyone else feels this shitty?'

'No one's rung in sick. I think you should go home. I don't think you're fit to fly.' Andy gave her another hard stare. 'And you're sure you didn't have a drink?'

Kate, feeling deathly, didn't need this sort of interrogation on top of everything else. She wished Andy would leave her alone. 'I told you, I was on bloody orange juice.' Suddenly she felt her stomach heave more violently than before and knew exactly what this presaged. She dashed from the crew room, clutching a hanky to her mouth. A second or two later the sound of retching was heard. Andy grimaced and went into the corridor, where he found Kate hunkered down on the floor, a pool of vomit in front of her.

'I'm sorry,' she mumbled, wiping her mouth with her hanky. 'I'll clear this mess up in a minute.' She rocked back on her heels and slumped against the wall. 'I just feel so awful.'

'Don't you worry about this,' said Andy. 'You need to be back home in bed. Stay here.'

Kate was too weak and ill to argue. Her stomach felt as though someone had torn it out of her, her head spun with dizziness and the feeling of nausea was still strong despite the fact that there was nothing left to bring up. Oh God, she was going to be sick again! This time, though, she heaved and heaved and nothing appeared. How could that be? she wondered. Her stomach ached even more from the straining.

Andy reappeared with a bucket and mop and a roll of kitchen towel. Deftly he cleared up the mess and washed the floor.

'Thanks,' said Kate weakly. She leant against the wall, wondering when she would begin to feel better. Surely if it was food poisoning she would be all right once she'd got everything out of her system. There couldn't be much left now, she thought grimly.

'I'm going to drive you home,' said Andy. 'You're in no state to be on the road on your own. But first I'm going to take you to the MO to see if he can give you something.' Kate, feeling too lousy to argue, could only comply.

'It's nothing sinister,' said the doctor. 'You're pregnant, that's all.'

That's all! Kate couldn't believe what he was saying. 'I'm what? I can't be. It's ridiculous. I haven't been married long enough.' Shock, amazement and disbelief left her feeling stunned and bewildered.

'I don't usually make mistakes, and I can assure you I haven't this time,' said the MO coldly, unused to having his word doubted quite so vehemently. 'Anyway, what on earth do you mean, you haven't been married long enough? There's no time limit on this sort of occurrence.'

'I suppose not.'

'Most women are usually quite pleased at the news, especially married ones.'

'But I can't be pregnant.'

'Why not? Are you using any form of contraception?'

'Yes, I'm on the pill.'

'And you're sure you've been taking it?'

'Yes.'

'Have you been ill at all recently? Diarrhoea, vomiting, that sort of thing?'

That was the explanation then. 'I ate some dodgy seafood when I was on my honeymoon. I had a fairly violent tummy upset for twenty-four hours.'

'Well, there you are, then.'

Kate sighed. Not only an explanation but a bun in the oven to boot. Perhaps when she got over feeling quite so dreadful she would be pleased with the idea, but right now all she was experiencing was shock and nausea.

Eddie was over the moon when she broke the news to him that evening.

'But that's wonderful! Clever, clever girl.'

Kate, feeling sick still, and now exhausted as well, smiled wanly. 'It's come as a bit of a shock to me. And I thought pregnant women were supposed to feel wonderful and fulfilled. All I feel like is a wrung-out dishcloth.'

'You put your feet up. I'll make supper. What is it?'

'Spag bol.'

'Tremendous. How do you make it?'

Kate explained.

'That sounds easy enough. Right, I'll get cracking on it. Is there anything I can get you?'

'What I'd really like is a stiff drink, but that's off limits now. How about orange juice and lemonade?'

'Coming right up.'

Eddie bustled off to the kitchen and Kate heard cupboard doors being opened and slammed shut.

'Where do you keep the lemonade?' he yelled through.

'In the cupboard by the oven, bottom shelf,' Kate called back.

'Got it.' He appeared shortly with her drink. 'I'll get on with supper now. You just relax and take it easy.'

Gratefully Kate took a sip, sank back in the armchair and closed her eyes. With Eddie waiting on her, perhaps pregnancy wasn't too bad after all. She let her mind drift

'Sorry, darling . . .' Kate opened her eyes. 'Were you asleep?'

'Not quite.'

'Sorry. I can't find the garlic crusher.'

'In the pot by the sink.'

'OK.'

Kate finished her drink and shut her eyes again.

Two minutes later there was an appalling crash from the kitchen, followed by a stream of expletives. Kate put her empty glass on the table and went to see what was going on. The frying pan and its contents were on the floor and Eddie was holding his hand under a running tap. Kate didn't say a word, but took the cloth from the sink and began to clear up the mess.

'I'll do that in a minute,' said Eddie.

Kate ignored him and carried on, dumping the raw, oily onions back in the pan. 'What happened to your hand?

'I burned it on the handle of the frying pan.'

'How?'

'I don't know. It was red-hot when I touched it.'

Kate was puzzled. The handle was plastic and didn't get hot. 'Which ring did you put the pan on?'

'That one.' Eddie pointed to the left-hand front one.

'Well that explains it. You switched on the wrong ring. No wonder the handle got hot if it was over something belting heat at it.'

Eddie smiled sheepishly. 'Tell you what, suppose I nip into town and get a takeaway?'

'That sounds more sensible than you cooking supper.' Kate finished clearing up the onions and tipped them into the bin. 'I'll ring and order' – she paused as she got the mop and bucket out of the utility room – 'while you wash the floor.'

By the time Eddie got back from collecting their supper Kate was fast asleep on the sofa. He wasn't sure whether or not to wake her but reasoned that she ought to eat properly. She needed to keep her strength up especially now she was eating for two.

'You don't have to resign,' said Andy. 'You're entitled to maternity leave you know.'

'I know but I just feel that it's all wrong. I'm completely useless to the squadron, I can't fly because I get airsick, I'm not even able to come into work most days because I feel too lousy. You can't get anyone else posted in to replace me unless I leave and the baby isn't even due until April. If I resign now, on family grounds, it'll be fairer all round and I can rejoin once I've had the baby. I just think it's wrong for me to keep on getting paid when I'm frankly incapable of performing a useful task.'

Andy gazed at her from the other side of his desk. He didn't think that feminists would agree with her moral stand. It had taken quite a fight to allow pregnant women to stay in the armed forces and Kate was about to let all the hard work go for nothing. And anyway he didn't want her to leave. 'What if we found you a ground job?'

'It's not that. I can't cope with work at all the way I feel at the moment. I feel such a wimp for admitting this. Loads of women carry on till the end, but I just don't seem to be able to. By the time I've spent half the morning with my head down the loo, I feel too knackered to want to do anything other than crawl back to bed. I'm just not up to doing anything.'

Andy looked at her sympathetically. It wasn't like Kate to be devoid to energy; she was one of the liveliest people he knew. And she did look awful: pinched and drawn, with big dark shadows like bruises under her eyes. 'It's your decision, of course.'

'Eddie agrees with me. We can manage on his pay quite easily. He's terrified that I'm going to overdo things and make myself ill.' She smiled wanly. 'As if I could feel iller than I do right now.'

'Poor old Kate. What does the doctor say?'

Kate sighed dejectedly. 'That it should pass. This sort of reaction is not that uncommon, but unless I really start to lose weight there's not much they are prepared to do for me.'

'You poor kid.'

'I'm not really. I should feel lucky that I can fall pregnant at the drop of a hat. There are plenty of women who'd give their back teeth to be in my position. Just ask Emma. She works in a maternity hospital; she'll tell you I'm right.'

'What will you do all day? I can't imagine you sitting in a rocking chair and knitting.'

'I'll find something. Well, I will if I can keep my head out of the loo for more than a couple of minutes at a stretch.'

'How are you getting on with your CPL?'

'I've applied to take the exam next week. I was wondering,

if I pass, would you give me a check flight and sign up my logbook? It's just I'd like to get it all done and dusted before my resignation is accepted – I sort of feel it'll be like a safety net in case anything goes wrong in the future. You know, if the army decides it doesn't want me back after all.'

'I'd be delighted, as long as you promise to bring plenty of sick bags with you.'

'How did you get on?' asked Eddie.

'Andy passed me.'

'So you're fully qualified to fly helicopters commercially now?'

'That's the general idea, although I'll need loads more hours before I can fly fare-paying passengers.'

'So why bother?'

'It's another string to my bow. I mean, with Options for Change, the peace dividend and all the redundancies, it's not inconceivable that it may be harder for me to rejoin than I think it will be.'

'But you're still going ahead with your resignation?'

Kate sighed. 'I can't stay in. We've been through it all. I know that I could if I wanted, but I just hate being a dead weight to the squadron. The other pilots don't say anything but I know that they resent the fact that I can't do any duties and that I'm still drawing my pay. They see it as unfair, and frankly I don't blame them. And anyway, if I've stopped work then I don't have a mad rush after I've had the baby to get a nanny organised and get back into harness again. We can get by on your wages; goodness knows, there are loads of married captains with families whose wives don't work.'

'True, I don't dispute that for a minute. I just can't see you taking up knitting somehow.'

'Funny, that's exactly what Andy said to me.'

Kate's resignation was accepted, and as the days and weeks passed she found that the worst of the feelings of sickness began to pass. There were days when she felt quite bright and sparky and she began to look forward to the rapidly approaching festive season.

'We ought to invite Mummy over here for Christmas.

You've only got a couple of days' leave so it isn't enough to be worth flying back, and I don't like the idea of her being all alone.'

'You don't think that she might have made arrangements to spend it with some of her bridge friends?'

'We can only hope, I suppose.'

With a superhuman effort Kate summoned the energy to coax her mother over to Ireland.

'If you don't come, we'll be all on our own,' she pleaded.

'Well, I'm sure you and . . . Eddie' – again Kate noticed the deliberate pause before her mother enunciated his name – 'will be only too happy not to have me under your feet.'

'Not at all. We wouldn't be inviting you if we didn't want you to come.'

'Supposing you came here?'

'We can't. Eddie's on duty on Boxing Day and we're stuck here.' Silence. 'Please, Mummy. I could do with a hand, especially if I get really tired again.' She distinctly heard her mother sniff and then sigh. Do be careful you don't over-whelm me with enthusiasm, thought Kate snakily.

'Well, I suppose I could fly out,' said Honour. 'But only for a few days. People will be expecting me to host my drinks party. It's becoming quite a fixture on the social calendar here.'

Bully for it, thought Kate.

Still, having her mother arriving made Kate focus on the preparations for the holiday and she threw herself into baking mince pies, decorating a cake and trying her hand at making her own Christmas pudding.

'You'll be making a *Blue Peter* Advent crown next,' said Eddie one day as he came home from work and found her stitching lengths of red felt to make stockings.

'You're taking the piss out of me,' said Kate with a grin.

'*Moi!*' Eddie, standing beside her as she fed the fabric through the sewing machine, dropped a kiss on her forehead and assumed a look of injured innocence. 'As if such a thought would cross my mind.'

'Beast.' Kate took her foot off the switch and put her arms round Eddie's waist. She snuggled her face against the khaki wool of his uniform sweater. 'And you're sure you really don't mind having my mother for Christmas?'

'I thought we had agreed on turkey, besides she'll be old and tough.'

Kate laughed. 'But seriously?'

'No. Honestly.'

'Uncross your fingers and say it again,' mumbled Kate, her face still buried in his midriff. There was silence. Kate released her grip slightly and looked up at him. 'You *do* mind, don't you.'

'I don't. I'm just afraid that she may say or do something to upset you and I don't want that to happen. I can't bear the thought of anything spoiling our first Christmas together.'

'She won't. Remember, I'm used to her. I don't think there's anything she could do that would upset me. She's mostly pretty harmless these days.'

Eddie raised his eyebrows and remained silent. From what he'd seen of the old bag, he'd put nothing past her, but then he could hardly say that to Kate.

In the event Honour, although not the perfect house guest, was mostly pretty innocuous. She was demanding and unhelpful, expecting Eddie to wait on not only Kate but also herself. Her excuse was that she didn't know where anything was, although she seemed to be able to find the sherry bottle on the dot of six o'clock in the evening if Eddie hadn't got in from work.

On the morning of Christmas Eve, as he and Kate lay comfortably entwined in bed, Eddie, now more used to the kitchen and its appliances, demanded that he should be allowed to cook the turkey.

'Will you be able to manage?' asked Kate. 'I mean, grilling a couple of chops and mashing some potatoes isn't quite in the same league as rustling up the full monty for Christmas lunch.'

'Don't you worry, I've checked out your recipe books and they all give a blow-by-blow, minute-by-minute account of how to do it. I mean, everyone must cook their first Christmas dinner at some stage. Please can this be mine?'

'But why?' Kate was perplexed. His only forays into the kitchen so far had been because Kate had been too poorly and he'd been keen to ensure both his and her survival. He'd hardly been elbowing her out of the way of the cooker since she'd been feeling better.

'I'm sorry, Kate, but if I'm in the kitchen cooking I don't have to talk to your mother. If I have to spend a whole morning with her while you are closeted in the kitchen I'll either go mental or I'll deck her.'

Kate began to giggle. She had a delicious but incongruous image of Eddie and her mother wrestling on the floor. 'OK, but just this once. And it had better be edible or there'll have to be a forfeit.'

'Like what?'

'How about having my mother visit for Easter as well?' Eddie pounced on her and began tickling until Kate begged for mercy.

'All right, all right,' she squealed. 'Not another visit from her.'

'Promise,' said Eddie. He tickled her even harder.

'Yes, yes, on my honour,' shrieked Kate, tears of mirth running down her face.

'Good grief, let's keep Honour out of this,' said Eddie, releasing her.

From across the corridor they heard the sound of the spare room door closing. 'Oh God, please don't say she overheard,' whispered Kate, suddenly sober. Then both of them had to dive under the duvet to smother the fresh waves of laughter that engulfed them.

Once they had pulled themselves together, which took quite a while as for several minutes one or other of them would be assailed by a fresh fit of giggles, Eddie went to make them both a cup of tea. Kate sat up in bed and wondered why she should have been blessed with such a wonderful man for a husband. She was so happy she felt she must have cornered not just more than her fair share of the market, but the entire supply of happiness worldwide. It wasn't only that he was scrummy to look at, or that he was intelligent, articulate and undoubtedly good at his job. It was also a dozen intangible little things: the fact that in some ways he was romantic, despite once declaring that he wasn't the sort to give women flowers 'because why on earth are you giving a gift the recipient just sits and watches die?'; that he didn't laugh at her when

155

she got sentimental over weepy films; and that, unlike any man she had ever known, he folded his clothes up and left the bathroom tidy. But most of all he made her laugh. He was such a buffoon sometimes; coming out with ridiculously funny comments that made her laugh out loud. And then he was always so thoughtful, noticing when she felt tired or her back ached, and doing endless little things to help her or to make her feel better. She loved him so intensely it almost hurt and she found that when he was at home she had to make a real effort to keep her hands off him, as she wanted constantly to touch him or hug him or ruffle his hair. She knew that the other officers in the mess took the mickey out of them and had dubbed them 'the Young Lovers', a nickname that had been shortened to 'the YLs' and adopted by just about everyone in the barracks. Kate smiled as she recalled Eddie telling her about a briefing his boss had given the GOC about an incident that had happened near their house involving a guard dog and a civilian contractor. When the General had asked where exactly it had occurred, Eddie's boss had replied that it had been on the path that led behind the YLs' garden. Apparently the General hadn't batted an eyelid.

Eddie returned with two mugs of tea.

'What are you grinning like a Cheshire cat about?' he asked.

'I was just thinking about the General knowing that we're called the YLs.'

'I expect he was young once.' Eddie put both mugs down on the bedside table and climbed under the bedclothes again. He snuggled up next to Kate and warmed his cold body against hers.

Kate shivered slightly and said, 'Yes, but I can't imagine him as a lover.'

'Do you spend much of your time imagining what senior officers would be like in bed?'

'I might do.' Kate smiled impishly.

'You're weird,' said Eddie.

'Don't you fantasize, then?'

'Not about senior officers in the buff.'

'Oh, so you admit that you do fantasize, though. Do you have these little dreams before, during or after sex?'

'I can't remember.'

'Shall we jog your memory?' asked Kate, sliding her hands down his chest.

'The tea will get cold,' mumbled Eddie, nibbling her ear.

'Stuff the tea.'

'I'd prefer to stuff you. I don't want to scald my willy.'

Kate's giggles were silenced as Eddie's mouth closed over hers.

Chapter Sixteen

Honour decided to return to Windsor on the day after Boxing Day.

'Thank God for that,' Eddie had whispered to Kate as Honour went upstairs to finish packing. 'Do Belfast International have handling facilities for jet-powered broomsticks?' He clamped his hand over his mouth and spoke into an imaginary microphone. 'Hello, tower, this is Broomstick Airways, request permission to taxi.'

'Shh,' squealed Kate. 'She'll hear you.' As she spoke, Honour materialised on the landing halfway down the stairs.

'Eddie, could you give me a hand with my luggage?'

Kate felt herself blushing at the thought that she had overheard, but Eddie didn't turn a hair.

'Certainly, I'd love to.' He took the steps two at a time.

Honour swept down the last of the stairs and into the cloakroom by the front door. Kate followed Eddie to the spare bedroom to check that nothing had got forgotten.

'Has she got her PPL for the broomstick?' continued Eddie, unperturbed. 'What about her instrument rating? Isn't it a bit cloudy for her to be flying on visual flight rules?' Kate was torn between enjoying Eddie's gentle mockery and a horror of being overheard by her mother.

'Oh, do stop, please,' she begged.

'What's it worth?'

'Anything.'

'Rampant sex in front of the fire?'

'Yes, yes, yes, just stop taking the piss out of Mummy.'

'I'll think about it.

They heard Honour calling from below. 'Is there a problem?'

'Not as long as her broomstick doesn't melt the runway,' said Eddie, *sotto voce*. Then, louder, 'Just checking we haven't missed any of your things.'

Kate helped Honour put her case, umbrella, coat and handbag into the car, and then reversed down the drive. As they set off to the gate out of the barracks, Eddie waved them off.

'I'd have thought Eddie would have let you rest this morning instead of allowing you to drive,' said Honour sniffily.

'He's got an important phone call he's expecting,' lied Kate. She could hardly tell her mother that Eddie had flatly refused to take her; he'd been worried she would say something that would make him finally lose his temper.

Kate parked the car and helped her mother into the terminal. The queue for the British Airways desks seemed endless and Kate's feet and back began to ache, but she kept quiet about it, knowing that if she complained, her mother would launch into another diatribe against Eddie. Finally it was her mother's turn to check in and Kate was free to go.

As she was so close to Aldergrove she decided to pop in just to see how everyone was and catch up on the gossip. She had to admit that she missed them all: the banter, the camaraderie, the lively atmosphere of the place.

'Hiya, stranger,' said Andy as she put her head round the door of his office.

'Hello, Andy, how's things?'

Andy's face creased into a broad smile. 'To what do we owe this honour?'

'I had to go to the airport.'

'And you thought you'd grace us with your presence?'

Kate nodded.

'I've missed you, Kate.'

The serious tone of Andy's voice gave Kate a frisson. Deliberately she lightened the atmosphere.

'Well, I've only been gone a matter of weeks, and I've hardly been on the other side of the earth. Lisburn is only down the road.'

'It's not been the same without you here.' He gazed at Kate with sad eyes. Sheep's eyes, thought Kate. She felt faintly annoyed. What had happened between them had been over for ages. She had moved on and it was about time he did too. Goodness, what would Emma think if she knew that her fiancé still lusted after an old flame?

'Of course it's been the same here,' she said tartly. 'Just a bit quieter.'

Andy took the hint and dropped the subject. 'Good Christmas?' Kate told him about her mother's visit. 'So, the answer to my question is no, then?'

'Not really. She could have been worse.'

Andy looked horrified. 'Worse! Thank God my future in-laws seem quite nice in comparison.'

Kate laughed, 'Eddie says she's an escapee from the Addams family.'

'Ahh, talking of weirdos – no offence to your mother – the mess is having a party. Come along and join us. It'll be a combined New Year's Eve bash and leaving party for me. I'm posted to London in a few weeks, so I don't suppose our paths will cross again for a bit.'

Kate considered the offer. Andy noticed her slight hesitation. 'Emma will be there.'

Kate came to a decision. 'That would be brilliant. I'll have to check that Eddie hasn't got anything else planned, but it sounds great. How about if I give you a ring?'

'Party? At Aldergrove? Sounds good, as long as you don't think it'll be too much for you.'

'I'm going as a guest, I'm not organising it. If I get tired I'll sit down. Besides which, we haven't much else planned for that evening, have we? And Emma is going to be there and I want to meet her.'

'It's not fancy dress or anything?'

'Andy said the dress is casual. You know what he's like – he gets nosebleeds if he has to wear anything other than jeans when he's off duty.'

'In which case I think we'll definitely go. There's a bash here but it's black tie – I can't be arsed to get dressed up just to get pissed.'

'Do I take it from that that you would like me to drive home?'

'Well, there's no point in us both staying sober, now is there? Tell you what, I'll drive there, how about that?'

When Kate and Eddie walked back into the mess at Aldergrove she felt as though she had barely been away. Most of the old faces were still there and she was greeted effusively and enthusiastically. The mess was packed to the eaves with members of the regiment plus guests, girlfriends, wives, hangers-on and anyone who the mess members liked enough to invite.

'Hello. Welcome to the YLs,' yelled Andy over the hubbub of voices and music. 'Come and have a glass of punch.' They squeezed along the corridor and into the anteroom. He was standing at a table near the door, supervising the distribution of a tureen full of a fizzy golden liquid and floating slices of fruit. Beside him stood his fiancée, Emma. Kate appraised her with one glance. She was certainly an extremely pretty girl, but Kate detected a tough streak in her. She struck Kate as the sort of woman who wouldn't tolerate Andy mucking about. She most certainly wouldn't be impressed if she thought that Andy was hankering after another woman. Kate introduced herself and Eddie. Emma greeted them both warmly.

'It is so nice to be able to put faces to names. Andy has talked about you a lot, and I often wondered what a female pilot would look like. The male ones always seem to be so glamorous – obviously the same applies to the female of the species too.'

'Hardly,' said Kate, but she was flattered all the same. 'I don't think anyone looks glamorous when they're five months pregnant.'

'You forget, I only ever get to see pregnant women. I've seen some absolute frights in my time, I can tell you, and you are at completely the other end of the scale.'

'Can I break up this mutual admiration society and offer you a drink, Kate?'

'Do you mind if I pass on that?' asked Kate. 'I'm on the wagon.'

Andy put a hand dramatically to his forehead and pretended to swoon. 'Teetotal? Kate, what's happened to you?'

'I'm just being good,' said Kate smugly. 'I was told to give up the booze for the baby, so I have.' Emma nodded approvingly. 'It wasn't that much of a hardship. I hardly drank for Britain before, did I?'

'Meantime, one of us has got to keep the family reputation alive,' said Eddie hopefully, picking up a glass. Andy ladled some punch out. 'What's in this?' asked Eddie cautiously.

'God alone knows. The subalterns made up the recipe. All I can say is that it doesn't taste too bad and so far no one has gone blind, so I don't think they've put too much aviation fuel in it.'

'That'll do me then,' said Eddie, taking a swig. 'Come on Kate, we mustn't monopolise the OC. Let's go and get you a lemonade.' They fought their way through to the bar, where Kate was greeted by yet more old friends, each of whom commented on her increasing girth and how happy she looked. Kate was worried that Eddie might feel a little jealous over the amount of attention she was receiving, but judging by the indulgent expression on his face, no such thoughts had entered his head.

'Let's go and dance,' he suggested after about twenty minutes.

'OK, as long as it isn't too hot and crowded in the disco.' They excused themselves from the gaggle of Kate's admirers and elbowed and wriggled their way through the press to the television room, where the disco had been set up. When they got there, Tina Turner was belting out 'The Best'.

'They're playing your song,' said Kate. She gazed at him adoringly, her hands resting on his shoulders as she swayed to the music and sang along to the words. Eddie looked sheepish and put his arms around Kate, hugging her close to him. They swayed and moved in time to the music and it was obvious to anyone with half an eye that the YLs were still utterly and completely besotted with each other. Andy, dancing with his fiancée, watched them over her shoulder and felt a renewed pang of jealousy. Kate could have been his if he hadn't been so annoyed at the way she'd left Cyprus without even saying goodbye to him. If he hadn't let his stupid pride get in the way it could be him she was looking at with such adoration. He sighed heavily.

'Are you all right, sweetheart?' Emma asked.

'I'm fine.' He forced his gaze away from Eddie and Kate and smiled at his fiancée. 'Let's go and get another drink.' He led Emma to the bar and ordered a double brandy for himself and a glass of wine for Emma.

'A double?' said Emma.

'Hell, it's New Year's Eve. I'm not flying in the morning, I can tie one on if I want, can't I?'

'Yes, of course you can.' Emma hadn't meant to sound so disapproving and backtracked fast. 'Oh, look. Here come Kate and Eddie. Why don't you buy them a drink as your chit is still open?'

'Kate,' yelled Andy above the noise of the disco in the next room and the hubbub of voices in the crowded bar. 'Kate, over here! Let me buy you and Eddie a drink.'

Kate, smiling and flushed, elbowed her way expertly through the throng, Eddie following in her wake.

'A drink? Wonderful, I'm parched. I could kill for a really long lemonade and lime.' Eddie arrived at her side.

'And a pint for me, please.'

Andy ordered the drinks and Kate gulped gratefully at hers. 'I'm pooped. I'm going to sit down for a few minutes.'

'I'll join you if I may,' said Emma. 'I wore these shoes because they look so fabulous but they cripple me after a few hours.' Kate wasn't surprised. The heels must have been getting on for four inches high, and the little straps that made a filigree pattern across Emma's toes must cut into her flesh like wire. Kate waddled and Emma tottered through to the conservatory by the bar, which was cooler, emptier and quieter.

'Phew, that's better.' Kate collapsed on to a rattan sofa.

Emma sat down beside her and surveyed her shoes ruefully. 'I'd take them off, but if I do I won't get them back on again.'

'That's the one good thing about being pregnant. It's legal to look a frump.'

'You don't look a bit of a frump. I love that dress.'

'Do you?' Kate was wearing a pearl-grey silk dress that was pleated at the shoulders and cascaded to her calves like a waterfall. 'I've had it for ages. It really should be worn with a belt, but without it it makes quite a good maternity outfit.'

'Quite good? It's lovely. Promise me that if you ever want to get rid of it you give me first refusal.'

Kate liked Emma. Her friendliness and charm were completely natural and Kate could see why Andy wanted to marry her. If anyone was going to stop him from hankering after an ex-girlfriend it would be her. Kate thought that his move away from Ireland was exactly what he needed to start appreciating what he had got rather than thinking about what he hadn't.

'So,' said Kate, 'when's the big day?'

'In the spring. After Andy has got settled into his new job. He didn't think it politic to arrive and instantly want a fortnight's leave for a honeymoon.'

The sounds from the bar became more boisterous and raucous. Both women turned to see what was going on. The men had formed themselves into two teams, sitting on the floor like a rowing eight. As each crew member downed his pint and put his inverted glass on his head the next man in the crew began to drink his.

'Oh God,' groaned Kate. 'They're playing boat races, the silly buggers. Why do men think it's so clever to be able to drink a pint in a few seconds flat?' A huge cheer from the victorious team drowned Kate's last comments.

'Rematch,' yelled Eddie from the losing side. 'I demand a rematch.'

'Best of three,' bawled a tipsy officer from the sidelines.

The pints were pulled, the teams settled back into their starting positions and Kate and Emma looked on shaking their heads in despair.

'The only consolation is that when Eddie feels ghastly tomorrow, I can give him what-for for being such a prat,' said Kate.

The noise rose to a climax as the two teams battled it out once more, then, with a roar, Eddie's team snatched victory.

'Shit,' said Kate. 'They're going to have to go again.'

'Enough's enough,' yelled Emma. 'You're all going to be as drunk as skunks.'

'We already are,' yelled back Andy. His voice sounded slurred and his stance was a trifle unsteady.

'It's no good,' said Kate pragmatically. 'They're all pissed. They're beyond reason.'

'I suppose this is one aspect of army life I shall just have to get used to.'

'Too right. Still, your nursing skills should come in handy coping with an unconscious patient. And always remember to remove his spurs before shoving him under the eiderdown. That is, if you don't want to wake up in a room that resembles a hen house after a raid by a family of foxes.'

Emma grimaced. 'Just great.' The two women returned to their seats and ignored the antics at the bar. An audience would only encourage their partners further, they decided.

The final boat race ended and the teams staggered to their feet. Eddie belched loudly as he clapped Andy on the shoulder.

'Not bad for a crap hat,' he said a little indistinctly.

'I should bloody well hope not,' said Andy genially. 'I nearly joined the Paras. I almost passed P Company.'

'That's what everyone who fails says. The truth is that if you're good enough you pass.'

'No, honestly,' Andy insisted, swaying slightly as he tapped Eddie's chest to emphasize his point. 'It was only because I tore my hamstring that I failed. I did it in the log race.'

'Yeah, but if you had been fit enough you wouldn't have had the injury.'

'That's bollocks,' said Andy. 'It could have happened to anyone. Even you.'

'No. It wouldn't have happened to me, because I was properly fit.'

'So was I.'

'Stands to reason you couldn't have been.'

'Now, you just look here,' said Andy, getting close to losing his temper. He leaned forward belligerently. 'You weren't there, you have no idea how I got my injury. Until then I'd been flying through the course.'

'I'm not saying you weren't, but you obviously didn't have the stamina, otherwise you'd have been all right.'

'Yes, well at least I've got the brains to be more than just a grunt.' Andy deliberately chose the pejorative word for members of the infantry.

'Come on, it can't take that many brains.' Eddie wanted to defuse the situation. He could see that Andy was out to pick a fight and thought that if he made a joke of the whole conversation everything would calm down. Unfortunately his attempt at the sort of macho humour he thought might appeal to Andy was in pretty bad taste. 'I mean, if it took brains, Kate wouldn't be able to do it.'

'What do you mean by that? She's a bloody good pilot. In fact,' Andy paused and chose his next words with deliberate care, wanting to score a point off Eddie to even things up for the slight about his fitness, 'in fact, she's as good at flying as she is at fucking. And I should know.'

He had gone too far. Without warning Eddie swung his fist back and landed a punch squarely on Andy's jaw. The smack of skin and bone connecting sounded like a starting pistol being fired. The lively racket in the bar was killed as if someone had hit the mute button on a remote control.

'What on earth's happened?' Kate asked Emma. The pair of them stood up and went to the door of the conservatory.

The scene required no explanation. Andy was on all fours, shaking his head groggily and massaging his jaw, and Eddie, restrained by a couple of fellow officers, was rubbing his knuckles.

'Eddie! What the blue blazes have you done?' said Kate, almost spitting with anger that her husband could have been so crass. 'Good God, what on earth possessed you to hit Andy?' She turned her attention to Andy, who was being helped to his feet by his fiancée. 'Are you all right? I'm so sorry. I'll take Eddie home straight away.' Kate was mortified, but both men looked shamefaced. Neither was proud of the incident. Drink and jealousy had been the driving forces and they both knew that they should not have succumbed to either. Kate waited for some sort of explanation from Eddie, her anger rising. How could he have done this? These were her friends; this was, or rather had been, her mess. Who was he to come in and start brawling like some drunken squaddie?

'It's OK, Kate,' mumbled Andy, still nursing his jaw. 'It was six of one and half a dozen of the other.' He held out his hand to Eddie.

'That's very magnanimous of you, Andy,' said Kate. She glared at Eddie. Sheepishly, Eddie took the proffered peace offering.

'Sorry,' he said.

'I'm sorry too. I was out of order,' said Andy.

'We both were,' agreed Eddie.

'Are you boys going to tell us what this was all about?' asked Kate.

'No,' said Andy quickly.

'It was nothing,' said Eddie.

'It didn't look like nothing to me,' said Emma.

The noise level in the bar began to return to its previous level as the other party-goers finished speculating on the cause of the fight and drifted on to other, more interesting subjects of conversation. Emma took Andy off to his room to administer a cold compress and some TLC, and Kate decided that it was time she took Eddie home. The effect of all the drink he'd consumed earlier, together with the three gulped pints, was beginning to take hold.

'Let's just wait for midnight,' he said, leaning on her shoulder rather heavily as she tried to steer him out of the bar.

'I'm not sure that's wise,' said Kate. God, he reeked of booze. How much had he drunk?

'Don't be such a killjoy. Just 'cos you're the only sober one here.'

And that's the truth, thought Kate. There's nothing more depressing than being the one missing out on the fun; although the fun had rather gone out of the evening. She looked at her watch. It was only fifteen minutes till the New Year was going to be rung in. They might as well wait, especially as the men had apologised to each other. But she was going to get to the bottom of that fight. What on earth had they found to bicker about?

As soon as it was decent after midnight had struck and everyone had toasted everyone else and wished all and sundry a happy 1995, Kate dragged Eddie away.

'I know you're having a good time, but I'm knackered.'

'It's all righ'.' He swayed slightly as he spoke.

'Come on, the walk to the car will be good for you,' said Kate, tucking her arm through his to prevent him from stumbling. 'You're going to snore all night now, aren't you.'

'Me? Snore? Never!'

'Huh,' said Kate, propping Eddie up by the car while she

fumbled in her bag for her keys. She unlocked the driver's door, thus releasing the central locking, and supported Eddie round to the passenger side.

'Come on, make an effort,' she grumped at him, half out of exasperation and half out of tiredness. He managed to pull himself together enough to climb in. Kate pulled the seat belt half across him and handed it to him. 'Make yourself useful and put that on.' Eddie took it but still hadn't plugged it into its socket by the time Kate was in the driver's seat and ready to start the engine. 'What are you doing with it?'

'I can't get it in the hole,' he slurred, shutting one eye to try to improve his focusing and then roaring with laughter at the smutty innuendo of what he'd just said.

'Oh, for God's sake get a grip,' said Kate, her patience wearing thin.

Eddie made a big effort and complied. 'Done it,' he exclaimed triumphantly, as if he'd just achieved some major feat.

'Great, let's get home then and get you to bed.'

At the barrier to the base, the guard found some excuse to make her wind her window down.

'It's all right,' said Kate, as he apologised for having to stop her. She realised that the airman had been briefed not to let anyone on to the public roads who might have celebrated a bit too much. 'I'm stone cold sober; he was drinking, I'm driving.'

'OK, ma'am. Drive carefully now.'

'I will,' said Kate cheerfully, winding her window back up. The barrier was raised, Kate slipped the car into gear and set off on the twenty-minute journey to Lisburn.

'So, come on. Now we're on our own I want to know what happened between you and Andy.'

Eddie groaned. He'd known he was going to get the third degree but had hoped that Kate would wait till morning. 'Honest, it was nothing.'

Kate changed down a gear to negotiate the winding road through the village.

'Look, you two hardly know each other. In my book virtual strangers don't just happen to take a dislike to each other and start brawling for the hell of it. So what did he say that made you so angry?'

Eddie realised that he wasn't going to get any peace unless he came up with some sort of explanation. 'He was boasting about how he'd nearly passed P Company,' he said.

'So you dropped him because he stretched the truth a bit? Because you didn't believe him? Come on! You don't expect me to swallow that?' They had reached the main road. Kate turned on to it and began to accelerate. She was tired and wanted to get home. She yawned heavily.

'I just got fed up hearing the same old story trotted out by everyone who fails. The one where it's not their fault.' Eddie belched and closed his eyes.

Kate drove competently along the main road to Lisburn. There was little traffic, and the conditions weren't too bad. She put her foot down. 'So you actually *told* him you didn't believe him?'

'Yeah, OK. Maybe it wasn't the most tactful thing to do. It made him bloody angry.'

'So if it was Andy who was so mad, why didn't he hit you?'

'I don't know.' Eddie opened his eyes again and glanced at Kate to see if she had swallowed his tale. He saw her staring at him – and even in his fuddled state he could recognise her expression of utter scepticism.

'I don't buy that,' she said, still staring at him.

'Look out,' yelled Eddie. Kate returned her attention to the road. She was approaching a corner far too fast. Luckily, being sober, her reactions were as hot as ever. Simultaneously she braked and changed into second gear. Feeding the wheel through her hands, she just managed to get the car round the corner, under control and keep all four wheels on the ground.

'Oops,' she said, not the least bit flustered.

'For God's sake concentrate.'

'How can I when I know I'm being sold a dummy.'

'We both said things.'

'What things?'

'Stupid things.'

'Not stupid things. It was enough to make you deck him.'

'OK, if you must know, Andy told me he'd slept with you.'

'He told you? Oh, God.' Kate felt as though she'd been kicked. It wasn't as if she'd been unfaithful – it wasn't a crime to lose one's virginity before marriage, and to someone other

169

than one's future husband – but she still felt as though she'd betrayed him. She hadn't told Eddie because she hadn't wanted to upset him. She knew he would have found the idea that she was working for her ex-lover hard to stomach. She hadn't lied to him, but now she felt as though she had. And how could Andy have done that to her? He must have known he was going to hurt both of them terribly. No wonder Eddie had hit him. She took her eyes off the road again and stared at him in horror. Eddie stared back at her, a look of abject sadness and pain in his eyes.

Chapter Seventeen

Kate was on a shingle beach in Sussex. She could hear the swish and suck of the waves. For some reason she didn't appear to be able to open her eyes although she could tell through her eyelids that it was light. Or perhaps a sea mist had rolled in. She felt cold, and so tired. The mist would explain why she felt cold, but why was she so tired? And there didn't seem to be an explanation for how she had got there. She hadn't been to this beach for years, not since she had been quite young. But she was too tired to think right now. She needed to rest. If only she didn't feel so cold. She could sense she had some sort of covering over her. Perhaps it was a towel. She felt so cold she needed to pull it about her, but for some reason her arms wouldn't obey her command. It all seemed too difficult. Thinking was making her feel even more drained. She had to sleep. Perhaps when she woke up again she would understand.

She was aware of sounds. The swish and suck of the waves was still there. And a higher-pitched noise, more staccato. Birds? Gulls? But she couldn't see them, as she was still surrounded by the mist. At least she felt warmer now. Perhaps the sun was going to break through. She could tell it was still light, which was puzzling. She felt as though she'd been asleep for hours. And why wasn't anyone with her? How had she got here? She couldn't remember. She had no recollection of anything much and yet she knew this wasn't right. She felt fear strike. What had happened to her? The gulls screamed louder, the staccato noise became almost incessant. She felt as though there were people near her, but why couldn't she see them? She tried to shout, but her mouth refused to work. The terror mounted and the high-pitched cries of the birds filled the air. She wanted to get away from wherever she was; find peace and safety. But, she thought, it was like being in one of those dreadful dreams when there's a threat but your legs refuse to move. She felt something touch her arm. A prick. She was wondering what had stung her when the fog of oblivion swept around her again.

She opened her eyes and the light hurt terribly. She shut them again. But in that fleeting moment she had seen a woman, wearing a nurse's uniform, standing beside her. Who was she? It wasn't Emma, Kate was certain of that. Emma? Where had that name come from? Who was Emma? The stranger stroked Kate's face and then gently started to wash her. The feel of the soft flannel and the warm water was delicious. Kate wanted to thank her, whoever she was, but she felt too tired still to speak. Why was a nurse here – wherever *here* was? Suddenly she remembered that Emma had been at Aldergrove. She remembered flying at Aldergrove. But this wasn't Aldergrove. She wished she knew what was going on. She wondered if she was dreaming. She wondered when she'd wake up.

It was still light. When was night going to fall? She was sure hours and hours had passed but it was still bright through her shut eyelids. She'd been thinking about something earlier. What had it been? Emma, that was right. But Emma was at Aldergrove – with Andy. Kate's remembrance of Aldergrove brought back other glimpses of memories, but glimpses too faint to grasp, like a barely remembered dream. She had been there recently, but why? She hadn't been flying, she knew that, but she couldn't find a reason for having visited the base. Why couldn't she make her brain work properly? Everything was such a blur. Why couldn't she remember things? She listened to the noises around her, hoping to make some sense of them. She was so used to them now she almost had to make an effort to hear them. Whenever she woke up, there they were, all around her. She listened to the sounds for some minutes with a growing awareness that she'd been mistaken about the seaside. The high-pitched noses weren't bird cries, they were electrical blips and bleeps, and the swishy-sucky noise wasn't the sea, it was far too regular and with a mechanical click keeping a beat. But she knew she'd heard these sounds before. She knew they were familiar. Where had she heard them? She let her mind drift and suddenly she had a vision of Eddie after he'd been caught in the bomb. That was it. She remembered now. It was the noise of the equipment in the ward when she'd been visiting Eddie. Eddie, her husband. That was it. They'd got married. And they'd gone to a party together. That was right, they'd been at a party. So where was she now? Tiredness engulfed her again. Why was she so tired? Why couldn't she wake up? Was there something the matter? Her mind became foggy again. As she lost consciousness she wondered why she felt so alone.

Maria was calling her. Why? Was she late for parade? How could she have missed reveille? Why hadn't the duty cadet woken her? Kate tried to open her eyes. She felt them flicker but the light hurt them as it had before and she blinked them shut again.

'Kate, Kate? Can you hear me?' Maria's voice sounded urgent. 'Squeeze my hand if you can.'

Kate didn't understand what was going on or why the urgency, but the instruction was clear enough. She felt Maria's warm, smooth hand slip into her own. Kate tried to make her fingers function but she didn't seem to be able to work out how to send a message to them.

'Come on, Kate, you can do it. Give me a squeeze.' Making a huge effort, Kate willed her fingers to work. She was rewarded by an ecstatic yell from Maria. 'Mrs Hayleigh-Ffoulkes, Mrs Hayleigh-Ffoulkes, she responded, honestly she did. She squeezed my hand.'

Kate tried to open her eyes again but the light was so bright. She screwed them up and opened just one a tiny fraction. She hadn't imagined things, Maria was there, and her mother too. Why on earth . . .?

'Hello, darling,' said her mother, leaning over her. 'How do you feel?'

Kate didn't know. But her mouth was dry. Yes, she felt

thirsty, terribly thirsty. She tried to tell Honour but her mouth seemed all gummed up. Then, inexplicably, both Honour and Maria began to cry. Kate, her eyes now used to the light, tried to focus beyond them on the machines around her, the curtains that surrounded her bed and the neon strip lights on the ceiling. She was in a hospital, but why on earth? What had happened?

'Don't try to talk, Kate,' said her mother. 'You'll be well enough for that soon. You just concentrate on getting better.'

Beside her, Maria had tears streaming down her face. Kate wondered why everyone was crying if she was getting better. And why wasn't Eddie there? Why was it only her mother and Maria?

Kate's recovery was slow. Her progress each day was barely recordable, but she didn't care. She didn't care that she was alive, she was not the least bit comforted when she was told that the baby was unharmed. As if any of that mattered when all she could think about was that Eddie was dead. What reason was there to find any joy in life? What reason was there to go on? She wished she had died in the crash too. Why was life so unfair? What had she done that was so wrong that he had been taken from her? She had lived and breathed for him, he had been her every waking moment, her reason for living. And she had killed him. She had been driving the car. It had all been her fault. She was the only one to blame. Dry-eyed, too numb with shock and anguish for tears, she turned her face to the wall and wished that they would unplug the drips, the tubes, the monitors – everything – and let her slip away.

She was too sick to attend the funeral, so Maria told her about it, at Kate's insistence. Maria's voice quavered as she tried not to cry, but when she saw huge, silent tears rolling down Kate's face, she broke down. Kate implored her to continue but Maria was so overcome with emotion that she was barely coherent. Everyone hoped that this display of grief would have a cathartic effect, but when Maria left, Kate withdrew once again into her silent, wretched world of misery where physical and emotional pain were indistinguishable.

'Come on, Kate,' said her mother one morning. 'You've got to try and eat something.'

Kate's response was the same toneless reply that she had given every morning for days. 'I'm not hungry.'

Honour sighed. What could be done to tempt her daughter to try nibbling at a piece of toast? 'But you must eat. Think of the baby.'

'How many times do I have to tell you, I don't care?'

Honour tried again. 'Please then, do it for me.'

Kate turned her eyes, huge now in her pinched white face, to her mother and said with deliberate slowness, as though explaining something to a small child, 'I said, I am not hungry.'

Honour stood up and left. She was close to losing her patience. She went into the corridor and walked angrily over to the big window that looked out across the dull view of the hospital car park. As usual, it was raining.

'Good morning, Mrs Hayleigh-Ffoulkes.' Honour turned round at the sound of Maria's voice. She didn't really like Maria – she thought she was rather brash – but she couldn't doubt her loyalty to Kate. She had taken leave to come over and be with her, and spent most of her free time sitting with Kate, talking of this and that, endlessly, patiently listening to Kate's guilt-ridden conversation; sympathising, comforting, caring.

'So how is Kate this morning?' asked Maria.

'Much the same,' sighed Honour. 'She is still being difficult about food.'

'Do you want me to try?' Honour shrugged, as if to say there wasn't much point. 'Well,' said Maria, 'I'll give it a shot, see how I get on.'

Maria opened the door of the ward and peered round it. 'Watcha,' she said cheerily. Behind her, Honour winced. *Watcha*? How vulgar.

'Hi,' said Kate.

'Mind if I come in?'

'Suit yourself.'

Maria plonked herself down on the hard chair by the bed. She eyed the tray. 'Oh, yum! Breakfast. Aren't you having any?'

Kate shook her head.

Maria picked up a slice of toast and spread butter and

175

marmalade on it thickly. She took a big bite. 'This is delicious,' she said indistinctly. 'You ought to try it.'

'No thanks.'

'Go on.' Maria thrust the slab of toast up to Kate's lips. A blob of marmalade adhered there and Kate, involuntarily, licked it off. 'There, it's nice isn't it?'

'No.'

'You fibber!' Maria took another bite, then buttered another piece and held it out to Kate. Wordlessly Kate took it and began to nibble at it half-heartedly. Maria, although she felt glad she'd managed to achieve this small victory, made no comment.

'So,' she said instead, 'how are you and junior today?'

Kate just shrugged. Why should anyone care? She certainly didn't.

As Kate's health began to improve, so memories about the accident slowly returned. She remembered Eddie being drunk, she remembered leaving the base, she remembered Eddie owning up to the reason for the fight, but she couldn't recall anything after that. Was that why she had crashed? Because she had been worrying about that and wasn't thinking about driving? She asked Maria for more details.

'You don't want to know, do you, Kate?'

'If I didn't I wouldn't be asking.'

Maria consulted the doctors, who concluded it was unlikely to do Kate's psychological state much harm. In fact, they thought it might even help. So Maria told her that because of the evidence of skid marks, it was thought that another vehicle might have come around a bend on the wrong side of the road, and that Kate had swerved to avoid it and had collided, head-on, with a telegraph pole. As a result of the impact, Eddie's improperly fastened safety-belt had given way and he had gone through the windscreen.

'I don't remember another car,' said Kate.

'It doesn't mean there wasn't one. The doctors are all agreed that loss of memory for a short time before such a dreadful event is perfectly normal.'

Kate shook her head. She wasn't convinced; furthermore, she didn't want to be convinced.

'The police are certain another car was involved, that it forced you off the road. You were not to blame for the accident and you are to get that thought out of your head.'

'But I was driving. I should have been able to stop. It's all because I wasn't concentrating,' said Kate miserably.

Maria didn't know what to say. Kate seemed determined to shoulder all responsibility for Eddie's death and nothing was going to convince her otherwise.

Honour and Maria visited her every day, and both did their best to comfort her. They tried to encourage her to talk about Eddie, as they had been told that it was bad that Kate was bottling all her emotions up inside her, but despite their best efforts Kate would stare blankly past them, barely acknowledging their presence or answering their questions. Others came to see her bringing their best wishes and flowers or gifts, which Kate would accept with polite thanks and then ignore.

Kate lost track of time. The lights in the intensive care unit were never switched off, and beyond sometimes noticing that the nurses had changed shifts, it was irrelevant to her whether it was day or night. She took no interest in her condition and expressed no pleasure as slowly she was weaned away from the plethora of equipment surrounding her. She barely even noticed when Maria's leave came to an end and she had to fly back to England to return to work.

Not long after that Kate, although her leg was still in traction, was pronounced well enough to move to an ordinary ward.

'It won't be long before you'll be well enough to come home with me,' Honour told her. Kate stared at her blankly. What did her mother mean – go home with her? Or did she mean go back to her quarter in Lisburn. And then realisation struck. Her home was an army quarter and she lived there because she had been married to an army officer. But he was dead, she was unemployed and her entitlement to live there had ceased. She had lost her husband and her home. She had no job and she was pregnant. Could life get any grimmer? she wondered.

When she contemplated her bleak situation, she decided that, in reality, there really was no choice. How was she going to cope with her damaged leg, a new baby and no support? It was unlikely that her mother could stay until the birth – that was still some months away – and Kate couldn't face being alone, except for memories, in the quarter. The only sensible thing to do would be to pack everything up, put it in store and hand the house back to the army.

'But no one has said you have to move out. As far as the army is concerned you can stay in the house for as long as you want – until after the baby is born, if you like.'

'No.'

'No, what?'

'No, I don't want to stay in it. I can't. I just want to get rid of everything.'

'Don't be hasty. There's no hurry.'

'Yes there is. I've decided. I don't want to see the house again. I want it all dealt with before I get out of here. Could you pack up the house? Shove it in store somewhere, anywhere. I don't think I could face it.'

The prospect of packing Kate's things and preparing the quarter for march-out didn't faze Honour at all; after all, she'd moved from one RAF quarter to another often enough herself to know exactly what the form was. 'It's only Eddie's personal things in the house now,' she said. 'His unit have already held the Board of Adjustment and dealt with all his military kit.'

'Oh.' What else was there to say? 'There won't be much to pack. All the furniture was issue and we hadn't got round to buying much in the way of pictures and ornaments.'

'I know.' With a rare flash of maternal sympathy, Honour patted Kate's hand and said, 'You didn't have enough time together to accumulate much.'

Enough time, thought Kate. They'd barely had any time at all. For want of anything else to occupy her mind, Kate totted up the days. Three hundred and eleven days; not even a whole year. They hadn't even been allowed to have a complete year together. She stared, unseeing, at the ceiling. It was so unfair. Why? Why her? Why Eddie?

A nurse bustled past, saw Kate looking close to tears and stopped.

'Why don't you listen to the hospital radio?' she suggested. 'Some jolly music might take your mind off things.' And without waiting for a reply she picked the headphones off their hook and plonked them on Kate's head. The radio was playing Tina Turner singing 'The Best', and Kate was transported back to the last time she had danced with Eddie. She remembered how they had clung together, how they had been so idyllically happy. She remembered his smell, his strength, the way he made her laugh and the way he made love. The tears rolled unchecked down her cheeks and the pain, the misery, the anguish surfaced with an intensity made stronger by being suppressed for so many weeks. Her sobs – huge, gulping, rasping sobs – shook her whole body; her face, contorted with the pain of her loss was running with tears and Kate didn't care. She was so shut up in the awfulness of her loss, she didn't notice the concerned stares of the other patients in the ward.

'Eddie, Eddie!' she cried.

Spring was at its height when Kate, although still suffering from a fairly pronounced limp, was at last discharged from hospital. Her mother had returned to Ireland with the sole object of accompanying her daughter back to England, and Kate was touched by her concern.

'I lost my husband, and I thought I was going to lose my daughter,' Honour explained. 'When something like that happens you discover what your family really mean to you.'

Kate remained silent. She hadn't had to suffer bereavement to discover what Eddie meant to her, but she held her tongue. Her mother was displaying more kindness towards her than she had previously known and Kate had no intention of alienating her now, especially as they had arranged for her to move into Honour's house until the baby was born, at which point she could think about finding a house of her own. But Kate didn't think she could face that hurdle for a while.

To be honest, she didn't seem to be capable of facing any sort of hurdle. She didn't know if it was the aftermath of being so ill, or her pregnancy, but she felt completely drained and exhausted all the time. It was as much as she could do to raise the energy to get dressed in the morning. Most of her time she spent sitting on the window seat in the sitting room, staring blankly into the garden. If Honour tried to chivvy her into doing anything Kate would either burst into tears or silently rise from her seat and disappear back to her room.

'You'll feel more yourself when the baby arrives,' said Honour.

'Why?' asked Kate expressionlessly.

'You will have to think about someone else other than your-self.'

Kate sighed and stared at Honour. 'I'm not thinking about myself. Don't you understand? All I ever think about is Eddie.'

Honour tried to make her daughter take an interest in the impending arrival of the baby, but Kate barely seemed to acknowledge the fact that she was pregnant, let alone show any concern about the birth. Honour bullied and cajoled her into attending doctor's appointments but nothing would make Kate go to the antenatal classes.

'They expect your partner to attend too,' Kate said flatly. 'I can't face seeing all those happy couples, all smug about being a family.'

'But Kate—'

'No,' Kate shouted. 'This isn't a matter for discussion.' She stormed up to her room and lay on her bed, staring blankly at the ceiling. When she finally returned downstairs, Honour had the sense not to raise the subject again.

With Kate showing so little interest in the baby, Honour took matters into her own hands. She ordered a cot, bought nappies and baby clothes and packed a case ready for Kate. The day the baby was due came and went despite a number of Honour's friends insisting that first babies were often early. When the contractions started the next day Honour was more excited than Kate.

'Don't fuss so,' said Kate, still walking with a limp, as her mother helped her towards the car. 'I'm not ill.'

'But you must look after yourself.'

Kate shook her mother's hand off. Honour, reluctantly, allowed her to walk unaided down the path, and wondered if Kate would ever regain her previous zest and enthusiasm for life. Perhaps the baby would help – give Kate something to love again.

Kate's labour was difficult and protracted and it wasn't until some thirty hours later that her son was finally born. Any hopes that Honour had had that the baby would magically cause some change in Kate's condition were shattered when Kate refused to hold him when the midwife placed him on her tummy while the cord was clamped and cut. The nurse looked horrified and took the baby away again to wash and dress him in a minute hospital gown.

'What name should we write on the band?' she asked, pen poised, wishing to label the new arrival immediately in accordance with hospital policy.

Kate didn't answer. Honour, who had been at Kate's side from the start, jumped in to try to cover up her daughter's increasingly obvious and unconventional lack of interest in her baby. 'I don't think Kate has made a final choice yet. Why don't you just put Baby Thomas?

'As you wish.' The midwife scribbled rapidly on a couple of slips of paper, inserted them into two plastic tags and fastened them securely to the baby's ankle and wrist.

'Right,' she said briskly, returning to Kate with the infant. 'How about seeing if this little chap would like his first feed?' And without waiting for Kate to answer, she thrust the baby into her arms and then gently pushed the baby's face so his tiny mouth connected with her nipple. Instantly the baby latched on.

'There, said the midwife with satisfaction. 'He knows what to do.' She would have liked to add, *even if his mother doesn't*, but refrained.

It took some while to tidy Kate up and repair the damage that her son had done during his lengthy entrance to the world. By the time she was ready to be wheeled down to a ward, the baby was fast asleep in his perspex cot and Kate had turned her face away from him again. Because of her recent bereavement it had been decided to put her on a side ward, and Kate was thankful that she didn't have to communicate with anyone. She didn't feel as though she could be bothered. And she certainly didn't want to have to pretend to be happy about the arrival of her own son, let alone coo over any of the other babies.

'I'll leave you to get some rest,' said Honour when she had

seen her daughter safely installed in her room. It was a cheerful enough place, with bright curtains and a matching bedspread. 'You'll feel quite different when you've had a sleep.'

'If you say so.'

A nurse came into the room as Honour left. 'Would you like me to take the baby away while you sleep?' she asked.

'Yes,' said Kate. As far as she was concerned she could take the baby for ever, not just for the night. Kate lay down on the pillow and willed sleep to come, but it wouldn't. Her mind was filled with irrational, disjointed thoughts about Eddie, her father, flying and Ireland. She kept trying to empty her head but these thoughts kept muscling back in again. The minutes and hours passed. The muted bustle of the main ward stilled to silence; everyone else must now be sleeping, so why couldn't she? The door opened.

'Mrs Thomas, your baby is crying. Would you like to come to the nursery to feed him, or would you like us to bring him back here?

'No.'

The nurse looked taken aback. 'I'm sorry, which would you prefer?'

'Neither. You feed it.'

'But I thought you wanted to breast-feed. I was given to understand . . .'

'Well, you were given to understand wrong.'

The nurse withdrew in silence. She'd come across cases like this before, but it still shocked her. Kate settled back to her sleepless night. She supposed she'd be made to look after the baby tomorrow, but at least she'd get left in peace for the rest of the night.

The next day Kate was brought breakfast at what she felt was an unnecessarily anti-social hour. Her tray, plonked on her bedside table, contained juice, cereal and scrambled egg and toast. Kate looked at it with disdain. She hadn't asked for this. A piece of toast would have been more than enough.

The door to her room opened and a cheery young nurse wheeled in the baby.

'I expect you missed him, didn't you? I brought him along as soon as I knew you were awake. He's had a feed but it was a couple of hours ago. I expect he might be hungry again soon. When he wakes up, if you press your call button I'll pop along to make sure that he takes his bottle properly and show you how to change a nappy.' She smiled at Kate, who stared expressionlessly back. 'He's a dear little thing, isn't he?' Was he? Kate hadn't noticed. She wished this woman would go away. She really couldn't be doing with this sort of chit-chat; she couldn't be bothered to join in. 'Now, what about some breakfast? Your eggs are going cold. You must eat to keep your strength up. You can worry about your weight in a week or two, but it's not a good idea to try to get your figure back too quickly.'

Kate had had enough. 'Go away,' she said. 'Just bugger off.'

The nurse looked as though she'd been slapped but quickly regained her composure. 'I'll leave you to get to know your son, then.' And then she swept out.

Kate knew she had been dreadfully rude but she just couldn't be bothered to care.

A ward orderly crept in and removed the tray. In its place she left a menu for the meals until breakfast the next morning. As she went, she asked in a rather scared voice if Kate could fill it in before nine o'clock, then she scuttled away. Word of Kate's shortness of temper had obviously got round.

A sudden urge to go to the loo made Kate get out of bed. She slipped on her dressing gown and slippers and hobbled down the corridor in search of the bathroom. The way some parts of her body felt, going to the loo was the last thing she wanted to do, but nature was clamouring. When she had finished, she braced herself for the walk back to bed. Every movement hurt, partly because she was so bruised, and partly because a couple of the stitches were tugging most uncomfortably. She was thinking about this rather than anything else when a voice said rather tentatively, 'Kate?'

Kate looked round. 'Emma? What are you doing here?'

Emma ignored the question. 'Oh, Kate. I can't get over the dreadful news about the accident. I was so upset when I heard what had happened to you. I barely knew Eddie but it was so obvious that the two of you adored each other.'

'We did.' Kate wasn't sure she could cope with this encounter. If it hadn't been for Andy, things might be so different now. She wasn't sure she wanted to get too chummy with his fiancée, and she certainly wasn't sure she wanted to have anything to do with Andy again. This wasn't the moment to talk about her feelings for Eddie. She changed the subject. 'Are you working here?'

'I'm doing agency work. Andy and I got married a few weeks ago but we ended up getting a quarter miles out of London. There was no way I could carry on working at Queen Charlotte's, so here I am.' She glanced at Kate's stomach. 'And you must have had the baby.'

'Yes, last night.'

'How wonderful. Congratulations! Is everything going well? And did you have a boy or a girl?'

Kate didn't want to sound too graceless. 'Come and see for yourself.' She led the way to her room.

Emma peered into the cot and noted the blue blanket. 'Oh, Kate, he's beautiful. You must be so proud. Oh, look! He's waking up.' And the baby began to move, stretching his tiny arms and splaying his minute, perfect fingers. 'Can I pick him up?' Kate nodded. Emma cradled the infant expertly in one arm and stroked his cheek with a finger. Instantly the baby began to nuzzle for food. 'He's hungry. Let me give him to you to feed.'

'I need to get a nurse to bring a bottle.'

'Oh, I'd have thought you would have been feeding him yourself.'

'No.'

'Tell you what, you hold him and I'll go and rustle up a bottle. How about that?' And without waiting for Kate's reply, she plonked the baby in her arms. When she returned with the bottle, however, the baby was once more in its cot and yelling furiously. Kate seemed oblivious.

Chapter Eighteen

Emma came to see Kate as often as she could in the few days she was in hospital, and although by the second day Kate was going through the motions of looking after the baby, Emma could see that she was doing it because she had to, not because she wanted to.

'You haven't really got to grips with this motherhood thing, have you?' she said sitting on the edge of Kate's bed.

'Is it a crime?' said Kate warily.

'Not at all; in fact it's pretty natural. It's just that you mustn't think of yourself as a failure if the whole bonding thing doesn't kick in straight away.'

'What if it never kicks in?'

'It will,' said Emma reassuringly.

'What if I don't want it to?' Kate stared at her blankly. 'There are two people I have really loved: one was my father and the other was Eddie. They're both dead.' She wasn't being melodramatic, just stating a fact. Emma didn't know how to respond, so she leaned over and gave Kate a big hug.

'You've had a terrible time recently. But don't you think that this might be a new start?'

'Why should I?'

There was no answer to that. 'Andy was wondering if it would be OK to visit you. Would you like that?'

Kate turned her face away. She didn't think she could face him; it was knowing that he had told Eddie about their relationship that had distracted Kate from her driving. He was as responsible as she was for what had happened.

'He would really like to see you,' continued Emma. 'He

has been so worried ever since he heard about the accident. He was completely devastated when he heard.'

As well he should have been, thought Kate in an uncharacteristic moment of savagery.

'Shall I say that it's OK for him to come in tonight?'

Suddenly Kate felt completely weary. She couldn't be bothered to turn him away, she couldn't be bothered to carry on with this conversation, she couldn't be bothered to care one way or the other about anything. Everything was hopeless, everything was a waste of time, nothing had any point to it at all.

'Whatever.'

'I'll tell him.'

Emma left, very concerned about Kate's state of mind. Lots of women got post-natal depression, but Emma thought there might be more to Kate's lethargy and withdrawal than that.

Andy arrived bearing a large bunch of flowers. He sat on the chair next to the bed and took Kate's hand.

'How are you?' he asked.

Kate disengaged her hand. 'What do you think?' she asked. 'Life hasn't been a barrel of laughs recently.'

'I know. You can't imagine how saddened I was when I heard the news.'

'I think I can,' said Kate bleakly. 'I've done a lot of *saddened* myself since New Year.'

'God,' said Andy. 'I'm sorry. I didn't mean to be so stupid.'

'No, well . . .' Kate tailed off. She thought bitterly that if he hadn't been so stupid the last time they had met, things might be different. She thought about telling him that she knew about the cause of the row between him and Eddie. But why bother? It wasn't going to bring Eddie back.

'She looked ghastly,' Andy said to Emma later. 'Her hair was dreadful, her skin looked positively grey – I thought new mums were supposed to bloom. I tried to be cheerful and not to dwell too much on Eddie but I couldn't even get her to smile.'

'Knowing that your idea of being cheerful usually involves telling dubious jokes, that doesn't surprise me,' said Emma. But her levity hid a real anxiety about Kate.

After Kate was discharged, Emma made a point of dropping in to see her whenever her hours at the hospital allowed. It seemed to Emma that, more often than not, Honour was doing everything for the baby and Kate might have been no relation at all to the child. She certainly didn't behave like its mother. About a fortnight after Kate had come home, Emma rang the doorbell to be told that Kate had taken the baby out in the pram, at Honour's insistence, to go to the local shop and get a pint of milk.

'I'd offer you a cup of tea, but until Kate gets back I've not got a drop of milk in the house.' Honour led Emma through to the kitchen.

'How is Kate today?'

'Much the same. She just won't make any effort with her appearance, she ignores the baby, and if I insist that it's her responsibility to feed or change him, she bites my head off.'

'And has she thought of a name for him yet? She's got to call him something soon.'

'I know. I keep reading the birth announcements out to her to try and give her some ideas, but she won't listen.' The doorbell rang. Honour stood up and went over to the kettle to switch it on. 'That'll be Kate. Let her in would you, please, Emma.' As Honour got the tea cups and tea pot ready in the kitchen, she could hear Kate and Emma talking in the hall followed by the sound of someone stamping upstairs. Oh dear, thought Honour, Kate's in a mood again.

Emma returned to the kitchen alone. 'Did you say Kate took the baby out in the pram?'

'Yes.'

'She hasn't come home with him. I asked her where he was and she just flounced upstairs.'

'Dear God. Where is he?'

'I think he's probably outside the shop. I don't think she's done him any harm – just forgotten about him.'

Without saying another word, Honour flung off her apron, grabbed her car keys and ran out of the house. In less than ten minutes she had returned with the baby safe and well, but it was some time before she felt calm enough to resume making tea.

'Can I give you a word of advice, Mrs Hayleigh-Ffoulkes?

Kate hasn't just got a case of the baby blues. I think she's suffering quite badly from clinical depression, and I suspect it's getting worse. She's becoming more and more withdrawn; she's right down in a pit of misery. She's neglecting herself, she's neglecting the baby, she rarely speaks, she doesn't eat. If she didn't have you to look after her, goodness knows what state she would be in. I think she needs medical help and I think she needs it sooner rather than later.'

Honour nodded. 'I have been thinking along those lines. We've got to do something. I've put my life on hold for weeks now, and frankly I don't feel inclined to carry on like this indefinitely. Not that I could say that to her – she'd accuse me of being selfish. Something is obviously very wrong with her even if she won't admit it herself. Although God knows how we'll get her treated, because I don't think she will co-operate. You know how angry she gets these days if we suggest she isn't well, and I certainly won't be able to get her to the doctor without her smelling a rat.'

'Supposing I had a word with the health visitor. Perhaps if she agrees with us she could persuade the doctor to visit. The thing is, the sooner we get Kate on to some sort of medication, the sooner she may return to normal; but the longer we leave it, the harder the job will be.'

With a prescription of Prozac, Kate began the long, slow road to recovery. The first sign that she was getting better was her deciding on a name for the baby.

'I'm going to call him Edward,' she announced out of the blue and at a point when Honour had almost given up on him ever being called anything. Honour half expected Kate to go on to say that she would call him Eddie for short, and had already prepared her expression to look pleased, even though she hated the idea, but no. It appeared that Edward was going to be Edward, for the time being at least.

After that there seemed to be a gap of several weeks before there was any other noticeable improvement, and even then Kate had good days and bad days. Emma and Andy called round regularly, and at weekends they often planned short trips out for Kate and the baby; picnics, walks along the Thames, lunches in pub gardens and even an evening at the cinema, although for this the baby was left at home. It seemed to Emma that as Edward learned to smile, so did Kate. And by the time summer had turned to autumn, Kate, although prone to times of introspection and sudden, deeply morose silences, was almost fully recovered not only from the accident but also from her depression.

It was on one of their outings that Kate mentioned that she was bored. They were sitting in the warm autumnal sunshine in the attractive garden of a village pub just outside Marlow. The remark was almost an aside, but Emma seized on it as it meant that Kate was at last taking a healthy interest in her own well-being. In an instant she decided that Kate should be encouraged to take her off-the-cuff remark further.

'You ought to consider getting a job,' she said. Kate looked horrified. 'Oh, nothing too stressful. Perhaps a little part-time pin-money earner. I mean, look at it this way, your mother seems to be more than happy to give you a hand with the baby at the moment, but don't you want to regain some independence? It's all very well living with her, but you say yourself that the pair of you don't always see eye to eye. Getting a job would be the first step towards independence. I know you don't need to earn a bean to support yourself . . .' Here Emma paused in embarrassment, since the reason Kate was well off was almost entirely due to Eddie's life insurance. She tried to cover up her gaffe. 'But it's getting back into harness that's important.' Kate didn't appear to notice Emma's *faux pas*. 'Anyway, I'm sure there's lots of jobs around – what about that new hotel that's being built near Runnymede; don't they want staff?'

'Look, I've had a holiday job in a hotel and it's damned hard work. Besides which, an operation like that would only be looking for people who know all about the business, unless they're applying for jobs as chambermaids or bellboys – and I don't fancy either of those,' protested Kate, worried that she was being railroaded into something she wasn't sure she was ready for.

'I don't imagine that the average receptionist has a degree in hotel and catering management.'

Kate shrugged. She wasn't convinced.

'I think you ought to get back in the air,' interjected Andy. 'How long is it since you flew? Your CPL will have lapsed because you haven't done enough hours since you qualified, but you ought to keep your private pilot's licence current at the very least. You know, if you don't get paid, there's nothing to stop you working as an instructor if you can find a flying club to take you on. Your hours on fixed-wing aircraft aren't enough to allow you to charge for your time, but what the heck?' Kate looked interested, so he carried on. 'I would have thought that would have suited you to a T. You could pick and choose your hours, you'd get loads of flying for free, and you'd be doing something you love. I can't think of a better job – that is, if you're serious about doing something other than being a mother.'

Beside them the baby in his pram began to stir. Kate got a small thermos out of her bag, unscrewed the top and poured out a bland-looking mixture of mashed potatoes and carrots into the cup.

'That looks disgusting,' said Andy, peering at the mixture.

'Edward likes it,' answered Kate. Then she turned her attention on her son. 'Did you have a nice sleep then poppet? Are you ready for your lunch?' The baby rewarded her with a wide gummy grin and Kate smiled happily back.

'Mummy,' said Kate in a faintly wheedling tone later that evening. The baby was asleep upstairs in his cot and Kate and her mother were relaxing in the sitting room, half watching the news.

Honour knew that tone. 'Yes,' she said warily.

'How would you feel if I went back to work? Did something part-time?'

Honour contemplated this prospect. She certainly thought that Kate ought to do something with her time, but would this mean that she would be left holding the baby – literally? Even more warily she said, 'What have you got in mind?'

'Perhaps a little work as an instructor at my old flying club.'

No, that was not an option. Not after what had happened to Kate's father, Philip.

'Flying? Must you? I've never liked the idea of you flying for a living. One pilot in the family was enough. To be honest I was only too glad when you gave it up. Please don't go back to it again.'

Kate knew that if her mother wanted to she could make life difficult for her. If she was going to work part-time, she needed help with Edward. If she alienated Honour, that help would be withheld. She backed down. Perhaps if her mother got used to her working she could take a job which involved flying at a later date. 'Maybe not flying then, but I would really like to do something. Emma suggested that that new hotel over at Runnymede might need staff – receptionists, that sort of thing. I can't say I fancy stripping beds for a living.'

'Oh, I think that sounds a much better option.' Honour couldn't hide her relief that she had diverted her daughter away from flying. 'Why don't you pop along there tomorrow and ask if they are recruiting staff?'

'And you won't mind looking after Edward now and again? I shan't take on a full-time job, I really don't think I want that, but it would be nice to get out and about again and talk to other grown-ups.'

'No, that should be all right. But I would like you to remember that I like to do things too. While you were ill I had to stop many of the activities that I used to enjoy. I want to get back into some of them again, so whatever you apply for, please remember that I won't be able to look after Edward all the time. Now that you're so much better I want to pick up some threads in my life too.'

Kate couldn't blame her mother for this. She remembered, in the days before the accident, how difficult it had been to reach her mother on the phone. She had often been out gallivanting around then and it was only natural she should wish to rediscover her freedom. Kate could only hope her mother wouldn't revert completely to her old lifestyle.

Kate walked from the lift across a pale grey carpet – goodness, was that a Kandinsky on the wall above a bright red sofa? – to the single office door. She could see her reflection in a large recessed mirror on a third wall. She thought she looked pretty composed considering how nervous she felt. She opened the door and went straight in, as the woman in reception had directed her to. A smartly dressed secretary looked up as she entered.

'I'll show you in right away,' said the woman. Kate gulped

as she held the door open for her and she was confronted by a huge expanse of yet more pale grey carpet, on the far side of which was a thirty-something well-groomed woman seated behind an enormous desk in front of an even more enormous window. She had a cap of short glossy hair and a bright red mouth that was turned down at the corners. It gave her the expression of a bad-tempered cat

'Mrs Thomas?' she said briskly. Kate nodded. 'Come and take a seat.' There was an unpadded plastic dining chair facing the desk, incongruously stark amidst all the opulence of this large and lavish office. Kate knew that it had been chosen deliberately so interviewees would not be able to feel at ease. She walked as coolly and as confidently as she could across the room and sat down, arranging her skirt carefully and crossing her legs. She was blowed if this hard-faced glossy female was going to intimidate her. The brass nameplate on her desk said she was called Miss Ionescu.

'Right, I see from your application that you are a widow.' She looked across the desk as if she expected Kate to elaborate on the details.

'That's right.'

'And you have a young son?'

'Yes. But as I live with my mother now, childcare arrangements will be no problem.'

'Mrs Thomas, your childcare arrangements are entirely your own business. All I expect of the people I employ is that their family affairs do not interfere with their work.'

Bitch, thought Kate, taken aback by this frosty little statement. But despite her nerves, and now her antipathy, she smiled to show how friendly she could be.

'I also see that you were in the army for some years, and before that you had a holiday job in a tourist hotel in Torquay.' Kate nodded. 'So what do you think, looking at your past experience, you could bring to the Spyrou hotel chain?'

Kate explained that her time in the army had made her very adept at social skills, that she was good with people, outgoing, skilled in the field of administration and very well organised. Miss Ionescu studied the papers in front of her and then her nails; anything, it seemed, to relieve the boredom of listening to Kate. But Kate smiled at her as she talked, although her palms were itching to smack the immaculate but expressionless face in front of her. When she'd finished, she waited for some sort of acknowledgement of her skills.

'And you think that these will be the sort of assets that we are looking for?' The tone was unmistakably sneering.

'I would think so, yes.' Kate was feeling herself getting increasingly annoyed with this supercilious and superior cow. She wasn't sure that she wanted the job now, if it meant working for the likes of her. However, she had the sense to keep her annoyance hidden. After all, it might be some sort of test. As a receptionist she was bound to come across similar people and it wouldn't do to lose one's rag with the paying customers.

'You do appreciate that the sort of guests we attract at our hotels are extremely demanding. In your capacity as receptionist, you would be the first impression they get of the hotel. Do you think they would find such an impression favourable? Dealing with wealthy businessmen is hardly the same as ordering a few soldiers around.'

Kate flatly refused to be intimidated by the cold woman opposite her. She smiled sweetly again. 'I quite agree, but in my last job I spent a lot of time dealing with VIPs, including, on several occasions, government ministers, and I think you will agree that such people can probably be just as demanding and expect a similar standard of deference as your clients.' So yah-boo-sucks, thought Kate, still smiling engagingly.

The woman opposite looked at her with a clear expression of disbelief. 'And what, exactly was your last job in the army?'

'I was a pilot. I flew helicopters in Northern Ireland.' Kate was delighted to see that her answer wiped the superior smile off the face of her inquisitor.

A voice spoke behind her and Kate jumped.

'A pilot? How interesting.' Kate swivelled round in her seat to look at who was speaking. It was an undeniably good-looking olive-skinned man. He was seated in a corner, and would have been hidden by the open door and a large pot plant when Kate had entered. Obviously he didn't want his presence made known to the interviewee unless he intended it.

'Yes,' she said. 'It was a great job.'

'What did you fly?' She noticed that he had a slightly foreign accent but couldn't identify its origin. She didn't think it was French – Italian, maybe.

'Gazelles.'

'Ah, small but powerful.' This man obviously knew a bit about aviation. 'And do you still fly?'

'I haven't done for a while, but I would like to again one day. Perhaps do some part-time instructing if I pass my instructor's exam.'

'Why?'

'I don't know; some vague idea about flying professionally again one day. If I keep my PPL current and build up my hours, it might just be possible to get back into the air again.'

There was a slight cough from Miss Ionescu. She was being ignored. Kate switched her attention back to her.

'I'm sorry,' she said, although she didn't feel in the least like apologising. She'd much rather talk to the man – whoever he was.

'Well, I think we've heard all we need,' said Miss Frosty-features. 'Have you any further questions, Mr Spyrou?'

Mr Spyrou! Good God! No wonder he knew about aviation – he didn't own just a chain of hotels but an airline, a package holiday company, loads of restaurants and goodness only knew what else. Kate felt rather foolish. He must have thought that she was angling for a job as a pilot, not just a few mornings a week as a receptionist. Well, she'd probably blown it. Heigh-ho.

'No, I think we've covered everything Mrs Thomas,' said Mr Spyrou. 'We'll let you know shortly.' He stood up, indicating that the interview was at an end, and proffered his hand. Kate shook it and left the large, sunlit office.

'How was it?' asked the secretary kindly.

'You didn't tell me Mr Spyrou himself was in there too,' said Kate indignantly.

'It's his policy to sit in on interviews for people doing front-of-house jobs. He can't always spare the time, but when he can, he always eavesdrops.'

'You might have warned me,' muttered Kate, unplacated.

'I'm not allowed to because it stops the interviewees from

acting naturally. If people know he's there they get even more nervous. Anyway, good luck. This company is pretty quick about letting people know the result of their interview. You should hear before the weekend.'

Chapter Nineteen

Kate quickly settled into work at the Spyrou Golden Crown Hotel. On her first day there she discovered that Miss Ionescu was head of personnel in the south-east region. As such, their paths were bound to cross, and Kate had a feeling that when they did she would have to tread carefully, although she was relieved to hear from some old hands, transferred from other hotels in the chain, that the woman didn't stray from her offices in London too often. Kate was certain that Miss Ionescu, or Magda as the others all called her, had taken an instant dislike to her at the interview and that she would not have got the job but for the intervention of Mr Spyrou himself. Still, she thought, it wasn't her problem if the boss had overridden the decision.

Her work at the hotel wasn't difficult, and she found that her main requirement was to be organised. It was no good thinking that she would find the time to pigeon-hole messages or hang up keys later; it was by far the best thing to get everything squared away as it happened. She quickly learned how the computer system worked; she made friends with the rest of the staff equally swiftly, and she had only been in her new job a month when she began to see some of the guests for a second time. Both they and the management noted that she greeted them by name without having to be prompted, a feat of memory that improved her stock all round. She worked odd hours, sometimes coming on duty in the evening and sometimes starting work early in the morning but after her time in Ireland and the weird hours she'd worked there she found it easy to adjust. What was more it suited her as it meant she was often around either in the mornings or the afternoons –

depending on her shift – and could therefore look after Edward herself.

As much as her working hours permitted, life settled into a routine of sorts. Kate and her mother, although not exactly close, achieved a fairly easy-going co-existence unlike anything they had enjoyed before. Edward thrived on having two devoted carers and was a happy, contented baby who achieved every milestone in his development bang on schedule. Christmas, coming as it did less than a year after Eddie's death, would have been subdued but for his presence, and although there was none of the laughter and tomfoolery of Kate's only Christmas with Eddie, she enjoyed watching her son attempt to rip off the cheerful paper and then ignore the gifts in favour of the wrappings. Edward gurgled with delight as he played with the pretty paper and even Honour had to admit how much Edward's eyes, intensely blue and fringed with thick lashes, were like his father's. Maria, invited by Honour, who, in a rare moment of thoughtfulness, was worried that Kate might find the first anniversary of Eddie's death difficult to deal with, came to stay for the latter half of the holiday. When she arrived she was sad to see how quiet and subdued Kate had become. The old *joie de vivre* had disappeared, and although outwardly Kate seemed capable of putting on a show of being fairly happy, Maria sensed that there was still a deep sadness within her friend. She tried to jolly her along and make her smile and laugh and fool around as she had done before, but although Kate laughed politely at her jokes and feigned amusement at some of Maria's anecdotes, Maria could see that it was really an act.

'You needn't worry,' said Kate to Maria the evening she arrived. They were sipping sherry in the sitting room as Honour prepared supper.

'Worry about what?' asked Maria innocently.

'That I'm going to have some sort of breakdown.'

'I didn't think you would. Well, not really. Your mother just thought you could do with some company your own age.'

'It was kind of her. And kind of you to come, and I do appreciate all your efforts to make me have a rip-snorting good time, but New Year's Day isn't going to be any harder to bear than any other day of the year. Hardly a moment goes by

197

when I don't think of Eddie; a million things happen all the time to remind me of him, so I don't think that particular day will be any worse than any other.'

Maria wasn't sure what to say. She felt so sorry for Kate, but sympathising wasn't going to make things better for her. Clucking or patting her shoulder was not going to make a difference to Kate's life. They sat in silence for a couple of minutes, both contemplating their drinks and thinking about how things might have been so different.

'How's your flying?' asked Maria after a while.

'I haven't been in the air for over a year now.' Kate paused, trying to analyse her reasons for having given it up, and failing. It was lethargy really, if she was honest, but she wasn't going to admit to it. 'Oh, I don't know, I just don't seem to want to fly like I used to.'

Maria could scarcely believe that. 'But you must miss it?'

'Not really. Worse things can happen to a girl than giving up flying.' She didn't have to elaborate. Silence descended again and in it Maria thought about how much Kate had changed. She wondered when her friend would find the strength to pick up the tattered threads of her life and move on again. Working for the hotel was a step in the right direction, as it gave Kate a reason to get up in the morning, take a pride in her appearance and interact with the world in general, but Maria didn't think that this was enough for her friend; Kate had always lived life to the full, given everything to the things she loved. For as long as Maria had known Kate, her flying had taken priority over almost everything in her life, and she found it very hard to believe that Kate didn't want to get airborne again. In some ways she hoped that this wasn't a permanent state of affairs; she felt that perhaps, as it had given Kate so much happiness in the past, it might bring some light back into her life in the future.

Maria returned to her unit and Kate returned to work on the day after New Year's Day. It was nice to get away from her mother. Mostly they rubbed along tolerably well, but they both had their own ideas on childcare and these weren't always the same. Discipline was a particular area where they disagreed, and Kate knew Edward found life much simpler when there was only one grown-up in charge.

The hotel was relatively quiet and Kate enjoyed the ordered and leisurely pace of the main lobby. The head receptionist, Mrs Arkwright, was busy sorting out bills at the computer terminal so Kate was left to man the desk and try to look busy with not much to do. She checked the reservations for the day and noted that the penthouse was booked but no name was mentioned – no doubt some mega-rich tycoon who could afford the extortionate rates and who wanted to remain anonymous. She wondered who it might be; they sometimes got people staying whom she recognised from the press: minor rock stars, actors and sporting types. The phone ringing nipped her curiosity in the bud, and then she had to sort out a problem regarding a disabled guest and his bathing requirements. Everything was running smoothly, the departing guests had gone and the new arrivals had yet to appear, whilst those doing neither appeared to have taken themselves out for the day. Mrs Arkwright had gone off on some errand or other and left Kate on her own. Bliss – utter silence. She was just thinking about getting herself a cup of coffee while all was quiet when she heard footsteps approaching across the marble lobby. She looked up to be confronted by Mr Spyrou and Magda Ionescu. Behind them was a porter with several expensive looking suitcases.

'Good morning, Mr Spyrou. And Miss Ionescu, how nice.' Kate smiled her best smile, hoping it would cover up her insincerity.

'Mrs Thomas!' Mr Spyrou sounded genuinely pleased to see her. 'And how is the job? Worth the trauma of the interview, I trust.'

'Yes thank you. I enjoy my work very much.'

'Good. I'd like the keys to the penthouse, please.' Aha – well, she was right about the mega-rich business tycoon. 'I'm going to be staying here for a few days. And don't worry, I haven't come to check up on you.'

That might be true, Kate thought, but she suspected that he *had* come to check up on the hotel as a whole. And why shouldn't he? He owned it, when all was said and done. She handed over the keys and ordered a bellboy to take the luggage up to the top floor. She longed to know if any of the bags were Magda's but knew it would be inappropriate of her to quiz the porter when he returned. Anyway, why shouldn't Magda stay in the penthouse with Mr Spyrou? Even if either or both of them were married, it did have two bedrooms, two bathrooms and a sitting room, and his personal arrangements were no business of a part-time hotel receptionist. All the same, she was curious about his private life, although she didn't stop to wonder why she envied Magda.

A couple of hours later Mr Spyrou came down the short flight of stairs from the lifts and into the main lobby unaccompanied by Magda. He approached the desk and instantly Mrs Arkwright leapt into action, ready to answer his questions or carry out his orders. He ignored her and approached Kate. Mrs Arkwright, straight out of Magda's mould – glossy, humourless and frosty – looked daggers at Kate.

'Mrs Thomas, I'm glad you're still on duty. I have a question for you.'

'Yes, Mr Spyrou.'

'It's about your flying. Are you managing to get some in?' What was it with everyone that they suddenly wanted to know about the state of her aviating? 'Not really, Mr Spyrou.'

'Why? What's the problem? Ah, I know, I don't pay you enough.'

Kate could see out of the corner of her eye that Mrs Arkwright looked as though she was about to blow a gasket.

'No, honestly, it's nothing like that.' Mr Spyrou raised his eyebrows. He obviously wanted her to elaborate, but really, her private life didn't have anything to do with him. She decided to make him drop the subject and said, looking as mournful as she could manage, 'It would upset my mother; my father died in an air accident.'

'My dear lady, I had no idea.' He looked stricken. 'How terribly tactless of me. Please forgive me.' He flashed Kate such an apologetic and engaging smile that Kate couldn't help herself from smiling back. She felt a bit of a heel – what she had done was rather mean. She guiltily tried to soften her words.

'It was a while ago now, Mr Spyrou—'

'Please, call me Andreas.'

Quite unexpectedly Kate felt herself blushing furiously.

'I'm, I'm . . .' she stammered. 'I'm not sure that is appropriate,' she managed to say eventually.

'Isn't it up to me to say what is appropriate in my own hotel?'

Kate could see Mrs Arkwright manoeuvring herself into battle stations.

'Mr Spyrou,' said the head receptionist coldly, 'I do think I should point out that such a move might be *extremely* bad for discipline.' Her disapproval was almost tangible. Kate watched as Andreas's eyes widened at the woman's audacity. She had to bite the inside of her cheeks to stop herself from smiling.

'Thank you for your opinion, Mrs Arkwright, which I value as always,' he said graciously. He was the soul of diplomacy, Kate thought.

Mrs Arkwright didn't look particularly mollified but Andreas decided to ignore her.

'As I was saying, I am so sorry for my *faux pas*. But is it *just* your finer feelings for your mother that are the reason you don't fly, or is it that you haven't the time, the money or the desire any more?'

Kate wasn't sure that her reasons were any of his business, but all the same, she was intrigued to know why he wanted to know. In her experience generals usually weren't particularly interested in knowing too much about the foot soldiers, beyond that they had enough of them to fight the next battle. And in the context of Spyrou Hotels, he was a field marshal and Kate was quite definitely a lowly squaddie.

He noticed her hesitation.

'I'm sorry,' he said. 'This is a personal matter. I shouldn't pry.'

'No, not really. I don't quite know myself. I suppose it's just that a lot has happened to me recently, a lot a big changes in my life, and flying has slipped a long way down my list of priorities.'

'Would you like to tell me about it over a drink at the bar?' said Andreas.

Kate was horrified. 'But I'm on duty! I can't possibly.'

'And I say you can. Mrs Arkwright can hold the fort for a few minutes.' He turned the full force of his charm on the head receptionist. 'I know you'll be able to cope. I'll only keep Mrs Thomas for a short time.'

201

Mrs Arkwright nodded and smiled, but Kate could tell that inwardly she was seething. Kate didn't blame her; she felt she'd be as cross if the roles were reversed. Really, Andreas Spyrou wasn't scoring ten out of ten for his man-management skills right now.

'Look, I'm not sure . . .'

'And I insist.'

Andreas Spyrou took her by the arm and led her firmly away from reception. As they walked across the lobby Kate shot what she hoped was an apologetic smile at Mrs Arkwright, but it was rebuffed by a stony stare. Kate was sure that her boss, despite the fact that he owned the place, was getting her into trouble – big trouble – with Mrs Arkwright.

Although it wasn't her place to say it, Kate always felt that the bar was at odds with the décor of the rest of the hotel. The lobby was light, airy, simple and elegant in its design. It reminded her of the hotel she'd stayed in in Cyprus – cool and clean, with its marble floor, high ceiling and bold, bright soft furnishings in brilliant reds and yellows. This theme was carried through the rest of the hotel except for the bar, which tried, and in Kate's opinion failed, to emulate an English pub. The ceiling was artificially low, the settles and banquettes were covered in red plush, there were fake beams in abundance and copper warming pans and horse brasses were festooned like bunting around the walls. Still, Andreas Spyrou presumably liked it or he wouldn't have let the designer get away with it.

'What would you like to drink, Kate? I may call you Kate?'

'Of course. Orange juice, please.'

'Are you sure? I promise I won't tell Mrs Arkwright if you have something alcoholic.'

Kate smiled. 'Thanks, but I've got to drive home later.'

'OK.' He ordered her juice and a mineral water for himself. Kate went and sat at a table and he joined her an instant later, sitting opposite her so Kate had to look at him. Not that looking at him was unpleasant. He was extremely attractive, although how he looked was completely immaterial, Kate told herself. But he did have nice eyes. She always liked men with nice eyes. Eddie had had lovely eyes. The barman hurried over bearing the drinks on a tray. Not the sort of treatment the

202

ordinary punters got, but then, thought Kate, rank does have its privileges.

'So, tell me about yourself,' said Andreas.

'There's nothing much to tell,' said Kate, still wondering furiously why he was taking such an interest.

'Now, I just can't believe that,' he said. 'Anyone – and forgive me for saying so, but especially a woman – who flew helicopters for the army has to be special.'

So Kate told him about the gliding and her time in the army; she told him about the death of her father and then the death of Eddie; she told him about her mother and her baby son, and every time she paused he told her he wanted to hear more.

'But there isn't any more to tell,' she protested finally. 'Absolutely nothing. Besides which, it's getting late. You promised Mrs Arkwright that I'd only be away a few minutes and I've been gone over an hour. I must get back.'

'In a minute. I want to know if you want to fly again.'

'I don't know. I mean, I do like flying but it seems rather a lot of money just to indulge a hobby. Keeping a PPL current costs hundreds of pounds, and as I don't have much reason to have a licence, well . . .' She shrugged to underline her point.

'Supposing you could fly for free, would that change things?'

'Well, of course it would, but that's not likely is it?'

Andreas smiled at her but didn't say anything.

'Look, Mr Spyrou . . . Andreas, I really must get back to work. I know you call all the shots and I know Mrs Arkwright is your employee, just like I am, but she is my immediate boss and I don't want to fall out with her.'

'Yes, I'm sorry. You're right, of course. I will accompany you and apologise for detaining you for so long.'

Kate was grateful for this gesture, but even so she had a nasty sneaky feeling that as soon as his back was turned Mrs Arkwright would allow her disapproval to manifest itself.

It became clear the next morning that while Andreas was staying at the Golden Crown, Magda would travel here daily from London. For reasons that she didn't stop to analyse, Kate was glad that the head of personnel wasn't staying in the penthouse suite with Andreas. He was much too nice to be having a relationship with a cold, hard woman like that.

The summons to see Magda which awaited her when she arrived at work the following day didn't come as much of a surprise to Kate. Mrs Arkwright had obviously decided that telling tales was going to be the most effective form of revenge.

When she got to Magda's office, she was forced to listen to a diatribe from Magda about her sloppy time-keeping (she'd been late once due to an accident which had blocked the road), her attitude to the guests (Kate was unaware of any complaints) and finally about leaving her post and drinking in the bar when she was supposed to be on duty.

'But I tried to refuse his hospitality,' said Kate, cross and indignant.

'Apparently not hard enough.'

'I don't see I was in a position to do more.' Magda didn't answer. 'Well, what do you suggest I should have done?' Magda smiled. Kate noticed that her sharp little white teeth pointed inwards very slightly and was instantly reminded of a shark. Not a bad comparison, she thought. Definitely a predatory creature.

Kate returned her attention to what Magda was saying. She spoke very slowly, as if to an imbecile. 'In the first place I wouldn't have set my scheming little cap at Mr Spyrou if I had only been employed as a part-time receptionist.'

'I beg your pardon?' Kate couldn't help herself. She was incensed.

'You heard.'

'You have no right to make such an accusation. Retract that at once.'

'No.' Magda smiled again.

Kate wasn't going to stand for this but she had little room for manoeuvre. 'In which case, I quit.'

Magda shrugged. 'You are contracted to give me a week's notice while I find a replacement.'

'Fine. I'll leave a week today then.' Kate knew that Magda had deliberately got her into this position, but what the hell. The job wasn't worth the hassle. Magda had obviously resented her from the instant they had met at the interview, and with Kate so junior to her in the company, she had been bound to lose out if ever things came to a show-down. A point which had just been proven.

'That's that then. Shut the door on your way out.'

Kate was tempted to slam it but decided not to give Magda the satisfaction of seeing how much she'd got to her. Cow!

She returned to the desk, smiled sweetly at Mrs Arkwright, and pretended nothing was wrong. Her reward was to see her supervisor nearly popping with curiosity that she would be unable to assuage until she ended her shift and could go and quiz Magda.

Andreas Spyrou appeared in the lobby shortly after lunch. Kate was due to knock off at three and was watching the clock. After her earlier interview she was keen to get away.

'Kate, how are you?'

Kate wasn't inclined to be particularly chatty. Presumably as he'd taken an interest in her recruitment, he now knew about her resignation. Or did he? Magda could hardly tell him, as there was implicit criticism of him in the dressing-down she'd given Kate which had prompted her to give in her notice.

'All right,' she said grudgingly.

'Good. Would you come with me, please?'

This time Kate didn't argue. She'd already lost her job – what else could Magda do to her? Andreas headed towards the front door and Kate followed.

'I want you to come for a drive with me.'

'Excuse me?'

Andreas stopped just beside the revolving door. 'A drive, in my car.'

'Why?'

'I want to show you something.'

Kate was feeling very wary and rather vulnerable.

'What?'

'It's a surprise.'

She shook her head. 'No thank you.'

Andreas tilted his head to one side. 'You don't think I've got some dark fate planned for, do you?' Kate smiled sheepishly and shrugged. The thought had crossed her mind. 'Look, I promise my motives are innocent. Please, will you trust me?'

Kate was on the spot and she knew it. What could she say –

I wouldn't trust you as far as I could throw a grand piano? Or should she put her instincts to one side, go along out of politeness and end up regretting her gullibility?

'My chauffeur will be with us; he'll protect you.'

Oh yes? And who paid his wages?

'Please?' He was begging her.

Kate gave in. If he really had something terrible planned for her, she didn't think that he would be standing here, in a very public place, entreating her. 'OK, then.'

Andreas grinned broadly and led the way through the revolving doors to his waiting limousine with its personalised numberplate – HOT3L. As she followed him, Kate hoped that she wouldn't live to regret her decision – or rather, she hoped she would live to regret it. No, that wasn't right either. Oh hell, was she making a terrible mistake?

Kate stepped into the Rolls-Royce. She'd never travelled in one before and was struck that this was what money smelt of – leather, a hint of expensive perfume or aftershave, a whiff of polish and the merest hint of cigar smoke. She sank into the deep rear seat and tried, for the benefit of a group of guests arriving at the hotel, to look as if she did this every day of her life. The chauffeur shut the door behind Andreas with barely a sound, then climbed in himself. The engine was so quiet that Kate had to strain her ears to hear it. So, the rumour about the loudest thing in a Rolls being the ticking of the clock was true. The big car purred away down the long gravel drive and then turned on to the road that led to Windsor.

'Where are we going?' asked Kate.

'You'll find out soon enough; it's a surprise. It's not very far, though. Now would you mind if I'm terribly rude, but there are a couple of papers I need to look at.' He opened his briefcase and extracted some thick bundles of documents.

'Don't mind me,' said Kate, and contented herself with looking back at the people who stared curiously at the car as they wove through the heavy traffic leading to Windsor.

The chauffeur skirted round the town itself before turning on to the M4 heading westwards. It seemed to Kate that they had barely joined the motorway before they were off it again, but the territory was familiar. They were heading towards Marlow and, if they kept on going, High Wycombe. Kate had been to school near here and a little part of herself rather hoped that she might be spotted by one of her old teachers now that she was travelling in the company of such a fabulously wealthy man. Her hopes were dashed, though, when they turned off before reaching her school and purred down a lane that cut across the Chiltern Hills, beautiful as always despite it being winter, cloaked in wonderful beech woods; the trunks, tall, straight and grey, always reminded her of the interior of a cathedral. When the car turned in to the entrance to a small airfield, Kate began to have an inkling as to what the surprise might be. Her suspicions were confirmed when the chauffeur drew up beside a Cessna 150.

Andreas put his papers away and dug a couple of keys out of his case.

'Come on then,' he said with a smile. 'Let's see how much you've forgotten.'

Kate didn't know what to say. 'Thank you,' she managed to stammer out eventually.

The chauffeur was holding her door open so, still in a daze, Kate climbed out.

'Don't we have to book in with anyone?' she asked.

'As this is my plane and I have already told the control tower that I will be doing some local flying this afternoon, I don't think it is necessary.'

'Your plane!' Kate was impressed, but then she remembered that he owned a whole fleet of Boeings. She felt rather foolish.

'Right then, external checks. Off you go.'

Kate unlocked the cockpit door and leant inside. She had been taught that the first thing to check was that the park brake was on and the magneto switches were off, because if they weren't the aircraft was lethal to anyone standing near the propellers. That done, she flicked the master switch for the electrics and a couple of other switches to make sure the strobe and navigation lights were working. She completed the few other internal checks and then turned her attention to the outside of the aircraft. She began to walk slowly round the plane looking for any visible signs of damage, checking that the tyres looked as if they were properly inflated, that nothing had bashed or dented the aircraft, that things that should move

207

could and that it was all in good working order. She ran her eyes and her hands over the surfaces, made sure the ailerons had full and free movement, that the flaps were OK and that everything was in place and working properly. Satisfied, she moved along the side of the aircraft to the tail and then finally the other wing. Then she went to the front and checked the engine for loose wires and that the oil level was adequate.

'Everything seems fine,' she reported to Andreas.

'I should hope so, otherwise I would sack my mechanic.'

Kate grinned. She couldn't imagine the luxury of being able to employ people to look after your every need. She was reminded of the Victorian landed gentry who expected to have horses saddled and ready whenever they wanted and never gave a thought to looking after the animals themselves.

'Right, let's take this baby for a spin.'

Kate clambered into the left-hand seat of the cockpit. It was like being reunited with an old friend, for it had been a Cessna that she had flown at Blackbushe. She did her start-up checks, made sure they were both securely strapped in and that the doors were properly shut, and then switched the engine on. The plane came to roaring, throaty life. It took a few minutes for the engine to warm up and for all the instruments to settle down, then she called the tower and asked for permission to taxi.

'Roger Zulu Delta. Clear taxi, runway two eight left,' came back the voice, distorted by a slight crackle. She listened carefully as she was given the local prevailing met conditions and then began to taxi towards the runway. As she taxied, she completed some other checks, which included making sure the compass was working, the altimeter was correctly set and the brakes worked.

When she arrived at the holding position she began to go through the pre-flight checklist.

'When I first learned to fly I was taught "Too Many Prostitutes For Good Health" to help me remember the checks,' said Andreas.

'And how did that work?'

'"Too" was for trim for take-off and throttle friction set. "Many" was mixture rich, mags on both and carb air cold . . .'

Kate began to laugh. 'I get the picture. God, I'm glad

things are more sophisticated now.' She flipped open the checklist again and began to go through it, mentally ticking off each stage.

'Happy?' asked Andreas as she finished.

'Everything is fine.'

'Good,' said Andreas. 'I can't fault you so far.'

'It's amazing how it has all come back. It's almost as if I last flew yesterday.'

She opened up the throttles to rev the engine up to full power and then throttled back again. Then she called the tower for permission to depart.

'Zulu Delta, clear take-off,' acknowledged the voice. Kate released the brake and the plane crept on to the runway; then, as she turned it into wind she eased the power on and the plane sped forward. Kate felt a familiar thrill of exultation as the aircraft took to the sky. For an hour she flew around the Chilterns practising landings and take-offs, doing some navigation work, going over procedures for emergency landings and all manner of basic aviation skills. When she finally climbed out of the cockpit she couldn't believe that she had gone for so long without allowing herself the thrill of being in the air.

'Did you enjoy that?' asked Andreas.

'It was wonderful, and thank you.'

'Then you must do it again, next week.'

Kate's heart sank. Next week? Next week she would no longer be one of his employees. Bugger! 'I can't.'

'Of course you can. If it's a problem about work I'll sort it out with Mrs Arkwright.'

'It's not that.'

'Well?'

'I had a row with Magda and I quit. By next week I won't be working for you any more.'

'Ah.'

Silence followed. What else was there to say? She could hardly tell him the reason for the row. The silence lengthened.

'Are you going to tell me what happened?'

'No.'

'I see. If I asked you not to resign, what would your answer be?'

Kate had a short think. She had enjoyed her job, but she couldn't face seeing Magda again. Apart from anything else, she was so angry with the woman she felt she might hit her if their paths crossed again.

'I've made my bed. I'd better lie in it.' She didn't add that it was unlikely that Magda would agree to reinstating her either.

'I see.' He didn't look or sound pleased.

'I don't want to appear ungrateful. It has been a wonderful afternoon and it was terribly kind of you to take me flying. I really appreciate it. I can't think . . .' she stopped. She had been about to say, *I can't think why you felt you wanted to*, but it would have sounded so unbelievably rude and ungrateful.

'I wanted to do something to bring you a little happiness. You have had such a dreadful time in the last year. I just wanted to see you enjoy yourself.'

Kate blushed and felt quite overwhelmed that he should take such an interest in her welfare.

'I'm sorry,' continued Andreas. 'I appear to have embarrassed you.'

'No. It's just you've been so kind and . . .' Kate faltered. She wasn't quite sure how to continue. 'I mean you are a multi-millionaire, you own dozens of hotels, and I'm just a receptionist. Someone in your position doesn't usually even notice someone in mine – let alone take them flying.'

'But I wasn't always in this position. I wasn't born into a dynasty of hoteliers. And there's something of myself that I recognise in you. It must have taken a lot of single-minded ambition to achieve what you did. I admire that.'

Kate shrugged. She knew he was complimenting her but to what end? Was he just being kind and generous or was there something else behind his actions? She felt that he had to have some sort of motive for encouraging her to get back in the air, but she was blowed if she could see it. After all, if he needed another pilot, all he had to do was advertise for one to join the other dozens in his employ flying his holiday charter jets around the Mediterranean.

'Come on, it's time we got back to the hotel,' said Andreas, signalling the Rolls to come forward and pick them up.

On the return journey Andreas returned to his papers and

Kate wondered whether she did have any future with Spyrou Hotels. She faintly hoped that Andreas might take Magda to task about her resignation, but even if he did it would hardly make her position within the group more tenable. Magda and Mrs Arkwright were bound to make sure that if she made the least slip she would be out on her ear, and next time they would do it when Andreas was safely out of the way. She sighed quietly; the reality was that Magda was obviously a powerful influence, and Kate couldn't expect Andreas to back her in favour of such a senior employee.

When they arrived back at the hotel, Kate thanked him again before going to collect a couple of personal possessions and knocking off for the day.

'And where have you been?' said Magda from the office in reception.

Kate jumped at her voice and, to her chagrin, felt herself blushing guiltily. 'Mr Spyrou wanted me to accompany him. I didn't think I was in a position to refuse.'

'A position to refuse?' hissed Magda. 'Just who do you think you are? You've been with this company for no time at all and yet you think that you have some sort of privilege that none of the other employees enjoy. Just because you used to be able to fly a helicopter, you think you are superior to everyone else. Perhaps you think that the terms of your contract don't apply to you because of this. Well, let me assure you that they do, and even though you will be leaving shortly – and not a moment too soon, in my view – you needn't think that you can swan off as and when you want.'

'Mrs Thomas was not *swanning off*, as you put it,' said Andreas from the doorway of the office. 'She was accompanying me at my express insistence.' His voice had an edge to it that Kate hadn't heard before. But she felt that anyone who had built up such an empire by his age – and she didn't think he could be much more than forty at the most – had to have more than a streak of ruthlessness.

'Mr Spyrou! Naturally I didn't mean to imply—'

Andreas cut her off. 'You meant to imply exactly that, Magda.' He paused for a second, then said, 'My suite. Now.'

Mrs Arkwright looked on in horror as Magda Ionescu followed him across the lobby to the bank of lifts, then turned to Kate, a look of pure venom on her face.

'What do you think you're playing at? What have you done to get Magda into trouble?'

Kate refused to rise. 'I've done nothing. I've been carrying out the instructions of Mr Spyrou, and considering that this hotel belongs to him and not to Miss Ionescu, I would have thought that it was not a matter for interference or conjecture from anyone.' Mrs Arkwright looked as though she had been slapped. Kate picked up her umbrella and briefcase that she had left behind earlier and departed. 'I'll see you tomorrow, Mrs Arkwright,' she called over her shoulder. 'Have a pleasant evening.'

Chapter Twenty

Kate was feeding Edward his breakfast of porridge and banana when the doorbell rang.

'I'll go,' she called upstairs to her mother, who was still dressing. She left Edward happily slapping his spoon into the gooey mess in his bowl and ran to the front door. At this time of day it would most likely be the postman and it wasn't fair to keep the poor man hanging about in the cold, miserable January weather. She nearly exclaimed with surprise when, on opening the door, all she could see was a massive bunch of unseasonable, and doubtless expensive, flowers.

'Mrs Thomas?' said a female voice from somewhere on the other side of the bouquet.

'Yes.'

'Sign here, please.' A hand appeared from around the bunch and proffered a clipboard with a list of deliveries on it. Kate found her name and signed as directed.

As she did so she said, 'Good heavens, I didn't think florists made deliveries this early.'

'We were given very exact instructions about the delivery time,' said the voice, which sounded rather put out about the whole business. The bouquet was then thrust at her. It was with some difficulty that Kate manoeuvred it through the door.

'Good heavens,' said her mother, descending the stairs. 'Who on earth sent those?'

'No idea. I'll have a look at the card when I can find it.' Kate went into the kitchen, followed by her curious mother. She placed the giant bouquet on the work surface by the sink and peered amongst the blooms for the customary little white envelope. It took her a couple of minutes to find it.

'Well?' said her mother.

'It's from Andreas. The card says, "Don't go, I've got high hopes for you."'

'What?'

Kate repeated it.

'How very enigmatic. What do you think he means?'

'It looks as though he doesn't want me to leave my job.'

'I'm surprised you didn't do more than just walk out. From what you said, that Ionescu woman sounds perfectly bloody.'

'She's not my cup of tea and that's for sure. Although I've no doubt she is very efficient.'

'Hmm,' said Honour. 'Is that a euphemism for being a prize bitch?'

'Mother!' Kate was horrified. She couldn't ever remember hearing her mother be quite so direct.

'Well, is it?'

'It is, actually.'

'Then you're probably better off out of the job.'

'But Andreas has sent these to try to persuade me to stay.'

'It's up to you then, but Andreas won't be around except on rare occasions, and Magda will be much more visible.'

Kate knew her mother was right; after all, she'd come to much the same conclusion herself on the way back from the airfield the day before.

'I don't know. I'll think about it. In the meantime I must finish sorting Edward out and then get myself ready for work. Could you be a darling and bung these flowers in some water?'

Kate got a damp flannel and mopped porridge from Edward's face, then she swiftly fed him what was left in the bowl and took him upstairs to dress him and get herself ready. It was just before eight, and she was about to leave for work, when the phone rang.

'Hello,' she said.

'Have the flowers arrived?'

'Andreas! Yes, they have. They're beautiful.'

'Did you read the card?'

'Yes.'

'And?'

214

'And what?'

'Are you still going to go?'

'I don't know. It's not as simple as just going or staying.'

'Why?'

'It just isn't, that's all.'

'You mean Magda?'

Kate couldn't dodge that question. 'Yes.'

'Well that's not an issue you need to worry about any more.'

'Why?'

'Because she's no longer in my employ.'

'You mean . . .?'

'I sacked her.'

'Why?'

'Because of the way she treated you, because of her attitude and because I can.'

Kate wasn't sure about the last bit of his statement. She had a feeling that employees couldn't just be dismissed out of hand like that but then maybe Magda had had her written and verbal warnings and yesterday had been the last straw. Whatever, it was none of her business, except that she no longer had a reason not to work for Andreas.

'So are you still quitting?'

'It would be dreadfully ungrateful if I did – after all your efforts to persuade me otherwise.'

'Good. Then you'd better stop chattering on the phone or you'll be late for work. And that would never do.'

Kate couldn't stop herself from laughing.

When she got to work there was a note waiting for her saying that she was to report directly to Mr Spyrou's penthouse suite. Mrs Arkwright wasn't on duty at that early hour but Kate knew that if she had been she would have given her one of her disapproving looks. After making sure that the reception desk was manned sufficiently – it got extremely busy between eight and nine in the morning – Kate crossed the lobby to the lifts with mixed emotions. Certainly it was very flattering that such a rich and powerful man was taking a personal interest in her welfare, but she was still worried about his motives. And this dilemma was further compounded by the very fact that she *did*

215

find his interest flattering and she therefore felt disloyal to Eddie. By the time the lift got to the ninth floor, Kate was feeling a very odd mixture of guilt, apprehension, smugness, worry and excitement and her system was complaining that all this was making it difficult to digest her rather hasty breakfast properly. As she knocked on the door of the penthouse, she realised that added to everything else, she was also feeling slightly sick.

Andreas opened the door. 'Kate, my dear, come in. Breakfast?' He indicated a large tray containing cups, croissants, butter, jam and a huge cafetière of piping hot coffee. Kate's stomach grumbled a soft warning that it was already under enough stress.

'Just a coffee, thanks.' There was a pause while Andreas poured her one and handed it to her. 'You look nervous. Don't be. I'm not going to bite.' Kate smiled awkwardly. 'I want to apologise for the way you were treated yesterday. Magda had no right to accuse you of the things she did.'

Kate blushed. She was embarrassed that Andreas knew of them. Perhaps he thought that she had been setting her cap at him and now wanted to take advantage of her interest.

'Anyway,' he continued, 'you needn't worry about her any more. But of course I have a problem. I no longer have anyone in charge of personnel in this area of my operations.'

From worrying that he was about to proposition her, Kate suddenly had a different inkling of where this conversation was heading but didn't trust herself to look at him. She took a sip of her coffee to give herself an excuse to focus her attention elsewhere.

'I spent last night studying your file in depth. Magda glossed over most of your army career in the interview, didn't she? I didn't realise how extensive it was. Much more than just flying Gazelles.'

'Well, it probably wasn't very relevant to the post of receptionist,' mumbled Kate.

'But it seems extremely relevant to the post of head of personnel. You spent a lot of time administering troops, sorting out personal and personnel problems – before you began to fly, that is. So?'

Kate looked over her coffee cup at him. Although she'd

seen this offer coming, she still felt bewildered. She didn't know anything about his hotels – well, not enough to look after all the people who worked in them. No, it was a ridiculous offer. 'But I can't do Magda's job. I don't know anything about the business; I wouldn't know how to interview a chef or an accountant. And I don't know what all the people who work for you are supposed to do or if they are doing it well or badly.'

'Maybe not, but I do, and so do lots of other people who work for me. Your job is to make sure the staff are happy, that there are enough of them to make my hotels run efficiently, that their personal problems get sorted out, that they are polite to the guests and that the ones who let standards slip and become rude, dirty or fraudulent leave as soon as possible. You could do that. What do you say? There's a big pay rise involved.'

Kate had no doubt about the pay rise, but that wasn't the issue. Apart from her doubts as to how well she would be able to carry out this job, it was a long way from the stress-free part-time number she had originally applied for. 'I'm terribly flattered by your offer, of course I am, but I have a young baby, and apart from anything else I just don't think I can take on this sort of commitment while Edward needs me.'

'I thought your mother looked after him for you while you're at work?'

'She does, but I only work part-time at the moment and she has things to do too.'

'Will you think about it, will you discuss it with her, please?'

'OK, but can I ask that if I turn it down I can still have my job in reception, that there'll be no hard feelings about this?'

Andreas held out his hand. 'You have my word on it. And I also promise that we will go flying together again next week. I'll be away till then; you can give me your answer about the job when you see me next.'

'You're a fool if you turn it down,' said Honour when Kate returned with the news that afternoon.

'But it's too much.'

'And this from the girl who was going to go back to flying helicopters after the baby was born.'

'But this is different. It means travelling up to London every day and it means asking too much of you.'

'Does that mean you don't think I'm capable of looking after Edward?'

'No. Not at all.' God, her mother was contrary. If Kate had assumed that Honour would automatically take on Edward's care, she would have hit the roof and complained that there would be no time to pursue her own life. Now she was trying not to take her mother for granted, and Honour was getting stroppy about being left out of the equation. Kate tried to placate her. 'It's just you have things you like to do too.'

'Just because I will have Edward in tow doesn't mean I can't do other things. And if you're so worried about me, why don't you employ a nanny?'

'I didn't have a baby to give him to a stranger to look after all the time.'

'That's not how you felt in Ireland. You were quite set on returning to work then.'

Kate's anger flared. 'That was before Eddie died.' Honour didn't reply. Kate was right, of course. Priorities changed when you'd lived through a personal tragedy.

'Well, I think you should do it. I think you are perfectly capable of this job; it will give you a challenge that you could do with. You are wasted as a receptionist – ridiculous that a woman with your abilities and qualifications fritters them away taking messages and handing out keys.' Kate didn't tell her mother that there was rather more to the job than that – Honour would have dismissed the notion anyway.

'I'll think about it. Except I'd really rather not get involved with hiring nannies. Do you really, truly mean that you wouldn't mind taking care of Edward?

'I said so, didn't I?'

Kate smiled gratefully at her mother. She knew from her own childhood that small children had never really been Honour's cup of tea, but over the last year or so she had mellowed rather – or at least had seemed to. Kate had noticed that her mother seemed less set on social climbing and the gains that might bring, and more content with making the most of what she actually had: her daughter and grandson, her home and her health. It would be nice to think that Honour had come to the conclusion that these were the things that really mattered, but Kate knew in her heart that it was more likely that this had been brought about involuntarily through having her and Edward to care for. Still, if Honour was prepared to carry on in the same vein and to forgo organising the lavish luncheon and dinner parties which would ingratiate her with the social scene, Kate wasn't going to complain. Perhaps the bridge club and an occasional overseas holiday would be enough to keep her mother happy. And neither of those was likely to interfere with Kate's job and Edward's welfare.

Kate mulled over Andreas's offer in almost every waking minute over the next few days. Did she want the responsibility that this post would bring? Could she cope with the hassle and the stress of such an important job? She rang Maria, who was now an adjutant of a divisional signals regiment in Germany.

'Of course you can do it. You're just suffering from cold feet because you've been out of harness for a while.'

'But there are so many employees in this area. He's got hotels at Runnymede, Gatwick, Marylebone, to name but a few. Then there are another half-dozen further out in the Home Counties, and they all employ at least a couple of hundred staff.'

'Yes but doesn't each hotel have its own personnel manager?'

'Yes, but . . .'

'*Yes, but* nothing. Think of each hotel as a platoon . . .'

'Bloody big platoon,' muttered Kate.

'As I was saying, if you think of each hotel as a platoon and each on-site personnel manager as the platoon commander, and each hotel manager as a company commander, then your job is no different to mine really – you are the adjutant and Andreas is the CO. Think about it. Most of the time the companies in the regiment sort out their own problems. I only get involved if it is a really serious problem or breach of discipline and then I tell the CO because he needs to know what is going on in his empire. It'll be just the same in the hotel business, I'm sure.'

Put like that, Kate could see that the job wasn't as daunting as she had first thought. Maria was absolutely right, but even so it was a giant step away from being a simple receptionist, and she said so. Kate was obviously having a crisis of confidence even though it was clear to Maria that she was more than capable of holding down the post successfully. Maria thought of another ploy to try and persuade her.

'OK, let's put it another way,' she said. 'Is Andreas a hugely successful businessman?'

'Yes, but . . .'

'Right. And did he get to that position by making duff decisions?'

'No, but . . .'

'So what makes you think that his decision to appoint you to the job of personnel manager is a duff decision?'

'Because I worry about his motives. It doesn't seem to be as straightforward as employer and employee.' There, she'd said it now.

'You mean, you think he fancies you?' said Maria, astonished.

'Well, thanks very much for the vote of confidence. I'm not completely hideous.'

'No, I didn't mean that, but – I mean, God, what *do* I mean?'

'You mean exactly what I've been thinking: he's rich and powerful and I'm just a lowly receptionist.'

'In a nutshell, yes. So why do you think he fancies you?'

Kate told her about the flying lesson.

'That's not conclusive.'

'Oh, come on! Why should he concern himself about either my welfare or my flying?'

'Because he's a pilot and he's got his own plane and he did it out of generosity.'

'OK,' said Kate. 'Perhaps if we use you analogy of the CO and the regiment . . . Supposing your CO took one of the company clerks – a female one – out in his car to give her a driving lesson, what would you say?'

'Hmm.'

'I should think it would be a bloody sight more than *hmm*.'

'I take your point.' There was a pause. 'Is he married?'

'What's that got to do with it?'

'Quite a lot.'

'No it hasn't. I'm not the least bit interested. Anyway, I don't know. I haven't asked and I'm not going to.

Maria sighed and Kate knew why. If she started taking an interest in other men it would be an indication that she was beginning to heal, beginning to move on, but she wasn't ready for that. Not yet. Perhaps in another year or so, who knew?

'Anyway, you're still the right person for the job whether or not Andreas is after more than a replacement manager.'

'Do you really think so?'

'Would I lie to you?'

Kate told Andreas of her decision when she saw him the following week.

'I am so pleased,' he said. 'Let's celebrate by going flying.'

'With all the extra money you're going to be paying me, I would have thought you would expect me to fork out for my own flying.'

'But I haven't paid you yet. It's still a few weeks before you take up the post.'

Kate couldn't resist asking, 'Does Magda know who is taking over from her?'

'Yes.' There was a slight pause. 'She didn't take it well.'

I bet, thought Kate, trying and failing not to feel smug and vindictive.

'In fact I don't advise that you meet her again before you actually take over. I will make sure you know everything you need to know, and of course your PA will brief you. You mustn't worry about it at all. In the meantime I'm going to take you off reception and let you understudy the personnel manager here at Runnymede.'

Kate breathed an involuntary sigh of relief. Life with Mrs Arkwright had been more than a little tricky these last few days. Obviously the woman wasn't bosom buddies with Magda but when it came to the issue of taking sides she wasn't on Kate's. Which would have been fine, thought Kate, if she had been leaving as planned. But as things were now, Mrs Arkwright was busy allying herself with the wrong side. Not that Kate cared as long as Mrs Arkwright didn't try to undermine her once she assumed her new post. And if she did then Kate would deal with it if and when that problem arose.

When Kate and Andreas arrived at the airfield the cloud was low and there was a light but persistent drizzle. However, such conditions were ideal for Kate to practise flying on instruments. Again she was surprised at how little she had forgotten despite the fact that it had been quite a while since she had had to fly exclusively on instruments.

'It just shows how well you were taught,' said Andreas, as they taxied back towards the pan.

Kate agreed that her army training had been very thorough.

'I am going to be away for a few weeks from Thursday.'

'Somewhere nice?' asked Kate conversationally.

'Cyprus.'

'Oh, lucky you!'

'Not really, it's business.'

'But business in lovely surroundings.'

'Do you know the island?'

'Not terribly well but I've been there once.'

'Did you get to Kyrenia?'

'I did, and I thought it was the most beautiful harbour I'd ever seen.'

'I agree. But maybe I am biased, I was born there.'

'Oh, lucky you! How fantastic to grow up in a place like that.'

'You have no need for envy. In 1974, when the Turks invaded Cyprus, we lost everything.'

'I'm sorry, I didn't realise.'

'Well, I don't advertise the fact that I spent several years in a refugee camp on the outskirts of Larnaca.'

Kate turned the little aircraft into wind, applied the park brake and began to shut down the aircraft's engine, radio and fuel system. As she went through the procedure Andreas kept silent, not wishing to distract her.

'Happy?' he said as she finished and began to get out of her harness.

Kate wasn't sure whether he was enquiring after her overall state of mind or asking if she was satisfied with the aircraft. She assumed it was the latter.

'Yup. I don't think I missed anything off the checklist.'

The Rolls drew alongside. Kate prepared to get out.

'No, I meant are you happy? You seem,' he searched for the right word, 'less melancholy than when I first met you.'

'I probably am. You know how it is; things get a little easier every day. The pain when you lose someone doesn't go away, but you do get used to it. You learn to live with it. And I think that going flying again has been good therapy.'

'I'm glad.' He smiled at her. Kate smiled tentatively back, acutely aware that she didn't want to encourage this man into thinking that there was anything more to their relationship than employer and employee, but also aware that because he was treating her differently to all his other thousands of staff, it wasn't that simple. 'Anyway, while I'm away I've arranged for an instructor to take you flying, and Mark here,' he indicated the chauffeur, 'will collect you and bring you back in the Rolls.'

'But that's too much,' Kate protested.

'No it isn't. This plane sits here idle for much of the year. You enjoy flying, the plane is a waste of money if it isn't used regularly, so why shouldn't you make use of it? All I ask is that you think about requalifying as a private pilot. I would like to feel that I have helped you get back into the air again. I want to hear that you've gone solo.'

'Of course.' Kate was still feeling bowled over by his generosity. Flying privately cost a bomb, and this was a heaven-sent opportunity. She made up her mind to repay him by getting her PPL as quickly as possible and by being the best personnel manager ever.

By the spring Kate had taken and passed her general flying test, regained her PPL and got to grips with her new job. She had suggested that it would make more sense for her to have an office in the hotel at Runnymede rather than commute into London every day, a suggestion that Andreas had agreed to. After all, she was dealing with hotels across the south-east and it made no difference to the other employees where they could contact her or where she travelled from when she visited them. This arrangement suited Kate, although she had to admit to herself that it did have one drawback – which was that she didn't see much of Andreas. She tried to convince herself that her feelings for him were simply because it was immensely flattering to have been singled out for special treatment by someone so rich and powerful, but really she knew in her heart of hearts that given any sort of encouragement she could easily fall in love with him. More and more she found herself thinking about Andreas, not Eddie, when she lay alone in her bed. She tried to ignore how her heart quickened when her PA told her that he was on the phone. And she dismissed her mother as imagining things if she suggested that Kate had taken special care with her appearance because she was meeting Andreas that day. Perhaps it was best that their paths didn't cross too often, she thought.

Chapter Twenty-One

Edward's first birthday was a week away.

'Is he having a party?' asked Maria. She had phoned Kate to find out what he would like for a present.

'Not really. I don't know many other children his age. To be honest, I don't think there's any point until the kids are old enough to enjoy them and have fun playing games. But Andy and Emma are coming over to help him cut his cake.'

'Great. Am I invited?'

'Of course. I didn't ask you because of the distance.'

'No sweat. I've got to come over to go to Manning and Records to discuss a whole load of problems we've got with a lack of suitable personnel in some jobs and then I've promised to support the regimental swimming team in the inter-unit finals in Aldershot.'

'So you'll be in the area.'

'I most certainly will be – and in need of a bed for the night.'

'Then look no further. The Hayleigh-Ffoulkes Hotel is happy to accept your reservation.'

As Kate had predicted, Edward was largely unimpressed by his birthday party, preferring to mash his cake around on the tray of his high chair rather than eat it.

'But he loved his presents,' said Maria, engrossed in building a large tower with the brightly coloured bricks she had given him. Edward clapped enthusiastically as she balanced the last one on the top. 'Come on, young man,' she said, swooping across to him, wiping his hands and lifting him out of his chair. 'Let's see what damage you can do to this.' She put him on the floor and obligingly Edward instantly crawled to the pile of bricks and gave the bottom ones a shove. The tower clattered down and Edward rocked with laughter.

'You'll have to build it for him again,' said Andy.

'Absolutely,' agreed Emma. 'You'll be stuck doing that for the rest of the day.

'More champagne, anyone?' offered Kate picking up a freshly opened bottle.

'Yum, please,' said Maria, leaving the bricks and picking up her glass. 'Champagne and Marmite sandwiches. What a combination!' As Kate filled her glass, the doorbell rang.

'Who can that be?' said Kate. 'We're not expecting anyone else, are we, Edward?'

'I'll go,' called Honour from the kitchen.

The conversation in the dining room ceased as they unconsciously strained to listen to the voices at the front door and determine who the visitor was.

'We've a surprise guest,' announced Honour. And through the door of the dining room stepped Andreas, clutching the biggest teddy any of them had ever seen.

'Shit a brick,' murmured Maria, catching sight of the little button in its ear. 'And it's a Steiff too.'

'Huh?' whispered Emma.

'Fucking expensive Toys 'R' Us,' explained Maria quietly.

'Andreas, let me introduce you to everyone,' said Kate, moving forward to greet him.

Maria's eyebrows shot up to her hairline. Andreas! So this was Kate's sugar daddy. What a hunk!

'First of all, you must meet Edward, the birthday boy.' Kate lifted Edward off the floor and Andreas took his tiny hand.

'I know it's your birthday young man. Look what I've got for you,' and Andreas thrust forward the huge bear. Edward's face crumpled then he turned and buried it in his mother's shoulder.

'Oh dear,' said Kate, embarrassed.

'Don't worry. I probably scared him with it. Look, let's sit teddy on the floor and perhaps Edward will make friends with it later.' Even placed on the floor, the toy still managed to dominate the room.

'This is too generous of you,' murmured Kate. 'How did you know?'

'I tried to get hold of you at the office but your PA told me you'd gone home early for your son's party.'

'I didn't think you'd mind.'

'I don't.'

'And thank you for this wonderful gift. This is terribly thoughtful.' She smiled at him shyly. 'Now you must meet everyone else.' Swiftly she completed the other introductions.

'Do I gather that Edward and I are the only ones who haven't joined up?' asked Andreas.

'And me,' said Emma. 'I'm just married to a soldier.'

'Ah, good. That evens things up rather.' Edward, ignored and left to his own devices, crawled hesitantly towards the teddy, then thought better of it and hastened away again.

'Let me get you some champagne,' said Kate to cover her embarrassment at Edward's lack of appreciation of Andreas' kindness. She opened the sideboard to find a glass while Maria retrieved the bottle from the table.

'Thank you,' said Andreas watching the bubbles subside.

Kate was anxious to know why Andreas had been trying to get hold of her. She drew him to one side.

'Am I right in assuming that you haven't just come here to wish Edward many happy returns; presumably you wanted to talk to me about something?'

'Yes, but it's nothing bad.'

'Can you tell me here?'

'If you don't mind. I'm selling the Cessna.'

'Oh.' Kate couldn't keep the disappointment out of her voice.

'But don't worry. I'm buying something else.'

'What?' Brighter.

'A Citation.'

'But that's a jet.' The disappointment was back. She almost added, *and I can't fly those, so that's no good to me*. But she didn't, after all, she'd had plenty of flying at his expense already, and she really couldn't expect any more. That would just be greedy.

'A twin-engined jet, to be precise.

'Nice. You'll be able to get to your overseas operations in style now.'

227

'That's the general idea. Of course I'll need someone to fly it.'

'You'll be swamped with applications. I'm sure there's loads of pilots with the right qualifications that'd jump at the chance. Do you want me to write the ad and interview the applicants?' Now this was a field Kate would be able to shine in; she never felt too happy about quizzing newly qualified catering students and prospective hotel managers about their credentials – what did she know about them? And even if the head of the particular department did sit in on the interviews with her, she knew her ignorance was blatantly obvious.

'I wasn't planning on advertising.'

'Oh, you've got someone lined up then?' Kate wasn't surprised. He ran a package holiday business, for heaven's sake – of course he had a pilot for the job.

'Yes. It's you.'

Kate opened and shut her mouth. 'But, but . . .'

'But you're not qualified? Is that what you're trying to say?'

'Um, yes. I suppose so.'

She was prevented from saying anything else by a huge crash and a wail from Edward. Everyone had been so intent on eavesdropping on the conversation that no one in the room had noticed Edward grab the edge of the tablecloth and use it to haul himself upright. Unfortunately the food and drink on the table proved no contest against the weight of his sturdy little body, and three feet of cloth was pulled over the edge, taking with it half a dozen plates, knives, forks, a platter of Marmite sandwiches and a jug of juice. Edward howled with fright, surrounded by smashed china and spilt squash. Everyone rushed to the scene of the disaster, pandemonium reigned and Kate's new job offer was forgotten.

Honour swept in from the kitchen. 'What on earth is going on? Good grief! What's happened?' She surveyed the mess and the screaming child distastefully and then swept out again, returning a short while later with a bowl of soapy water and a cloth. Kate placated the miraculously uninjured toddler and Maria gathered up the broken plates, while Andy and Emma straightened the tablecloth and rescued the remains of the sandwiches before they were trodden into the carpet.

'Here, take Edward, will you, while I go and get the Hoover,' said Kate, thrusting the baby into Andreas's arms. She didn't wait for a reply and Maria had to suppress a giggle at the expression on Andreas's face as he struggled to hang on to a squirming and tearful child whilst keeping his suit away from the danger zone of Edward's nose.

'You don't look very happy,' she said.

'I'm not used to this sort of thing.'

'No kids of your own, then?'

'Not that I'm aware of,' said Andreas with a gleaming smile. 'I'm not married.'

Maria tucked this piece of information away. So Mr Megabucks was available. She bet that Kate still hadn't found out about his marital status – well, it was about time she knew. And good luck to her.

Edward squirmed and struggled harder. 'Would you like me to take him?' she asked, taking pity on Andreas.

'Please.'

Edward was more than happy to go to Maria, who deftly dried his eyes and wiped his nose with a paper tissue. 'There, that's better, isn't it, poppet?' Edward smiled in agreement and Andreas grinned with relief.

Kate returned with the Hoover and all talk ceased as she whizzed it across the carpet, slurping up crumbs and tiny shards of porcelain. Emma took the broken crockery away, and within a couple of minutes order had been restored.

'Now,' said Andreas, 'as I was saying before we were so rudely interrupted, you are not currently qualified to fly this plane, but part of the package when you buy something like this is a pilot training programme. It seems silly to waste it. So, if you would like to learn to fly this plane and you could face having me as your passenger, all you have to do is say yes.'

'But you've just made me personnel manager.'

'And now I want you to be my pilot.'

'Yes, but . . .' Kate couldn't see the logic in any of this.

'Look, personnel managers are two a penny. Finding someone professional enough in this field for me to trust implicitly is much harder to find. Let's face it, if anything goes wrong at thirty-five thousand feet, there isn't much in the way of a breakdown service. I've flown with you, and I have no doubts that you are a superb pilot. I am certain that the army trained you to the highest possible standard, and if I'm going to be stuck in the air for hours on end with just one other person, I would rather it was you than some hairy man with indifferent personal hygiene.'

Kate couldn't help smiling. 'I don't know. This is such a shock. What about all those other pilots you already employ?'

'I have to say that your rate of pay would start off at some-what less than they earn, and I don't think any of them would be happy to take a pay cut just for the privilege of flying the boss.'

That wasn't much of a surprise. The captain of a large passenger jet might be earning double what she could expect – still, that would probably be more than she was getting at the moment. A thought other than money crossed her mind: this sort of job would mean being away from home a lot.

'I don't know, I need to think about it.'

If Andreas was disappointed that she hadn't leapt at the chance, he didn't show it.

'Take as long as you want. Well, within reason,' he added. 'Now then, how about drinking a toast to the birthday boy?'

The toast was duly drunk, Edward chortled happily at being the centre of attention, made friends with the giant teddy and experienced his first taste of champagne. And Maria managed to corner Kate.

'You're well in there,' she said in a low voice so the others couldn't hear. Even so her admiration, verging on envy, was apparent.

'What on earth do you mean?' hissed back Kate.

'Come off it,' Maria snorted in disbelief at Kate's naïvety. She spelt it out. 'He really fancies you. Why else would he be singling you out for this sort of treatment? How many other employees' houses does he roll up at, clutching wildly expen-sive gifts for their offspring? And as for this business of buying a plane so he can have you as his own personal pilot . . .' Maria rolled her eyes heavenward. 'That's a pretty pricey way of having you around and unchaperoned. How much does a private jet cost?'

'I don't know,' said Kate a little sulkily. She didn't want to believe what Maria was saying, but similar thoughts had crossed her own mind. No, really! It was too ridiculous.

'I bet you do. One million, two million?'

'More like five or six.'

'Christ!' Even hard-as-nails Maria was impressed. She lowered her voice again and played her trump card. 'And because I knew you still wouldn't have done it, I've found out that he's not married.'

'How?'

'I asked him.'

'You did what?' Kate's voice rose to a shriek and everyone stopped their own conversation and stared curiously. Kate ignored the enquiring looks, the interest subsided and conversations were resumed.

'You did what?' she repeated more quietly but with the hint of a threat in her voice.

'Well, not right out.' Maria related how she had elicited the information.

Kate was not mollified. 'Well, I don't see what you think it has got to do with me.'

'Don't be so stupid. Think about it. Think of the lifestyle. Think of the holidays, the houses, the yachts.'

Kate gave her a withering look. 'You need to get out more, join the real world. Men like that don't take up with girls like me.'

Maria just shrugged and sashayed away to join Andreas, Emma and Andy.

But after all the guests had departed and Kate was bathing a very sleepy Edward, Maria's words refused to go away. Perhaps Andreas did fancy her; perhaps there was more to his generosity than met the eye, perhaps ...? Oh, get real, she told herself. He could have his pick of the world's beautiful women and most of them would be only too ready, willing and able to throw themselves at his feet – and they certainly wouldn't come complete with a whole load of emotional baggage and a fatherless child. All the same, he had encouraged her to fly again, he was offering to pay for her to learn how to fly a jet, he had taken the trouble to buy a present for Edward and he had singled her out from the rest of the staff on two occasions now. Her mind was in turmoil as she lifted

Edward from the soapy water and wrapped him in a warm towel. And beneath the turmoil she was aware that she also felt slightly nervous and excited, as she had so many years ago when she had been besotted with Mike. It wasn't like when she'd realised she had fallen for Eddie. She could still remember the first time he had touched her and it had been like receiving an electric shock – a sudden convulsive tingle that had jolted her heart into life. And then the second time – when he'd returned to Ireland and she'd blown the unit's chances at the quiz night because she had been so completely distracted by knowing he was just a few yards away. What she was feeling now wasn't in the same league, but then, she reasoned, how often does a love affair have that sort of intensity? She had to ask herself the direct question now: was she falling for Andreas? Or was it his money and his lifestyle that she found so attractive? Was she just flattered because an attractive man with pots of money was giving her more than the time of day? The nearest she came to giving herself a direct answer was that it could be either. She tried to analyse her feelings as she dried Edward and then dusted him with talcum powder, but it was all too complicated. Oh God, she just didn't know.

And then there was the problem of his job offer. Under any other circumstances she would have jumped at the chance. It was a fantastic opportunity. But was his motivation for his offer and her motivation for wanting to take it up quite as they should be? Why wasn't anything straightforward? Why did life have to be so complicated? Why did Maria have to go putting thoughts into her head? Why, why, why? And anyway, what would Eddie think? She rewrapped Edward ready to carry him to his bedroom, and then buried her face in the towel as she held him close.

'I don't know,' she whispered to him, 'I don't know. What do you think I should do, Edward?' Edward just yawned sleepily at her and blinked. She dropped a kiss on top of his damp curls. He, of course, was yet another complication. She loved him to bits, naturally, but was being Edward's mother going to be enough for her? Could she focus her entire fore-seeable life on providing for his needs and emotions and putting herself second all the time? She knew the answer should be an unequivocal yes but she also knew that she could not do it. She had to have more in her life; she had her own needs and emotions too, her own hopes, ambitions and dreams. If she put everything on hold for Edward's sake, would she wind up resenting him? Wouldn't life be a lot simpler if you came into the world with your own personal crystal ball, she thought sadly, so that you knew the outcome of your decisions?

She carried Edward into his nursery and dressed him in his pyjamas before tucking him up in his cot. Then she read to him till his eyes shut and he drifted off to sleep looking as angelic as could be. Kate sat beside him for some time, letting her thoughts range over the problem. Eddie had understood about her flying and her need to do it. He'd always supported her in whatever she'd chosen to do. He'd been concerned when she had resigned her commission and had been adamant that once the baby had been born she should join up again. He knew that flying was as much a part of her life as breathing. He would have supported a new career for her in commercial flying. He would have wanted her to take the opportunity.

'You've got to go for it,' he'd always said. 'Opportunities, once missed, don't come round again.'

Kate made her mind up. She wasn't going to miss this opportunity. The only problem now was to tell her mother. As she headed down the wide stairs to the kitchen where Honour was preparing supper, she hoped she could put off breaking the news until she had thought of a strategy.

'Are you going to take up Andreas's offer?' asked Honour icily as soon as Kate walked through the door. Kate groaned inwardly. She didn't want this, not now, not today. Honour had her back to Kate and was busy chopping onions. Kate grimaced in frustration and then arranged her features into something blander.

'It's very tempting,' she said noncommittally, she really didn't want a row. 'I promised Andreas I'd give it some thought and I will.'

'Why? You don't need the money. And you'll be away a lot. You don't want to be away from Edward, now do you?'

Kate sighed. She'd known this would be her mother's reaction. 'I know, but . . .'

'You've always been selfish about your flying. I would

have thought that after what happened to your father it would have been the last thing you would have wanted to do. Even if only for my sake.' Honour sounded angry rather than sad. Kate remained silent. 'And what about Edward? What if something happens to you? He's already lost one parent.' She put down her knife and swept the onions into a pan of melted butter on the stove. They hissed and sizzled and Honour quickly clamped the lid on them.

'Can I do anything to help?' asked Kate.

'No, and don't change the subject.' Honour attacked the meat next, wielding her knife with ferocity. 'What is wrong with being a personnel manager anyway? It's a nice safe, steady job. You're not always stuck in one place so you can't complain about monotony. Why on earth do you even want to *consider* taking up flying professionally again? After all, you can afford to fly as a hobby if you want to. I wouldn't object if you did that.'

Kate felt a range of emotions. Annoyance and frustration with her mother, certainly, but stronger than these were guilt and despair. Guilt because she knew, despite all the arguments about being away from Edward and the effect it would have on his welfare, that deep down she wanted this job. And despair because she had no idea how she could ever convince her mother that it was a good idea, that it would make her happy, that it was what she wanted to do more than almost anything. Her mother lifted the lid on the pan and added the chopped steak.

'Get the sour cream and the mushrooms out of the fridge, will you?' Kate did as she was told and handed them across. 'Andreas would understand if you told him you wanted to put your family first. Of course he would; he's Greek, and the family is very important to the Greeks. Just tell him that you have to think about what's best for Edward.'

'But what about me?' said Kate. 'What about my hopes and ambitions? What about my life?'

'But you're a mother now. You've got to put all that behind you.'

Kate wasn't going to let that go. 'Oh yes. Like you did when you shipped me off to boarding school so you could help hoist Daddy up the promotion ladder? When did you put me ahead of your plans?' She glared at her mother, who glared back.

'That was different. It wasn't my ambitions I was nurturing; I did it for your father. And it would have been impossible for you to get a decent education with all the moving around that we did if you hadn't been sent away.'

'Bollocks. You didn't move that often. That wasn't your excuse. You wanted me out of the way so you could socialise with all the right people without worrying about me.'

'Don't you *dare* talk to me like that.' Honour was white with anger.

'I bloody well will. You wanted him promoted so you would be Lady Hayleigh-Ffoulkes. As far as you were concerned I was a tedious distraction and the more time I spent at school the better.'

'That's not true.' They were both shouting now.

'Huh. I can hardly remember a time when I didn't come home to find you holding some sort of social function and to be told that I was to eat in my bedroom so I didn't get in the way.' Honour reddened. Scored a direct hit there, thought Kate.

A thread of smoke wafted out of the heavy frying pan. 'Damn! The supper.' Honour whipped the lid off the pan and stirred the steak and onions, which were dangerously close to burning. She lowered the heat and tipped in the mushrooms.

'Now it's you changing the subject,' accused Kate.

'I'm not.'

Kate sighed. She hadn't wanted to row with her mother. Over the past months they had got on better than at any time she could remember. They still weren't anywhere near as close as Maria and her mother, but at least they seemed to be able to talk. Kate knew that the personal tragedies in both their lives had given them some common ground, and Edward provided a shared source of joy.

The mushrooms sizzled in the pan, Honour checked on the progress of the rice on the back burner and the tension eased fractionally.

'So, do I gather from your reaction that you *have* made up your mind? That you have got further than merely giving it some thought?'

'It's a wonderful opportunity, Mother. You have to see that. Offers like this don't come around more than once in a lifetime.'

'And what about Edward?'

'I don't expect I'll be away all that often. Andreas doesn't spend that much time overseas – half a dozen trips a year, from what I can gather.'

'You must realise that I won't be able to guarantee that I will always be available to look after Edward for long periods of time. You must surely realise that I may very well need some help. And I can remember what you said when you got the job as personnel manager; when I suggested that, if you were worried about me looking after Edward, it might make you happier if we employed a nanny. You completely dismissed the idea.'

Kate coloured. She remembered too and she seemed to recall that her exact words had been, *I didn't have a baby to give him to a stranger to look after*. And now she was planning to take a job that might mean she was away for days at a time. In all fairness to her mother, she would have to look seriously at this idea. 'But Edward is older now,' she said sulkily.

'Not that much.'

Kate tried another tack. 'Look, I've got to move on from where I was immediately after Eddie's death. I'm still young – I'm only twenty-six. I don't want to lock myself away and let life pass me by. And when I'm not flying I'll be around quite a lot.'

'You really want to do this don't you?' Honour's voice was hard. She obviously wasn't the least bit swayed by her daughter's arguments. She stirred the tub of soured cream into the stroganoff and vented her anger on the wooden spoon, bashing it against the side of the pan.

'Yes.'

'So I doubt that anything I say will make any difference.' Kate didn't know how to answer this. The honest answer was *no*, but it would sound so selfish. 'I see,' said Honour. The silence was enough of a reply. 'Get the plates out of the oven, would you?'

Honour dished up and they carried their meal through to the dining room. The atmosphere was hardly convivial or chatty.

236

It was no better the next morning when Kate left for work.

'Are you going to ring Andreas and tell him your answer?'

'I expect so, yes. He needs to know my decision.'

'Huh. Well, I'm sure he'll be pleased. And how long will it be before you have to go off to do the training?'

'I've no idea. Let's cross that bridge when we come to it.'

Andreas was, predictably, delighted with her news.

'That's great. I'll fix up a training course and get back to you with the dates. I believe it'll be fairly intensive, over several weeks. There won't be a problem with that, will there?'

Kate confidently said no but she had her fingers crossed just the same.

Chapter Twenty-Two

'Florida!' said Honour. 'I had no idea you'd have to go to the ends of the earth to do this. Of course you can't go, it's just too ridiculous. What about Edward?'

'Please shut up and listen,' said Kate. She had known this was going to be the reaction <u>as soon</u> as Andreas had told her all about it.

'Four to six weeks they reckon, depending on ability,' he had said, handing her the details of the flying course. 'They run these ones in Florida because the weather is guaranteed. At the end of it you'll get an American Federal Aviation Authority rating, but it's perfectly acceptable over here.'

'Wow,' said Kate, examining the glossy brochure with all the details. 'This looks fantastic. Much more glitzy than the School of Army Aviation.' There were pictures of all the amenities – the accommodation, the facilities, the local countryside, everything – and it seemed more like an up-market holiday resort than a flying school. And she'd always wanted to visit the States. This was wonderful, and she was being paid to go. She almost had to pinch herself.

'Of course I couldn't expect you to be separated from Edward for that long,' Andreas had continued. 'I'll make arrangements for both him and your mother to fly out with you.'

Kate explained to her mother about Andreas's generous offer, but Honour wasn't placated.

'You must be out of your mind even thinking about taking a child of his age to a country where they have shoot-outs on the streets and the entire population is on drugs.'

'Don't exaggerate, Mother, please.'

'I'm not exaggerating. I see stories in the papers all the time. Only the other day some poor holidaymaker in Miami was shot dead by a gang of muggers. You can't possibly expose Edward to that sort of danger. What would Eddie say?'

That was below the belt, thought Kate. Honour had never taken into consideration any of Eddie's opinions when he was alive. 'I think Eddie would think it a fantastic opportunity. If you're so worried about your own personal safety you can stay behind. I'm sure I'll be able to arrange for some sort of child-care while I am there. Edward will have the time of his life with all those wonderful facilities, to say nothing of the fact that he loves swimming and they seem to have two, if not three pools.'

'Anyway, we'll need visas.'

Kate could sense that her mother was weakening. 'That'll be quite straightforward to arrange. People visit the States all the time.'

'There's still all those people who carry guns.'

'I'm sure there will be more than adequate security arrangements around the airfield. They're going to be a little picky as to who they allow to wander around it, with millions of pounds' worth of aircraft sitting around.'

'I'll have to buy some new clothes. I haven't anything suitable for such a hot climate.'

Yes, she'd won, but Kate was careful not to look smug or triumphant. 'Let's go shopping at the weekend and find some nice outfits.'

'I can manage on my own, thank you.' Honour was obviously sulking. Kate didn't push it.

America was everything Kate had imagined, only bigger. Even the spaces in the car parks were huge, she thought as she gazed from the window of their spacious suite of rooms. Everything was big, from the size of the beds to the size of the meals. If she lived here for any length of time she would become vast too she mused as she recalled the enormous breakfast she had been offered that morning. Really, the amount of food that constituted an American portion was obscene. No wonder obesity was such a problem. She regarded a couple of extremely large ladies – obviously employees of the flying school, because they wore the uniform blazer – walking along the path that led to the main administrative building. Kate wondered how much they each weighed – fifteen, twenty stone? She felt like a stick insect in comparison. Funny, though, she thought, if you were to judge Americans from the people who featured on the TV, you would think they were a nation comprised entirely of beautiful, bronzed sex gods and goddesses. You didn't see any fatties on the *Baywatch* beach, for a start.

She turned away from the window and looked at Edward sitting happily in front of the TV, glued to the cartoon channel. Here he was, only just over a year old and already addicted to the box. She'd have to be strict about the amount of television he watched here, with so many channels to choose from. Still, if that was her only gripe about the place, things had to be good. Their accommodation certainly was. It was a fabulous suite of rooms – goodness only knew how much it had cost Andreas to put them up in such luxury. The mind boggled.

'Do you fancy a swim, Edward?' she offered. He didn't budge. She walked across the vast expanse of pale apricot carpet to his room and collected his trunks and water wings. 'Come on, darling, let's get you changed.' She switched off the TV and instantly there was a wail of complaint. 'Look, we're going swimming. That's nice, isn't it?' Judging by the way Edward was yelling, she was alone in this opinion.

'What's the matter Edward?' asked Honour, appearing from her room.

'He'd rather watch TV than swim,' said Kate, pulling off his shirt.

'Don't be silly, Edward. You know you love swimming, don't you?'

Kate finished undressing him and began to try to insert his flailing legs into his trunks. By the time she had finally succeeded she was sweaty and breathless. 'Goodness me, you're a prize fighter when you don't want to do something,' she panted. She plonked him on a towel, in case of accidents now he was nappyless, while she went to get herself changed. Edward was still protesting vociferously when she returned a few minutes later. She gathered him up into her arms, grabbed the suntan lotion, towels and armbands and stepped from the air-conditioned apartment into the sizzling heat of the Florida sunshine.

The pool, only a few yards away, glimmered and shimmered enticingly. Edward perked up when he saw it and began to struggle again, this time in eagerness to be in the water.

'Hold on, young man,' said Kate with a laugh. 'We have to get some sun cream on you first and get your armbands blown up.' She laid him on a sun lounger in the shade of a large umbrella while she dealt with these matters. Edward's struggles made things tricky but it wasn't long before they slid into the delicious and refreshing water. Edward gurgled delightedly, the television, and his earlier anger at being thwarted, forgotten.

Kate and Edward played happily in the water together. Once they'd been in the pool a while she began to let some of the air out of his bands to try and get him used to the idea that, like walking, swimming was something that he could do if only he put his mind to it. He's a real man, she thought indulgently; he's bone idle. He'd much rather be carried or pushed in a buggy by a woman than go to the effort of doing things for himself.

'Come on, Edward. it's not that difficult,' she implored him, but Edward was having none of it.

'Isn't he a little young to be training for the Olympics?' said a familiar voice.

Kate spun round in the water, and a shiver of something – excitement? – zinged through her. 'Andreas! What on earth are you doing here?'

'I came to see how you are getting on.'

Kate felt terrifically flattered. She laughed out of nervousness and pleasure. 'Wouldn't a telephone call have done?'

'Possibly, but then I would have missed out on seeing you in a swimming costume.' Kate felt her face burn and it was nothing to do with the sun beating down. Her discomfort was reflected in her expression. 'I'm sorry,' said Andreas, 'that was a very improper comment to make.'

'No, no, don't worry.' Kate was too flustered to think of anything much else to say. Edward had probably had enough time in the water and exposure to the sun. She wanted to get out of the pool but felt incredibly self-conscious. It was ridiculous, she told herself. She wouldn't normally give a toss who saw her in her cossie, but she really didn't feel able to expose herself to Andreas. It wasn't proper somehow. But it was obvious that he wasn't going to move away, and she could hardly admit to her embarrassment by asking him to go or look away. Perhaps if she distracted him with Edward . . .

'Could you bring over our towels and take Edward into the shade? I think he's had enough sun.' There, that should do it. She could get out of the water and hide immediately behind a towel while Andreas was busy sorting out Edward. But Andreas must have misheard her or deliberately ignored her request, and only picked up a towel for Edward. Bugger. She handed the slippery infant out of the water and into the fluffy confines of the towel. Hoping that Andreas's mind would be concentrating on not dropping Edward, she swiftly hauled herself out of the pool and scuttled across the paving slabs. She couldn't resist casting a swift glance at Andreas to see if he was watching her. He was. She felt her face flare red again. Well, best to ignore it and try and behave with as much dignity as possible. She wrapped herself in the luxurious fabric, tucking the edge over on itself so it was like a sarong.

'Thanks,' she said, strolling over to Andreas to collect her son. 'Now, we must get this chap ready for his supper.' Edward cooed and gurgled as Kate made to return to their apartment. 'Would you like a cup of tea? I'm about to put the kettle on for myself.'

'So you haven't become Americanised yet?' said Andrea with a smile. 'You still drink tea rather than coffee.'

'Only when we're in our rooms. It's too much hassle when we go out, and it always tastes disgusting.'

They returned to Kate's rooms, and Andreas was left to amuse himself while Kate sorted out first Edward and then herself. She felt much more comfortable once she was in slacks and a shirt. Really, she told herself, you're behaving like a lovesick teenager, thinking that he was really interested in how you looked in a swimsuit. He was probably only ogling out of disgusted fascination at the amount of cellulite, like someone at a freak show. But even as she thought this, she knew that she was deceiving herself.

She returned to the sitting room and opened the double doors which led to a tiny kitchenette.

'Hardly the equipment to knock up a Cordon Bleu meal but just the job for beans on toast for Edward's tea,' she said, filling the kettle and plugging it in. She busied herself at the counter making their tea and preparing Edward's supper.

'So when do you eat?' asked Andreas.

'Mummy and I wait till Edward is asleep and then go to the hotel restaurant. They have a natty little baby monitoring device so if he wakes up one of us can be back here in thirty seconds.'

'It sounds wonderful.'

'It is, but all this fantastic food is doing my waistline no good.' Kate stopped herself from saying any more. Would Andreas think she was fishing for compliments? Oh God! Please, no.

'If you are eating there this evening, may I join you?'

'Yes, yes, of course.' She could hardly say anything else. At least he hadn't responded to her inadvertent comment about her figure.

'Then we can talk about the course and how you are finding it.'

At the restaurant Kate found she had the usual problem of being bewildered by the choice offered by a menu the size of an English Sunday broadsheet. She had tried some of the more unusual dishes on the menu but tonight she fancied something relatively simple. The easy option of course was steak, but they were always so big and she hated the waste. Perhaps the deep-fried prawns with blue cheese dressing? Yes, that would do, and a salad but no fries.

'No fries?' said the waitress, who had informed them that her name was Karen and that she was here to help them. The fact that Honour and Kate knew this perfectly well from their numerous previous visits to the hotel restaurant was obviously irrelevant. Her training had programmed her to greet all the clients in this way and nothing was going to alter it – even the fact that Kate now said 'Hi, Karen' before she had a chance to spout her lines.

'No fries,' emphasized Kate.

'But the meal comes with fries,' said Karen, a note of despair creeping into her southern drawl.

'Could you ask the chef to leave them off?'

Karen looked nonplussed. Her programming hadn't taught her how to deal with a customer who didn't want fries. Didn't everyone eat fries?

'I don't know.' But the customer was always right. She smiled and made the big decision. 'Heck, I'll try.'

Kate suppressed a smile. Honour and Andreas made their selections and Karen, still looking worried, withdrew.

'So what is it like to fly the Citation?' asked Andreas.

'Wonderful. Fantastic. And so fast. I can't get over the speed of the thing. After the Cessna 150 it's like the difference between riding a moped and driving a racing car.'

'But you've never ridden a moped,' interjected Honour.

'I can imagine, though.'

'So you are enjoying it?'

'It's brilliant. A lot of what I've been doing is revision, but no less important for all that. I seem to be getting on OK. All being well I should qualify by the end of next week.'

'That's great.' Andreas and Kate discussed the finer points of the flying course for a while.

'And have you had time to see many of the sights, when you haven't been flying?'

'We've been to Disneyland – where else? – but I think Edward was more bemused than enthralled.'

'Perhaps a bit too young.'

'I think so. But we enjoyed the Everglades, and Mummy persuaded me to go to Charleston. That was nice but dreadfully hot. How the Southern belles coped with corsets and bustles in the old days beats me.'

'They bred them tough in those days.'

'They must have done.'

Their meal arrived, brought by Karen, who still looked worried about Kate's lack of fries. For her part Kate was thankful she'd resisted the temptation of chips, as the oval platter was heaped with massive prawns and she doubted that she would be able to manage them all. Silence fell as the three of them tackled their various gastronomic challenges.

Eventually, sated, Kate pushed her plate away.

'That's it, I'm stuffed.' Then she failed to completely suppress a burp.

'Kate!'

Andreas smiled indulgently. 'I like to see a woman with a healthy appetite. So often young girls these days eat nothing but salad and crispbread. Will you be able to manage some pudding?'

'If I let the prawns go down for a minute or two I may be able to.' Kate had a sip of wine. 'So come on, tell me, you didn't really come all the way out to Florida to make sure I wasn't flunking the flying?'

'Not entirely. I have some business associates in Miami I needed to see, and while I was in the area . . .'

'Are they in the hotel business too?'

Andreas looked suddenly uncomfortable. 'Why do you ask?' he said, sharply.

'Forget it.' Kate felt hurt. God, it was only small talk. His associates could be Mafia for all she cared. A faintly awkward silence fell.

Honour, with her impeccable social skills, stepped in. 'When are you planning to return to the UK?'

Andreas's frown cleared. He smiled at Honour. 'Tomorrow night. It will be good when I have Kate to fly me and I am not bound by the timetables of the commercial airlines.'

'But surely there are dozens of direct flights to choose from each day?'

Andreas shrugged. 'Look at it as the difference between taking your own car to the shops and going on the bus. Which would you rather do?'

Kate couldn't help a slight smile. She didn't think her mother had ever taken the bus anywhere, let alone to the shops.

As Kate had predicted, she passed the course at the end of the following week and received her FAA licence. To celebrate they flew, courtesy of American Airlines, to New York for a shopping spree before returning to the UK. Honour, who had become noticeably less paranoid about America, its crime rate and its drug culture, unbent so much that she admitted that she found Fifth Avenue almost as good as Knightsbridge,

'If only they didn't all have these terrible American accents.'

By the time they had returned to Windsor, Edward, despite Kate's best efforts, had got into some bad habits. His sleep pattern had been disrupted by jetlag, he had developed an addiction for the TV and refused to eat his meals if chips were not included – even breakfast.

'No,' he would say, pushing his cereal away.

'Yes,' Kate would counter, pushing it back. More than once the food ended up on the kitchen floor.

'I've got to get him sorted out before Andreas takes delivery of the plane and I start working properly again,' Kate moaned to Emma one day.

'How's the sleep going?'

'His sleep isn't really the problem; he's naughty at bedtime, but he knows he can't get out of his cot and he does settle down reasonably quickly. No, it's this business with bloody chips. Come on, you're the qualified paediatric nurse, what do you suggest?'

'If he were mine I would refuse all chips and if he doesn't eat let him go hungry. When he's hungry enough he'll eat anything, chips or no chips.'

Kate looked horrified. 'I can't do that.'

'You can. Look, he's perfectly healthy, he's a good weight and size for his age, and this is just a question of his will against yours. It'll only take a few meals, honestly. And think about it: in the long run you'll be doing him a big favour, because otherwise he's going to get fat, and a fat toddler isn't a healthy toddler.'

By the time Edward gave in and ate mince and mash for his lunch with no protest, Kate felt completely wrecked. Three days of tears and tantrums had been exhausting both emotionally and physically, but Emma had been right. Of course it was partly her own fault, she should have spotted earlier that Edward had gone from eating most of his meat and vegetables as well as the chips to just eating the chips. But as they had been eating out so much it had seemed easier to give in than risk having a scene in a restaurant. Big mistake. Still, it was as well she had tackled the problem when she did, because Andreas phoned the next day to say that the jet had been delivered to Farnborough.

'There's a company there that will hangar it, and provide all other basic services. All you have to do is inform them when we want it and where we want to go, and they'll do pretty much everything else.'

'That sounds terrific. I can go with that. So when is my first assignment?'

'I need to get up to Edinburgh tomorrow. I've got a meeting scheduled with some investors for a new leisure and golf complex at midday.'

Kate did some rapid calculations. 'Suppose I try and book a slot for us at nine thirty? That gives us plenty of time to get there, and then for you to get into Edinburgh for your meeting.'

'That sounds fine. And I'll need a car at the other end. Arrange that too please.'

'OK.' Kate wasn't too sure about the car. But his PA would know. She would probably even book it if Kate asked her. 'Fine then. I'll see you at Farnborough at about nine.'

'Till tomorrow. *Ciao.*'

Kate phoned the agents at Farnborough to ask them to have the aircraft ready. A trip to Edinburgh and back would be a great way of acquainting herself with her – oops – Andreas's new toy. Kate was so excited she could hardly sleep that night. She hadn't felt this sort of buzz about flying since she'd been on helicopters. That seemed a lifetime away now, but the reality was that it was not even two years ago. She wondered what Eddie would say if he could see her now. Her excitement popped like a soap bubble as she remembered him, and instead she suddenly felt deep sadness. She did miss him so much; the ache was still there although time had blunted the pain. She wondered if it would ever go away. Even if she moved on, found another man, would Eddie always be in her mind? She tried to be grateful for the little time they had had, but it was difficult not to feel bitter. Bitter and guilty. She should have checked his seat belt, she should have realised he wasn't capable, she should have kept her eyes on the road, she should have driven more slowly ... If only she could go back in time. If only.

Chapter Twenty-Three

When she awoke the next morning some of her excitement had returned. She dressed carefully in a neat trouser suit that she thought would be ideal as an unofficial livery. She hoped Andreas would approve. She'd asked him what he wanted her to wear and all he had said was 'something suitable.' Was this suitable? Probably, but she would have liked a bit more guidance all the same. Having dressed with a care she hadn't exercised since the last time she had been on a parade square, Kate woke Edward and went down to get her breakfast.

'Now, don't you dare splash your cereal today.'

''Day,' repeated Edward with a disarming smile.

'That's right.'

Honour was already in the kitchen sipping a black coffee and perusing the *Telegraph*.

'You look very smart, dear.'

'Thanks. I hope Andreas thinks so too.'

Kate efficiently gave Edward his breakfast, scanned the headlines on the front page of the paper, downed a piece of toast and a cup of coffee and then finally checked her watch.

'Right, it's time to see if all my new technical equipment works.'

'I should hope so dear. I'm sure it must have cost Andreas a fortune.'

Kate nearly said, rather snakily, that she was sure he could afford it, but stopped herself. That wasn't the point; the point was that he had funded an expensive computer, modem and fax machine all to make life easier for her. She lifted Edward out of his high chair and put him on the kitchen floor with a toy while she went into the study and settled herself on the chair facing her new computer. It was the latest in laptops and was immensely powerful considering its diminutive size. She switched it on and clicked on the flight plan program provided by the Jeppesen Company – a firm that, from the early days of aviation until the electronic age, had specialised in air navigation charts but which had now branched out to take advantage of the computer revolution. The program flickered up on to the screen. First she typed in her point of departure, Farnborough, then her destination, Edinburgh, and in a few seconds the program produced the optimum route. So far so good, she thought, as she copied the information on to the relevant section of the official flight plan form. Next she filled in the bits about the aircraft she was going to be flying; the height she wanted to fly at – thirty-three thousand feet; her cruising speed – three hundred and fifty knots or about four hundred miles per hour; the time she wanted to take off and her estimated flight time. That done, she dialled Farnborough's parent air traffic service unit at Heathrow and faxed the flight plan over to them. Kate knew how her plan was then processed, but despite her understanding of it she still found it bizarre, because ultimate approval of the flight plan happened in Brussels. Still, that was computers and the EEC for you, she thought. Having sent her flight plan on its way, she then phoned the parent ATSU to make sure it had gone in OK, and the aircraft's handling agents at Farnborough to make sure that the plane would be ready and refuelled for nine. All she had to hope for now was that the slot she'd asked for would be free and she would be allowed to fly that route at that time. It would be tough if she wasn't, but there would be nothing she could do about it. If there were too many aircraft wanting the same section of sky at the same time, things could get dangerous, so the authorities would control the flow by refusing some aircraft their preferred take-off slot time.

She switched off the little computer, unplugged it and put it back into its carrying case ready to take with her to the airport. She checked her charts, made sure she had all the relevant paperwork and checklists, and then returned to the kitchen to make sandwiches for her lunch and a big thermos of coffee for herself and Andreas to drink en route. The one thing an executive jet lacked was in-flight catering, unless the pilot provided it.

'I'd better be off then,' she said as she screwed the top on to the flask.

'So soon?' said Honour. It had only just turned seven thirty. 'I didn't think you were going until later.'

'Well, I want to check out a few things. And the last thing I want is to make a mess of the first flight in the boss's new toy.' She didn't add that she was longing to take command of the shiny new aircraft. She remembered when she had been about twelve and had gone with her dad to collect his new car; it had been pristine, gleaming and virginal. After a few weeks the novelty and the smell of newness wore off and it had become like every other car, but the memory of those first days with it had stuck. If that had been such a big deal, then what would five million quids' worth of brand spanking new aeroplane be like? She was longing to find out.

She gathered together her flask, her charts and her brief-case, kissed Edward and her mother and set off for the airport. She tuned to the local radio station, ostensibly for the traffic reports but also because she felt she wanted some jolly music to match her mood. She hummed along happily as she drove skilfully along the M3. For once the traffic was moving relatively smoothly and it only took her half an hour before she breezed off the slip road and on to the dual carriageway that led to Farnborough itself. At the gate of the business aviation park she showed her pass and was waved through. She tried to look cool as she swung her car into a parking bay at the offices of the handling agents, but no matter how hard she tried she couldn't wipe the smile off her face.

She opened the door of the office and approached the girl at the reception desk. Her hair was the most unlikely shade of blonde Kate had ever seen and her nails were like long red talons. Kate didn't think she had been recruited for her brains but was prepared to give her the benefit of the doubt.

'Hello,' she said. 'I'm Kate Thomas, Mr Spyrou's pilot.'

'Hello,' said the receptionist with a simpering smile and a voice like Betty Boop. 'My name is Amelia. Mr Spyrou is the owner of the new Citation?'

'Yes.'

'It's being brought round now. Would you like a cup of coffee while you wait?'

'I'd love one. Just milk, please, no sugar.'

'There's a machine over there.'

'Oh.' This wasn't quite what Kate thought she was being offered, but never mind. She fished in her handbag for the right change and the machine clunked and sploshed and eventually produced a cup of piping-hot coffee. Hot and wet, thought Kate, and the right strength. It would do nicely.

'Have you filed your flight plan or would you like us to do it?'

'I did it first thing this morning, thanks. I'm not sure it's been approved though.'

'I'll check for you.' Amelia picked up a pen to press the digits on the keypad of her phone. Obviously with nails as long as hers she couldn't dial in the ordinary way. 'Your requested take-off time is . . .?' she asked as she paused over the last number.

'Nine thirty,' answered Kate.

Amelia's pen hit the last digit and she was through almost instantly. It was obvious from the conversation that it was all OK.

'Yes, that's fine,' she said in unnecessary but polite confirmation to Kate as she replaced the receiver.

'So far so good,' grinned Kate. 'May I make a call? I'd like to ring Mr Spyrou and tell him we can take off on time as planned.' Amelia pushed the phone across so Kate could make her call. She couldn't get Andreas on his home number so she tried his mobile. When she replaced the receiver Amelia simpered at her again.

'Is this your first job with Mr Spyrou?'

'It's my first job in commercial flying full stop.'

Amelia smiled encouragingly. 'You'll be fine. I'm sure you won't have any problems.'

Kate went right off her. Patronising cow, she thought. What would a dimbo-bimbo like this know about flying? She knew as much about aircraft as the girls who hung about the pit lane ogling the Formula One drivers knew about piston engines. But she smiled all the same and said in a saccharine voice, 'I'm not really worried about the flying. That bit is easy. I just

251

don't want to get any of the paperwork wrong, cause a delay and annoy the boss.'

'We can do all that side of things for you if you want,' offered Amelia.

Kate nearly snorted at the use of the word *we*. Amelia didn't look as if she could do joined-up writing, let alone fill in a flight plan. 'I know. But I like to do it myself.' She didn't add that then she would know it had been done properly. She trusted herself but she was never too sure about other people – even professional set-ups like this one might not be quite as meticulous as she would be herself. She could rely on herself to check and double check – other people might not.

A buzzer sounded discreetly on the desk. Amelia pressed a button and a distorted voice crackled noisily, informing them that Golf Alpha Bravo Zulu Yankee was outside on the apron. Kate recognised the registration as that of the new plane. She felt a surge of excitement – like a kid at Christmas. She tried to look really cool, as if she was bored with flying executive jets and this trip was going to be marginally less interesting than a journey on the M25 in the rush hour, but she couldn't stop her mouth from smiling.

'I'll just go and check it over,' she said, trying to sound casual and knowing she was failing.

'OK. Go through the lounge and out of the far door and it should be parked dead ahead.'

Kate wandered through the rather basic waiting area that Amelia had called the lounge and noticed that the pilots weren't offered much in the way of comfort. Being employees of the super-rich or the extremely famous didn't necessarily mean that they merited any consideration. Their bosses could turn up and walk straight on to their planes and not have to set foot in this faintly dreary building, so there was no point in providing any frills. The pilots, chauffeurs and other lackeys who might have to hang around here could make do with plastic chairs, scuffed tiles and dog-eared magazines on scratched tables. As she stepped out of the door on to the airfield, she instantly saw the gleaming new Citation in front of her. Goodness, it was shiny, and so sleek and beautiful. She felt a thrill of excitement knowing that it was hers to fly. Who would have thought that learning to fly gliders would have led to this!

The truck that had towed it over from the hangar was departing, dark fumes belching from the exhaust. Kate hoped they weren't going to leave dirty marks on the sparkling paintwork. She walked slowly towards the plane, savouring the anticipation of actually getting into it and taking control of it. It wasn't a big plane, not even fifty feet long, and except for the tail, not much higher than her head. But the size wasn't important. What counted was its range and performance. She took the key out of her pocket, opened the cabin door and flipped down the little steps. She peered into the cabin. She knew roughly what it would look like – after all she'd spent four weeks in one in the States – but this one was hers, her toy. She corrected herself. It wasn't hers at all; it was Andreas's. She really mustn't forget that. She pushed her charts and briefcase through the door and climbed in. It was fabulous. A pearl-grey carpet covered the floor and the six seats were covered in matching leather. It could take up to eight seats but obviously Andreas wanted the extra leg room. The ceiling of the cabin was quite low, so Kate had to stoop as she pushed her case and other bits and pieces into the storage space by the door.

She checked her watch. She had plenty of time before take off but she wanted to familiarise herself with every aspect of the plane. She jumped out on to the ground and began to check the exterior. Her first task was to remove the blanks from the engines – protective covers inserted into the inlet and outlet vents to prevent birds or other small creature from entering the engines when the plane was left unattended on the ground. These she took back into the cabin and stowed in another storage compartment. Then she began her walk round. She wasn't expecting to find anything wrong but she wasn't going to take any chances. She double checked that there were no chocks under the wheels and that the tow-bar had been removed; she took off the pitot covers and made sure that there were no dents; she checked that the tyres were fine, the oil was OK and the plane looked fit to fly. She took her time; the weather was pleasant, there was no need to hurry and there was no way anything was going to be missed on this inspection. As she finished, she patted the plane on its nose like a jockey making friends with a mount before a race.

'Its beautiful, isn't it?'

Kate spun round. 'Andreas! I wasn't expecting you here for another hour.'

'The traffic was unusually light this morning and anyway, I was keen to get here to see what I got for my money. Have you been inside it?'

'Only to dump my kit. But it's lovely. I adore the colour scheme you chose.'

'Thank you.' Andreas stepped up into the plane. 'Hmmm. Very satisfactory,' he said.

Kate poked her head round the door. 'I shall have to be careful to wipe my feet. This carpet will show every mark.'

'Carpets can be cleaned,' said Andreas casually.

That's the luxury of being filthy rich, thought Kate: not having to give a thought about practical details. Andreas moved around the cabin, opening storage compartments, examining the little loo, trying out the luxurious seats and generally making sure the plane exactly matched the specifications of his order. Kate kept out of his way in the cockpit. At length he appeared satisfied. 'As I'm here early, there are a few calls I would like to make. You finish here and let me know when you're ready to start engines.'

'It won't be long now,' she said.

'Fine.' Andreas disappeared across the apron and back into his Rolls.

In fact Kate had nothing much left to do now except wait for their allotted slot. She killed the time by scanning the manuals and bumf that had been delivered along with the plane. But she couldn't concentrate, and every few minutes she glanced at her watch, willing the hands to move faster so she could be off.

At last it was time. She walked swiftly back to the car and caught the eye of Mark, the chauffeur. She gave him the thumbs-up and saw him turn and say a few words to Andreas. Her excitement that the moment for departure had arrived was infectious, as Andreas thrust his mobile and his papers into his case, snapped it shut and was by her side in seconds.

'Let's go then,' he said.

Once inside, Kate shut the cabin door and settled herself in the cockpit. Then she reached forward and flicked on the battery master switch. Instantly a whole array of warning lights lit up, telling her about all the things that weren't working. But this was normal – without the engines running, naturally nothing was working yet. She checked that amongst these lights the ones indicating that the exterior storage area was not locked and that the cabin door was not properly shut weren't on, then she switched the radio to get permission to start engines.

'Hello, Farnborough tower, this is Golf Alpha Bravo Zulu Yankee, request start.'

'Golf Alpha Bravo Zulu Yankee, this is Farnborough tower. Start approved. Temperature is twenty-one degrees.' The air temperature was important because it could affect the engines. On a balmy early summer's day such as this it wouldn't be a problem, but procedures demanded that this information be given out as standard, regardless of prevailing conditions.

Kate acknowledged. 'Zulu Yankee, roger,' then turned her attention to the control panel. She ran through her pre-start checks to make sure all the switches were set correctly, that there was sufficient fuel and that everything was ready to go. Then she pressed the button to get the first of the little aircraft's two jet engines running. The starter whizzed round in the turbine of the engine. Once it hit the right speed, she put the fuel in. *Whoosh.* The plane began to judder slightly. Number one engine was going. She made sure the oil pressure was rising, the generator was coming on line and everything looked as if it was behaving normally, then she did the same with the second engine. As both engines spooled up so the warning lights began to go out. It was all going exactly as it had on her training course and as per the textbook. She set her radios and navigation equipment, and checked the oxygen – 'In the unlikely event of an emergency . . .' she said to herself, mimicking the patter of countless airline stewardesses – and that was it.

'Farnborough tower, this is Golf Alpha Bravo Zulu Yankee, request taxi.'

'Golf Alpha Bravo Zulu Yankee, taxi to runway two five. The QNH is one zero one three.' Kate logged the number and set her altimeter. This then showed her how high the airfield, and thus also her aircraft, was above sea level.

She switched on the taxi lights, released the brake, eased on a little power and the aircraft began to move forward smoothly. As they progressed around the taxiway she checked that the brakes worked, that the instruments recorded the correct change of direction as she turned corners, and that the gyros were working. She looked out of the windows to make sure that the rubber de-icing boots on the leading edge of the wings inflated properly when she pressed the appropriate button. They did, and, just as importantly, retracted again. She set the flaps for take-off. The radio burst into life.

'Golf Alpha Bravo Zulu Yankee, are you ready to copy your clearance?'

Kate had a notebook and pen ready for this message.

'Ready to copy.'

'London clears Golf Alpha Bravo Zulu Yankee for Edinburgh. Initially maintain runway heading, climbing to two thousand feet, then turn right towards Luton climbing altitude four thousand feet.' Kate copied down the details as they were read out to her. 'Contact London when advised on one three four decimal one two. Squawk five four one two.' As the tower finished giving her the essential details of her clearance, she read them back, more or less word for word.

'Read-back correct. Call ready for departure,' responded the tower. By this time she'd reached the holding point. She set on her transponder her squawk frequency of five four one two so that this number would appear above the blip that represented her aircraft on the radar screen. In this way the air traffic controllers would know where she was amongst all the other jet-propelled lumps of metal flying around the sky – a comforting thought. Ahead of her lay the giant piano keys at the threshold of the runway. This was it; this was the moment.

'Farnborough tower, this is Golf Alpha Bravo Zulu Yankee, ready for departure.' She checked her watch. Bang on nine thirty.

'Zulu Yankee clear take-off. The wind is two four zero, fifteen.' Kate automatically translated this into direction and strength – a light south-westerly breeze, so nothing to worry about.

She pushed the throttles forward and almost instantly the plane responded, leaping forward up the runway like a horse coming out of the starting gates at a big race. She knew what to expect, but this time it felt different. This was her plane to fly – hers exclusively. She was in command. This was no course, there was no instructor; it wasn't a training flight or an exercise. This was the real thing. She'd joined the élite world of being a commercial pilot.

The journey to Edinburgh couldn't have been smoother. As she progressed, she was handed over from one set of controllers to another, each time squawking her identification so they could see where she was on the screen. After forty-five minutes she began her descent into Edinburgh, and fifteen minutes later she was taxiing towards the terminal and her allotted parking space on the apron.

'They've sent a car,' she called back to Andreas. 'They promised they would, but never having met the agents at this end I wasn't sure how reliable they'd be.'

'I'm sure they're always very reliable.'

Kate was pretty certain of this too. As a general rule, the sort of people who flew around in their own executive jets wouldn't take kindly to being mucked about or let down and would have the clout, the money and the lawyers to make it very uncomfortable for those who failed to provide top-notch service.

Andreas unbuckled his seat belt and leaned forward into the tiny cockpit as Kate switched everything off and shut down the engines.

'That was remarkably smooth. My faith in you has obviously been justified.' Kate found herself swelling with pride. She knew she had flown well, but it was lovely to have it acknowledged. 'What are you doing about lunch?'

'Oh, don't worry. I've packed some sandwiches.'

'Don't be ridiculous. I can't possibly expect you to stay here with just some bread for lunch while I go off into Edinburgh.'

'But you've got a business meeting.'

'Yes, but it won't take that long. If you can find something to amuse yourself for an hour or two, I'll make sure you get a proper meal before we return.'

'Well, if you're sure. Thank you.' Kate remembered something. 'Talking of our return, what time do you want to leave? I need to file a flight plan.'

'Will it take long?'

'Just a few minutes.'

'Make it three thirty.'

Kate gathered her laptop from where she'd stowed it, and sitting at one of the tables in the cabin she quickly got the program to tell her the best route back to Farnborough and filled out the form as before.

'I'll hand this to the handling agents as we go past. They can fax it through for me. OK, that's it. If you want to leave, I'll lock up.'

Once the plane was secured and Kate had dispatched her form, they got into the shiny black Mercedes that was waiting for them and were driven swiftly and smoothly into the centre of Edinburgh. Andreas's meeting was in a large house set in a smart square just behind Princes Street. With the shops of Edinburgh's main thoroughfare beckoning, Kate didn't think she'd have the least problem killing any amount of time.

'I'll meet you back here at one thirty,' said Andreas as they parted on the steps of the imposing Georgian house.

'One thirty,' acknowledged Kate as she sped off down the road, heading for some serious shopping.

It was with more and more desperation that Kate searched through her handbag in the first shop, trying to find her little black wallet containing her credit cards, cheque cards, loyalty cards, store cards – everything that made shopping possible. As the queue of customers behind her began to tut and shuffle in impatience she tipped everything – purse, pens, keys, tampax, hanky, old receipts, lipstick, the lot – on to the counter. No wallet.

'Bugger,' swore Kate through her clenched teeth. 'I'm sorry,' she said to the shop assistant. 'I've left my banker's card at home.'

'Well, if you like, I could put these things to one side if you want to go back and get it.'

Kate smiled ruefully. She didn't think it was worth explaining why this simply wasn't possible. 'Thanks, but it's best I leave it for another day.'

'As you please.'

Kate scooped her ramshackle possessions into her bag and cleared out of the way of the solvent customers. So now what?

She had never been a great one for window-shopping. Either she wanted to buy stuff or she didn't. There didn't seem to be much point in just looking at things. She thought about going for a walk, but it was hot and the idea of tramping crowded streets aimlessly didn't appeal. She got out her purse and checked how much cash she actually had on her – a shade under seven pounds. What she wanted was a long cold drink or an ice-cream, and something to pass the time. She decided to go to the big bookshop next door and use the small amount of cash she had to buy a book, then she would find some refreshment and somewhere pleasant where she could sit and while away the time. There were a dozen books that Kate had been promising herself for some time that she should read, so making her choice was tricky. Her intelligence told her that she ought to pick something of literary worth that would improve her mind, but in the end she plumped for something which looked light and frothy and promised lots of laughs. Her change afforded her just enough for an ice-lolly from a street vendor, and thus equipped she made her way back to the shady square to wait for her lunch date. She spotted a bench in the cool gloom beneath a giant lime tree from where she could keep an eye on the front door of the house where Andreas was conducting his business. Eagerly Kate gave herself up to the dual sybaritic delights of licking the cold sweetness of her ice-lolly and immersing herself in the book.

The book didn't live up to expectations. The shout lines on the cover that had promised so much appeared, after Kate had trudged through the first chapter, to have been written by someone who hadn't read a word of it. She finished her lolly and flicked through the pages of the next chapter in the hope that the author had just got off to a bad start. Apparently not. She threw the book down beside her on the warm wooden slats, yawned and prepared to give in to the heat of the day. She leaned back and let her mind drift as she gazed up through the green, gold and blue of the skyscape above her. The buzz and hum of the city faded, she stopped noticing the clack of shoes on the pavement, even the song of a nearby blackbird went unheard. Her eyes closed . . .

A sudden burst of voices awoke her. With a start Kate opened her eyes and guiltily looked at her watch. She hadn't meant to drop off. Was she late? She had a horror of unpunctuality. Thank goodness for that. It was only one twenty-five. Her eyes turned towards the voices. A group of about five men, all dressed smartly in dark suits, were standing outside the door of the house Andreas had entered. They were talking animatedly but Kate couldn't catch a word of it, as whatever language they were using wasn't English. Kate couldn't tell what it was. She'd only done French till she was sixteen and she hadn't been brilliant at it. Flying was one thing; speaking foreign languages was something else. And as they talked, they all kept looking over their shoulders as if they were on the look-out for something. Andreas appeared at the door and shook each man in turn by the hand. As he did so, the bright sunlight made their flashy signet rings and bracelets sparkle. Kate thought with a giggle that they all looked like a bunch of Hollywood gangsters. The word *hoods* sprang to mind. The fact that most of them were wearing sunglasses only made them look even more suspicious, although given the fact that the sun was blazing down, there was no reason why they shouldn't. They were probably perfectly respectable businessmen, but for all that, for some reason, they looked slightly shady. A couple of them walked off into town, another hailed a taxi and two others drove off in a smart car parked in the square. Andreas didn't see Kate and returned into the building.

As the men disappeared, Kate thought that they didn't look at all like the sort of people who would be interested in funding a leisure complex. Not that she had ever met anyone who made those sorts of investments, but this lot just didn't look the part at all. More like spivs or second-hand car dealers. There was something a bit too sharp about all of them; sharp, and also slightly furtive in the way they had been constantly checking behind them.

The square regained its tranquillity and Kate checked her watch. The limo should be returning soon. Right on the dot of one thirty, it rolled to a stop outside the building. Kate gathered together her few things and arrived by the bonnet of the car just as Andreas emerged.

'Perfect timing,' he said as he opened the door of the car for her. 'How was your shopping spree?'

'Oh, I didn't see anything that really caught my eye.' She wasn't going to admit to being an idiot.

Andreas gave the driver the name of a restaurant and they moved off. Judging by his expression and the tone of his voice he seemed in a good mood.

'Did you have a good meeting?' asked Kate conversationally.

Instantly Andreas's face darkened.

'No,' he snarled.

'Sorry,' mumbled Kate. She felt crushed. It wasn't her fault if things hadn't gone his way. What did she care about his meetings and wheelings and dealings as long as he had enough money to keep the Citation in the air? There was no need for him to take it out on her. Then as suddenly as he had snapped at her, Andreas's mood changed again.

'I'm sorry,' he apologised, giving her one of his devastating smiles. 'I shouldn't have been so rude.' But despite the apology, Kate wasn't going to ask any more questions, and she certainly wasn't going to mention his dubious-looking friends, although her natural feminine curiosity was urging her to find out who they had been. They really couldn't be as shady as they looked, could they?

Chapter Twenty-Four

All through the meal Kate found her mind wandering. Between snippets of conversation her thoughts kept going back to the two things that concerned her: one was Andreas's motive for entertaining her to lunch, because when all was said and done, she was just an employee; and the other was the odd people that he seemed to be associating with. Kate supposed that his attention to her welfare could, at a pinch, be put down to old-fashioned chivalry, but somehow it didn't quite ring true. He didn't look after his chauffeur in the same way. Kate had often seen Mark making do with a snack in a car park while Andreas had a solitary but sustaining meal courtesy of one of his hotel restaurants. The fact that he was now entertaining her to lunch seemed smack of wanting to win her over, to gain her approval for some reason; the same with his interest in her past, the flying lessons, the toys for Edward, his championing her in the showdown with Magda. But why? It wasn't just because she was a pretty girl. He hadn't done this for any of the other young women in his employ. In the short time that she had spent as head of personnel, she made it her business to check out all the other female staff to see if any had come even close to her in the receipt of favours. And no one had. So why her? Kate had sufficient self-knowledge to realise that she was pretty but not stunning; that she was bright but not a genius; that she was a good and loyal employee but then so were most of the people who worked for Andreas; and that all in all she really didn't merit this treatment. It could be that he wanted more from her than her flying skills, but if that was the case he was being extraordinarily patient. He'd been paying her serious amounts of attention for well over six months and hadn't even attempted to hold her hand. Perhaps he didn't want to. Perhaps he didn't find her attractive. But then why *was* he paying her all this attention? Kate felt bemused. She didn't think she'd mind if he didn't proposition her but she really did want to know where she stood. *What* a mystery. And what about the other mystery – those odd men Andreas had been consorting with? Most peculiar! Working as she had in the London office for the weeks before she'd decided it would make no difference if she worked from Runnymede, she had come across a number of his associates and they had all looked like perfectly normal businessmen: grey men in grey suits, and not a medallion or a diamond ring between them. So what did this lot do? Andreas had said that they were investors in a leisure and golf complex, but Kate couldn't imagine anyone wanting to trust that crew with anything involving money. There was no way she could quiz Andreas about them, though. She wasn't going to risk another outburst of anger. In fact, she thought, she didn't think she would even mention that she had set eyes on them.

She was suddenly aware that Andreas was staring at her oddly. He didn't look best pleased.

'You haven't listened to a word I've been saying.'

Kate blushed guiltily. No, she hadn't. She'd been miles away and she could hardly tell Andreas what was on her mind. She thought fast.

'I'm so sorry. I was reliving the flight up here. I can still hardly believe that I'm a proper commercial pilot.'

Andreas's face softened. 'What a big kid you are with your new toy.'

'It isn't my toy,' protested Kate.

'No?' Andreas was smiling indulgently.

Kate shook her head. 'I won't forget that it's yours.' He really was a nice man, she thought, and then immediately felt a surge of guilt that she had been having such unforgivable thoughts about his motives, his friends and possibly even his business practices. To cover her shame she looked at her watch. Time was getting on.

'How about a coffee?' offered Andreas.

'I think we need to keep an eye on the time,' she reminded him. 'We don't want to miss our slot.'

'Let's go then. I didn't really want coffee.' He paid the bill and escorted her to the car. As they returned to the airport Kate had to remind herself that she was actually getting paid for this – flying, riding round in a shiny Merc, and an expensive lunch in a swanky restaurant. Life really couldn't be much sweeter than this, she decided, so to hell with Andreas's motives. She had probably got him all wrong. Perhaps he was nice to her out of the goodness of his heart, he wanted nothing more than her happiness and his meeting had been with a group of men who were Methodist lay-preachers in their spare time.

The journey back to Farnborough was completely uneventful; the weather was clear, air traffic control gave her a straight run into the airport and they arrived bang on schedule.

'I should have invested in this years ago,' said Andreas as they parked on the apron. 'Talk about hassle-free flying! This is so much easier than all the fuss of Heathrow. Just walk on and walk off, no check-in, no crowds, brilliant.'

'I'm glad you think so,' said Kate with a smile. 'It would be an expensive mistake if you didn't.'

Andreas's Rolls was parked by the handling agent's office, and as he had another meeting that day in London he headed off leaving Kate to finish tidying up the aircraft. She made sure everything was shipshape, filled in her logbook, collected her bits and pieces and locked up. When she walked into the offices by the apron, Amelia was still sitting looking vacuous behind the reception desk and a couple of what Kate took to be drivers waiting for their employers were hanging around in the lounge reading magazines. The front door banged open and a young man in a Customs and Excise uniform hurried in.

'Hi, Martin,' purred Amelia. Kate was amused. Did she greet all men using this pussycat voice, or was Martin something special? She certainly hadn't used it on Kate, but then somehow Kate didn't think she was Amelia's type. She had to admit, though, that if Amelia fancied Martin, her taste was pretty good. This bloke was a hunk. Tall, square-jawed, tanned – the sort of man who could play the part of James Bond and look absolutely right.

'Hi, Amelia. Has the flight from Amsterdam landed yet?'

'No. They're not due in for another ten minutes.'

'Good. When I saw that Citation coming in I thought I'd missed it.'

'That was mine, and I don't think it's worth your while checking it,' said Kate, easing her way into the conversation and noting with glee Amelia's filthy look. 'We've only been to Edinburgh and back today.'

Martin turned and noticed Kate for the first time. Kate could see approval written all over his face.

'Well, unless Scotland had broken away from the rest of the UK since yesterday, I think I can dispense with the formalities.' He stuck out his hand. 'Martin Brayfield, Customs.'

Kate took it. 'Kate Thomas, Citation pilot.'

'Pilot, eh?' He looked suitably impressed. It wasn't often he met pilots as tasty as Kate. 'Who do you fly for?'

'Andreas Spyrou.'

'Is he the hotel magnate?'

'One and the same.' Kate noticed smugly that Amelia was irritatedly tapping her fingernails on the reception desk. Obviously she didn't like a bit of competition.

'No doubt we'll run across each other again. Presumably you go abroad for him fairly regularly?'

'I imagine so, but I really have no idea at the moment. I only started today.'

'Nice to meet you.'

'And you.' Kate went on her way. Nice bloke, she thought, and then forgot about him.

'How was your first trip then?' asked Maria eagerly on the phone that evening.

'It was OK, actually,' said Kate, trying to sound cool and blasé.

'I bet it was better than that,' said Maria, refusing to be taken in by Kate's tone.

'OK,' conceded Kate. 'It *was* better than that. It's hard to believe that he actually pays me to do it. I shan't tell him, but I would almost do it for free.'

'We're still talking about flying here,' said Maria wickedly.

'Maria! I've told you before, it's not like that.'

265

'But you wouldn't mind if it was?' Maria said it as a throw-away remark, but even so Kate didn't want to get into this discussion. She didn't know the answer herself and she wanted to come to a conclusion on her own and not be swayed, one way or the other, by Maria's opinion.

'I'm not looking for a relationship, Maria. Eddie's only been dead for eighteen months and I'm not ready to move on yet.'

'But one day . . .?'

'We'll see when "one day" comes, but it's pretty unlikely. Not many men want a girlfriend who comes complete with a ready-made family.'

'Hmmm,' said Maria in apparent agreement. Kate stayed silent, thinking to herself, *ain't that the truth*?

'So tell me all about it,' said Maria realising that her agreement had been less than tactful. 'I want to hear every detail.'

Kate related every moment, from the feeling on take-off to what she'd had for pudding at the restaurant.

'Go back a bit,' said Maria. 'Tell me more about the gangsters.'

'I'm sure they weren't' said Kate with a laugh. 'You know me, never one to spoil a good story for want of a bit of exaggeration.'

'But you did think they looked odd.'

'Only because they were wearing sunglasses. And let's face it, with the weather we enjoyed today, everyone was wearing shades.'

'But wouldn't it be exciting if you discovered you were really working for Mr Big?'

'I haven't checked him out in that department,' replied Kate, sounding absolutely serious, before she and Maria dissolved into helpless smutty giggles.

Kate had never been happier. Every day was a joy and she constantly found it hard to believe that she was actually being paid for doing what she herself had had to pay to do in the past. There were a few drawbacks: boredom could be a problem once she had landed, but she always made sure she was armed with a couple of good books; and her social life had gone to pot because she never knew when Andreas would phone up and ask her to fly him somewhere. Mostly they did short hops – over to France or Spain – and came back the same day, which suited Kate down to the ground because she didn't like to be away from Edward for too long. Honour had calmed down on the subject of his care, as Kate was home most evenings to take over, thus allowing her to go to her bridge club. It seemed that as long as she could see her cronies at bridge she would tolerate giving up some of her other social engagements. On the few occasions when Honour and Kate couldn't sort things out between them, there was the nineteen-year-old daughter of a neighbour whose gap year arrangements had fallen through and who was only too pleased to earn a bit of pin money now and again.

Kate didn't always fly just Andreas. Quite often he asked her to ferry friends and clients about, and on occasion she was asked to act as a courier for bundles of documents or parcels of supplies of specialist equipment that hotels overseas couldn't acquire locally. But even so she still only had to work a few days a week on average, and the work could hardly be described as arduous. OK, she was really little more than a glorified chauffeur, and meals in some smart restaurant, after that first occasion, weren't part of the deal, so a large portion of her diet was now sandwiches and coffee. But on the plus side, whenever they did have to stay away overnight, Andreas always made sure she had a first-class hotel room and insisted that whatever she wanted in the way of food and drink was on the house.

Quite often, in moments of boredom, Kate still wondered about the nature of her relationship with Andreas. It certainly hadn't become any easier to fathom. In the beginning there had been his very overt interest in her flying, his incredible encouragement to get her back into the air again and his apparent display of favouritism. Then there had been his attentiveness when she'd been out in the States, and little peculiarities like buying the huge teddy for Edward and taking her out for lunch when they'd flown to Edinburgh for the first time. But that was over a year ago now and since then he'd had virtually nothing to do with her. To begin with she hadn't really noticed – their paths still crossed, they still talked – but then she realised that when he spoke to her it was nearly always just to tell her where he wanted her to fly to, and when they were on board together he seemed almost to ignore her. The special attention that she had enjoyed in the first few months of their working relationship no longer seemed to exist; the meals, the presents, the compliments seemed to be things of the past. Kate decided that she had to be realistic about this. Right at the start, when Maria had been suggesting that there was more to Andreas's intentions than business, Kate had said that people with Andreas's wealth didn't marry girls like her. Being a pragmatist, she knew that this just proved she'd been right all along, but she couldn't help feeling a tiny bit disappointed all the same – there was no denying his good looks and charm, and it had been immensely flattering to think that he might have fancied her once.

As the months passed and Kate clocked up the flying hours, she thought less and less about what might have been between her and Andreas. Much to Maria's disgust, relationships slipped further and further down her list of priorities.

'You'll turn into a bitter and twisted old crone,' she told Kate.

'Thanks for the vote of confidence,' replied Kate, not the least bit put out. 'And less of the old. I'm only twenty-seven.'

'But you ought to be meeting loads of glamorous people in your line of work.'

'I wish. It seems that most of the men I fly are fat, balding bankers—'

'Sorry, that was *bankers* you said?'

'Bankers,' emphasized Kate. 'Or else they're people in the holiday business who seem to be all fake tans, fake jewellery and fake sincerity.'

'Ugh,' shuddered Maria with feeling.

'Precisely.'

'But what about the other pilots?'

'On the way up and arrogant, or on the way down and past it,' summed up Kate.

'No hope then.'

'None at all.'

Kate told herself she didn't mind – after all, she lived for flying – but her bed at night seemed dreadfully big, and just occasionally it would have been nice to have someone to snuggle up next to. And besides, Edward was rapidly turning from a toddler into a little boy and she worried about him not having a man to look up to. Perhaps she should start to think about finding someone, but where?

It was the autumn when Andreas phoned and asked her to take him to Cyprus. He gave her the dates he wanted to fly out and return – he would be there for over a week.

'Is this going to cause you any problems?' he asked.

'I don't think so.' But Kate could never be completely sure how her mother would react.

'Don't you worry about me,' said Honour huffily when Kate broke the news. 'Edward and I will manage fine. You just go off and leave us.'

'This isn't my idea. It goes with the job. And think of all those times when I've been free. Last week I only worked two days.' But Honour was in a sulk and wasn't to be placated. God, she was so unreasonable.

'We could always ask Gilly from next door if she could stay that week. She always seems to need the money.'

'And I'd have to put up with her taste in music. No thank you.'

'It was just an idea.'

'Well, I'd rather manage without her.'

'What about your bridge evenings?'

'I've missed them before.'

Kate didn't pursue the matter. Honour was working herself up into a temper and Kate knew that whatever she suggested would just make matters worse.

She was still pretty frosty a week later when Kate set off for Farnborough and then Cyprus.

'I promise I'll ring when I get there,' she said.

'I don't want you putting yourself out. I'm sure you will have dozens of duties once you are there.'

Kate doubted this. As far as she could see, once there she would have nothing whatsoever to do until the return journey. Andreas certainly hadn't mentioned anything. It was such a crying shame Edward couldn't come along too –he'd love the sunshine and the sea – but, considering she was just the pilot, Edward tagging along was completely out of the question.

The flight was a doddle. They left Farnborough in foul

conditions: cold, wet and windy. Shortly after they crossed the coast and she was handed over to Paris air traffic control, the weather began to improve. As she flew south it got progressively better until, over the Alps, the clouds finally disappeared altogether and the crystal-clear air meant the view was spectacular. She called Andreas forward for him to admire it too.

'I shouldn't have any problems finding Cyprus,' she said. 'We'll be able to see it from miles away.'

'It is such a beautiful island. Call me again when it comes into view.'

'You must miss living there very much,' said Kate.

'After 1974 life there was spoiled forever,' said Andreas bitterly. 'Everything changed once the Turks invaded. We lost everything: friends, home, business, the lot. You have no idea what it was like.'

'It must have been terrible.'

Andreas nodded. 'It was.' He returned to the cabin and his papers.

From thirty-two thousand feet Cyprus was clearly visible from miles away. The dark green of the pine-clad Troodos Mountains contrasted with the neat patterns of emerald orange groves and the dusty khaki of the grassland, not yet refreshed by the winter rains, which had yet to begin. The whole was fringed with white beaches and a startlingly blue sea. Andreas came forward again just as Nicosia control gave her instructions for starting her descent into Larnaca. Beneath them Kate could see the towns of Paphos and then Limassol, and she could also pick out the runway of RAF Akrotiri. It seemed a lifetime since she had flown out there to visit Maria although in reality it had only been a few years. The southern coast of Cyprus slipped beneath them with the details getting progressively clearer as Kate headed to Larnaca, losing height all the time. Ahead of her was the airport and just beyond it Larnaca itself. Just east of the town, further round the bay, Kate could see the neat rows of houses that constituted the quarters of Dhekelia Garrison. Goodness, it was going to be fun to have a spell out here again. She knew she wouldn't know anyone on the island but it would be lovely to return to some of the tavernas and beaches where she and Maria had had such good

270

times. She made herself concentrate as she began her landing procedure and her plane was brought in on a safe glide path by Larnaca's instrument landing system. Easy-peasy, she thought as she slid down the imaginary slope that led to the runway threshold; then a thump and they were down. A few seconds later she was directed off runway two-two and on to the taxiway. On one side she could see Tekke Monastery on the edge of a salt lake; and on the other side was the sea. Five minutes later she was standing at the open door of the little jet, breathing the same smell of citrus groves, warm tarmac and aviation fuel that she had smelt at Akrotiri on her holiday with Maria. She inhaled deeply. Oh, it was good to be away from the autumnal gloom of Britain and here in the glorious bright sunshine of the Mediterranean. She flicked down the steps and stood back to allow Andreas to descend. She could see a small car approaching across the tarmac – customs, she suspected.

The questioning was routine – they had nothing to declare – and in a couple of minutes the car sped off again and a large limo pulled up in its place. The driver collected their luggage and placed it carefully in the boot before ferrying the two of them to the handling agent's offices beside the main terminal building. There, an immigration official checked their passports and Kate made arrangements for the plane to be hangared and generally looked after for the next few days.

As they drove away from the airport, Andreas gave the driver some rapid instructions in Greek. Instead of taking the direct route round the back of the town, he had directed the driver to go along the sea front. Despite the fact that it was mid-autumn, the main palm-fringed road that ran along between the beach and the town was crowded with tourists seeking some late sunshine. The shiny car drew to a halt outside a tiny and rather unprepossessing restaurant.

'There, that was my family's first step up the ladder back to achieving some self-respect,' said Andreas.

'You mean you used to own this place?'

'My father did, yes. After three years in the refugee camp, and with him and my mother working every hour God sent, they finally had enough to be able to afford the down payment on this place. In those days, Larnaca wasn't much of a resort – nowhere at this end of the island was. All the hotels were in

271

Kyrenia, Nicosia and Famagusta, so the land around here was still relatively cheap.'

'You say your parents worked hard to raise the money for this; what did they do?'

'My mother was a cleaner for some British army officers' wives. They liked her because she could speak English. Of course she could – she had run a beautiful hotel for international tourists for twenty years.' His voice was harsh with bitterness as he spoke. 'And my father was employed driving a lorry for a fruit exporter. They hated it; they were proud people,' he said simply.

'It must have been a terrible time.' Kate was at a loss to know what else to say.

Andreas flashed an unexpected smile at her. 'Well, at least it taught me never to take anything for granted.'

'So how did you get from owning one little taverna to being a multi-millionaire?'

'Hard work; and of course a little bit of luck.'

'Tell me.'

'It's a long story. Some other time perhaps.' His smile disappeared and his expression hardened.

Kate, remembering past, unaccountable flare-ups if she showed too much curiosity, decided to let the matter rest. Still, how wonderful. A real rags-to-riches story. What a man!

As they drove eastwards out of the town and towards the resort of Ayia Napa where they would be staying, Andreas pointed out to Kate the site of the refugee camp he had lived in twenty years previously. There was nothing to see now except offices and houses, but he explained to her how squalid and depressing it had been when the refugees had first arrived with nothing but what they had been able to carry.

'I was seventeen when we finally got out of the hovel we called a home. I swore then that I would never have to live in such conditions again.'

They drove in silence along roads familiar to Kate, through the Eastern Sovereign Base Area and out through the rich potato fields, citrus orchards and olive groves to the coast just west of Cape Greco.

'Of course, most of the land you see around you didn't exist like this when the Greek Cypriots were forced out of the north,' said Andreas. 'Most of this soil was imported from Egypt. This land is really quite barren – just rock until we Greeks took it in hand.'

'I didn't know that.' Kate was astounded. As far as the eye could see were fields of rich red soil and lush greenery.

'We Greeks know about civilising places. Remember, we created civilisation.'

Again Kate decided that discretion was a good strategy. She wasn't quite sure if the Egyptians or the Italians would be inclined to agree, and she wasn't certain enough of her history to make an argument of it in any case. But either way, if what Andreas said was accurate, it showed remarkable diligence and enterprise to make an oasis out of what apparently had been a desert until necessity had forced such an undertaking.

'It was the same with the resorts all the tourists flock to now. When the Greek Cypriots lost everything in Kyrenia and Famagusta, we took a deep breath and rebuilt our businesses elsewhere.'

'Which was what your family did.'

'Absolutely.'

The weather was pleasantly warm and Kate felt none of the discomfort that she had on her first visit to the island, which was not surprising considering how it was late in the year. She commented on this to Andreas.

'The evenings will be too cold to sit out, but the days will be warm and so will the sea, although at this time of year we may get the odd shower. What will you do while I am working?' asked Andreas.

'Swim, walk, sightsee and generally laze about. There are a few places that I'd like to get to that I remember from last time, and on my previous visit I did very little to learn about the ancient culture of the island.'

'Well you must rectify that,' said Andreas in mock horror. 'If nothing else, part of your own history is connected with ours – Richard the Lionheart and Berengaria.'

'I know. I have promised myself that this time I won't be such a complete philistine.'

They were drawing close to the large resort where the original Spyrou hotel had been founded. Kate had been to this bay before but had no recollection of what the hotel had looked like. She didn't think it would be a good idea to admit this to her boss, though. Best to let him think it had been so magnificent that it had formed an indelible impression in her mind. When she did see it – Andreas excitedly pointing it out to her – she wasn't in the least bit surprised that she didn't remember it. It was the smallest hotel in the resort, certainly not half as big or imposing as the new one at Runnymede. In fact, if she was quite honest with herself, it was rather insignificant. But then she reprimanded herself. She was forgetting that this hotel must have represented a magnificent achievement for a family that had lost everything and who had had to start again from the very bottom. No wonder Andreas was proud of it. Who wouldn't be?

The car drew up at the entrance and an elderly flunkey immediately rushed forward and shook Andreas's hand effusively. Despite his years he seemed all arms and legs with enormous hands and feet tacked on so he resembled some outlandish cartoon character.

'This is Yannis,' explained Andreas. 'He has been in our employ since we opened this hotel.'

Yannis was introduced to Kate. He took her hand in one of his massive paws and shook it with so much vigour that Kate wondered if any permanent damage would be done to her shoulder and her elbow.

'Welcome, welcome, welcome, Mrs Thomas.' His smile, as huge as his extremities, split his face. 'If you need anything, anything at all, please, just ask Yannis. It will be my privilege to look after you.'

'Thank you, thank you very much.' Kate was lost for words. She'd never been greeted with such enthusiasm in her life before. She gazed about her. The hotel might have been unimpressive from the outside but inside it was beautiful, with cool marble floors, white leather sofas and expensive-looking oriental rugs. Kate didn't think that this was the sort of hotel for the lager-lout end of the market.

Yannis organised their bags from the car, and he and a porter and the manager of the hotel, who had been waiting for them in reception, escorted them to the penthouse suite, which was kept exclusively for Andreas, members of his family and his personal guests. The suite was vast, consisting of a spacious lobby with a door that led to a sitting room the size of a small ballroom, and two other doors that led to two bedrooms each with its own bathroom. The bedrooms in their turn also had doors that led directly into the sitting room. Of course Kate, having worked for Andreas for some time now, knew roughly what to expect, but she had never imagined that she would be staying in such sumptuous luxury herself. In fact on this trip she had automatically assumed that she would be staying in one of the hotel's perfectly standard rooms, with perhaps a sea view if she were lucky.

'But I can't stay here,' she exclaimed as her case was taken through to the adjoining suite of rooms.

'Why on earth not?' said Andreas. 'Surely you're not worried about what people will say. You can lock your door into the sitting room and use the other door if that makes you feel more comfortable.'

'No, no, that's not it at all,' said Kate, flustered. 'It's just that I'm an employee. I can't live at the same standard as you.'

'Why on earth not? And besides which, all the rooms downstairs earn money. The penthouse doesn't, for the simple reason that it's not available for rent. I don't want to sound miserly, but it would cost my business more if you didn't stay here with me.'

'Oh, well. Put like that . . .' Kate shrugged and smiled sheepishly. 'I'm sorry, I sound incredibly rude and ungrateful. It's wonderful. I promise I'll keep myself to myself and I won't get in your way at all.'

She went through to her room, carefully shutting the connecting door behind her. She was sure that Andreas, being the workaholic that he was, would be getting straight down to business and she didn't want the noise of her unpacking, opening and closing drawers and doors, to annoy him. It didn't take her terribly long, and once she was finished, she changed into a cotton skirt and blouse, picked up her book, threw open the door on to the balcony and went out into the fresh air to relax after her long journey.

Out on the balcony was a very comfortable sun-lounger. Kate sank on to it gratefully, feeling quite tired. The flight had taken more out of her than she had reckoned on. She had rather assumed that with the automatic pilot she would have little to do, but she had found that she'd been unable to relax. Every few seconds she had checked the instruments, looked at the gauges and strained her eyes into the distance to make sure there were no other aircraft anywhere near her bit of air space. Lying back on the comfortable padded bed she picked up her book meaning to read it, but found her eyes kept straying away from the page to admire the view. And even when she did manage to read a page she would then realise that none of the words her eyes had skimmed had actually made any sense. She gave up, let the book fall upon her chest and allowed the warmth of the sun and the beauty of the view lull her into a state of utter relaxation.

Chapter Twenty-Five

The swish of a patio door opening made her jump. Her book slithered off her chest and she grabbed at it wildly.

'I'm sorry, I didn't mean to startle you,' apologised Andreas. He came out of his sitting room and walked along the large balcony towards her.

'Don't worry. I was miles away.'

'I didn't expect you to be here. I would have thought you might have gone down to the beach or the pool.'

'I felt too tired to make the effort. Besides which, I can see the view so much better from up here.'

'Have you phoned home yet?'

'Not yet. My mobile needs to charge up. I was going to go to the lobby later and find a call box.'

'Don't be ridiculous. Use the phone in the room.'

'Are you sure?'

Andreas rolled his eyes in exasperation. 'Of course I'm sure.' Kate smiled in gratitude. 'Have you any plans for supper tonight?'

'Not really. I thought I might have some salad up here in my room.'

'That's what I had planned. How about we have some salad together? It would be silly for both of us to sit in solitude.'

Kate felt unexpectedly shy but it would be churlish to refuse his offer of some company. 'Thanks. That would be nice.'

'Good. I'll speak to the chef and get him to make you the best salad you've ever tasted.'

Kate looked forward to this; she loved Greek salad with its delicious feta cheese and olives. The phone rang in Andreas's room, and he excused himself and left Kate to enjoy the view again. But her previous state of repose had gone as once more she wondered exactly what his motives towards her were. Here he was asking her to join him for another meal. Was it that he was just naturally polite and charming and included her in some of his plans out of old-fashioned courtesy? There was no reason why she couldn't eat in the hotel restaurant – that wouldn't cost his business any more money than if she ate with him. She briefly considered that he might actually *want* her company, but then dismissed the idea. Surely there were plenty of wealthy Greek girls who would make much more suitable consorts. But as she thought about it, she realised that she'd never seen him with a woman. Another thought crossed her mind. Perhaps women weren't his thing – perhaps he was so nice to her simply because he *wasn't* interested in her except in a purely platonic way. Oh, what the heck! But then she thought that if her last assumption was correct, it was a shocking waste of an extraordinarily good-looking man. And she was still uneasily aware that if her latest thoughts about his sexuality were wrong, and he made the slightest pass at her, she wasn't sure she would be able to resist.

After an hour of lying in the afternoon sun, Kate decided that she had probably had enough and went into her room for a shower. The bathroom was breathtakingly luxurious. The bath was the biggest she'd ever seen – large enough for two people to bathe together. The tiles were marble, the bath sheets were so thick and fluffy they were more like duvets and the taps were gold. Real gold? Well, she wouldn't be surprised if they were. The shower was wonderful and she revelled in the needle-sharp jets of hot water that came from showerheads placed at every conceivable height and angle. No nook or crevice left unwashed, she thought cheerily. She washed her hair with care even though it didn't really need it, then asked herself sternly if she was doing this for the benefit of Andreas, and had to admit that she thought she was.

Finally she emerged from the steamy shower cubicle and into the magnificent bathroom. Between the twin basins was a large mirrored cabinet. Unable to resist the tug of her curiosity, she opened it to find it crammed with a magnificent range of soaps, shampoos, body lotions, and deodorants – every imaginable toiletry a girl could want. She noticed with interest that there were no 'own brands' here. Everything was Dior, or Chanel or Yves St Laurent. Had all this been supplied by Andreas or was it the leftovers from previous guests? Was it there for her to use or would that be taking liberties? She looked at the contents of the cupboard. There was so much no one would notice if she just had a little splash from a couple of bottles. She squirted a dollop of body lotion the size of a peach stone into her hand and rubbed it into her legs and arms. Umm, it smelt wonderful, and so it should considering what it had probably cost. She was more used to sharing Edward's baby lotion than being pampered with magnificent luxuries like this. She found a matching brand of deodorant and sprayed it under her arms, then determinedly shut the cabinet door. She mustn't be greedy, she told herself. Anyway, in all probability it wasn't hers to use. Feeling relaxed, pampered and happy she returned to her bedroom to dry her hair.

By the time she had finished styling her hair and putting on some light but effective make-up, she noticed with surprise that it was nearly dark outside. She hadn't realised how late it was getting. She went to her wardrobe and chose a simple but pretty wool challis dress. Feminine but not provocative, she decided. She scowled at herself in the mirror. What was she playing at? Scent, make-up, pretty dress. Was she trying to attract him? She sighed. She didn't know. She looked at her watch and wondered what time Andreas wanted to eat. It was past seven thirty. She dithered, should she disturb him or should she wait for him to tell her when their dinner arrived?

There was a discreet knock on her door.

'Come in,' she called.

Andreas opened the door. 'Are you going to stay in here all night or are you coming through to join me?'

'I'm sorry. I've only just realised what the time is.'

'It's time for a drink. Come through. I've quite a good bar up here.'

Kate didn't doubt this for a minute. She stood up from her dressing table stool and followed him into the massive sitting room.

'Champagne cocktails?'

'How lovely.' Andreas handed her a glass with sugar frosting around the edge. It looked so pretty. Kate took a sip. 'That's lovely.'

'I should hope so.' Andreas laughed. 'I haven't been in the hotel trade all my life without learning a thing or two.'

'Of course not.' Kate felt suddenly foolish. She wandered over to the window to hide her embarrassment. Out at sea dozens of little lights were bobbing about. It was very pretty.

'Do you see the fishing boats?' said Andreas. He was suddenly right behind her; she hadn't heard his approach. 'They shine lights to help attract the fish.'

Kate was acutely aware that Andreas was almost touching her. She could feel his breath on her neck. A thrill shot down her spine and made her shiver.

'Are you cold? Let me turn the heating up.'

'No, no, I'm fine.' Kate could feel her face starting to colour.

'But you're shivering.'

'No, I wasn't,' she protested. 'I think someone must have walked over my grave,' she said to cover up her discomfort.

'I'm sorry, I don't understand.' He moved to stand beside her so he could see her face. He was still very close.

'It's nothing; just a silly English proverb to explain why you sometimes get goosebumps or shiver for no reason.'

'You never shiver for no reason. There is always a cause,' said Andreas firmly. Kate felt suddenly apprehensive that he would demand that she tell him the real reason, and she didn't think she would be able to lie convincingly. 'So you're just being polite. It is a little chilly.' He walked across the room and adjusted the thermostat. In relief Kate took a large swig of her drink which polished off the last of her cocktail.

'Your glass is empty,' he commented on his return. 'Let me get you another. You can allow yourself to have a drink or two tonight. You're not flying again for days.'

'Well, if you are sure.'

'Of course I'm sure.' Andreas mixed her another cocktail. Kate took it but decided that she would take this one extremely steadily. She rarely drank these days and she'd never had a particularly strong head. Unlike many of her fellow officers in the army who could drink industrial quantities of booze and not turn a hair, Kate had always got quite squiffy on very little.

'Are you comfortable in your room?' asked Andreas.

'Comfortable! Are you kidding? I've never stayed in such luxury in all my life.'

'That's good.' There was a knock at the door. 'This should be our dinner,' said Andreas. In came a waiter pushing a large trolley. Swiftly and expertly he laid the table in the corner of the sumptuous sitting room. He put two large plates on it and then whipped the covers from the dishes with a flourish. Nestling amongst the various salad leaves and prettily cut tomatoes and radishes were two monster lobsters.

Kate boggled. Lobster! She was expecting some feta cheese, olives and tomatoes. Obviously her idea of salad and Andreas's differed somewhat.

'Is there a problem?' asked Andreas anxiously, misinterpreting the look on Kate's face.

'No, of course not, how could there be?'

'You might not like lobster.'

Kate raised her eyebrows. Was there anyone who didn't? Andreas pulled her chair out for her and Kate sat down.

'Wine?' he asked.

Kate nodded. He poured two glasses and then sat down opposite her.

'Come on,' he encouraged. 'What are you waiting for? Tuck in.'

Kate needed no second bidding. It was ages since she had had lobster, and it had to be said it was one of her favourite foods. With relish and skill she took up the silver-plated pliers and expertly cracked its claws. Silence reigned as they both tackled their meal with gusto. After several exquisitely delicious mouthfuls Kate stopped eating to announce how much she was enjoying it.

'I'm so glad,' replied Andreas. 'I do get fed up when the people I entertain are picky eaters.'

'No one has ever accused me of being that,' said Kate with a smile.

'I can imagine.'

Kate grinned. 'Are you implying that I'm fat?'

'My dear lady, how on earth could you . . .' Then he caught sight of her expression and laughed. 'More wine?'

'Yes please. It's delicious. I'm going to get pickled at this rate.'

'Would that be so bad?'

'It's not very dignified.'

'True, but it helps one lose one's inhibitions.'

Kate laid down her knife and fork. 'You think I have inhibitions?'

'I don't know. I haven't had the chance to find out.'

Kate's stomach was suddenly and unaccountably filled with butterflies and she was further aware that her heart rate had accelerated wildly. She lowered her eyes and fumbled for her napkin for something to do. She knew she should say something: rebuff him, encourage him. Good God, which?

'Well?'

She gulped. 'Well what?'

'Will I get the chance?'

'I ... I ... I don't know.' She suddenly realised she wanted him more than anything in the world, but it was ridiculous. He was her boss, for heaven's sake. It was impossible.

Andreas mistook the reason for her uneasiness. 'Ah, you don't find me attractive and you don't want to give me the brush-down.'

'Brush-off,' she mumbled.

'Brush-down, brush-off, whatever. It still comes to the same thing. I'm sorry. I shouldn't have said anything.'

'No, no, it's nothing like that. It's ... it's that you're my boss.'

'What has that got to do with it?'

Incredulity overtook all of Kate's emotions. 'Everything,' she said. 'You're worth millions. I'm your ex-receptionist.'

Andreas leaned forward across the table. 'For heaven's sake, Kate, don't you realise that when I first came across you at the interview I thought you were the most remarkable woman I'd ever met? Why else do you think I took you flying, promoted you, offered you this job?'

'I did wonder,' said Kate slowly.

'And you were always so correct, so proper. I've been despairing of ever getting to the real Kate.' Kate took her napkin off her lap and laid it beside her plate. Andreas reached across and grasped her hand.

'Oh, Andreas.' She gave a little sigh. Then, without being aware of moving, somehow she was standing up, in his arms and kissing him. He pulled her tight against his body and she could feel how lean and muscular he was under his shirt. Her hands moved up and clasped him around his neck, and the tips of her fingers could feel how luxuriant and thick his hair was. She was glad he was holding her so firmly because her legs seemed suddenly quite wobbly. She opened her eyes a fraction and found herself staring into his.

'You are so beautiful,' he murmured. Kate lowered her eyes again. 'Don't be shy, look at me. Let me memorise every tiny detail of your face.' He moved his hands so his fingers rested on either temple, then his thumbs traced the outline of her lips, the flare of her nostrils, the line of her eyebrows, the shape of her cheekbones, the curve of her chin. Kate turned her face so she could kiss the inside of one of his palms and rested her head on his shoulder. She felt so safe and so happy. She hadn't felt this way since Eddie. And she didn't think Eddie would mind. Yet she felt a twinge of guilt all the same. She told herself to ignore it; it was time for her to move on again. The past was past, gone – she had to think about her future. She gave a little sigh of happiness and pushed the guilt out of her mind.

'How are the inhibitions?' whispered Andreas.

'What inhibitions?' whispered back Kate.

'Come to bed.'

'What about supper?'

'It'll keep. After all, it isn't going to go cold.'

When Kate awoke the next morning, Andreas was already up, dressed and sitting at a table in the sitting room beavering away at some papers. Kate slipped on his dressing gown and strolled across the thick carpet. She dropped a kiss on his head.

'Don't you ever rest?' she asked resting her hands on his shoulders and massaging them gently.

'Hmm, that's wonderful,' said Andreas. 'You can do that as much as you like.'

'You haven't answered my question.'

'I do rest, sometimes. But the holiday business is not one

where you can afford to relax too much – you only have to upset a customer once and you can lose a lot of goodwill. As this is my business, I care more about it than I could possibly expect any of my employees to, so it's up to me to make sure everything meets my standards.'

'Do you think you'll get the chance to relax at all while you're here?' asked Kate.

'Maybe. We'll have to see.' He smiled up at her. 'Would you like some breakfast?'

'Please. Sex always makes me ravenous.'

Andreas laughed, picked up the phone and made a rapid order in Greek.

'It'll be here in just a few minutes.'

'Great. That'll give me time for a shower.'

When Kate emerged again, damp and smelling faintly of expensive toiletries – her reserve about using them had gone along with all her other inhibitions – her breakfast of orange juice, fresh bread, yoghurt, honey and coffee had been laid out on the table on the balcony.

'Wonderful,' she exclaimed. She tore hungrily at the still warm loaf and crammed a large chunk in her mouth. 'Are you joining me?' she mumbled indistinctly from the French window.

'No, I ate earlier.'

Kate swallowed and began to drizzle the honey on to her bowl of yoghurt. 'Tomorrow, when you wake up, will you wake me too, please? I really fancy a swim first thing, and when I've eaten this I won't be able to go into the water for hours or I'll sink.' She dipped her spoon into the honey and yoghurt and savoured it. 'This is heaven on earth,' she pronounced finally. 'I'm sure when the gods were dining on nectar and ambrosia, this was what they really ate.'

'I'm glad you are enjoying it. But please excuse me, I really have a lot of work to get through.'

Kate took the hint and continued her meal in silence, although she was faintly hurt by the rebuff, however gently it had been delivered. The she told herself sternly not to be such a stupid idiot – Andreas had work to do and she was interrupting him. Of course he wanted her to be quiet.

When she had finished, she crept off to her room to dress

ready to go out exploring. She didn't really fancy staying in the resort and had decided the night before that she would hire a car to get her to some of the more out-of-the-way spots that she had enjoyed visiting with Maria. She put on jeans and a T-shirt and threw an old sweatshirt over her shoulders. It was deliciously warm in the sun and where it was sheltered from the breeze, but she had no doubts that, being so late in the year, she could expect it to feel a little nippy if it clouded over. She wrapped her swimming costume up in a towel, stuffed that and her book into a beach bag and headed off. In reception Yannis greeted her effusively as she made her way across the expanse of marble floor over to the main desk. She waved at him in reply.

'Good morning, madam,' said a smooth and efficient-looking young man.

'I'd like to find out about hiring a car, please.'

'Excuse me, are you Mr Spyrou's guest?'

'Yes.' Word gets around fast, she thought. She wondered what else the hotel staff knew about her.

'Mr Spyrou has already organised a car for you. It's waiting in the hotel car park. I'll get Yannis to show you which one it is.' He raised a hand and imperiously beckoned to the hall porter. Yannis bounded over, grinning broadly, hands and feet flapping. Kate was reminded of the Andrex puppy. The receptionist handed Kate the keys to the car and Yannis led her eagerly out of the front door.

'This way, Mrs Thomas. Yannis knows which is your car. I show you. I show you.'

Kate had to half run to keep up as Yannis charged across the forecourt and down the path that led to the car park. He stopped in front of a smart little four-wheel drive with a soft top.

'This is perfect,' exclaimed Kate.

'You like?'

'I like very much.' This is exactly what I would have chosen for myself, she thought. Many of the roads, away from the main tourist routes, were little more than dirt tracks and unsuitable for ordinary cars. This little runabout would be perfect for going anywhere and everywhere. Kate wanted to run upstairs again and thank Andreas, but she was wary of disturbing him.

He was such a wonderful, thoughtful man in so many respects, but he did have a quick temper. Probably the Mediterranean temperament, she thought. All the same, it would be courteous to let him know how much she appreciated his kindness. She returned to reception, scribbled a quick note and asked it to be delivered when it would be convenient to Mr Spyrou.

'I don't know when that would be,' said the deferential receptionist, looking worried.

'He's bound to order coffee or lunch or something. Send it up on the tray then.'

Relief spread over the employee's face. Obviously he didn't fancy getting on the wrong side of Andreas' temper either.

Kate, feeling inordinately cheerful, bounced out of the lobby, unlocked her car, checked where all the various controls were and then zoomed out of the car park. She had a rough idea where she wanted to go; there were some secluded coves around Cape Greco. If her memory served her correctly, they didn't have much in the way of sand but the swimming was pretty good, and if Andreas was to be believed, the sea would still be fairly warm as it didn't really start to cool down until the winter storms set in properly at the end of December. She drove carefully, hugging the coastline until she neared the rocky headland that formed Cape Greco. She saw a rough track leading off the main road that looked hopeful. *Eureka*, she thought after a few minutes of hairy driving, weaving between potholes and rocks. In front of her was the expanse of the sea and at the foot of a low cliff was a tiny shingle beach. The breeze was so light here in this sheltered spot as to almost nonexistent. The waves, hardly more than large ripples, barely disturbed the gleaming blue of the water and, unusually for this tideless coastline, the shore was almost clear of any sign of litter. Gathering her bits and pieces, Kate scrambled the few feet down the sharp rocks on to a smooth rocky shelf. Contentedly she surveyed her little territory, then slipped off her shoes, rolled up her trousers and dabbled her toes in the water. Delicious, but she decided to wait a while before she went for a swim, both to allow her breakfast to be digested and to let the sun climb a little higher. Settling herself against a rock, she fished out her book and lost herself in its pages.

Her stomach brought her back to her senses by rumbling loudly. She looked at her watch. Good grief, lunchtime already and she still hadn't been swimming. But what the heck, what was the hurry? The sea wasn't going anywhere, she still had over a week here and she couldn't remember the last time she had felt so absolutely relaxed and peaceful. She yawned and stretched luxuriously, like a cat. She would find a nice taverna in a little backwater, the sort of place frequented by Cypriots rather than tourists, have a leisurely lunch and then think about swimming later.

She drove into the nearest village, which consisted of a church, a handful of houses and a bar. No shops selling tacky souvenirs, no hotels, no signs advertising local crafts for sale at inflated prices. Obviously the tourist industry hadn't found this place and begun to exploit it. This was exactly the kind of backwater Kate had in mind. Her perfect plan for a wonderful lunch looked like it was all coming together.

It was a perfect plan apart from one tiny flaw: Kate didn't speak Greek, and no one in the little bar spoke English. She gazed at the dog-eared menu hoping that she would miraculously discover how to decipher the squiggles. The café owner stared at her curiously, as did the handful of locals. Evidently outsiders were something of a novelty.

'*Bíra*?' he offered hopefully. Then, holding up a bottle, '*Keo*?'

Kate shook her head. It wasn't wise to drink and drive, and she had no idea how strong Cypriot beer was.

'*Krasí?*' He pointed at a bottle of the local wine. Again Kate shook her head. Then he held up a can of lemonade.

'Yes.' Kate nodded enthusiastically and the café owner smiled in triumph. The locals clapped. Kate felt a little as though she was providing the novelty turn. But however friendly everyone was, and however eager they were to help, it still didn't help with the problem of what was on the menu. She handed it back to the proprietor and shrugged. He smiled; he had a solution. Taking her by the arm, he led her into the kitchen. Kate decided to keep things simple and pointed to a jar of olives, some tomatoes and a loaf of bread. Obviously this was a good choice because she was rewarded with lots of smiles and a vigorous handshake. They returned to the bar and

287

the owner apparently relayed her choice to the villagers, because they raised their glasses to her and grinned. Kate did the same. She vowed that she would have to get Andreas to teach her some elementary Greek before she ventured out again.

Andreas was only too pleased to help and coached her in how to order a few basic dishes in Greek. He also got the hotel shop to send up a phrase book so that if she got into real difficulties she could just point to the words.

'So where are you planning to go tomorrow?' he asked her when they had finished with the Greek lesson for the evening.

'Probably back to the same place as today. It was wonderful just chilling out with a book. No hassle, no pressure. And the little taverna was a delight. The villagers were all so sweet to me despite the fact that none of us understood a word of what the other was saying.'

'You seem very happy, despite being left on your own.'

'I am. I'm having a lovely time.'

'I'm glad. You deserve some happiness after all that has happened.'

'Well, it's past now.'

Andreas smiled at her and said quietly, 'Did you love your husband very much?'

'Very much. We'd only been married a short time when he was killed.'

Andreas shook his head. 'Life can be so unfair.'

As he folded her in his arms, Kate pondered on the fact that he had known more than his share of unfairness too in his life, and that in that respect they were kindred spirits.

The next day she returned to the same taverna and stunned her audience by confidently asking for a *limonádha* and a *khoriátiki saláta*. The owner patted her on the back and the locals laughed and smiled. Kate determined to learn even more Greek, and besides, it would please Andreas that she was making such an effort to master his own mother tongue.

288

Chapter Twenty-Six

Her time on Cyprus was idyllic. During the day she had terrific fun exploring in her nippy little jeep. The solitude didn't bother her, and by acquiring a phrase book and with Andreas also helping her to add a few words to her vocabulary each day, she was able to get about with increased confidence. She would return to the hotel at teatime and in the evenings she and Andreas ate exquisite meals, sometimes in their suite and sometimes in a local restaurant, followed by nights of endless and delightful lovemaking.

On the last day Kate planned to go into Larnaca to buy some presents for Edward and her mother. She had got out to her car when she realised that she had left the keys in her room.

'Damn,' she swore and retraced her steps. She picked up her key from reception and then pressed the call button for the lift. It seemed to take an age to arrive. She had just stepped into it when movement caught her eye. She looked into the mirror that covered the entire back wall of the lift and saw two extremely ugly-looking characters in suits and shades enter the hotel. Whatever else they were, they weren't tourists. She stared at their reflection and the thought crossed her mind that they looked just like the men she had seen in Edinburgh. Don't be ridiculous, she told herself as the lift door closed. The lift zoomed up to the top floor and Kate stepped out. Quietly, so as not to disturb Andreas, she opened the door to the lobby. She needn't have worried, as the door into the sitting room was shut. She went into her bedroom. Where were those keys? She remembered distinctly putting them on her dressing table the evening before when she had returned from a day out but now they were nowhere to be seen. She rummaged around in her make-up bag: nothing. Bugger. She tipped out the contents of her handbag: again nothing. She sighed and sat down on the edge of the bed to think. In the silence she could hear voices. Andreas must have visitors. She remembered the characters she'd seen in reception. Surely not? Curiosity got the better of her. Kate crept to the door into the sitting room and pressed her eye to the crack. She couldn't see much, just a sliver of the room. This was hopeless, but then she realised that whoever Andreas's visitors were, they were all speaking in English. She listened.

'. . .in the oranges, as before.' The voice wasn't Andreas's.

'And when can I expect payment?' That was Andreas.

'When you deliver.'

Deliver what? thought Kate.

'And then I get the balance, a million pounds,' said Andreas.

Bloody hell, thought Kate. This is some deal he's negotiating. Still, hotels and land probably didn't come cheap. All the same – a million pounds. Then she realised that what sounded like a monstrous sum to her was probably just small change to him. She suddenly felt uneasy that she was eavesdropping and returned to her task of finding her keys. They came to light on the floor under a stool. She must have accidentally knocked them off her dressing table at some point. She picked them up and returned downstairs to her car.

As she drove into Larnaca, her thoughts kept returning to the two men she had seen in the lobby, and Andreas's conversation. It could be that none of it had anything to do with anything else. It was perfectly possible that the men were there to inspect the kitchens, or to deliver an estimate for carpet cleaning; but the thought that they were also the men who had met Andreas in Edinburgh wouldn't go away. And what about that conversation? What the hell did oranges have to do with the hotel business? As far as Kate was aware, Andreas had nothing to do with Cyprus's huge fruit industry. Well, perhaps he was branching out, she thought. After all, Richard Branson had gone from records to airlines to cola. Why not Andreas?

Suddenly there was a car in front of her in the middle of the road, indicating to turn right. She hit the brakes. Her tyres shrieked as she stopped just inches from the bumper of the vehicle in her path. Her hands were shaking as she unclenched her fingers from around the steering wheel. She felt sick as she realised she had almost been responsible for yet another crash. The car pulled across the other carriageway and, leaving two dark lines of rubber on the road, Kate drove on feeling very shaky. That had been a close one, and again she had not been concentrating properly.

When she arrived in Larnaca she found a parking space near the sea front and climbed out of the car, still feeling a little shocked by her lapse in concentration that had so nearly proved disastrous. She didn't feel like going shopping immediately – she wanted to calm her nerves first. She decided to go and find a café and have a quiet cup of tea. She looked about her and realised she was spoilt for choice. One of the surrounding establishments seemed a mite more welcoming than the others; the umbrellas were more jolly, the paintwork was brighter, the leaves of the potted palms greener . . . Yes, thought Kate, that one will do nicely. She found a table in the shade in the corner furthest away from the road and the faint smell of traffic fumes. In almost no time a waiter had taken her order and had returned with her tea and a plate of sticky cakes. Kate declined the buns and, as she sipped her hot drink, mused about how near a miss she had just had. Well, thank God, she thought, this time she had managed to brake. The calming effect of the tea began to work its magic and she felt her heart rate slow and her hands stop trembling. Around her were the sleepy sounds of a Mediterranean island at the end of the tourist season but approaching the heat of the day: the rasp of cicadas, the twitter of birds, the muted chink of crockery and the occasional ripple of laughter. Once or twice a motor scooter zipped past making a noise like a wasp in a jam jar, but it was muffled by the screen of shrubs that separated the terrace from the road. Her mind wandered peacefully through delicious memories of her stay in Cyprus, her nights with Andreas, her days on the beach, flying . . .

'I'm sorry, I won't stand for this.' An imperious voice cut into Kate's reverie.

Kate jerked out of her daydream in amazement. Magda! She was sure it was Magda's voice. She cast about her but couldn't see anyone remotely like Magda.

'I'm sorry, you can take it up with my superiors.' A pause; whoever it was seemed to be speaking on a mobile phone. 'No, I've told you. It is quite unacceptable.' Another pause. 'Yes, you do that.' Then, quite viciously, 'See you in court, then.' Silence. Kate craned her head in the direction of the voice but she still couldn't see the source. Suddenly she spotted movement from the other side of the plants that divided the adjoining café terraces. It was difficult to see the person clearly through the thick glossy leaves of the hibiscus and the fronds of a phalanx of small palms but the hair colour was right. Could it be Magda? Possibly. It certainly sounded like her. If it was, what was she doing here? It didn't sound as though she was here on pleasure.

Kate heard the plip-pleep of someone keying in a number to a mobile phone.

'Hello, Andreas? Yes, yes, I think I've dealt with the problem. I'll see you later and give you all the details. Yes, yes. Bye then.'

Andreas? Andreas! Kate felt the blood drain from her face. The waiter appeared.

'More tea, madam?'

'Sorry, what?'

The waiter looked perturbed. 'More tea?'

'Oh, no. No thanks.' Kate paid and fled, hurt and bewildered.

Magda still worked for Andreas? Surely not. Hadn't he sacked her as he had said? Had he lied about it? What was going on? A plethora of angry thoughts tumbled in her head as she stormed down the dusty pavement.

Suddenly she realised that to run away from the situation was an act of folly. You're being ridiculous, she told herself, and stopped dead in her tracks, having come to a snap decision. A couple of tourists walking behind her nearly cannoned into her and skirted round her mumbling things about lack of consideration which Kate didn't hear. She was going to return to the other café, waltz in and make certain one way or another if it really had been Magda, or another similarly hard-nosed cow. She wasn't quite sure what she would do if her worst suspicions were confirmed – she'd cross that bridge when she got to it.

Thirty seconds later she swept up the couple of steps leading to the other café's terrace, only to be confronted by two dozen completely empty tables. Her quarry had gone. Damn.

They flew back to England that afternoon. Kate was glad that Andreas seemed to be preoccupied with work and was disinclined for conversation. She was preoccupied with thoughts about Magda and whether or not she and Andreas still had dealings with one another. She wondered whether to ask Andreas about her presence on the island but decided against it. It sounded so – so jealous. As if she was checking up on him, his employees and his relationships. Anyway, she was probably wrong. She'd been in a state, after all, having just had that near miss on the road. And even if it had been Magda, it didn't mean she was still on Andreas Spyrou's payroll. How many men were there called Andreas on the island? It was like jumping to conclusions about a coincidence over someone called John in Britain. Really, she was completely overreacting. She came to the conclusion that it was just as well that the other woman had departed from her table at the café before Kate had gone crashing back; how embarrassing it would have been if she had stormed up to a complete stranger. Kate giggled at the awfulness of the idea and then, having provided herself with a rational explanation for the incident, put the whole affair out of her mind.

The journey went slickly, the weather was calm and they landed on the dot of their scheduled arrival time.

'When will I see you again?' asked Kate as Andreas prepared to depart.

'I'll call you,' he promised as he collected his briefcase. Mark, the chauffeur, had already extracted his suitcase and put it in the back of the Rolls. 'Our relationship . . .' He paused.

'Yes?' said Kate. Things suddenly seemed different now they were back in England.

'I don't think it would be a good idea if we were too obvious in public.'

293

'Bad example to other employees, right?' said Kate without malice.

'Something like that. And I don't want you to be subjected to any nasty gossip.'

'Don't worry, I'll be incredibly discreet.'

'Of course, when we are away together – on business – it'll be different then.'

'I understand.'

'But back in England . . .' He let the sentence hang.

Kate got the picture. On home ground she would revert to being the hired hand. She felt a little deflated. What he was telling her was that she mustn't expect to be a significant part of his life. She knew in her heart of hearts that this was to be expected. All along she'd been telling herself that men like him didn't take up with girls like her, and now she knew it for certain. But she didn't mind. She would have him to herself on business trips; she could be patient and wait for those. It didn't make him any less adorable. He stroked her face and was gone. No kiss. She sighed. Somehow she'd expected more than that as a farewell but hadn't he just spelt out the way things were to be? She sighed again and got on with tidying up the interior of the aircraft before locking the door and making her way to the handling agent. Her thoughts strayed back to the past week and she couldn't help smiling. She could live with Andreas's terms in exchange for making love with him now and again. Anything was worth it for that.

She made her way through the offices with a light heart. She was smiling broadly, and looking a picture of radiant health, when she ran into Martin, the customs officer, again.

'Hi,' she said beaming at him, more to annoy Amelia than for his benefit.

'Goodness, what a tan,' said Martin. 'Been somewhere nice?'

'Cyprus. Business, of course,' she added smugly.

'Nice work if you can get it.'

'It's a dreadful job, but someone's got to do it,' said Kate, absolutely deadpan.

'I admire your courage,' replied Martin equally gravely. Then they both burst out laughing. Amelia looked daggers.

'Seriously, is he a good boss to work for?'

You'd better believe it, thought Kate smugly, recalling the recent shift in her relationship with Andreas from employee to lover. 'He's a great man to work for. Very considerate,' she added.

'That's nice,' said Martin. 'I'd always imagined these Greek tycoon types to be completely ruthless bastards.'

'Aren't you thinking of Italian Mafia, not Greek hoteliers?'

'You're probably right. Anyway, I must go. Got to see a man about a dog – sniffer dog. Catch you again soon,' he said hopefully as he left.

'Sure, bye.' Kate finished off the last of the paperwork – noting as she did so that Amelia looked particularly put out – passed on a few messages about some routine bits and pieces that she wanted checked out by the maintenance section, and then left the airfield for home.

As she drove she wondered about telling her mother about Andreas. Perhaps it would be better not to, it might spark a row. Andreas hadn't told her she couldn't tell her nearest and dearest, and it wasn't going to be the sort of thing she would be able to keep under wraps indefinitely, especially as she was still living with her mother. She knew that Honour approved of Andreas as Kate's boss, but how would she react to the news that he was now her lover?

'I'll think about it tomorrow,' she muttered under her breath as she turned her car into the wide gravel drive. And then all thoughts of Andreas were swept away in her joyful reunion with Edward.

'I'd like you to meet Henry,' said Honour.

'How do you do?' said Kate assessing her mother's guest. Fifty-something, three-piece suit, gold watch chain, silk tie – apparently well heeled. So this was the man who had phoned almost every night since her return from Cyprus.

'Delighted to meet you, young lady,' said Henry in the plummiest drawl Kate had ever heard. Good heavens, even some of the really far-back cavalry officers she had known at Sandhurst hadn't managed to strangle their vowels that much. Kate struggled to keep her eyebrows from rising. Henry extended a beautifully manicured hand. Kate took it. It was like holding a lettuce leaf, limp and faintly damp. She took an instant dislike to him. *A friend from the bridge club* was all her mother had said when Kate had asked her about him. And when Kate had pressed her for more information, she had rather coyly asked Kate if she would like to meet him. Looking at him now, Kate rather wished she hadn't answered yes. Still, he was her mother's friend, not hers, so her feelings towards him really didn't enter into the equation. And furthermore, considering recent developments, she was hardly in a position to criticise her mother for having a fling. She was aware that Henry was staring at her curiously.

'I'm sorry,' said Kate. 'Is there something wrong?'

'Not at all. I just can't imagine a pretty girl like you flying an aeroplane.'

Kate was tempted to retaliate with a comment about not being able to imagine an upper-class twit like him playing a complicated game like bridge, but bit her tongue. She forced a smile and said that it was only like driving a car.

'Kate,' said Honour, 'would you be so kind as to get Henry a sherry while I go and get my coat.'

Kate did as she was told but declined to join him. Irrationally, she had no desire to make him feel at ease in her mother's house. She knew she was being selfish and childish but she couldn't imagine that his continuing presence was going to be an asset.

Cold damp autumn turned into a miserable and wet winter and Henry seemed to spend more and more of his time around Honour.

'Really,' said Kate to Maria on the phone one day, 'I can't tell you how ghastly he is. I'm sure his intentions are honourable – you know, he's not going to rape her or anything – but there's something about him that strikes me as phoney. He's trying too hard to be the archetypal English gent. The thing I remember about the really upper-crust blokes at Sandhurst was that they didn't try – they just did it naturally.'

'And this has nothing to do with the fact that you don't like him?'

'I have to admit I don't.' Kate paused. 'Can men be gold-diggers?'

'I can't see why not. But your mother isn't loaded, is she?'

'She's not short of a bob or two,' said Kate. 'The house must be worth about half a million, and Daddy had a few stocks and shares that have done all right over the years.'

'And you think he's after that?'

'I don't know,' said Kate miserably. 'It's just he's a good bit younger than my mother—'

'And you're worried about your inheritance.'

'No, I couldn't give a stuff about that. I just hate the thought that she is being conned somehow.'

Maria didn't say that she thought that whoever Henry was, he'd have to get up very early to catch Honour out.

'Why don't you have a word with him, then? Ask him what his intentions are.'

'You must be joking. Can you imagine what Mummy would say if he told her that I'd quizzed him.'

Maria conceded that Kate had a point. Honour on the warpath was a scary thought.

'And I don't like him being one of the very few males that come to the house. The last thing I want is Edward thinking that he is some sort of role model.'

Throughout the winter Kate ferried Andreas and his business associates around Europe. And where only a few months before this had seemed like money for old rope, life at home was now becoming increasingly difficult, which made Kate start to wonder if the responsibilities of the job and the irregular hours made it worth what she earned. It was the odious Henry who seemed to be entirely responsible for the difficulties in Kate's life. It was bad enough that he seemed to have virtually moved in, but Honour's almost total absorption in him meant that she was becoming increasingly unreliable in the matter of looking after Edward.

'This can't go on,' Kate complained one day.

'What?' said Honour.

'Me not knowing if you can take Edward for me or not.'

'I'm sorry, darling,' Honour said, not sounding the least bit apologetic. 'Henry isn't awfully good with small children and it isn't always appropriate to have Edward trailing around with us.'

'And it isn't always appropriate for Edward to have a virtual stranger looking after him.'

'But I thought you said the nanny agency was very good.'

'They are, but when you let me down at a moment's notice it makes life very difficult all round. They try and send either Kelly or Hilary, but sometimes they can't, and I really hate leaving him when it isn't one of those two.' She didn't add that her worries about Edward's welfare were affecting her relationship with Andreas. A few months earlier Kate would have been overjoyed at the prospect of having Andreas to herself for a night, but now she sometimes found herself resenting having to stay away, especially if she felt that Edward wasn't being properly looked after at home. She was going to have to resolve the situation very soon.

'I'm going to have to find some permanent arrangement,' she confided in Maria, who was over on a spot of leave from Germany. 'It isn't just that I need a full-time live-in nanny, but I can't go on living with mother. Henry is driving me to distraction.'

'Your mother isn't going to like that.'

'Mother isn't likely to notice, she's so wrapped up in that tame creep,' said Kate icily. 'I've done some sums and providing I only buy a small place I should be able to pay the mortgage and a nanny. The trouble is that it has to have three bedrooms, and round here that isn't going to come cheap.'

'Do you want some help looking?'

'Would I!' Kate paused as a thought crossed her mind. 'The only problem is, Mother is bound to smell a rat. A whole load of bumf arriving from estate agents is bound make her wonder.'

'I thought you said she was totally engrossed in horrible Henry.'

'Perhaps I exaggerated a bit. Supposing I ask if Andy and Emma would act as a post office for me?'

'That's a great idea if you don't think they'll mind.'

'I shouldn't think so. They've met Henry themselves and will understand my motives.'

'It'll be a few weeks before I'll be able to get away again, probably not till Easter. Can you manage until then?'

'I'll just have to.'

Maria changed the subject. 'So tell me about Andreas.'

'Tell you what about him?' asked Kate.

'Well, the last time I saw him he was the original Greek bearing a gift. Since then you've spent weeks with him in foreign parts. Has he made a move yet?'

Kate didn't answer but blushed deeply.

'Aha,' shrieked Maria triumphantly. 'I told you he fancied you. So, tell me, what's his house like?'

'I don't know.'

'Hasn't he taken you there yet?'

'It's not like that. We only see each other on business trips. Once he lands back here then he only contacts me about my next job.'

'So you're his bit on the side?'

'I'm not,' said Kate indignant at the idea.

'Why are you kept in the background then?'

'I'm not. It's just the way it works out.'

Maria raised her eyebrows, unconvinced.

'He said he wanted to keep me out of the way of malicious gossip.'

'OK, I believe you,' said Maria, although it was patently obvious that she didn't. Still, it was typical of Kate to believe that a man was acting in her best interests just because he told her he was. Maria sometimes thought that for someone so bright and intelligent, Kate was remarkably blinkered when it came to men. She supposed that was what happened if you allowed the notion of romance to cloud your vision. She hoped Kate wasn't going to be hurt by this man.

Chapter Twenty-Seven

Maria, as good as her word, arrived the week before Easter. Kate had already been to a number of estate agents in the area and asked them to send her, care of Emma and Andy, details of houses in her price range. They were now in Emma's sitting room going through the dozens of envelopes that had plopped through Emma's letter-box.

'No,' said Maria as she scanned a sheet of A4. She flicked it on to the discard pile and picked up some more. 'No, too much for that. They'll be lucky to get anywhere near that amount. No, no garden; no, too small; no, it's got a downstairs bathroom; Good God, no!' The pile of houses that didn't meet Kate's exacting requirements grew. Edward, unaware that what was happening might shape his future, was building with Duplo bricks.

'Look, Mummy,' he said, holding up a box shape with a flat roof. 'It's a house.'

'It's wonderful, darling,' cooed Kate indulgently.

'Which is more than can be said for most of the rubbish we've been sent. I mean, why do they bother asking details of what you want if they don't pay any attention? What's the use of you specifically saying three bedrooms, gas central heating, garden and upstairs bathroom if they then send you dozens of houses that don't even remotely fit the bill? There's no point in even considering these,' said Maria, gesturing to the pile at her feet.

'The perfect house is around somewhere,' said Kate. 'It has to be.'

'You're right. If you're prepared to pay this sort of money, what you want must be out there somewhere. It has to be.'

'Yes.' Kate sounded doubtful. She picked up one of the sets of details that Maria had binned. Maria sensed that Kate's resolve was wavering.

'I know you are looking for a bolt hole, but it has got to be a home too.'

'I know, it's just that escaping has become a bit more of a priority.'

Emma breezed into the sitting room carrying a tray loaded with mugs of tea and a plate of biscuits.

'Horrible Henry getting more horrible?' she asked.

'I didn't think it was possible, but yes. He hit Edward yesterday.'

'He did what?' chorused Emma and Maria together. Emma put the tray down on the table and passed the tea around.

'I know Edward can be a bit of a handful sometimes . . .'

'It's only because of his age,' said Emma loyally. 'All children go through it at three.'

'I know, but he can be naughty all the same.'

'Still, it's nothing to do with Henry,' said Maria sternly.

'Well it was – sort of. And what he did was pretty bad. But it was partly Mummy's fault. She shouldn't have left the scissors lying about.'

'So what did he cut up?' asked Emma, smiling at Edward who at that moment looked a picture of angelic innocence.

'Henry's cashmere scarf,' admitted Kate.

Maria and Emma dissolved into giggles.

'Serves him right for being such a pretentious git and owning one in the first place,' said Maria.

'And it still isn't any reason for him to hit someone else's child. You could have him done for assault,' said Emma.

'I know, but really I don't want the hassle. I just want to put space between him and us.'

'Then let's keep looking,' said Maria, turning to the task with renewed determination. 'Now, what about this one?'

'How soon can you arrange the mortgage?' asked Kate.

'I'll get on to it straight away,' said the pretty girl in the building society whose badge on her bosom announced that she was 'Debbie, here to help you'. 'I just need to have details of your earnings confirmed. You're not in a chain – it's always less complicated when it's like that – so assuming everything goes according to plan you should be in your new house by the beginning of the summer.'

'Brilliant,' said Kate with feeling. The sooner she and Edward got away from Mother and Horrible Henry the better.

Debbie picked up a piece of paper from her desk and handed it to Kate. 'This is the breakdown of your mortgage and details of your monthly repayments.'

Breakdown was a good word to describe it, thought Kate. She felt like having one herself when she looked at what she had to pay back each month. What with that and what a full-time nanny was going to set her back, there was going to be precious little left over for any luxuries. Holidays and nice clothes would have to be forgotten for the time being. Still, she could manage it, just, and it would be worth it for Edward never to have to cross paths with Henry again. All she had to do now was break the news to Honour.

'Penny for them,' said Martin.

Kate, sitting by the window of the lounge at Farnborough, was staring sightlessly out of the window.

'Sorry?' She had been miles away, reliving Honour's reaction to the news.

'Oh, nothing. You were obviously lost in thought.'

'Yes I was. Sorry.'

'Problems with the boss?'

'No, why?'

'No reason. It's just it can't be easy working for someone as rich and powerful as that. Some of the pilots tell me they work for complete bastards.'

'Andreas is OK.' She didn't want to discuss Andreas. She was feeling too vulnerable.

'Would you like a coffee?'

Kate checked her watch. She still had loads of time before she was due to take off. She'd come here early to get away from the atmosphere of simmering resentment at home. Honour had said some horrible things to her. Kate was trying to convince herself that she wasn't really spiteful and ungracious, as Honour had told her in no uncertain terms. Perhaps a few minutes in Martin's company would make her feel better. 'Yes, I'd like one very much indeed.'

Martin went over to the machine. 'Black? White?'

'White, no sugar, please.'

Martin inserted the money, the machine clunked and whirred and he returned with two plastic cups. Kate looked completely miserable.

'Do you want to talk about it?'

Suddenly Kate found that she did. She spilled out all the details about Henry, Honour and her escape.

'So you've saddled yourself with this almighty mortgage just so you can get away from your mother's boyfriend? He must be dreadful,' said Martin as Kate finished.

'That's about the size of it.'

'And your mother isn't happy that you're going?'

'A classic understatement.'

'Poor old you.'

Kate, confident, competent Kate, was suddenly aware that she was dangerously close to tears. Her lip trembled as she tried to blink them back. A wave of self-pity swept over her.

'I know what you're thinking,' she gulped. 'Poor little rich girl; wonderful job, nice boss, she's got everything.'

'Not at all. I feel incredibly sorry for you. It can't be easy being a single parent and holding down a job like this with all its odd hours and the days away from home.'

That did it. The floodgates opened, and tears spilled over and rolled down her cheeks.

'Hey. It can't be as bad as all that,' said Martin handing her a handkerchief.

'But it is,' wailed Kate. 'I'm so worried I can't sleep properly, and that's no good. Everything seems to be getting on top of me: the mortgage, Edward, my mother. I seem to be making such a terrible mess of everything. I sometimes feel as if I can't go on. And now I've burned my boats at home so I've got to move out even though I'm not entirely sure I can really afford to.' She snuffled noisily into the hanky.

'You'll make it up with your mother.'

'You don't know her. And poor little Edward hasn't got so many relations we can afford to alienate the few he does have.' A fresh wave of sobs overtook her. Amelia looked up from her desk just in time to see Martin put a comforting arm around Kate's shoulders. She looked at Kate as though nothing would please her more than to see her drop dead on the spot.

'There, there,' he said, not sure what else to say. Comforting damsels in distress wasn't in his repertoire. But it seemed to be the right thing, judging by the way Kate buried her face in his chest and clung to him so tightly he could hardly breathe. Amelia looked as if she was going to explode.

Martin suddenly seemed to be around a lot more than she had remembered in the past. Perhaps she noticed him now because he always had something nice to say to her when they met.

'I think he's made keeping me cheerful his mission in life,' she told Maria during one of their regular gossips on the phone.

'He sounds like a nice bloke. Have you shagged him yet? I mean, if Andreas only wants to play with you when you're away from home . . .'

'Maria!' shrieked Kate in indignation. 'I'm not like you. I don't go to bed with every man I meet.'

'I don't go to bed with everyone.' Maria giggled. 'Just most of them. Anyway, enough about my rampant sex life. How are things with you?'

'Not too bad at the moment. Henry is still horrible, but Mummy has calmed down a bit. I've found a nanny – a wonderful girl called Julie who's just like Mary Poppins – and I move into the house next week.'

'I shall have to come and stay as soon as you are settled.'

'You'll be very welcome, although God knows what you will sleep on. I've only bought the bare minimum of furniture. I just can't afford more than that at the moment.'

'Don't worry about that. I'm a rough, tough soldier remember, and I can probably cope with a sleeping bag and a floor. And when I do come to stay I shall want to meet this Martin bloke.'

'I don't know he's up to coping with a man-eater like you.'

'Not for me, silly. I want to check out his suitability for you. It's about time you got yourself a proper man again, not just someone who wants you on stand-by.'

After she put the phone down Kate thought about what

Maria had said. She was right; she didn't really have a man, did she? She loved it when she and Andreas were together but for some time now she'd begun to acknowledge to herself that the set-up was far from satisfactory. And she'd also acknowledged that Andreas might feel affection for her but it almost certainly amounted to nothing stronger, not if she had to keep their relationship a secret. It was such a weird arrangement she sometimes felt as if she was going to end with a split personality. It was tricky pretending that she was nothing more than his personal pilot every time they flew in from overseas, when the instant they landed in whatever resort he was checking out she assumed the role of his lover. But she was in a cleft stick. She could hardly end their affair – not while she still worked for him. And she had to keep on working for him or how else could she afford that effing great mortgage? There wasn't much chance of her finding another job which paid as well as this, because outside aviation she had no qualifications. And she had to admit that, for her age, she was extremely well paid – which was just as well considering her outgoings. As long as this situation continued, she could hardly expect another man to want her on the days Andreas didn't, despite the fact that in her current state of disillusionment she could fancy having a proper relationship with someone else. Thinking about it, she had to admit that Martin was quite a fanciable option, but it wasn't really on the cards if all she had to offer was a time-share arrangement, with Andreas getting all the best slots. Let's face it, she told herself, I'll just have to make do with being Andreas's mistress when he has the time and the inclination. And much as she loved it when Andreas *did* have the inclination she knew in her heart that it wasn't what she was looking for. For the moment, though, it would just have to do.

On the day of the move, Kate had been hoping that Honour would look after Edward while all the upheaval was going on. It wasn't that she had much to take, but she didn't think that a boisterous three-year-old and busy removal men were a good combination. But Honour had other plans and sniffily told Kate that she would have to cope.

'I'll be glad when Julie takes over,' muttered Kate. 'At

least then all I'll have to worry about is flying.'

'And that ridiculous mortgage,' added Honour sourly.

Well, thought Kate, as long as I keep this job I can manage. And it didn't look as though there was any likelihood that Andreas would want to get rid of her.

Despite Honour's dire warnings about her finances things seemed to pick up for Kate. Edward adored Julie, Maria was posted back from Germany to a job on Salisbury Plain, there seemed to be less flying, which meant more time off for Kate, and best of all there was no Horrible Henry. Martin hung around enquiring anxiously about her welfare but Kate didn't go out of her way to encourage him. Sure, he was a really nice guy and definitely quite a hunk, but as long as Andreas still wanted her it would be unfair of her to lead him on. Amelia could have him if she could get him, although Martin seemed oblivious to her overtly heavy hints.

Occasionally Martin or one of his colleagues would take a professional interest in Kate and would meet the aircraft to ask her or her passengers if they had anything to declare, but they never asked to inspect their bags or to search the plane itself. In fact, wherever they went in Europe the customs officials were all remarkably uninterested in them. Kate assumed that it was because they realised that Andreas was so loaded he was hardly likely to risk all by trying to slip a couple of extra bottles of duty-free gin into the country. And she certainly wouldn't risk smuggling. All pilots knew for a fact that if the CAA caught them doing anything in that line they would remove the miscreant's flying licence with the speed of light. The thought of being grounded for the rest of their life was more than enough to keep a million miles between pilots and contraband.

As the summer progressed, Kate finally felt as if she had got everything in her life under control. The job was great, she loved her independence, Edward was happy and contented, and her income and her bills just about seemed to balance out. She should have guessed that with her track record, a spanner was bound to be heading for the works to mess things up again.

The day had begun in a completely routine way. Kate, as usual, had arrived at Farnborough in plenty of time, having filed her flight plan from home. She had checked her slot time, checked the aircraft, made sure that everything was in order and was going through the met reports, cup of coffee in hand, when she noticed that there were warnings for clear air turbulence along her proposed route to Turin. She sighed and prepared to file an amendment to her route so they would avoid the area. Clear air turbulence was not to be trifled with, as it could strike with terrifying strength out of a clear blue sky. Jumbo jets had been thrown around by it and passengers had been killed after planes had been tossed around like ping-pong balls in a fountain. What it would be like for the little Citation to get caught up in such wild atmospheric conditions didn't bear thinking about.

Andreas arrived twenty minutes or so later, and it wasn't long after that they were in the air. He came and sat next to Kate in the cockpit for a while, and told her about some deal he had pulled off, netting a big contract to provide holiday accommodation for one of the big UK-based tour operators.

'That's terrific,' said Kate.

'I am very pleased. It's guaranteed business and it's up to them to rent the rooms. I get the money anyway.'

'Sounds cool.'

'And today I'm hoping to close a deal with a winter sports outfit in the Italian Alps.'

'Hey, fantastic, winter holidays.' Kate fell silent, thinking that it would be a long time before she would be able to afford any sort of holiday, winter or otherwise. The silence lengthened, so Andreas made his excuses and returned to the cabin, ostensibly to do some work.

They flew on for a further twenty minutes, until suddenly, and without a hint of a warning, the aircraft was kicked violently upwards with such force that Kate felt herself being physically slammed down into her seat and crushed against her straps. Shit, clear air turbulence. What the hell was it doing here? The forecast had said it was supposed to be over a hundred miles away. Bloody met men. She felt her heart rate double and tasted bile in her mouth as fear gripped her. The plane was bucking and jumping all over the sky, like a mustang in a rodeo. It wouldn't be able to take too much of this sort of punishment – the wings simply weren't designed

307

for such abnormal stresses. She yelled over her shoulder for Andreas to put his seat belt on, but as she did so the plane dropped five hundred feet vertically and Kate felt her body try to hit the ceiling. She thanked God for her retaining straps and hoped Andreas had managed to get his on. It was like the most violent roller-coaster ride imaginable and twice as frightening. From the cabin came a loud crash.

'Are you all right?' she called. No reply. She wanted to go back and check him but she had to get out of this wild air stream first. The Citation was still leaping about the sky, jinking madly up, down and sideways. She knew that her priority was at the controls and not administering first aid. She called up air traffic and, as calmly as she could, requested clearance to lose two thousand feet. Clear air turbulence only occupied a narrow piece of air, like water flowing down an invisible tube, and by diving or climbing she would get out of it.

'Golf Alpha Bravo Zulu Yankee you are cleared to level three three,' came the laconic reply. 'Maintain current heading.'

Thank God, thought Kate as she pushed the stick forward and allowed the plane to slide down two thousand feet. Within seconds the buffeting and shaking stopped as they entered smoother air. Kate breathed deeply a few times, flicked on the automatic pilot and then shakily climbed out of her seat to check on her passenger.

Andreas was sprawled across the cabin floor, blood oozing from a gash on his forehead and his skin ashen. Kate knelt on the floor beside him, swiftly loosened his tie and opened the neck of his shirt. He seemed to be breathing, that was something. He'd obviously been thrown around considerably during those violent few minutes. Her army first aid training had instilled in her the necessity not to move an injured person, but she really needed to check him over. She carefully felt all his limbs for any obvious signs of broken bones. They seemed all right. She was worried about his skull and neck, and although there was nothing she could do there – she didn't have the equipment or the expertise – she felt carefully round to make sure that there was nothing obviously drastically amiss. She felt she ought to immobilise his head so that if he did have a neck injury it wouldn't get any worse. His jacket was lying on one of the seats. Kate grabbed it, rolled it up and wedged it against the left side of his head. Too bad if it creased the expensive fabric; she hoped Andreas would understand. She cast about her looking for something to wedge the other side of his head and spotted his briefcase upturned on the floor. That would do. She tugged on the handle to pull it towards her, and as she did so the lid opened and dumped its contents in a heap on the floor.

'Shit,' swore Kate under her breath. Still, this was not the time to worry about the mess. She pushed the case gently against Andreas's other temple. Providing they didn't meet any other violent weather conditions he should be OK now till they landed and she got some proper medical assistance.

She stood up and gathered up the contents of Andreas's briefcase. In amongst all the papers she could feel his mobile phone and she pulled it out so that she could stack the documents neatly. She began to straighten the papers but there was something else amongst them: a clear plastic bag of white powder. She stared at it uncomprehendingly for a minute. What on earth . . .? Then a nasty suspicion began to form in her mind. She knew what it looked like but it couldn't be, surely . . .? There must be some other explanation – maybe it was sugar, or some sort of food additive – but a horrible creeping feeling seemed to be telling Kate otherwise. She turned her gaze from the bag and looked at Andreas. He didn't look like a junkie. She'd never seen any sign of a drug habit. Surely if he was into that sort of rubbish she would have noticed? Track marks, mood swings, something. Not that she knew anything about weird substances and their side-effects. The dodgiest thing she had ever put into her body was an entire bottle of disgustingly cheap Liebfraumilch when she had been a cadet – and she'd been sick all the next day. She returned her gaze to the bag of powder. What was she to do? She could hardly ask Andreas what was in it. If it was something innocent then he wouldn't appreciate the suspicious turn her thoughts had taken, and if it was an illegal substance he wouldn't want her to know about it full stop. Oh shit, what a problem! With trembling hands she put the papers back on the floor and spread them out so they looked as though they had fallen out of his case that way. Then she carefully tucked the bag and the mobile phone in amongst them so they couldn't be seen. As a final touch she removed his briefcase from where she'd wedged it to keep his head still, stripped off her jacket and replaced it with that. Then she dumped the case, open and upside down, over the papers. It looked pretty OK to her. When Andreas came round, if he said anything, she would tell him that she'd been so busy tending to him and flying the jet she hadn't had a chance to tidy up. Would he believe her? All she could do was pray. She really didn't want to have anything to do with what she had just seen and she certainly didn't want any awkward questions.

Kate checked Andreas's pulse and breathing, both of which seemed to be pretty normal, and then returned to the cockpit to monitor their position and weigh up the pros and cons of diverting to a slightly nearer airport. She decided that Andreas's condition didn't look life-threatening, and thought that if he were in a position to make the decision himself, he would probably rather reach his intended destination, even if it took a few more minutes, rather than divert. She radioed ahead to the airport to request a medical team to meet them and then began a gentle descent towards Turin.

They were about ten minutes from landing when Andreas began to come round. Kate was aware of a low groan from the cabin.

'Lie still,' she called over her shoulder.

'Huh?' came the confused-sounding reply.

'We hit turbulence. You got knocked unconscious.' There was a silence of several minutes, then another, louder groan.

'How do you feel?'

There was a further pause, then Andreas said gruffly, 'How do you think?'

Kate broke off her conversation to respond to Turin air traffic control and changed her heading and speed slightly as she had been directed. She heard a noise behind her. Andreas was struggling to sit up.

'I thought I told you to lie still,' she said, worry making her voice terse.

'And since when did you give the orders in this outfit? Stop worrying, woman, I'm all right.'

310

She glanced over her shoulder, aware that this stage of an approach into a busy international airport was not the best moment to be distracted by what her passenger was up to, and saw him lean groggily against one of the leather seats. He reached across, pulled his case and papers towards him and stuffed everything away. Once he had packed the case he seemed to go through the contents more carefully, then snapped the locks shut. Kate realised she had been holding her breath and let the air out of her lungs with a sense of relief. He looked as if he believed that that was how everything had landed after the accident. And talking of landing . . .! Kate flicked her concentration back to her flying.

The ambulance was there to meet them as Kate trundled to a halt at her allotted place on the apron.

'What the hell do we want that for?' snapped Andreas.

'I wasn't sure how badly hurt you were,' said Kate. 'Supposing you were still unconscious? Or you'd broken something?'

'I'm sorry,' said Andreas, realising his anger was misplaced. 'But apart from a bloody awful headache I don't think anything permanent is wrong.'

But the medics wouldn't let him go, despite his protestations, until they had checked him over for symptoms of concussion.

'And you understand what we say?' said the paramedic in halting English. 'You feel sick, you feel dizzy, you cannot see too good, you go to hospital.'

'Yeah, yeah,' said Andreas impatiently, anxious to get away for his meeting.

'OK. Take these for the headache.' They handed Andreas a couple of painkillers, which he knocked back gratefully.

'I should be finished by about four this evening, can you arrange a slot for about five?' he asked Kate.

'Shouldn't be a problem,' she replied. She watched him climb into the waiting Merc and depart for whatever business he had come to Turin to complete. As the car disappeared, she wondered again about the little packet in his briefcase. She had read enough in the papers about the lifestyles of the rich and famous to know it seemed to imply the regular use of recreational drugs. She supposed that it was perhaps not so

311

odd, given Andreas's bank balance, that he indulged in such a pursuit but her strict upbringing and her disciplined life in the army would not allow her to condone it. In fact, she found the thought that he was involved in any way with drugs quite abhorrent. It didn't matter how attractive he was; Kate didn't think she could carry on a relationship with someone who took drugs. She resolved to make a big effort to look for another job.

Chapter Twenty-Eight

When Kate got home that evening feeling absolutely drained, Maria was sitting in her kitchen drinking tea and feeding Edward biscuits made by Julie. Julie had apparently retired to her room to watch an early evening soap as Maria had informed her that she would be only to happy to help with Edward's bath and bedtime tonight. Kate made herself a cup of tea and flopped on to a kitchen chair. She was tired and hungry, and her mind was in turmoil over what Andreas had had with him in his case. She was about to confide her worries to her friend and ask for some advice when Maria announced she had some momentous news.

'I'm being sent out to Bosnia. I go next week.'

'Oh, Maria! That's terrible.' Kate was horrified. This was all she needed after the events of the day.

But Maria was too buoyed up with her own happiness to really take any notice of Kate's less than enthusiastic response. 'It's not really. It's a good job and it's real soldiering; you know, out in the field with troops, not admin and paperwork. I'm sick of running a bloody desk.'

Kate felt selfish about her reaction. Maria was right. She'd felt the same way when she'd been sent to fly helicopters in Ireland rather than in Germany. Ireland was the real McCoy; Germany was playing war games and taxiing VIPs about. Even so, she had been so looking forward to having Maria living close enough to visit, and now she was being sent further away than ever. Selfishly, Kate didn't want her friend's happiness; she wanted her here, near her.

'But you've only just been posted back here.'

'I know, but you know what the army's like.'

Kate did, only too well, but she didn't relish the disappearance of her closest friend for the next six months. And unlike Germany, there was precious little chance of Maria being allowed back except for a few days' R&R in the middle of her tour.

'I shall miss you so much,' said Kate with heartfelt feeling.

'And I'll miss you and little Edward. Goodness, by the time I get back he'll be almost four.'

'We'll write to you, of course.'

'Too damned right you will,' said Maria with a grin. 'And I expect it'll be possible to phone. It's not like I'm going to the dark side of the moon.'

But the way Kate felt, it might almost be as bad as that. She valued Maria's support, humour and judgement so much and she wasn't relishing being without her for a whole six months.

'Can you stay the night?' asked Kate. If she wasn't going to see Maria for ages she wanted to make the most of her while she was still around.

'Tonight I can, but I must nip home tomorrow and say goodbye to Mum. After that I shall have to go back and get myself ready to go. I don't suppose there'll be a chance of my being able to drop by again before I'm off.'

'That's great. I can only offer you the dining room floor and a sleeping bag and pillow, but if that's OK . . .?'

'I'm a soldier, remember. That'll be fine, especially if you ply me with a drink or two to help me sleep.'

'Let's see if Andy and Emma want to come round. We can get a curry and have a couple of bottles of wine. It won't be much of a send-off but we haven't time to plan anything better.'

'That would be great. I'd like that. And what about inviting that bloke of yours, Martin?'

'He's not my bloke. I just know him through work.'

'But you told me how nice he was to you.'

'He was, but it doesn't mean . . .'

'Well, why not give him just the merest hint that you might be interested. You know what I think about you keeping faithful to Andreas just because he might fancy a roll in the sack when you fly him abroad.'

'I'm not saving myself for Andreas, not really.'

'You must be, otherwise you'd be out looking for something more permanent. I know you, and I know that however much you are kidding yourself that Andreas is God's gift, this cannot possibly measure up to your romantic ideal of a wonderful love affair. And for what it's worth, I think you deserve better than that – even if Andreas is filthy rich.'

Kate looked at the floor and said, rather coolly, 'Look, if it's all the same to you, I'd rather not discuss that right now.'

Maria got the hint. 'OK, no Martin at the party. And I won't mention him again.'

'Good. Then you order the curry; I'll phone Andy.'

'Maria's not the only one with news,' said Andy when he and Emma arrived half an hour later clutching two bottles of rather good claret.

Kate ushered them into her sitting room. 'Tell me when we've all got a drink,' she said. She scuttled about, finding the corkscrew, getting glasses from the kitchen, offering some peanuts about, until Andy told her to sit down.

'We're all quite capable of fending for ourselves. You don't need to wait on us hand and foot.'

'Sorry,' said Kate and instantly plonked herself down on a chair. She was grateful for the chance to stop; she was pooped.

'And now you're sitting comfortably,' said Andy with a grin.

'Oh yes, I forgot, you said you had some news too.'

'Maria's not the only one to be posted. We're going out to America. I've landed an exchange posting over there.'

Kate knew she should be pleased for Andy. It was obviously a terrific opportunity for them both, and judging by the look on Emma's face, she might as well have won the lottery, but all Kate could feel was a sense of utter abandonment. First Maria, now Andy and Emma. Her mother would barely speak to her, her friends were posted – there was no one for her to turn to now.

She forced herself to say, 'That's great,' but she knew it sounded false. In the excitement of the moment no one noticed.

'America!' said Maria with enthusiasm. 'That's terrific. Can I book in for a holiday as soon as I get back from Bosnia?'

'Of course,' said Emma, laughing. 'We're hoping to have loads of visitors. It'll be so exciting. I can't wait to go. I've never been outside Europe so this is going to be a wonderful adventure. And it's all happening so suddenly. The poor bugger who was supposed to be going has got some awful illness and we're having to fill in. Andy reckons we got chosen because we don't have kids so we don't mind being mucked about at short notice.'

'How short?' asked Maria.

'Three weeks. Hardly time to find out about where we're going, what we can expect when we get there or anything. But you could tell us all about it, Kate. You've spent some time out there, haven't you?'

'Yes. Yes I have, but it's a huge place so I hardly saw much of it.' She didn't think she wanted to talk about it right now. All she could think about was how everything seemed to be going wrong again: she'd had a lousy flight, God alone knew what Andreas was up to, she'd rowed with her mother again, her friends were leaving the country . . . And what was in store for her? More worries about her rocky finances, a relationship that was going nowhere, the problems of a single mother, no social life to speak of and no shoulders to cry on. Four years ago she had had everything: a glamorous job, a wonderful husband, a large circle of friends, plenty of money. She'd been the envy of many. Well, who would envy her now? She felt her eyes stinging as self-pity got the better of her. Oh God, she was going to cry. She couldn't let the others see. What explanation could she give them?

Stifling a sob she said, 'I thought I heard Edward. I'll be back in a minute.' She raced out of the sitting room and up the stairs to the bathroom. She locked the door and sat on the loo and let the tears stream down her face. Why did life seem to be so unfair? What had she done to deserve losing Eddie? Why was her love life so unsatisfactory? Why couldn't her friends do jobs that meant they stayed near her? And as she cried huge sobs that she muffled with wads of tissues, she knew she was being unreasonable. She knew that in the eyes

316

of many she was quite privileged. She had a good job, a lovely son, a nice house; she got to travel, she had a good boss if you ignored his dabbling in an illegal habit, and even if her love life left a bit to be desired, at least it existed after a fashion. So why was she feeling so lonely and miserable?

Downstairs she heard the doorbell ring. The curry had arrived. Hurriedly she blew her nose and dried her eyes. Brace up, she told herself, looking at her reflection in the mirror. You're supposed to be giving Maria, Andy and Emma a good time, so stop behaving like a wet weekend. She splashed water on her face and dried it roughly on a towel. She hoped no one would notice that she had been crying.

By the time she got downstairs, Maria had already taken charge of the delivery.

'Hey,' said Kate trying to feign cheerfulness. 'This is my treat. How much do I owe you?'

'No way. Save your dosh to keep the bailiffs at bay.' Maria carried the large plastic bag containing their meal into the dining room and dumped it on the table next to a pile of plates and some knives and forks. 'Grub's up,' she called to the others. Everyone was famished and there was a good-natured scrum for the naan bread, poppadoms, curry and rice.

'Pass me the chutney,' said Andy to no one in particular.

'Hey, don't take all the lamb pasanda,' called Maria to Emma.

'Wine, anyone?' offered Kate.

'Mmm, this is to die for,' enthused Emma, licking her fingers as she finished filling her plate.

Everyone piled back into the sitting room and a contented silence descended, occasionally broken by a comment on how good a particular dish was proving to be or a request for a refill of wine. Finally the plates were emptied, the last of the poppadoms were nibbled and the four friends slumped back in their chairs.

'God, that was wonderful. That's got to be one of the best curries ever. I feel stuffed,' said Maria, and then followed it up with a loud belch. 'Oops. Sorry.'

'That good, eh?' said Andy.

'Absolutely,' agreed Emma. 'I know what a python feels like when it has just swallowed a goat.'

'Hey talking about swallowing things, I heard a really disgusting joke the other day,' said Andy. And without further ado he told them it.

'That was awful,' said Maria, wiping her eyes, as the guffaws died away. Even Kate, feeling better now she had relaxed with a glass of wine and was full of good food, had found herself able to laugh. Perhaps things weren't so bad after all, she thought. Perhaps she'd just been overwrought and had got things out of proportion. All the same, she wouldn't mind asking her friends for some advice about what she had found in Andreas's possession and what she should do about it. But before she could, Emma remembered her own favourite joke, and that sparked off Maria, who had a stream of politically incorrect but nonetheless extremely funny stories. As the evening continued, the wine flowed and the sitting room rang with laughter, Kate became less and less inclined to bring a serious note into the proceedings and foist her worries and problems on the others.

Emma, sober because she was driving, eventually managed to persuade Andy that one o'clock was quite late enough for them to be staying, especially as he had to go to work in the morning. Reluctantly he allowed himself to be dragged away.

'Last glass of wine?' offered Kate, waving the bottle vaguely in Maria's direction.

'Why not?' Maria hauled herself out of her chair and tottered across to where Kate was sitting. She swayed slightly as she held out her glass. 'I think I'm pissed,' she announced.

'I think you are too.' Kate smiled at her fondly. 'Not that it's a first.'

'I should bloody well think not. And I don't suppose there'll be much to drink out on the Bosnian front line, so best I make the most of it while the going is good.'

'Always the opportunist.'

''Cept where men are concerned.' Maria suddenly looked completely miserable.

'But you always have loads of blokes hanging around. I'm the one who's back on the shelf.'

'I know.' Maria took a long swig of her wine. 'But they all think I'm just a good-time girl. They love me and leave me. I've never had a really steady relationship and now all the

318

blokes that are my age are married with kids. I sometimes think there's no one left for me.'

Kate felt a wave of sympathy for her friend. Maria was right, of course; she could attract men just by batting her eyelashes at them but they never seemed to hang around.

'You'll find someone one day.' Kate tried to sound convincing.

Maria looked at her over the rim of her glass. 'Huh.'

'You will. Look at me. At one stage you reckoned I was the oldest living virgin, and I managed to find Mr Right.'

'That's probably exactly why you did find him. But who wants me? *Shop-soiled* is the phrase that springs to mind. I think I've missed the boat if I'm going to get married and have kids. I've always wanted lots of kids, like my mum, but I think I've blown it.'

'You're just a bit maudlin,' said Kate. 'How about a nice cup of coffee?'

'No thanks. And don't change the subject. I envy you, Kate, I really do. Look at you, you've got it made.'

Kate felt stunned. She didn't see her life like that at all; in fact, quite the reverse. 'You just think the grass is greener.'

'No I don't.' Maria finished her glass of wine and looked up hopefully. Kate passed her the bottle to help herself. 'Look at you: you've a gorgeous son, a house of your own; you're settled, you've got a job doing what you love—'

'I've got money worries, I've got no social life, it's not all a bed of roses,' interrupted Kate.

'Yes, but when I look forward to my future all I can see is me ending up as one of those terrifying single senior female officers, whose only companion is some sort of yappy little dog.'

Maria's picture of her future self was so improbable that Kate couldn't stop herself from laughing. 'Hardly. For a start you haven't got a moustache, and isn't that a prerequisite?'

Maria started to laugh too. 'I'd forgotten. Perhaps you're right. Perhaps it is just a case of the grass being greener.' She knocked back the rest of her wine. 'And now you've put me straight and made me cheer up, it's time for bed.'

Maria weaved her way out of the room and disappeared into the dining room. By the time Kate had given the sitting room a perfunctory tidy, she was out for the count and snoring hard.

Kate made her way up to her room thinking back over the evening. She'd started off by feeling so sorry for herself, seeing only the things that were wrong in her life, and yet Maria had come as close as she ever would to admitting that things were far from right in her own life. Perhaps, Kate admitted to herself, things weren't so bad after all. Perhaps she'd just got everything way out of proportion. She'd had a lot to worry about recently, what with her finances, the move and then that awful scare earlier on today. She had just been overwrought and getting everything out of proportion. She didn't approve of Andreas, or anyone, taking drugs, but it was his life he was mucking up. It wasn't as if she had suddenly discovered he was a mass murderer or anything. As Kate pulled off her clothes, she decided that although she would definitely look for another job, there wasn't any particular hurry. She would wait until she found something exactly right before she moved on. Just because she felt as she did about drug misuse there was no reason why she should end up being the one who ultimately lost out by taking the first job that came along.

Kate said farewell to Maria the next morning with a heavy heart. What she'd said the night before about missing her friend was completely true, and six months seemed an age to wait before they would be able to get together again.

'You will look after yourself properly?' said Kate as she helped Maria load her few bits and pieces into the car. Edward was riding his tricycle round and round the tiny square lawn that had been ambitiously described by the estate agent as the front garden.

'Have you ever known me not to?'

'Well . . .' said Kate, thinking of all the occasions that Maria had punished her body with excessive quantities of food or drink.

'I know, I know,' laughed Maria, knowing what Kate was thinking. 'But life out in the Balkans is hardly going to be the equivalent of a Club 18–30 holiday.'

'Apart from the ratio of women to men.'

Maria was suddenly serious. 'No. I'm turning over a new

leaf in that department. I'm giving up men for a bit, see if I can't patch up my tattered reputation.' She grinned ruefully at Kate. 'It's probably too late, of course but one can always hope.'

Kate hugged her friend on impulse. 'I'm sure it isn't. You'll find some gorgeous hunk. Honest you will, and then you can have a dozen kids.

'A dozen!' shrieked Maria. 'Five at the absolute tops.'

'All right, five then. But you'll have them, just see if I'm not proved right.'

'And remember what I said about Martin.' Maria saw Kate's expression. 'I know, I know I said that I wouldn't mention him again, but please think about what I said. I honestly believe Andreas is just using you and I really think you deserve more than that. And if Martin isn't right, then . . . Oh, forget it. It's none of my business.'

'No, it's not,' said Kate, but she wasn't angry. She knew Maria was only saying these things because she cared so much for her. 'Now stop worrying about my love life and go and see your mum.'

The two women stood staring at each other for a second before throwing their arms around each other.

'You will write,' said Maria, her eyes looking suspiciously moist.

'Of course I will.' Kate blinked rapidly, disentangled herself and called to Edward. 'Come here darling, and say goodbye to Auntie Maria.'

Edward clambered off his trike and ran forward. 'Bye Auntie M'ia. Will you bring me back a present?'

'Edward!' said Kate in horror. 'Maria, I'm so sorry. I can't think what put such an idea into his head.

Maria knelt down and gave Edward a big bear hug. 'I'll see what I can do, sweetheart.' Then, over his shoulder to Kate, she said, 'Don't worry about it. He's just a born go-getter. You should take a leaf out of his book and do some go-getting yourself. Remember, you should be most loyal to yourself – if you don't get the things in life you most want, the only person you are letting down is yourself.'

As Maria finally drove away, Kate waved goodbye to her thoughtfully. Perhaps she had a point.

*

Kate had been told that her take-off was going to be delayed by at least an hour due to industrial action by French air traffic controllers. Her three passengers – business associates of Andreas's – had sloped off to the bar of a smart hotel only a quarter of a mile away, leaving instructions to ring them on their mobiles if the situation changed. Kate was left with nothing better to do than kick her heels and thumb through out-of-date copies of *Flight International* magazine.

'How's life?' said a familiar voice.

Kate recognised it as Martin's and looked up, smiling.

'Not too bad, thanks.' She hadn't come across him for a while and she felt a pleasant little buzz of happiness at seeing him again.

'And the mortgage?'

Kate grimaced. 'Still like a millstone, but at least the interest rates are now going down, not up.' How nice of him to ask. 'Can I get you a coffee?' she offered. 'Or are you about to make a swoop on a gang of international drugs smugglers?'

'International drugs smugglers? Here? Hardly.'

'You never know. I mean, why not?' She dropped some coins into the coffee machine. 'White, sugar?' she asked.

'Just white, please.'

Kate hit the relevant button. Two plastic cups of hot coffee were duly dispensed.

'So, why not?'

'Because most of the people who use this place are far too respectable. OK, we get the odd celebrity living life in the fast lane coming through with a stash for their own use, but not much more than that.' Kate suppressed the urge to make a comment. 'Besides which,' continued Martin, 'the big boys tend to go for very busy entry ports where customs are really stretched. It's much easier to bring a consignment through on a route that is used for freight.'

Kate could see that he was flattered by her interest in his job, but that wasn't surprising; most people liked to talk about themselves. She remembered Maria's advice about go-getting and thought that she could do worse than Martin. She threw him another question to keep him chatting and to give him more opportunity to notice her feminine charms. 'But don't these drugs barons sometimes employ people to bring stuff through?'

'Mules, you mean?'

'Yes, if that's what they're called.'

'Yes, it's perfectly feasible, but you've got to remember that because they know they are carrying the stuff, they tend to be easier to spot than the poor innocent lorry driver who thinks he's got frozen meat on his load but hidden somewhere in it is half a ton of heroin or coke.' Kate nodded to encourage him a little more. 'The innocent driver will act like he hasn't a care in the world, because he hasn't. He hasn't a clue that he's got something on board he hadn't bargained for. Of course, that isn't too bad if he gets caught in a country where they believe in the concept of innocent until proven guilty, but the poor bastards that get caught crossing from Romania into Hungary or Turkey into Greece may find they get stuck there for months or even years. And Mr Big just writes off the deal he had planned and looks for some other poor bugger to stitch up.'

'So go on, what does the average Mr Big look like?'

'Pretty normal, from my limited experience.'

'They don't go around wearing dark suits and shades and carrying guns in shoulder holsters, then?'

Martin laughed. 'Not that I've noticed. In fact the couple I've come across have looked remarkably normal.'

'How would you spot a big-time drug-dealer, then?'

'Quite often we get a tip-off. More often than not someone from the organisation with an axe to grind approaches us and grasses up the others. Sometimes it's as a result of months or years of surveillance, intelligence work and luck. But what doesn't happen is that we see someone coming into the country and think, aha, here's a shady-looking hood, let's nick him.'

'Oh.' Kate sounded disappointed.

'Ruined your illusions?'

'Not really.' She laughed. 'It seems to be what happens on the TV.'

'Yes, well . . .' They both laughed.

'Silly me,' admitted Kate.

'Not really. I've probably got all sorts of misconceptions about flying.'

323

Kate was about to extend the conversation when Martin's pager bleeped.

'Sorry,' he said, reading the message. 'You'll have to excuse me, I'm required elsewhere. I'll catch you another time.'

'Bye,' said Kate, returning to her magazine, which had suddenly become a lot less interesting. Shame he had to go; she'd been enjoying their chat. But perhaps being a customs officer wasn't the most glamorous of professions. It sounded like a lot more like hard graft and painstaking investigation than she had thought.

About a fortnight later she had just returned from a trip to Nice when Martin approached her.

'Seen any big-time smugglers recently?' he asked with a wicked grin.

Kate laughed. 'Push off,' she said. 'Just because I make one mistake.'

'Sorry,' he said. 'I shouldn't make fun of you. It's not fair.'

'I don't mind. I'm glad I gave you something to laugh about.' She continued to walk through the offices towards the door to the car park. Martin fell into step beside her.

'Really?' he said, sounding surprised.

'Why not? I mean, it's no big deal. As you said yourself, there's probably a great mound of things that you have got completely the wrong idea about when it comes to flying a plane.'

'So tell me about it.'

'What?'

'Flying, of course.'

'Well, actually, the biggest secret about flying is that once you can do it, it's easy, just like driving a car.' Kate extracted her car keys from her bag and jangled them as if to prove her point.

'I bet it isn't. I mean, how on earth do you work out what the plane is doing in the first place? I can't imagine how you can tell if it's going up or down when you've got nothing but fresh air around you. At least in a car or on a bike you can see whether the countryside is flat or hilly.'

Kate's jaw dropped. Of course you could tell what the plane

was doing in the sky; your sense of balance and all sorts of sensations told you that. The only way you wouldn't know that was if . . . She had to ask. 'You mean you're telling me that you spend your life hanging around light aircraft and you've never once had the desire to get in one?' She reached her car and unlocked it. Martin opened the driver's door for her, looking faintly bemused by her tone of complete astonishment.

'No, why should I? I'm sure flying can't be that great.'

Not that great! How could anyone say that? Another realisation dawned on Kate as she got behind the wheel. 'You don't know what you're missing out on at all, do you?'

'Come on. It can't be such a thrill.'

'Have you *never* flown?'

'No.'

'You're joking?' Martin shook his head. 'But what about holidays?' Kate could scarcely believe that there was still someone in Britain who had never been in a plane.

'I go to the Lakes and go hill-walking.'

Kate shook her head in disbelief. Good heavens above! Maria's words about being loyal to herself and going out to get what she wanted suddenly pushed themselves to the forefront of her mind. Almost before a thought had formed in her mind she found herself issuing an invitation. 'Well, it's about time we put this to rights.'

'What do you mean?'

'What are you doing on Saturday?'

'I'm on the late turn.'

'So you're free in the morning.' Martin nodded. 'Right, I'll meet you here at ten o'clock.' She braced herself for a rebuff as she turned the key in the ignition.

'Why?'

'For the experience of a lifetime.'

'OK,' he grinned. 'You're on.'

For some reason that she didn't want to analyse, Kate felt hugely pleased that her offer had been accepted. 'Great. Till Saturday then.' And with that she slammed the car door and zoomed off, leaving Martin looking slightly puzzled.

It was only later that Kate realised that she had never once considered that Martin might not wish to go flying or that he might have a long-term relationship with someone whom might conceivably resent Kate making a date with him. Heigh-ho, she thought as this notion flitted across her mind, too bad. He could always have told her to get lost if he hadn't wanted to find out what she was offering. Maria had said she ought to be more of a go-getter. Well, so far so good.

Chapter Twenty-Nine

Saturday morning dawned overcast with a stiff breeze, which was faintly disappointing. Kate wasn't fussed; she'd flown in far worse, but Martin wouldn't like it much. However, her spirits lifted a little when she listened to the weather forecast, which promised that it would soon clear from the west and turn into a warm and sunny August day. That would be better from Martin's point of view; flying in cloud wasn't half as much fun as when you could see the view.

Martin was waiting for her when she arrived. She had half thought of bringing Edward along too, but he had a swimming lesson that morning and Kate had decided that it was more important that he should go to that than tool around in a light aircraft for an hour. As he hadn't any idea of the treat he'd almost been offered, he wasn't unduly upset.

'I'll give you a couple of days off next week,' Kate had offered Julie.

'That's fine. I hadn't any plans for today except to go shopping, so you're probably just saving me from spending more money than I could afford.'

'Thanks anyway,' said Kate, thinking that she was just about to spend a large amount of money that she could barely afford taking a man she scarcely knew for an hour's joyride in a plane. What was she thinking about?

She took him to the little club up in the Chilterns where she'd been a member since Andreas had sold his Cessna and her access to free recreational flying had come to an abrupt end. She rarely flew there now as the cost was a luxury she could not really justify, but just occasionally she felt the need to indulge in a few aerobatics and have a potter about in the sky for the hell of it. Besides which, she liked the other people who frequented the club and she liked the banter and the chat in the club room. Martin seemed quite ebullient on the journey there, so Kate was fairly certain that he wasn't suffering unduly from nerves. But as they drove through the gate and the car drew to a halt in the car park he fell silent.

'Nervous?'

'Not really.' But he didn't sound particularly confident.

'Don't worry. I've been flying for longer than I've been driving, and you haven't had the least qualm about my skills behind a steering wheel.'

'Yes, but if the car cuts out we roll to a stop. If the engine in the plane fails we plummet thousands of feet.'

'And how often do you hear of planes just dropping out of the sky?'

'Often enough.'

'Huh,' said Kate. They both climbed out of the car and headed across to the wooden hut that was the headquarters of the club. Kate booked in, collected the keys to the plane and took Martin across to where the little aircraft was parked. She unlocked the door and instructed Martin to get in and sort out his safety harness while she did the statutory checks. Satisfied that everything was in order, she started the engine and contacted the tower, and a few minutes later they were hurtling down the grass airstrip. Kate noticed that Martin's knuckles were white as he gripped the edge of his seat. She put out a hand and patted his arm reassuringly just before she pulled back on the stick and the plane zoomed upwards into the sky. They were cruising at three thousand feet before she could persuade Martin that the plane wouldn't nose-dive if he unclenched his fingers and relaxed slightly.

'OK?' she asked.

Martin nodded nervously.

'Look down there,' Kate said. 'That's Oxford, and if you look left you'll see Didcot power station. When I flew gliders and I got a bit short of lift I would head over to that and be guaranteed to get a good one to two thousand feet just by circling over the cooling towers.' Martin smiled at her but he

328

still didn't look anything like relaxed.

They pottered about over the Oxfordshire countryside, which was shimmering in the August sunshine, the breeze rippling across acres of ripening corn making the fields look like golden ponds. Kate kept Martin's mind off the fact that they were only supported by fresh air by pointing out various local places of interest, but she soon got bored with this.

'How about you take control for a bit?' she offered.

'Me?' Martin squeaked. Then he pulled himself together and repeated at a more normal pitch, 'Me?'

'Yes, you. You do the stick and I'll do the pedals. There's nothing to it, honestly. You see that?' Kate pointed to a little line drawing of an aeroplane floating against a black background. 'That's the artificial horizon. See if you can keep the little plane in the same place. You'll see that if I move the stick forward or back or to the left or right,' she demonstrated as she spoke, 'the little plane shows you your new attitude. Just hold the stick gently, no need to grip it, and move it ever so slightly to make any corrections you need to.'

Martin was a model pupil and was soon able to fly straight and level for a minute or two at a time. Next Kate allowed him to take over the rudder pedals simultaneously, but that wasn't a success. The plane yawed wildly around the sky and he concentrated so hard on trying to correct that that they lost height rapidly as he allowed the stick to go forward.

'OK, I have control,' said Kate, taking over the controls again. Martin looked relieved. 'Did you enjoy that?'

'I did, actually. It was great. And you're right, flying is wonderful.'

'I'm afraid it's time to head back now. I only booked the plane for an hour but perhaps we can do this again some time.'

'I'd like that.' Martin sounded genuinely enthusiastic, and for some reason Kate was really pleased.

She laughed. 'At least you look more relaxed than you did when we took off.'

'I am. Flying is cool. So how about I take you out to lunch somewhere to repay you for showing me what I've been missing all this time?'

'I'm sorry, I can't.'

'Oh.' Martin suddenly looked embarrassed. 'I'm sorry. I shouldn't have asked. It's just . . . I mean, I thought . . .'

Kate took pity on him. 'Honestly, normally I'd have said yes, but I owe it to my son's nanny to get back. Today should be her day off and she's doing me a big favour by looking after Edward this morning. It wouldn't be fair of me to stay away too long.'

'Oh.' Martin looked relieved if a little disappointed. 'How about a rain check, then?'

'I'd like that.' And she realised that she meant it.

The phone was ringing as she walked through the door of her house. She blew a kiss at Edward and waved to Julie as she raced into the dining room and grabbed the receiver before the caller rang off.

'Kate?'

'Hi, Andreas. How are you?' Kate felt her face reddening like a kid caught with its hand in the sweet jar. Did he know she'd been larking about with Martin? Was he ringing up to remonstrate with her?

'I'm fine. I just want to sort out some arrangements for the Turin trip next week.'

Kate gave a sigh of relief, and told herself not to be so silly. Of course he wasn't checking up on her. How on earth would he know what she was up to?

'Turin, sure. Fire away.'

'It would be easier if you came to the office. Can you come in on Monday morning? Eleven o'clock?'

'Of course. I'll see you then.'

'Till Monday. Bye, Kate.'

Kate replaced the receiver. He was always so formal and proper, even on the telephone – it was only when they were in one of his hotel rooms that he loosened up with terms of endearment and acts of tenderness – but as usual she felt a thrill of anticipation at being with him again. She had barely seen him at all recently, not since the last Turin trip, which had been three weeks previously. And when was the last time she had slept with him? She thought back. Nearly two months ago. Maria was right; their affair wasn't really going anywhere. She still liked Andreas, she would still go to bed with him if he wanted her to, she still felt immensely loyal to him, but their affair was reaching a dead end as far as she was concerned. Definitely time to move on. Just as soon as she found the right job. Perhaps next time she got stuck in the waiting room at Farnborough she would really have a proper look at the Sits Vac column in *Flight International*. She couldn't risk being unemployed, even for a few weeks, as she knew her finances simply wouldn't stand the strain.

On Monday, Kate got up early and dressed carefully as she always did when she was going to see Andreas.

'I thought you told yourself that Andreas was going to take a back seat in your life,' she said sternly to her reflection. She put her mascara wand down again, unused, and shoved her lipstick back in her make-up bag. Well, it's a start, she thought.

Downstairs Julie was giving Edward his breakfast with Radio One blaring over the noise of the washing machine climaxing on its final spin, bouncing around on the kitchen floor. Kate smiled at her and dropped a kiss on Edward's head. There was no point in trying to speak over the racket. The control dial on the washing machine clicked into the off position and instantly the deafening high-pitched whine ceased as the machine slowed to a stop. Gratefully Kate turned the volume control on the radio until the decibel level was just below the pain threshold.

'That's better,' she said with relief.

'What is?' asked Julie.

'Never mind.' It was probably an age thing, thought Kate.

'Coffee?' offered Julie.

'Please.' What an angel she is, thought Kate. Terrific with Edward, helpful, uncomplaining; what a paragon. She poured Kate's coffee and began to unload the machine.

'Come on, Edward. Let Mummy get her thoughts around what she's got to do today while we go and peg this lot on the line.' Edward clambered off his chair and ran out of the kitchen after Julie. Kate watched him go indulgently. He was growing up fast. She would have to think about the next step in his education soon. It was time for him to move on from his little playgroup and get used to the rough and tumble of a proper nursery school. She was afraid he was getting dreadfully spoilt with two doting grown-ups pandering to his needs. Perhaps she would start to make enquiries when she returned from London.

Kate looked at her watch. If she was going to get to London and be sure of not being late she ought to set out soon. The traffic could be appalling even when the rush hour was over. She went into the dining room and picked up her mobile, her laptop and her briefcase. If Andreas wanted to discuss routes and times it would be as well if she had the right charts and her trusty computer program so she could give him the definitive answer. Even if she was a particularly favoured employee, she knew he would not appreciate an inexact answer if he asked her a direct question. She loaded her car, said goodbye to Edward and Julie and drove towards London with nothing more on her mind than thoughts about local schools and how she would find out what might be best for her son.

Astoundingly, Kate didn't encounter a single jam, traffic lights turned miraculously to green as she approached and she sailed up Kensington High Street almost an hour early for her appointment with Andreas. She knew what a busy schedule he always had, so there was no point in going up to his office on the off chance that he might be able to fit her in early – it was a racing certainty he wouldn't. She parked in the underground car park and took the lift to the ground floor of the head offices of Spyrou International Hotels.

'Can I help you?' asked a pretty but intelligent-looking young girl.

'It's OK. I'm early for an appointment with Mr Spyrou. I'll wait here if I may.'

The receptionist glanced down at a computer screen and tapped a few keys. 'Mrs Thomas?' she enquired. Kate nodded in acknowledgement as she strolled across the gleaming marble lobby to the row of bright sofas opposite the reception desk. It was as comfortable a place to wait as any and at least there was a bigger choice of glossy magazines to be found on the glass-topped coffee table than was on offer at Farnborough. Kate sat in the sunshine and flipped desultorily through a copy of *Vogue*. Wonderful fashions but way out of her price range. She slid the magazine back on to the table and picked up *Country Life* to look at the property pages. Equally astronomical prices. She decided against making herself feel any more penurious and turned her back on the glossies and looked out of the huge plate-glass window. Across the bustling London thoroughfare she could see a sandwich bar. There was a constant trickle of people entering it and leaving again sipping from chilled cans of drink. As usual in high summer, London was swelteringly hot, and as Kate watched the comings and goings she was aware of how thirsty she was. She walked back across the expanse of marble to the reception desk.

'Is there anywhere I can get a cold drink?'

'I'm sorry. I can only offer you coffee. There's a place across the road, though.'

'Thanks. I'm going to get myself a coke. Can I get one for you while I'm there?'

The receptionist gave Kate a beaming smile but declined. 'It's awfully sweet of you to offer, but I'm on a detox diet so I'm only allowed water.'

Kate left the air-conditioned quiet of Andreas's headquarters and wondered if braving the fumes, bustle and heat of central London was going to be worth it for a can of coke. Perhaps she ought to take a leaf out of the receptionist's book and make do with water. As Kate dodged taxis and double-deckers to cross the road she couldn't think of anyone she had met recently who looked more radiantly healthy and less in need of detoxification. But then perhaps she was looking at the end result.

Kate reached her goal feeling even more frazzled, and perched on a stool by the counter while she waited to be served. She stared back across the road at the building she had just left. A taxi was drawing up outside it. Its fare got out and paid the driver, who then departed looking for a new customer. And there, standing on the pavement in a pale pink suit, was Magda. Kate took in every detail in a fleeting second, from her matching shoes and bag to the package clutched in her left hand. There was no mistake this time. Even though the figure was on the other side of a busy road, Kate knew she was right; she recognised the posture, the hair, even the suit was familiar. A bus thundered past, and when it had gone so had Magda.

'Yes please,' said a bored nasal female voice.

Kate looked round in surprise at being spoken to. 'Yes?' she said.

'What do you want?' The woman sounded even more bored if that was humanly possible.

'Huh?'

'What Do You Want?' said the woman loudly and slowly, going into speaking-to-stupid-foreigner mode.

'Oh, nothing thanks.' Kate made for the door.

'Next,' yelled the woman. Then, 'Care in the community, I ask you,' to no one in particular.

Kate legged it back across the road, getting hooted at several times as she caused a number of cars to brake suddenly. She dashed back into the cool calm of the head office and skated across the polished floor at full tilt.

'That woman,' she said, panting. 'The one in pink who just came in here.'

'Who?' said the receptionist.

'Miss Ionescu,' said Kate.

'I'm sorry.' The receptionist looked blank.

'But I saw her. She got out of a taxi just outside.'

The receptionist shook her head. 'No one has come in since you left.'

Kate couldn't believe this. There had to be a mistake. 'Are you sure?'

'Yes. Why, is it important?'

Kate shook her head. She had been so sure. 'My mistake. It must be the heat.' She went back over to the sofas and plonked down on the nearest.

But it had been Magda. She would stake her life on it. And if she hadn't come in here, where had she gone? Kate stared out of the window sightlessly, trying to make sense of everything. There had been that time in Cyprus when she had been certain that Magda had been just yards from her, and now this. Perhaps she was just paranoid. Perhaps it was just a figment of her imagination. She sighed heavily. Of course, if she had the courage to ask Andreas he could tell her for certain whether or not he still employed Magda, but Kate didn't fancy one of his angry outbursts.

'You didn't get your drink,' said the receptionist, puzzled.

'Oh no,' said Kate. 'I came charging back here to catch Magda and I forgot.' The receptionist gave Kate a stare that seemed to say that Kate needed to detox her brain. Kate looked at her watch. She was still forty-five minutes early. 'I'll go and get one now.' She felt very sheepish. She must look a right fool.

'Good idea,' agreed the receptionist silkily. Kate went right off her. 'Patronising cow,' she muttered under her breath.

Kate returned to the heat and noise and the traffic and this time made it into the sandwich bar and managed to buy a drink without being diverted from her task. As she left the shop she put the chilled can, glistening with dewdrops of condensation, to her forehead and rolled it across her skin. Delicious. This time she decided not to risk life and limb and walked the twenty yards or so to a pelican crossing. She crossed the busy highway in a group of about twenty other people. God, it was hot. She rolled the can across her forehead again. Then she froze. Not five feet from her, emerging from a shadowy doorway almost hidden from view between the imposing bulk of the Spyrou head offices and the façade of a major chain store, was Magda.

This time there was no mistake. Kate stood stock still, her can of coke held against her brow, her hand half covering her face as Magda left the discreet doorway and walked swiftly across the pavement, hailing a passing taxi as she went. Kate could see that she no longer had the packet. A crowd of tourists, chattering and clicking cameras, passed between them, and Kate lunged for the slowly closing door that Magda had just left. She got her fingertips to it just before it shut.

She slipped round the door and stood in the gloom, her heart thumping. What on earth was she going to say if anyone wanted to know what she was doing here? She didn't even know where *here* was. Her eyes adjusted from the brilliant sunshine outside and she saw she was in a tiny lobby with a lift door just in front of her. Nothing else, just the lift. Kate stared at it, mesmerised. She had this dreadful feeling that she knew where it led. She put out a finger and pressed the call button. Instantly the door slid open. Kate stepped into its stark interior. On the control panel were two solitary buttons. Taking a deep breath Kate pressed the top one and the door closed silently. She felt the lift start its ascent. After about ten seconds it stopped again with the slightest of jolts and the door opened. Kate took in the pale grey carpet that stretched before her, the Kandinsky original on the wall, the bright red sofa and the single office door to her left, and pressed the lower of the two buttons. She had seen all she needed to see. Instantly she wanted to know why Andreas had lied to her about sacking Magda. She was still working for him, but doing what? And why had Andreas engineered a situation where he could pretend to sack her? What on earth was he playing at? And, more worryingly, why did he think it necessary to indulge in such a peculiar subterfuge? Kate couldn't fathom it out. All she could think of was that he had sidelined Magda to run something for him that he couldn't trust any of his other employees to handle. Kate remembered the ugly types he consorted with, the overheard conversation and the fact that she was certain he used drugs, and suddenly a very nasty suspicion began to form in her mind.

Chapter Thirty

Her passengers for her flight to Turin arrived about fifteen minutes before they were due to depart. To a man they struck Kate as typical fat cats: expensively tailored business suits with the waistcoats covering the evidence of too many board-room lunches and club dinners; slicked-down hair; the flash of a Rolex and the residual whiff of cigar smoke. They were bluff and noisy, swapping tales of football matches as seen from directors' boxes, exchanging crude sexist jokes and coarse banter. She was reminded of badly behaved adolescents out on a school trip; overexcited and silly at being let out of the classroom. But then she thought that perhaps she was doing a disservice to badly behaved teenaged schoolboys. One of the four men she recognised as Andreas's lawyer, but the other three were unknown to her. She introduced herself to her passengers, showed them where to find the enormous insulated jug filled with fresh coffee, the refrigerator with cold drinks, wine, beer and sandwiches, and generally made them feel welcome, but knew that they considered her to have little more status than that of air stewardess or glorified chauffeur. She had encountered this attitude before and in the past it had amused her and even made her feel faintly superior as she knew it said more about their ignorance than anything else, but this time she had enough worries of her own to contend with without having to cope with this lot as well.

Fuck you, she thought as she ducked under the bulkhead into the cockpit. Behind her she heard one of the men say, 'Nice ass,' and she froze. Then she remembered she had promised herself that she would stay calm, that she would act perfectly normally. Good God, what with one thing and another that was going to be impossible. She tried not to think about it as she called the tower and asked for permission to start her engines. She was told to wait five minutes.

Why? Why today of all days when she just wanted to get the trip over and done with? When she just wanted to deliver Andreas's bloody package and get back to the safety of her home and shut the door. She'd been getting more and more worried since she'd left Andreas's office the previous day and she really didn't need any sort of delay now.

Since she had taken charge of the parcel she had felt she was living in a nightmare. She found it hard to believe that this was happening to her. After seeing Magda and discovering the concealed lift leading to Andreas's top-floor suite of offices, things had gone from weird, to spooky, to downright scary.

After she had left the lift she had returned to reception and hoped that her face had given nothing away about her recent discovery. It had seemed to take far more than thirty-five minutes before the receptionist had told her that Mr Spyrou was free.

'Do you know your way up?' she had enquired.

Kate had nearly responded that she probably knew more ways of getting to his office than most of his employees, but refrained in favour of just replying with a simple yes. She had taken the usual lift to the top floor and stepped out. There was the pale grey carpet, the Kandinsky, the red sofa and the recessed mirror. Taking a comb from her bag, Kate had pretended to neaten her hair as she'd examined the massive looking glass. After about fifteen seconds she had found what she was looking for: a tiny concealed button right at the edge. If you didn't know to look for it you would never spot it in a month of Sundays. No one would ever have guessed that the mirror was really the door to his own private executive lift. Any number of visitors could come and go and the front desk wouldn't be any the wiser. Kate had replaced her comb, straightened her skirt and gone through the outer office and into Andreas's sanctum.

'Hello, Kate.' Perfectly proper as always and no hint of affection. But wasn't that always the way when they were in the UK? Not that Kate had felt particularly affectionate in return. Why had he lied to her about sacking Magda? If he had moved her to somewhere else in his empire it would have been no business of Kate's. He hadn't needed to lie. It didn't make sense. She felt confused and hurt and betrayed.

'Hello, Andreas.' Kate had tried to sound normal.

'So, are you all set for your trip to Turin tomorrow?'

'I think so. There shouldn't be any problems with the weather. The only thing that might cause a delay is a threatened strike by French air traffic controllers.'

'How long a delay?'

Kate hadn't known. It was like wanting to know how long a piece of string was. 'I've no idea, but I'll try and by-pass it by routing through Germany.'

'Good. Do that.'

'I will, I promise.'

'Right, I've got a package for you to deliver.' Kate had felt a sudden sense of unease. This wasn't the first time she had been asked to deliver something for him, far from it, but in the light of the things that had happened recently she didn't think that she wanted to have anything to do with this package.

Andreas had been oblivious to her worries and had carried on with his bland and reasonable explanation for the necessity for her to act as postman. 'It's just a few documents, legal things, regarding the transfer of some property, but they are required by my Italian operation this week and I'd like you to take them over with you. A courier will collect them at Turin airport. There's no problem, is there?'

Kate had felt as though her insides were being churned by some sort of internal liquidiser. No problem? She had bet her bottom dollar there was a rat somewhere – she could smell it! A rat the size of Magda. Magda had been there to deliver a package and Andreas wanted her to fly it to Turin. Kate had been in an impossible quandary. She couldn't have admitted to spying on Andreas, but without such an admission she could hardly have refused to carry the package. So what could she have said? Use a courier firm? Send someone else? Of course she couldn't. This was one of the reasons why Andreas paid her, to fly whoever or whatever he asked her to around the world. She had wanted to convince herself that there was nothing wrong, that Magda's presence had been entirely innocent, that Andreas's business affairs were all entirely above board, but somehow a nagging doubt had pushed its way to the forefront of her mind. Kate had taken a deep breath and tried to smile, but her muscles hadn't seemed to want to work properly. 'No, no problem,' she had mumbled.

'Good,' Andreas had said perfunctorily. 'I am very glad.' This time Kate had managed to force a smile. She'd prayed it looked natural and not as false as it felt. 'We haven't seen much of each other recently,' Andreas had carried on smoothly. 'I am so sorry. Pressure of work. As you know, opening up the new chain in Italy has taken up a great deal of my time. I have had to neglect you, and that is unforgivable.' Kate had faked a smile again. 'I tell you what, when you get back from Turin, why don't we find some time to get away for a few days together?'

'Great.' Kate had tried to display an enthusiasm she certainly didn't feel.

Reaching into one of the drawers of his massive desk Andreas had withdrawn a large and weighty padded envelope. It was heavily sealed. Kate had recognised the size and shape.

'Goodness, you used enough tape,' she had exclaimed, looking at the package.

'Not me. This is how it arrived from our legal department.' You mean, this is how Magda delivered it, Kate had thought. And it was sealed like that to prevent anyone even thinking about making a casual investigation of its contents.

'It must be important,' she'd said out loud.

'Naturally,' Andreas had replied coolly.

'Great. Well, best I take good care of it then.' She'd attempted to sound carefree and cheerful. But inwardly her heart had sunk like a stone.

Kate had picked up the heavy envelope with as much relish as she would have handled a black mamba, tucked it into her briefcase and left the office. She had taken the lift down to the basement and then driven out on to Kensington High Street, almost expecting a police car to race out of a side turning and intercept her. Wasn't it obvious to everyone that she might be carrying something illegal?

Don't be ridiculous, she'd told herself sternly. Of course you're not. What an imagination, for heaven's sake! But she'd

340

noticed that when she moved her left hand off the steering wheel so she could change gear, it was shaking.

She'd driven home trying hard to concentrate on the dangers of London traffic but finding that her thoughts slipped far too often to Andreas and his lies. If he had lied to her about Magda, what else had he lied to her about? she had wondered. His feelings for her? The contents of the package? Goodness only knew. She had sighed, and glanced across to her briefcase lying beside her on the passenger seat.

'Take it to the police,' a little voice in her head had insisted.

'But what if I'm wrong,' she had answered. 'They'll open it and find it's a load of documents, as Andreas told me, and I'll look a complete fool. And how will I explain that the envelope has been tampered with? All I'll get is a very red face and my P45.' Just because he had some sinister business associates and snorted the odd line of coke – or whatever it was he was into – just because he had lied to her about sacking Magda and had a private lift to his office, it didn't make him an international drug-dealer, Kate had told herself very firmly. For God's sake, the man had so much money, the last thing he needed to do was to peddle drugs around the world in order to make ends meet. She was being paranoid because she had been worrying too much recently about her finances and her relationship with him. Get a grip, she had ordered herself firmly. The envelope contained documents, just as Andreas had said, and that was that. Except, deep inside there had been a small voice of doubt that refused to shut up entirely.

When she had got home she'd considered talking it over with Julie, but the more she thought about it, the more she felt she would sound like a drama queen. With difficulty she had put the whole thing out of her mind until the next day.

And now here she was, about to take off for Turin with the envelope and its contents stowed in one of the lockers. Andreas had told her that a courier would collect it at Turin. And suddenly, because she was at a point of no return, the little voice of doubt suddenly got a lot louder and asked her what would she do if customs got to it first. Just supposing it wasn't as innocent as Andreas had said. Her stomach lurched alarmingly, and yet again she told herself that she was being a complete pillock and overreacting; that she was the sad end-result of watching too many films and reading too many trashy thrillers. Brace up, she ordered herself. She took a deep breath, ignored her jangling nerves and shut out all thoughts of the parcel.

The radio burst into life. 'Hello, Golf Alpha Bravo Zulu Yankee, this is Farnborough tower. You have permission to start engines.'

Kate acknowledged. No going back now, she thought as she began her pre-start checks and then flicked the relevant switches. Christ, she hoped the package was OK. If it wasn't, would anyone believe she was entirely innocent? Martin's comment about mules being easy for customs officers to spot suddenly sprang, unbidden, into her mind. Shit! Her normal elation at flying the Citation was completely subsumed by the feeling of dread in the pit of her stomach. She hoped to God that nothing would go wrong.

The flight was mostly routine, the weather was unremarkable and there were no problems as she was passed along the line of air traffic controllers to her destination. But due to the French strike her route was more convoluted than it would have normally been, so she found herself kept busy for most of the flight. It was only as she began her descent into Turin that she suddenly remembered the envelope and its contents and she felt an icy thrust of fear in her stomach. Involuntarily her hand gripped the stick and the plane side-slipped to the right. Quickly she corrected the error and brought it back on course, but not before she'd heard an expletive from the back followed by a yell of protest.

'Hey, what the fuck is going on? You made me spill my coffee.'

'Sorry sir,' called back Kate. 'Just a spot of turbulence. Nothing to be worried about.' The protest died away to a disgruntled mutter in amongst which Kate could hear views being expressed about women being allowed to fly aeroplanes. Serves you right for being such a chauvinist bastard, thought Kate. She further hoped that the coffee in the Thermos had retained most of its heat – it had certainly been scalding when she'd filled it.

They arrived at Turin airport fifteen minutes later and the

men descended from the aircraft and were escorted to a waiting limo. Neither immigration nor customs seemed the least bit interested in either them or the plane, and Kate breathed a sigh of relief.

'Thank God for that,' she murmured. She extracted the envelope, put it in her briefcase and walked as nonchalantly as she could into the handling agent's office. The courier was to meet her there and she prayed that he would arrive sooner rather than later. She'd had this bloody thing in her possession for quite long enough now. And now that she was here in Turin she wanted rid of it as soon as possible before it caused her any more angst.

'Mrs Thomas?' Kate jumped; she'd been miles away. She turned to look in the direction of the voice. 'Mrs Thomas?' the young man asked again. Kate stared at the tanned youth, dressed in a T-shirt and jeans. He smiled a brilliant smile at her. Kate nodded in acknowledgement. 'You have something, yes?'

'Here.' Kate opened her briefcase and proffered the envelope. The young man took it and inspected it closely. Kate longed to say that he needn't worry, that she would have rather opened a jar of tarantulas than that envelope, but held her tongue.

'Good,' said the young Adonis. 'Thank you.' He strode off. It was as easy as that, thought Kate. She felt a huge sense of relief at the thought that her errand had been completed successfully.

When she returned to Farnborough the first person she ran into on the ground was Martin. Her guilty conscience made the pit of her stomach somersault alarmingly and she felt her cheeks burning.

'Good trip?' he asked conversationally.

'Fine.' Kate really didn't want to talk. Not now. She just wanted to get away and go home.

'Somewhere nice?'

'Italy, Turin.'

'I don't know it, so it doesn't answer my question.'

'It's OK. I don't get to see much outside the airport.'

'Oh.' Martin felt rebuffed by Kate's monosyllabic and unenthusiastic answers. 'Are you all right?' he asked.

Kate looked at him sharply. Her guilty conscience

screamed; why should he want to know that? 'Of course,' she snapped.

'Sorry. I shouldn't have asked.'

He looked so sheepish that Kate took pity on him. 'Pay no attention to me. I'm just a bit out of sorts.'

It was Martin's turn to redden. Kate suppressed a smile. He obviously thought she was alluding to her menstrual cycle and was embarrassed, like most blokes, by her answer.

'Oh, OK,' he stammered. 'Well, don't let me keep you. Bye,' he said as he fled.

As Kate drove home she realised how stupid she had been. She needed to talk to someone and that person had been there all the time. Martin would be able to advise her; he knew what he was talking about and he knew her and her circumstances. It would be so much easier to talk to him than go to a complete stranger. If she told him everything he would know whether she had real grounds for worry or whether she was just being paranoid. She had to get him to help her. The only thing she had to be sure of was that Andreas didn't get the slightest hint of what she was up to. God, if he knew she was thinking of telling a customs officer that she suspected him of drugs trafficking he was bound to sack her. It just didn't bear thinking about. How on earth would she and Edward cope if she lost her job? She wouldn't be able to keep on Julie, she wouldn't be able to afford the house and the prospect of having to move back in with her mother was awful. She would have to be absolutely sure that, if she did talk to Martin about Andreas, word never got back to him. It might be best if they met somewhere well away from Farnborough. In a flash the answer came to her: the flying club. Andreas didn't use it any more now he had got rid of the Cessna. It was perfect.

As soon as she got home Kate phoned Farnborough. Amelia answered. No, Martin wasn't on duty any more. No, she didn't have a number for him. Yes, she could try and get a message to him through the duty customs officer. And would Kate like to tell her what this was all about?

'No,' said Kate tersely, tension getting the better of her resolve to be pleasant to the woman.

'Suit yourself,' said Amelia frostily.

Kate instantly backtracked. Amelia wasn't a good person to

alienate. She needed to talk to Martin and the sooner the better – goodness only knew when Andreas would want her to carry something else out of the country for him. If she wanted to get hold of Martin quickly she needed Amelia's help.

'Sorry,' apologised Kate, hoping she sounded sincere. 'I didn't mean to be rude. But it is something important and I do need to speak to him. I really need to meet him today to discuss something. It's business,' she added, 'not pleasure.'

'Oh, OK then. I'll see what I can do.'

'Thanks. And if you can't get any joy, can you ring me back?' Kate rattled off her phone number and then hung up. Please let him phone me soon, she prayed.

'So what can I do for you?' asked Martin when he returned her call.

Kate suddenly felt frightened about what she was getting herself into. She tried to reply but her throat was so dry that no sound emerged.

'Hello, hello,' called Martin down the line.

'Hi,' Kate finally managed to squeak. She swallowed frantically. 'I was ringing just to apologise for snapping at you at the airport and to make it up to you by asking if you would like to go flying again?'

'The apology is unnecessary,' said Martin. 'I'd forgotten all about it.'

'I was still out of order. And what about the flying? How about this weekend?'

'I can't this weekend. I'm on duty.'

'Oh, but you can't be.' Kate hadn't mean to sound so disgruntled but her disappointment made her just blurt it out.

There was a pause before Martin replied. 'Is there a special reason why you want to fly this weekend?'

'Yes, no. Not really.' This was hopeless. Kate knew she was a lousy liar.

'So is that a yes or a no?' Martin sounded as though he was laughing at her.

'It's a no. Forget it, it was just a thought.'

'Just a moment. Don't hang up. What about that lunch I promised you? How are you fixed tomorrow?'

Kate thought rapidly about his offer. If they met in some out-of-the-way pub it would be OK, and she could think of a couple that would fit the bill very well. She didn't think for a moment that Andreas was spying on her, checking up who she associated with, but it was just conceivable that someone from the airport might see them and let something slip – best to be careful.

'I'm not scheduled to fly tomorrow, although that is always subject to change. How about you call me again in the morning just to check?'

'I'll do that. Bye.'

Kate replaced the receiver thoughtfully. There was no going back now, that was for sure. Tomorrow she had to spill the beans to Martin about her misgivings, and then what? Kate didn't know, but she knew she had to get an answer to her suspicions, she simply couldn't go on working for a man for whom she felt so little trust. She had kept scouring the job vacancies advertised in the back of *Flight International* but there had been nothing recently that she had felt even remotely qualified to do. And in her heart she hoped that she was wrong, that Andreas was innocent, that he was involved in nothing more socially unacceptable than developing unspoilt coastlines and possibly indulging in the occasional line of cocaine. But . . . That was the trouble – *but*. Things just didn't seem to add up, or if they did, they added up to an answer that Kate didn't like.

The next day, when the phone rang and Julie called upstairs to say that Martin was on the line, Kate almost felt like backing out of everything. She had had a sleepless night trying to convince herself that she was jumping to stupid conclusions and that Martin would laugh at her and tell her not to be such a silly idiot, that Andreas was nothing more than a perfectly respectable and rich businessman and that Kate's imagination was running riot. But as she descended the stairs her resolve to forget the whole business of involving Martin weakened. If she didn't sort things out now, one way or another, then she was going to wind up a total basket case. She took a deep breath and picked up the receiver.

'Still OK for lunch?' asked Martin.

'Fine, thanks. Why don't we go to that nice place between Farnham and Aldershot, the Windmill?'

'That sounds wonderful. We can sit outside if the weather holds.'

'Yes, that would be nice.'

'So what time shall I pick you up?'

'I'll meet you there.'

'Don't be ridiculous. I've virtually got to pass your house to get there. I'll collect you at twelve.'

And before Kate could protest, he had rung off.

Kate was upstairs getting changed when the doorbell rang. She glanced at her watch. He was early. Well, he'd just have to wait.

'Get that, will you, Julie?' she yelled downstairs.

'On my way,' called back Julie. Kate carried on applying her mascara. She heard the door open. 'Hello, Martin,' she heard Julie say.

'Hi Julie,' came Martin's reply. 'Where's the boss?'

'Upstairs getting ready. Coffee?'

Kate lowered her mascara wand thoughtfully. She wasn't aware that Martin and Julie had met before. Strange. She checked her appearance in the mirror then ran downstairs to join them in the kitchen.

'Hi, Martin,' she said breezily.

Martin gave a whistle of approval when he saw her. 'I've never seen you in a dress before.'

'Oh, haven't you? I suppose not. I always wear trousers to fly.'

Martin sloshed some more milk into his coffee and gulped it down.

'There's no need to rush,' said Kate. 'You'll give yourself hiccups.'

'I doubt it. I've got an iron constitution. Come on then,' he said, jangling his car keys. Kate picked up her handbag.

'Have a nice time,' called Julie after them as they left.

They drove along the busy roads, chatting companionably about the weather, personalities at the airport and flying, but as they talked two things kept muscling in on Kate's thoughts: firstly, how was she going to broach the subject of Andreas and his activities, nefarious or otherwise; and secondly, how did Julie and Martin know each other? When they arrived at the pub Martin went inside to order the drinks while Kate bagged a prize spot in the large sunny garden.

'I brought the bar menu for you to look at,' said Martin when he returned with a pint of Guinness and a half of cider for Kate.

She took her drink and relieved him of the laminated sheet that he proffered. She scanned it carefully then, quite casually, said, 'Have you known Julie long?'

'A few . . .' Martin stopped and then reddened. Kate looked at him with raised eyebrows. Was she getting paranoid? Had Martin been checking up on her through Julie? Did he already think she was mixed up with Andreas's activities? Couldn't she trust anyone any more?

'So I didn't imagine it. And I'm not going to believe that it is a coincidence. How, may I ask?'

'I walked into that, didn't I?' said Martin sheepishly. 'How did you find out?'

'You knew her name when you came to the house, but I've never talked about her at the airport. And you haven't answered my question,' added Kate coldly.

'I came over to see you a little while ago, but you were away flying for Andreas. Julie gave me a cup of coffee and we had a chat.'

'So why didn't she mention it to me?'

'I don't know. Didn't she? Anyway, what's the big deal? Perhaps she just forgot.'

'Perhaps.' Kate wasn't sure she was convinced. 'So what did you come round to see me about?'

'Just to see if you wanted to have lunch with me one day.'

'Oh.' Kate felt foolish. She *was* becoming paranoid. She had to stop thinking that the whole world was in a conspiracy against her. Poor Martin. She owed him an apology for snapping at him again. 'I'm sorry. I've had a lot on my mind recently.'

'How about you choose something to eat and then we sit here in the sun and you tell me all about it?'

Kate perused the bar menu. 'No contest,' she announced in a surprisingly short time. 'Toasted bacon and cheese sandwiches, my favourite.'

'Sounds wonderful. I think I'll join you.' Martin went off to the bar to order the food leaving Kate basking in the sun and wondering whether, since she had jumped to all the wrong conclusions about Julie and Martin, she was wrong about Andreas too. She sighed heavily. If only she knew the answer.

Martin returned in a couple of minutes. 'Penny for them,' he said, seeing Kate deep in thought.

'Not worth that,' said Kate dejectedly.

'Tosh,' said Martin. 'Come on. Tell Uncle Martin.'

This was why she had wanted to get Martin on his own. This was the moment. So Kate took a deep breath and told him the whole saga, and as the tale of the strange men in dark suits, the odd references to oranges and a million pounds, the reappearance of Magda, the envelope and all the other details spilled out, she felt an increasing sense of relief. She left out the details about her relationship with Andreas – she didn't think that it was of the least importance – but that was her only deviation from the truth, the whole truth and nothing but the truth. And Martin never once spoke, or laughed at her. 'So you can see why I'm not happy,' she finished.

'Absolutely.'

A waitress appeared with their food.

'Eat up,' said Martin. 'You'll feel better when you've got yourself around the outside of this.' Kate sniffed the sandwich appreciatively, like a wine buff with a glass of excellent red wine, and the worries about her boss were temporarily erased as her nostrils filled with the wonderful smell of fried bacon. She tucked in.

'Delicious,' she mumbled indistinctly through an overlarge mouthful, wiping bacon grease off her chin.

'Mmm,' said Martin equally unclearly. They munched on in silence, savouring their sandwiches.

'So what do you think?' said Kate, licking her fingers and then wiping them on a paper napkin.

Martin swallowed the last mouthful. 'Nicest lunch I've had in a long time.'

'No, silly. About what I think Andreas has been up to.'

'Ah, that. Well, if I were in your shoes I would probably have jumped to the same conclusions. But . . .'

'But you think I've got it all wrong,' Kate finished off for him.

'No, not at all. It's just there's not much I can do with what you've told me. I mean, you could just have made all of that up.' He could see Kate bristling. Quickly he added, 'I'm sure you haven't, but . . .' He shrugged, holding his hands out in front of him, palms upwards, in a gesture of helplessness. 'Now, if you had come to me with the package, it would have been a different matter.'

'I'm sorry. I wasn't really thinking straight. I was so worried about what I was getting into.'

'Have you had to deliver things before?'

'Oh, yes. It's not unusual. But in the past it has never crossed my mind that whatever I've had to take has been anything other than what I've been told.'

'And has it always been small packages?'

'Mostly, but I've had to carry some quite large boxes once or twice.'

'And what were you told was in those?'

'Once it was special curtain fabric for one of his hotels.'

'And was it?'

'I've no idea, I just delivered it.'

'And the other time?'

'Computer equipment. Or so I was told. But it could have been anything in either of them.' Kate drained the last of her drink.

'Here, let me get you the other half,' said Martin. Kate smiled gratefully. It was hot, and that and the bacon had made her thirsty.

As Martin walked away, Kate wondered if he was just humouring her. She could see his point of view. Without any evidence there wasn't much he could do.

Martin returned with the drinks in a couple of minutes

'Supposing I brought something to you?' said Kate. 'Would you be able to do something about it?'

'Would you be able to?'

'Probably. I sometimes have to collect stuff a day or so before I fly. Sometimes it is delivered to me at the airport.'

'On the days when you have to get the stuff, could you bring it to us? I mean, I don't want you to put yourself in harm's way . . .?'

'I think Andreas trusts me,' said Kate.

'Good, well see what you can do.'

350

Chapter Thirty-One

Martin left the room carrying the package Kate had brought. Part of her wanted to be proved wrong – a very large part – even if it meant that she ended up looking more than slightly foolish. Better that than to discover that she was mixed up with something extremely shady and possibly dangerous. Left alone with her thoughts in the unremarkable office, she wondered what was going to happen next.

It was twenty minutes before Martin returned, accompanied by an avuncular-looking man with thick wavy grey hair and a pleasant smile. Kate thought he looked more like a TV personality than a customs officer in his dapper suit and old school tie.

'Let me introduce you to Clive,' said Martin.

Kate said hello and extended her hand. Clive's grip was firm and warm.

'Hello, Kate,' he said. 'Martin has been telling me all about your quandary. It seems as though your boss has put you in a bit of a spot.'

Kate nodded. 'But I may be imagining all of it. I may be wasting your time.'

'Of course. That is always a possibility, but on the other hand . . .' Clive let the implication hang in the air. 'Would you mind telling me all those things you told Martin? I'd like to hear it for myself.'

So Kate repeated her story, and as she was going through the details yet again, it struck her that it seemed to sound more preposterous and unlikely than ever.

'I see,' said Clive slowly. 'You haven't forgotten any details?'

Kate shook her head. 'I don't think so.'

'And the conversation you thought you heard at the hotel in Cyprus? You've told me what you heard word for word?'

'I think so. I mean, when I heard it I didn't expect to have to recall it. But I think I've given you the gist of it.'

'You couldn't have misheard?'

'I suppose it's a possibility, but I don't think so. At the time I was pretty certain about it. It's just that since then I've had so many doubts and worries that I've begun to wonder which is real and which imagined.'

Clive nodded. 'Tell me about Mr Spyrou. Or rather, tell me what you know about Mr Spyrou.'

'I'm not sure I know that much.' But Clive smiled encouragingly, so Kate told him about how the family had fled from the north of Cyprus, how they had lived in a refugee camp, how they had got the money together to open a small taverna, and how the business had expanded from there. She recalled that Andreas had told her that the family had relied on hard work but had had one piece of luck, but that she had never discovered what that was.

'Weren't you curious?'

'Yes, but on a couple of occasions I asked him about his work or his business and he seemed really touchy, so I have always been careful not to look as though I was prying.'

'So you only ever knew things that he told you?'

'Yes.'

Clive and Martin exchanged glances. 'But,' asked Clive, 'you had a relationship with him. You and Andreas were lovers, weren't you?'

'Yes.' Kate looked at him. 'Excuse me for asking but how did you know that?'

'I surmised,' said Clive smoothly.

'Oh,' said Kate. What else could she say?

'Are you still involved with Andreas?'

Kate couldn't look at Martin as she answered. For some reason she felt acutely embarrassed at having to own up to this in front of him. 'Yes.' She added hastily, 'But I wish I wasn't. It's just that it's difficult to end it whilst I still work for him and I can't leave my job because I can't afford to. But,' she added quickly, 'we hardly see much of each other at all at the

352

moment – other than business. He's been very busy recently. He's got some new operation going on in Italy and it's taken up most of his time.'

'I see,' said Clive.

There was a knock at the door. A young man put his head round it. 'I've got the lab report, boss,' he said. Clive left. Kate could only assume that this was to do with the package.

After a few minutes Clive returned.

'Well, young lady,' he said. 'It seems your suspicions were well founded. We have found a packet of powder concealed in the wadding of the envelope. When we tested it we found that it was heroin.'

Kate felt a wave of horror sweep over her as her worst fears were confirmed. How could Andreas, how *could* he? He had led her on from the start. Had she looked so naïve? Was she really so gullible? Had he spotted that she might do as a fall guy from the day they had met at her interview? Was that why he had encouraged her to get back in the air? Was that why he had bought his private jet – so she would have to fly all round Europe delivering his illegal packages? She suddenly became aware that Clive was still speaking. He was pacing up and down the small office, his hands clasped behind his back, gazing intently at the floor.

'Of course the amount the parcel contained was small; certainly not enough for it to constitute trafficking. No, I am pretty certain that this is a sample to prove the quality of the main consignment that will, in all probability, be sent via another route. Naturally this larger consignment should be stopped, because although it is presumably destined initially for Italy, there is no knowing how widely it will ultimately be distributed through Europe. You see, if your Mr Spyrou' – Kate resented the connection between her and Andreas, but she was hardly in a position to object – 'if your Mr Spyrou is a big noise in the drugs trade, he won't just be moving the stuff into Italy. He'll be bringing it into Britain, Holland, Germany and anywhere else there is a ready market for this junk. He ships his consignment in, say, a lorryload of oranges and it can then be distributed throughout Europe in a matter of a day or so. We need the evidence to get the brains behind it all under lock and key, not just the small-time pushers and dealers. So it's important, if we want any chance of succeeding and if we're not to arouse any suspicion, that everything goes ahead as though nothing has happened.' Clive stopped his pacing and turned. He stared at Kate. 'You realise what I am saying.' Kate swallowed nervously. She might have been blind to what Andreas had been after but even she could see what Clive was getting at. Questions crowded into her head.

'But the envelope . . .?'

'Don't worry. Even Mr Spyrou himself wouldn't be able to tell that we have had a little look-see.'

Kate nodded, relieved. 'And customs at the other end?'

'This will have to be a joint operation with the Italian customs. They will be warned, and hopefully,' as he said this he grimaced, and Kate had the impression that his hopes had been dashed on previous occasions, '*hopefully* they will mount a surveillance operation and we will see whom Mr Spyrou is dealing with. Although, being Italy, I imagine the Mafia will have something to do with it.'

Kate felt a shiver of fear. The Mafia! God, what was she involved with? This wasn't what she had foreseen as part of her future when she'd gone for the job at the hotel. Anger overtook her feelings of fear. Bloody Andreas. What right had he to implicate and involve her in his shady deals? The old saying 'Beware of Greeks bearing gifts' sprang into her mind. The Citation had hardly constituted a gift as such, but he had known that she wouldn't be able to resist the thrill of flying such a stylish plane. And to think that she had worried herself sick about being disloyal to Andreas. Disloyal? God, she was still at Key Stage 1 SATS in disloyalty, while Andreas had obviously got a first-class honours degree in the subject and was now working on his PhD.

'So will you do it?' asked Clive.

Carried away on a tide of anger, bitterness and resentment, Kate nodded her acquiescence. What she wanted more than anything else now was to see Andreas get his comeuppance. He'd used her, and no one, *no one*, did that.

'Yes,' she said tightly, 'you tell me what to do and I'll do it.'

'Good girl,' said Clive. 'Martin will brief you. And Kate,' he gave her a warm smile, 'thank you. You're a plucky girl.'

As Clive turned to leave the room, Kate smiled wanly back. She didn't think she was the least bit plucky. Her own personal safety came very high up her list of priorities. Shit, what the hell was she agreeing to?

'Right,' said Martin once they were alone, 'the main thing is for you to act as normally as possible. I know this will be difficult now, but it really is essential that you do nothing to make Andreas or anyone else you come across suspect that you are aware there is anything out of the ordinary going on.' Kate nodded. 'When are you seeing Andreas again?'

'Not in the near future, except that he did mention a little while ago about the two of us going to Cyprus together, but nothing more has been said. Tomorrow's job to Italy is to fly out some bigwigs in the travel business to see the new resort. Andreas's representative is going to meet them there. Andreas is tied up at this end – or so he says. I expect I'll see him again some time during the week, but nothing is planned.'

'These people you are taking – do you know them?'

'I don't think so. I may have had them on board before, but to be honest, I don't pay that much attention to the passengers. I'm just the driver.'

'That's good. Try to keep out of their way as much as possible. They'll be less likely to notice if you are a little nervous, especially if they haven't met you before.

Great, thought Kate. Although she didn't think nervous was necessarily the word she would have chosen. Shit-scared was what actually sprang to mind.

'And you're sure no one will spot anything wrong with the envelope?'

'Trust us, we have experts. We've done this sort of thing before.'

Kate knew she had to put her faith in the abilities of Clive, Martin and the others, but her trust in men had taken a bit of a battering lately. Well, she reasoned, she had been dropped well and truly in it, and if the only way out was to go along with customs, then so be it.

The flight was routine, but the thoughts going through Kate's head as the little jet zipped across the skies of Europe were anything but. Supposing things went wrong at the Italian end? Supposing the message was all wrong and they arrested *her*? Supposing whoever was meeting her spotted the surveillance operation? Supposing that customs weren't as clever as they thought about concealing the evidence that they had had a poke around in the envelope? There were a dozen things that could happen, and in every scenario Kate visualised herself ending up either injured or in prison. By the time they landed at their destination Kate was feeling sick with worry. Her stomach was making ominous rumbling, churning sounds and she wondered if she was going to be physically sick.

She taxied to their allotted place on the apron and waited for the police and customs to arrive with arrest warrants and 'Do not pass GO, proceed directly to jail' cards, but nothing. Kate opened the cabin door, flipped down the steps and let her passengers off. A bored immigration official wandered over, but he could scarcely be bothered to open the passengers' passports. Then a limo drove across the concrete to meet them and whisked them off to their executive lunch and whistle-stop tour of the new resort.

And then Kate was alone in the plane. She sat down heavily on one of the grey leather seats and stared at the mess of dirty cups, crumpled newspapers and full ashtrays. She turned her gaze to the locker that contained her briefcase and the package. She really didn't want to walk across to the terminal and hand it over. She didn't care that it was such a small amount that it wouldn't, as Clive had so reassuringly put it, constitute trafficking. Whoopee, thought Kate. She could still be done for possession if everything went pear-shaped. She wondered what an Italian jail would be like. All she knew about prison, of any nationality, was what she had seen on *Prisoner Cell Block H*, and frankly, the last thing she wanted was to be able to compare fiction with reality. It would be so much simpler if she pretended that she had just forgotten about delivering the parcel and flew back with it. At least at Farnborough she was absolutely certain the authorities knew exactly what was going on. She only had Clive's vague assurances that it was all taken care of here.

Kate rubbed her hand across her face and stood up again. She tidied away the papers, emptied the ashtrays, washed up the cups in the tiny basin at the back of the plane and generally restored order in the cabin. She looked at her efforts. Not wonderful but she didn't think her passengers would notice, and anyway they would probably reduce it to chaos again a couple of minutes after take-off. Kate finished her chores and looked again at the locker. She really couldn't postpone the issue any longer. Slowly she opened the cupboard and withdrew her case. Then she sighed and made her way to the doorway. This was it. She made her way across the apron to the offices of the handling agency. She pushed open the door and walked into the modern but basic office. A few people were gathered there – a couple of pilots waiting for their passengers, a chauffeur in livery complete with peaked cap waiting for an arrival, a desk clerk or two, a cleaner mopping the floor – but no one who appeared to be the least bit interested in Kate. She wandered over to the desk.

'Excuse me, do you speak English?'

'Of course.' The clerk sounded faintly affronted.

Kate smiled in an effort to negate any offence her innocent question had caused.

'That's brilliant. Do you know if anyone has been asking for me? My name is Kate Thomas.'

The clerk shuffled some papers on his desk. 'There was a phone call.' He found a scrap of paper. 'Please would you ring this number.'

Kate took the paper. This hadn't been what she had been told would happen. She distinctly remembered that Andreas had said that a courier would meet her. Did this mean a change of plan? Oh God! And if so, did it mean that they knew she'd gone to see Martin? Her mouth felt uncomfortably dry and she swallowed nervously. She tried to work some saliva around with her tongue but all she succeeded in doing was making herself cough. Feeling desperately apprehensive, she took her mobile out of her case and dialled the number.

'*Si*,' said a man's voice almost instantly. He must have been right by the phone.

'Hello,' Kate tried to say but she was so nervous the word came out more as a strangled squeak. She cleared her throat and tried again. 'Hello, It's Kate Thomas here. I was told to call this number.'

'Ah yes. I can't get to the airport. I have been tied up with other business. I will send a taxi for you. It will be with you shortly. The driver will ask for you.'

'And I give him the package?'

'No!' The voice was sharp. 'No, I want you to bring it to me.' The voice softened slightly. 'These documents are important and I would rather you didn't give them to someone who might not understand their worth.'

'OK,' said Kate, trying to sound natural, but her heart was going berserk.

'*Ciao*,' said the voice and the line went dead.

Kate's hand was trembling as she switched off her phone. What about the surveillance operation that had supposedly been set up? How were they going to carry that out if she was being whisked away from the airport? What was going on? Was this some sort of set-up? What the hell was she getting into? These thoughts and more tumbled and jostled around her mind, until by the time the taxi came, she had worked herself up into such a state of apprehension that she felt sicker than ever. As she walked across to the car, accompanied by the driver, she had a discreet look about her in a hope that she might see someone taking an interest in her departure, someone from Italian customs, someone who might be on her side.

She got into the car, buckled her safety belt and then sat clutching her briefcase tightly on her lap like a child with a security blanket. She looked sideways at the driver. Was he detailed just to drive her to her destination, or had he been tasked with something more sinister? she wondered. He sensed her gaze and flashed her a smile. Kate didn't think he looked like a murderer, but then what did a murderer look like?

They drove swiftly along the main road that led away from the airport, but Kate was oblivious to the journey as she worried about what was in store for her. Suddenly the taxi swung into the car park of a roadside café and the Adonis who had acted as courier the last time approached from the café entrance. Kate got out hoping that no one would notice how much her knees were shaking. What was going to happen now? She had watched enough gangster movies to know the form: a bullet in the head and then her body dumped in a convenient river or used as part of the foundations in a construction site.

Adonis smiled. 'Mrs Thomas,' he said as he extended his hand.

Kate took it but didn't say anything. She didn't feel she could trust her voice. She couldn't remember feeling this scared before, not even when she'd had a couple of hairy moments in Ireland.

'I'm sorry to drag you away from the airport but I had business to attend to here and I couldn't get away. Do you forgive me for inconveniencing you?' Last time he had barely spoken, but this time Kate noticed that his English was almost faultless and virtually unaccented. He gave Kate a charming smile. She put her briefcase on the bonnet of the car and fumbled around in it for the package. As she did so she looked about her from underneath her eyelashes to see if there was anyone taking any sort of interest in the transaction. A couple of cars passed by on the busy road but there was nothing to suggest that they were being observed. She sighed inwardly, extracted the envelope and handed it over. She watched the courier to see if he examined it for signs of tampering, but he barely glanced at it before dropping it into his own case.

'Thank you,' he said. 'That should help wrap up the Cortina development.'

Kate forced herself to smile. 'I'm so glad,' she managed to say.

'Well, I'd better let you get back to the airport. Goodbye.' Another brilliant smile and then he walked from the car park and into the café. Kate, still nervous, got back into her vehicle. She wouldn't feel safe until she was back at the airport.

'Home, James,' she said to her driver.

'*Che?*'

'Never mind.'

When the taxi drew up outside the handling agent's office at Turin airport she got out of the car feeling saggy with relief. What she really wanted now was a large drink but of course that was out of the question. Twelve hours 'bottle to throttle' was a rule that no pilot would risk breaking. She had to make do with a cup of tea, and though it did little to help her frayed nerves, by the time her passengers returned she felt just about calm enough to fly. The return journey was smooth and uneventful, but even so as they landed at Farnborough Kate felt wrung out. She wondered where she was going to find the energy to drive home.

'Good trip?' It was Martin. Kate jumped. Her nerves were shot to pieces.

'It wasn't entirely as per my flight plan,' she said, hoping he would be bright enough to latch on to her veiled meaning. The airport wasn't the place to discuss the details. There were too many people who knew Andreas who might overhear.

'Oh?'

'No.'

'Well, no doubt everyone coped.'

'How can you be so sure?'

Martin smiled at her. 'Don't worry. I'll be in touch.'

For some reason, Martin seemed to make the awful day less ghastly. He was on her side; he would make everything all right. Thank God for Martin, she thought.

'You look bushed,' said Julie when Kate got in.

'Knackered,' said Kate with feeling. Edward, ready for bed and looking adorable in his stripy towelling dressing gown, was watching a video of Thomas the Tank Engine in the sitting room, while Julie got on with some ironing in the kitchen. Kate went to have a word with him but he was more interested in the antics of Thomas, Percy and the troublesome trucks than the attentions of his loving mother. Kate, too tired to make more than a token effort, returned to the kitchen and flopped on to a chair.

'Can I make you a cuppa?' offered Julie.

'Thanks but no thanks. I'm going to have a stiff gin. Do you want one?'

Julie's eyebrows went up in astonishment. 'But you don't drink.'

'I do sometimes, and I'm jolly well going to today.'

'Well, I hate to think of you having to drink alone,' said Julie with a grin. 'So yes please.'

'I don't think we've got any lemons. Can you cope?'

'I'll be brave.'

Kate got the gin out of the cupboard and poured a couple of industrial-strength ones while Julie unplugged the iron and put away the board.

'Cheers,' Kate said, raising her glass.

'Cheers,' replied Julie. She took a sip. 'Yum, what a treat. So what made the day so terrible?'

'This and that.' There was no way Kate was going to go into specific detail. 'The passengers were awful. Fat, rich, pompous businessmen with more money than manners.'

'Yuck,' said Julie with feeling. 'I've worked for that type, or rather their wives, and I know exactly what you mean.'

Kate took another slurp of her drink. 'At least I can be grateful that they mostly ignore me. Being up in the front they forget I'm there some of the time.'

'Your boss isn't like that, though, is he?'

'No.' Kate didn't want to talk about Andreas. She was still feeling too raw about everything.

'You really like him, don't you?'

'What on earth gave you that idea?'

Julie looked at her, her eyebrows registering her surprise. 'But . . .'

'But?' Kate's voice was chilly. Why didn't Julie get the hint that Andreas was off limits and was to stay that way?

'Nothing.' Julie, looked embarrassed, put her drink down on the table and glanced at the clock on the wall. 'It's Edward's bedtime.'

'I'll take him up,' said Kate. She felt awkward. Julie hadn't meant any harm; she wasn't to know how events were turning out. 'If you would like to peel some spuds. Please,' she added with a tentative smile. Julie smiled back. The incident was over. Kate drained her drink and left the kitchen calling to Edward that it was time for bed.

'No,' Edward shouted back from the sitting room. Kate realised that he wasn't just going to switch off the TV and do her bidding as she had hoped.

'Come on, darling,' she said, moving over to the television. 'It's getting late.'

'I want to watch Thomas.'

'Be a good boy and do as Mummy says.'

'No.' Edward was adamant.

Kate took a deep breath. She was tired, she was edgy, she was emotionally exhausted, she'd snapped at Julie who hadn't deserved it and now Edward was being naughty. This was the last thing she needed. 'I'm going to count to three and then I'm going to get cross,' she warned.

Edward pressed the volume control on the remote. 'Come along, Thomas,' roared Ringo Starr's Liverpudlian voice.

'One,' yelled Kate over the racket. She paused. 'Two. I mean it, Edward.' Edward completely ignored her. 'Three. Right, that's it.' Kate lunged for the remote but Edward saw her coming and threw it across the room. It hit the top of the bookcase and connected with a framed photo of Eddie. The picture toppled and fell, catching the edge of the waste-paper basket. The glass shattered. Before Kate could stop herself she'd smacked Edward, who screamed and ran out of the room to Julie.

Wearily Kate switched off the television and sank into an armchair. She could hear Edward's gulping sobs and Julie's soothing words. What was happening to her? thought Kate. She seemed to be losing control of her life. Everything seemed to be so dreadful. Her friends were overseas, this business with Andreas was a nightmare, the day's events had been terrifying and now she had taken it all out on first Julie and then Edward. She wondered if she was cracking up again. She heard Edward and Julie going upstairs. Edward seemed to have calmed down and Kate knew she ought to go and give him a hug and say she was sorry, but she was still angry. Angry that the picture frame had been smashed, angry at Edward's disobedience and angriest of all with herself for losing her temper. After a little while Julie came downstairs and returned to the kitchen, pointedly ignoring Kate in the sitting room. Kate sighed and went upstairs to Edward. She tiptoed into his room.

'Go away,' he said from under his duvet.

'I've come to give you a kiss and say I am sorry.'

Edward pulled the cover firmly over his head. 'Go away,' he repeated, his words almost smothered by the thick quilt.

'Please, Edward. Please let me give you a kiss.'

'No. I hate you.'

'I don't hate you. I love you very much.' There was

362

silence. 'I'm kissing where I think your nose should be,' said Kate. She leaned forward to plant a kiss on the lump under the bedcovers but the shape wriggled further down the bed. 'Good night, precious,' said Kate, feeling guilty and sad all at once. How could she have been so horrid as to hit him? Yes, he had been naughty but he hadn't deserved that. Well, he was punishing her now and she deserved it.

She returned to the kitchen. Julie was busy at the sink; the atmosphere was thunderous. Kate knew she had to make her peace with Julie too.

'I'm sorry, Julie,' she said. 'It's been a lousy day and Edward just made me see red.'

'You shouldn't have smacked him,' said Julie, not turning round.

'I know, I know. I feel awful. Nothing you can say will make me feel any worse than I do already. What I did was unforgivable. I've said sorry to him but he's refusing to talk to me. He's hidden under the duvet. But please believe me, I am truly sorry.' Julie threw her a fleeting smile over her shoulder. Kate felt as though she was being rehabilitated. 'I need another drink. How about you?'

'That would be nice.' Julie fished the peelings out of the muddy water and put them in the sink tidy. Then she tipped the water out and rinsed the spuds in some clean water before tipping them into a pan. Kate busied herself getting out the ice and mixing the drinks.

'Edward says he hates me,' announced Kate gloomily.

'He'll have forgotten about it by the morning,' said Julie.

'Do you think so?'

'Most likely.'

Kate handed Julie her drink. 'And what about you? Have you forgiven me?'

'Yeah.' Julie smiled. 'He can be a real little monster sometimes, can't he?' They both laughed.

'And I'm sorry I snapped at you earlier about Andreas. I was out of order.'

The jangling of the phone ringing interrupted their conversation. Kate went to answer it in the dining room.

'Hello, Kate, it's Martin here. Bad news, I'm afraid. The Italian end blew it.'

363

'You're joking?' Kate felt anger and disappointment. God, just when she thought things couldn't get any worse . . .

'I thought you said you would hand the stuff over at the airport.'

'Don't blame me for this,' whispered Kate furiously, acutely aware of Julie in the next room. The last thing she wanted was for Julie to know what was going on. She'd probably pack her bags in an instant if she got so much as a sniff of what Kate was involved in. 'That's what I thought would happen. When that car turned up for me I thought they had found out and were taking me somewhere to get rid of me. I was scared stiff. I really thought the worst.'

'I'm sorry, Kate, I really am. Clive wants to meet you again to discuss where we go from here. OK?'

Kate really didn't want to play any further part in this. Today's scare had been horrible and she didn't think she could cope with that sort of situation a second time. She simply didn't have the courage. The whole point of the Italian involvement was to get a lead on Andreas's contacts overseas so some sort of surveillance could be organised. Kate had assumed her part in it was going to be a one-off and then that would be that. Now they seemed to think that they had an endless call on her co-operation. She thought rapidly. If she wanted out of this she ought to meet them both and tell them, explain her reasons.

'How about tomorrow?' asked Martin.

'No, I can't make tomorrow. It's Julie's day off.'

'The day after?'

'Probably. I'll have to check. I'll ring you tomorrow.'

Martin gave her a contact number and apologised again for the cock-up.

'I just don't believe this,' said Kate when she returned to the kitchen. She picked up her glass and drained it.

'What?' asked Julie.

'Nothing.'

'It doesn't sound like nothing.'

'Just some people I work with mucked something up. A lousy end to a lousy day.'

'Does Andreas know?'

'About what?'

364

'This cock-up?'

Why did Julie keep bringing Andreas into the conversation? Kate was about to make a comment when she remembered that Julie was only asking out of polite interest. She didn't have a hidden agenda; not like Andreas did. 'No, no, it's nothing to do with him. I'm going to have another drink.' Kate sloshed a more than generous gin into her glass and waved the bottle in Julie's direction.

'I shouldn't.'

'Why not, you're not going anywhere.'

'But I'll get tipsy at this rate. I've not eaten anything since lunch.'

'Go on, be a devil.'

'OK, you've twisted my arm.'

Kate poured the drink, then turned down the potatoes, which were in danger of boiling over.

She didn't want to talk about work, Andreas or flying so she changed the subject to something that would directly interest Julie. 'I thought I'd look at nursery schools tomorrow,' she said. 'Edward should start in September. Have you heard anything about the ones in the area?'

'Well,' said Julie. And with that she launched into a complete and encyclopaedic guide to all of the ones Kate had heard of and a few that she hadn't. As she nattered on, detailing their size, facilities and catchment areas, Kate heated up some ready-prepared salmon in the microwave and bunged some frozen peas into a pan of boiling water.

'So basically,' said Julie, 'I would send him to St Bede's or Campion Hill.' She hiccuped and looked slightly embarrassed. 'I said you would get me tipsy. I feel quite sloshed.'

'Only a little bit.' Kate giggled. She tested the potatoes and then dished up. 'Blotting paper,' she said, putting the plates on the table and sitting down.

'A bit late for that.' Julie hiccuped again.

'Good job I'm definitely not flying tomorrow. Too much gin and jet propulsion don't mix.'

'So when are you seeing lover boy again?'

Kate was puzzled. 'Do you mean Martin?'

'No, silly; Andreas, of course.'

Kate froze, her fork halfway to her mouth. She had never

mentioned her relationship with Andreas to Julie. She couldn't have guessed; there had been no clues. The only people who knew, apart from her very closest friends, were Martin and Clive. So how did Julie know?

Julie reddened and stared at Kate, horror-struck. 'Oh God. I shouldn't have said anything.'

'No. Perhaps you shouldn't.' Kate suddenly felt very sober. 'But now you have, I would like to know exactly where you got that idea from.'

'It must have been something you said,' stammered Julie looking very uncomfortable.'

Kate put her fork down, her appetite gone. 'Julie, I know you are lying. I have never given you the least hint that I have had a relationship with Andreas. So where did you hear that I was involved with him?' Julie looked at her plate and didn't answer. Kate felt extremely vulnerable and very scared. Someone who knew a lot about her had been talking to her nanny. The only person who knew her really well, outside her family and her very closest friends, was Andreas. Had he been checking up on her? Had he been talking to Julie about her? More likely he would have sent a sidekick – and knowing the sort of people he was mixed up with, that was a terrifying thought. Kate said, as levelly and as calmly as she could, 'I want to know, Julie. Who have you been talking to about me?'

'I just guessed,' tried Julie.

Kate lost her calm and hit the table with the palm of her hand, making the nanny jump. 'Don't lie to me, Julie. I have had enough for one day. I want you to tell me and I want you to tell me now.'

'Martin,' said Julie in a barely audible voice.

Kate sagged. Martin. Martin? How could he? How could he sneak around behind her back and weasel his way into her private life? But why didn't he trust her? If he had been quietly checking up on her, did this mean that customs had already suspected that she was aware of what Andreas was up to and was conniving with him? She wondered fleetingly what would have happened if she hadn't gone to them with her suspicions. Another thought crossed her mind: did Martin think that the events at Turin airport had been engineered by her? That she had been involved in some sort of double bluff?

He probably thought that she had made up the fact that she hadn't had a clue that a car was going to meet her at Turin airport. He probably thought she had found it all a huge joke that she had escaped the scrutiny of the Italian surveillance team. If she went to them now saying she wanted out because being involved was too scary, they probably wouldn't believe her. How on earth was she going to make them believe that she had been so frightened she had almost been sick? Oh God! What a mess.

Kate became aware that Julie was asking her a question.

'Sorry?' she said.

'Do you want me to go?'

'No, eat your supper,' Kate answered dully.

'No, I mean leave, find another job.'

Kate didn't know. She sighed and rubbed her hands over her face. She didn't seem to know anything. She certainly didn't know whom she could trust any more. And if Julie left, would that make things any better? Kate doubted it. Besides, Kate herself had trusted Martin, taken him at face value, so it was hardly surprising that Julie had too.

Wearily she said, 'How about you tell me exactly what you have told Martin about me?'

'He came round to see me a while back. It was some pretext or other, I can't remember. He showed me his ID and said that he knew you from the airport at Farnborough. He seemed to be a friend of yours so I invited him in for a coffee. We chatted about this and that; he seemed to know so much about you – your row with your mother, your worries over the mortgage, Edward, everything. I just assumed you and he were really close. Anyway, he asked me about you and Andreas. He said he only wanted to know because he needed to find out if he had a chance with you himself.' Julie paused and looked at Kate, almost as if she expected Kate to lose her temper again.

'Go on,' said Kate. She didn't believe for a second the line about him wanting to know if he was likely to be able to pull her. If Martin knew she had been to bed with Andreas when their affair had only been conducted with the utmost discretion, then he had been doing some serious investigation.

Julie gulped. 'I didn't know anything about you and your

367

boss and I said as much. I asked him if was sure about his facts. He said that he was but under the circumstances it would be better if I pretended that I had never had the conversation with him. In fact he told me not to mention anything to you at all about our meeting. I thought it was a bit odd but he seemed such a nice guy that I agreed.'

'But you made a mistake that time he came to take me out to lunch.'

'Yes,' admitted Julie. 'Martin was OK about it but said I was to be more careful.' Suddenly she burst into tears. 'And now I've upset you and I'll be in trouble with him,' she wailed. 'And it isn't my fault. How am I supposed to remember all the time what I'm supposed to know and what I'm not?'

Even Kate had to concede that point. Poor Julie seemed to be as much a dupe in this game as Kate was herself. The only difference between the two of them was that Kate was the one who might end up in jail – or worse.

'No,' Kate sighed, 'it's not you fault.' Why was life so bloody complicated?

Chapter Thirty-Two

In the thirty-six hours between her conversation with Julie and her meeting with Clive and Martin, Kate had done a lot of thinking. She was supposed to be concentrating on choosing a pre-school for Edward, but most of the time she had found her mind turning to matters of trust and betrayal rather than facilities for rising-fives. That Andreas had betrayed her was bad enough, but almost worse was that it had caused her to fall under suspicion too. Given what Andreas was up to, and her relationship with him, she supposed that it was only to be expected, but she had thought of Martin as a friend and she felt that he had betrayed her too, by accepting her friendship when all the time he had another motive entirely. She found it very worrying that she had had no idea that the authorities had been investigating her personal and private life. Scary thought! And what else had been going on that she didn't know about?

By the time Kate switched off her light that night she had come to two conclusions: one was that Edward would go to St Bede's in the autumn, and the other was that she wanted nothing further to do with whatever Martin and Clive had planned for the future. She knew she had a duty to help but she also had a duty to Edward as a mother. Customs and Excise would have to get their information about Andreas from another source. They had already proved themselves more than capable of covert enquiries. Kate was quite certain they would be able to manage without her and she was pretty sure they couldn't force her to co-operate if it meant that she was being put at any sort of risk. It was also time to face the fact that she couldn't go on working for Andreas, and that the harsh reality was if she couldn't find a suitable job in aviation then she would have to look in other areas. Kate sighed when she thought how few skills she had outside flying. She knew a good bit about personnel management, but it was only the more senior posts that would pay enough to keep the house and Julie, and with her lack of experience she couldn't realistically expect to pick up such a position. There had to be some sort of job available that would pay her mortgage and leave her with enough to buy food. She would have to look harder than ever.

'I'm sorry things didn't go quite as we had planned,' said Clive smoothly, after the usual pleasantries had been exchanged.

'I don't remember that *I* planned anything,' said Kate. 'I think what you mean is that it didn't go as *you* planned.'

Martin and Clive glanced at each other. 'Quite,' muttered Clive. 'Anyway, I would like to try a similar operation the next time you are asked to deliver something.'

'I don't think so,' said Kate flatly.

Clive looked stunned. 'But you agreed.'

'I agreed to do it once. The operation was a mess, I thought my life was in danger, I have a young son and I'm not prepared to risk it a second time.'

'But Kate—' began Martin.

'But nothing,' she said angrily. 'You can't make me. You have no right to ask a member of the public to put their life in danger.'

'We could make things difficult for you,' said Clive turning nasty.

'And supposing I tell Andreas that I know you lot are on to him?' said Kate quietly.

Clive looked shocked.

'I don't understand,' said Martin. 'I just don't get this change of heart. Only a few days ago you were as keen as mustard to help us.'

'Only a few days ago I didn't know you'd been snooping around in my private life. Only a few days ago I was unaware that I was under suspicion too. Only a few days ago I trusted

370

you not to cock things up.'

Martin looked uncomfortable. 'I'm sorry, he mumbled. 'Perhaps I should have told you that we looked into your background too. But once we knew that you weren't being paid to act as a courier it didn't seem important.'

'I have to differ there. I think it's incredibly important. And I'd also like to hear what else you know.'

'OK, cards on the table.'

'That sounds like a good idea,' Kate replied icily.

'There have been rumours about Mr Spyrou for some time.'

'What sort of rumours?' asked Kate.

Martin knew she was upset but he was also beginning to get annoyed himself. 'If . . . *if* you let me tell the story without interrupting me, you'll find out.'

Kate backed down.

'Right, as I was saying, there have been rumours about your boss for ages. For example, in the eighties, when the recession was biting hard and holiday companies and airlines were, almost without exception, laying off staff, going bust, pulling in their horns and economising, Andreas Spyrou was expanding. Now that in itself is no crime, but there didn't seem to be a particular reason why he could afford to when every other company in the travel and holiday business seemed to be contemplating a very lean outlook. Also, you yourself have commented on his rags-to-riches story.' Kate nodded. 'It isn't that unusual over in Cyprus. A number of his compatriots did much the same, in about the same time frame – otherwise there wouldn't be the booming holiday industry in the southern half of the island that there is today.'

'So? So if he only did what other Greek Cypriots did, why the problem?'

'Because Andreas Spyrou did it without a bank loan of any sort. Unlike everyone else, he didn't seem to have any conventional financial backing.'

'So? He said he had a piece of luck.'

'You could call it luck,' said Clive drily. 'I would call it knowing a supplier in the drug trade.'

'But Cyprus isn't a big place for drugs, is it?' Not that Kate knew much about this sort of thing, but when she read about it in the papers it always seemed to be Colombia or Pakistan or

Amsterdam.

'No,' explained Clive, 'but Turkey is, and Andreas, unlike almost all the other Greek Cypriots who fled south, kept in touch with some friends in the north. We think this is where he gets his main supply. Andreas was very busy in the eighties. When the holiday industry was up against it he was buying up hotels left, right and centre. He even acquired his airline at that time. When Sunnydays, the charter company, went bust, Andreas got their fleet of 737s for a bargain-basement price, but we are still talking millions of pounds. This was when the rumours started and we began to have a look. But just as we did, it all went quiet and he stopped having anything to do with drugs. We couldn't prove the rumours about his past activities so that was that.'

'So if you know all this, why do you need to involve me?'

'Because we know where he gets the stuff from but we don't know how he distributes it. He seems to use a number of methods and as soon as we think we have found out how, he changes tack again. We were hoping that you might be able to help.'

'But you know so much about him already.'

'Not enough. And he is getting increasingly sophisticated.'

'Can you be sure he really is into this again? I mean bigtime, like before. Let's face it, he's made his millions. Surely with his wealth he doesn't need to deal in drugs any more?' Kate still wanted to believe that what was involved was just small stuff, tiny amounts that barely mattered in this monstrous international trade. She didn't want to face the fact that she might be involved with a major criminal.

'Things haven't been going too well for him recently,' said Martin. 'The resorts in Cyprus have been losing money – there has been some bad press resulting from a number of nasty incidents at the hotels he runs. There's a rumour that he's trying to build his way out of it and get into a new area – winter sports. His new complex in Italy is a massive deal, and they have encountered major problems that have cost vast amounts to put right.'

'And you think he's having to raise the money for this from drugs?'

'We do.'

'And Magda? Where does she fit into this?'

'We think she sets up the deals. She has a place in Turkey. When Andreas pretended to sack her she disappeared off there to renew his old contacts to finance his new expansion. She has been with him from the beginning and he probably trusts her more than anyone except himself. We're trying to find out the exact link between him and Magda because it is very unusual for a Greek Cypriot to be so friendly with a Turk.'

'But one thing you haven't told me is why you thought I was up to my neck in this. I mean, I don't exactly have a criminal background.'

'On the face of it, neither did Andreas,' said Martin flatly. 'At one stage we thought he had deliberately recruited you because you were a pilot. It was only later we discovered that your application to work for Mr Spyrou had nothing to do with being a pilot. Of course he must have seen it as a stroke of the most marvellous luck. Which was why he engineered your meteoric rise within his empire.'

'And there was me thinking that I'd done it all on the strength of my own ability.' Kate felt even more of a fool. 'I suppose he had an affair with me just to ensure my continuing loyalty. Business rather than pleasure,' she added bitterly.

Clive and Martin looked at her and shrugged. It seemed that they thought so too.

So if customs knew about her reasons for applying for a job with Spyrou Hotels, and if they knew about her affair, what else did they know? Kate felt her flesh creep. It was scary to think that they had been prying into every aspect of her life. Apart from Julie, who else had they spoken to? Had they quizzed Maria, and Andy and Emma? And what about her mother? If the authorities had been nosing around those who knew her best, would they now be wondering about her trustworthiness? Not that anyone had said anything to her, but then they were hardly likely to. It wasn't the sort of subject anyone would try and engineer into a conversation – 'Oh, by the way, what's this I hear about you being wanted by Interpol? What sort of sentence do you expect to get when they catch you?' It was a worrying thought that if Julie hadn't had her tongue loosened by too much gin, Kate would still be none the wiser that a finger of suspicion had been directly pointed at her.

'So you thought I was in this too?' she said slowly.

'We did.'

'And you don't now?'

'No,' said Clive. 'And we became absolutely certain when you approached us. Of course, we did wonder for a moment if it was some sort of double bluff, but everything we knew about you seemed to indicate that you were on the level.'

Great, thought Kate. The HM Customs and Excise seal of approval. She stared at Clive and Martin. She wondered how long they had been keeping tabs on her. No wonder Martin had been so happy to have her take an interest in him. How convenient for him to have her volunteer information about herself, therefore sparing him the trouble of finding it out. All the time she had thought that he had been taking an interest in her welfare, all the time she had thought that he was genuinely enjoying her company, all the time she thought he had been sympathetic and friendly, he had just been conning her so he could wheedle snippets of information out of her.

'So will you help us again?' said Clive.

'No,' said Kate. It wasn't the issue of the jeopardy her co-operation placed her in; it was also the sense of being used by someone she had regarded as a friend. First Andreas, and now Martin. What was it about her? Was she really so gullible? Did she have *sucker* written across her forehead? Well, she wasn't going to play the fall guy any more. Andreas could find someone else to do his dirty work and Martin and Clive could get their information from other sources.

'So what will you do if you're given something to carry?' asked Clive. 'He's more than likely to ask you again.'

'I'm going to have to tell him that I seem to have been stopped a lot by customs recently; that there's a risk they will want to examine anything in my possession and ask if it matters if it gets opened. That will make him think of another way.'

'That might jeopardise what we are doing,' said Martin.

'And it seems to me that you expect me to jeopardise my own safety. Whatever else you can expect of me, you can't expect that.'

Martin and Clive exchanged looks again. Kate knew they couldn't force her to co-operate against her will. She wasn't employed by them; she was a volunteer, and as such she could

374

un-volunteer any time she liked.

'Well, that's that then,' said Clive. He sounded disappointed. Kate felt a twinge of guilt that she was letting them down. He bade Kate a pretty chilly farewell and he and Martin left her to make her own way out. As Kate walked down the stairs of the anonymous block of offices towards the exit she began to feel annoyed. It wasn't as if any of this was her fault. She was just a pawn. Clive and Martin had no right to make her feel as if she was letting them down.

Once outside, Kate slumped against a wall feeling absolutely exhausted. At least she now knew exactly what Andreas had got her involved in. All she had to do now was get out of it. Wearily she made her way across to her car. Apart from Eddie, most of the men in her life had been absolute rats. Mike had ditched her for gliding, Andreas was using her for his drugs business and Martin had pretended to like her just so he could check up on her. Well, the great thing about junking Andreas's job would be that she wouldn't have to meet Martin again either, the bastard.

'I need to go to Cyprus again,' Andreas said to Kate from behind his imposing desk in his pale grey office.

'When?' she asked.

'Next week. I have to be there for at least two days so you had better stay over too. I trust that won't be a problem.'

Not in the way you think, thought Kate. Out loud she said, 'No, that'll be fine.'

'It will be good to see some more of you, Kate. I have been so tied up with the Cortina deal I've hardly had a chance to talk to you. I'll make it up to you in Cyprus.'

Peachy, thought Kate. She thought she would rather be promised a date with Dr Crippen. 'Great. I'll look forward to that,' she said, forcing a smile.

She returned home and told Julie. 'So do you mind working on your day off?' asked Kate.

'No. I had nothing planned anyway. Let me have another day when it's convenient.'

'Fine.' The doorbell rang. 'I'll get it,' said Kate, wondering vaguely who it could be. She wasn't expecting a visitor.

Her greeting died on her lips when she opened the door.

375

'Martin!' He had a cheek to come round here after what had happened. 'What the hell do you want?' Kate thought she'd made it perfectly clear at their last meeting that she wanted nothing more to do with him or his devious investigation.

'I want to have a word with you,' he said.

'And what if I don't want to listen? I can't think of anything that you might have to say to me that I would want to hear.'

'Aren't you going to invite me in?' asked Martin.

'I wasn't planning on it.' Kate felt extremely angry.

'Please. I would really rather we didn't talk on the doorstep.'

'I would really rather we didn't talk at all,' riposted Kate.

'Touché. I suppose I deserve that.' He looked so hangdog that Kate gave in.

'OK. Come in, but just for a minute.'

She led Martin through into the kitchen. Julie reddened when she saw him.

'Well,' she said with a small nervous laugh. 'At least I can own up to knowing you now.'

'I put you in an awkward position,' said Martin. 'I'm sorry.' He turned to Kate. 'I have to say, although you probably won't believe me, I never really thought that you were really part of Andreas's criminal sideline. Clive got a bee in his bonnet about it. It seemed the only way to convince him that you weren't was to prove him wrong.'

'I'm so glad you were proved right,' said Kate icily. 'It would have been unfortunate for your credibility if things had turned out the other way.'

It was Martin's turn to colour with embarrassment. The atmosphere in the kitchen became even more awkward.

'If you'll excuse me, I think I'll take Edward down to the swing park,' said Julie. She went to find him, leaving Martin and Kate staring at each other across the pine table.

'You must think I'm a bit of a heel,' said Martin.

'No,' said Kate. 'Actually I think you are a complete bastard. I know you were only doing your job, but you went out of your way to be friendly to me, to make me like you. Couldn't you have carried out your sordid little investigation without the social intercourse? Don't you think I've had enough to contend with recently without this as well?'

'I'm sorry.' He looked completely abject.

'You must have come round for a reason.' Kate wasn't going to make things easy for Martin. 'Tell me what it is, then you can go.' She was surprised at how brutal she was being but she didn't care.

'I want you to change your mind about helping us.'

Kate snorted. 'No chance. I have problems enough of my own without helping you solve yours.'

'Drugs are everyone's problem.'

'Hardly. Drugs are a matter of personal choice. I don't do them, you don't do them, thousands – millions – of people don't do them. If there are some sad, weak-willed people out there who think that self-improvement or happiness can be found as a result of taking a dodgy chemical, then why should I care? If there wasn't a market then there wouldn't be the suppliers.'

'How can you think that?'

'Because it's the truth.'

'But you were young once. Didn't you ever get drunk, have a few puffs of a cigarette behind the bike sheds, toke on a spliff? For loads of kids getting into drugs is the result of one little experiment – no worse than that.'

'Do me a favour. There's a huge difference between seeing what smoking is like and shoving a needle full of heroin into your arm.'

'You just don't see it, do you? That's the trouble with people like you. Kids don't start out on heroin or crack, like no one starts out smoking forty fags a day. No one plans to become a junkie. And it isn't just the kids in the ghettos and the inner cities. It can happen to anyone. It could happen to Edward.' Martin suddenly snatched the morning paper from the work surface. He thumbed through it impatiently, looking for a particular article. 'See,' he said, folding the paper and pushing it across the table to Kate. 'Read that.'

Kate scanned the article. It was about the daughter of a former cabinet minister who had been giving evidence at the inquest of an Oxford undergraduate, her well-heeled and privileged fiancé, who had fallen to his death from the roof of his college. Apparently he had been high on drink and drugs at the time of the accident.

'All that proves is that he had more money than sense. The poor lad probably had everything that money could buy except the attention of his parents.'

Martin suddenly looked tired, as if the fight had gone out of him. 'I can tell you it doesn't work like that,' he said sadly. 'If I can prove it to you, if I can convince you that even the most ordinary, loving, caring family can have their lives turned upside down by drugs, will you agree to help us?'

Kate thought about it. It seemed unlikely that he would sway her.

'What's the point?' she said. 'You won't change my mind.'

'If you are so sure, then you have nothing to lose by allowing me to try.'

'OK. What's the deal?'

'Are you free tomorrow?'

'I can be, as long as I'm back at Farnborough for the afternoon.'

'It won't take long.'

'What won't?'

'You'll see tomorrow. I'll pick you up at nine.'

'Where are we going?' asked Kate as Martin swung his car on to the M3 heading south-west.

'You'll see when we get there.'

'Go on, tell me,' wheedled Kate.

'No.' Martin switched on the stereo and pushed a tape into the machine, indicating that the conversation was at an end. Kate watched the Hampshire countryside slip past the windows. The trees were the dull, dusty, tired green of late summer, the verges were straw-coloured, the grass parched and desiccated, while in the fields the farmers were ploughing up the stubble, followed by flocks of seagulls hoping for succulent pickings. The air shimmered with heat and the horizon was hazy. They passed Basingstoke and then, as the tape in the stereo auto-ejected, Martin swung the car off the motorway and on to the A303. Kate looked around her with contentment – this was a part of England she probably knew better than almost any other. She had driven up and down this road constantly when she had been in the army; she had flown over it for hours on end during her helicopter training and she always had a feeling of homecoming when she neared this particular stretch of ancient, open, rolling country.

'Not far now,' he said. Kate was beginning to wonder. On this road they could be going as far as Exeter. Martin indicated again and turned off. The road undulated between high hedges until they came to a small village. It was an archetypal English village, with a pub, a green, a post office and a duck pond. The houses were made of stone with thatched roofs, and it looked as though it might be eligible for the dubious honour of being voted England's prettiest village. Martin turned the car off the road and into a driveway.

'We're here.'

The car scrunched on the gravel drive that led under a short avenue of tall chestnuts. At the end of the leafy tunnel Kate could see a pretty, double- fronted Georgian house.

'And *here* is?' she enquired.

'Home,' said Martin, stopping the car and pulling on the handbrake.

Nice, thought Kate as she took in the fanlight in the porch, the wisteria and clematis that clambered around the windows and the riot of lobelias and petunias spilling out of the containers on either side of the shallow steps that led to the door. She wouldn't mind living here, it was glorious. It certainly beat her tacky little overpriced suburban box into a cocked hat.

'Come and meet the folks,' offered Martin.

As Kate stepped out of the car the door opened and a grey-haired woman greeted Martin.

'You made good time,' she said. 'I wasn't expecting you for a while yet.' She turned to Kate. 'And how nice to meet you, my dear. I'm Martin's mother.'

'Hello, Mrs Brayfield. It's nice to meet you too.' Kate held out her hand.

Mrs Brayfield took it and shook it warmly. 'Call me Barbara, please. Martin tells me you fly planes for a living.' She guided Kate up the steps and into a spacious tiled hall.

Kate nodded. This was all very nice, but what on earth did it have to do with convincing her to help HM Customs and Excise with their fight against the drug trade?

'Show Kate into the sitting room, Martin, while I go and get some coffee. Or would you rather have tea?'

'No, coffee is fine.'

Barbara Brayfield bustled off, and Martin opened a door.

'Come and meet Gemma,' he said, and stood to one side to allow Kate to go through.

Several aspects of the room struck Kate almost simultaneously. One was the delightful fireplace with a wonderful overmantel and a glorious flower arrangement placed to hide the empty hearth. Another was the décor: warm pink and champagne tones; thick wool rugs over a polished floor; Colefax and Fowler curtains framing the windows. And lastly, and incongruously, an ugly electric wheelchair. It was positioned so its occupant could look out of one of the two floor-to-ceiling sash windows into the garden. They were both open, allowing the warm summer breeze to stir the curtains gently. As Martin came into the room, his footsteps noisy on the bare boards, the chair whirred into life and swivelled through one hundred and eighty degrees. In it was a young woman with long glossy chestnut hair. One hand, contorted and shaking spasmodically, rested on a control lever; the other, equally crooked, rested in her lap. Her head lolled at what looked like an uncomfortable angle and her mouth hung slackly, allowing spit to dribble on to a muslin square tied loosely round her neck to catch it. It was probable she had once been pretty, but now her features were so distorted by some sort of palsy that it was difficult to tell.

'Kate,' said Martin, 'this is my sister Gemma. Gemma, I would like you to meet Kate, a friend of mine from work.' If Gemma understood she gave no outward sign. Her eyes stared blankly ahead, her head didn't move, her vacant expression didn't change.

Kate felt awkward. She had never met someone with such a severe disability before. 'Hi, Gemma,' she said. 'How nice to meet you.' Then Gemma appeared to look at her but her eyes could have been focused on anything – she gave not a flicker of any sort of expression. Kate glanced at Martin.

'Kate flies aeroplanes,' said Martin. 'She's come here today especially to meet you.'

Hardly, thought Kate. She hadn't even known about Gemma's existence until she had walked into the room. Then the penny began to drop. Martin had said that he wanted to convince her about the effect of drugs on an ordinary family – and, outwardly, families didn't come much more ordinary than this one. Middle class, obviously comfortably off, well educated. So was Gemma's condition something to do with narcotics?

Barbara came into the room carrying a tray arranged with bone-china cups, a plate of home-made biscuits and a plastic beaker with a spout.

'I'll just go and get the coffee,' she said, putting the tray on the mahogany table. 'Martin, would you help Gemma?'

'Sure.' Martin picked up the beaker and put the spout to Gemma's lips. Gemma sucked greedily on it but seemed to dribble out as much of the liquid it contained as she swallowed. Martin wiped her chin with the cloth. 'Ugh, this is revoltingly damp. I'd better get you a clean one.' He left the room and Kate could hear him going upstairs. Gemma lost what little interest she had in Kate and swivelled her chair back so she could look out of the window once again.

Barbara returned carrying a cafetière of piping hot coffee.

'Martin didn't tell you about Gemma, did he?' she said, sitting down on the sofa and drawing the tray towards her.

'No,' said Kate. 'In fact he hasn't really told me anything about his family. Does he have any other brothers and sisters?'

'No.' Barbara handed Kate her coffee. 'Milk?' Kate nodded. 'Help yourself then, dear.' She handed Kate the jug. 'And have a biscuit.' She passed the plate. 'There's a picture of the two of them over there. It was taken just before Gemma's accident – about three years ago now.'

Kate looked in the direction indicated. The photo was in the centre of an antique side-table on the other side of the room. She got up to have a closer look. Martin and Gemma were sitting on the front steps of the house. The picture showed the pair of them laughing, Martin's arm draped casually across her shoulder, and Gemma looking stunning in a pale yellow frock which showed off her hair and her long, tanned limbs. In the picture it was possible to tell that there was about ten years between her and her brother, a big gap.

'Martin is a lot older than Gemma,' said Kate, stating the obvious.

'Yes. I don't know why, but I had endless trouble falling

pregnant a second time. It was only when I gave up and began to make enquiries about adopting that it happened. I was so thrilled that I had a little girl. It seemed to make our family complete somehow. Martin adores her.'

'I can tell.'

'Gemma was just about to go to university when that was taken. She'd won a place at Oxford to study French and German.'

'You must have been very proud of her.'

'We were,' said Martin from the door. 'But then she went to a party in Winchester and someone offered her an Ecstasy tablet. We can't be sure because Gemma can't tell us now, but we think that was probably the first time she had ever experimented with drugs. Just one little tablet.' Martin stopped, his face white with anger. He went over to his sister and carefully placed the clean bib round her neck.

Barbara continued with the story. 'By the time her friends realised something was wrong, Gemma had stopped breathing; that was when the real damage happened. By the time the ambulance crew got there and resuscitated her it was too late. At first the hospital didn't think she would ever regain consciousness and we prepared ourselves for the worst. But she always was a fighter and she pulled through.'

'If you can call this pulling through,' said Martin bitterly.

'Martin!' his mother rebuked him.

'Sorry,' muttered Martin. 'But it's all such a bloody waste.'

'It changed all our lives,' said Barbara.

'I can imagine,' said Kate, but she was lying. She couldn't begin to imagine what it had done to this family. She could remember what it had been like to look after her mother when she had been so helpless after her father died, but at least Honour had been able to talk, to tell Kate how she was feeling, to walk and to feed herself. She had no idea what it would be like to give total, twenty-four-hour nursing care to such a complete invalid. 'It must be quite a strain,' she added.

'Of course, the changes weren't just those to do with the care of Gemma. Martin threw up his career and applied for a job with the customs.'

Kate had no idea. 'Really?'

'It seemed to me that stopping the problem at source was

the best way to help prevent another life being trashed.'

'So what did you do before you joined the customs?'

'Martin was a geologist,' said his mother. Her pride in her son's achievement was obvious in her voice. 'He worked for a big American oil company, travelled the world and was tipped to do very well.'

Martin snorted. 'You don't want to believe everything you hear.'

'So why did they offer you a huge back-hander to stay with them when you said you were going?'

'Because it was cheaper for them to do that than to have to recruit someone new to the post.'

'Bunkum.'

Kate could sense that Martin's career move was a bone of contention between him and his mother.

'It must be nice for you to have Martin working more locally, though, surely, Barbara?' asked Kate, hoping she was saying the right thing.

Barbara's face softened. 'Yes, of course it is. Before he would be home for about one week every six months, just long enough for me to do his washing, and then off again to some other God-forsaken spot in the back of beyond. It makes a particular difference now Miles isn't around.'

Kate had this feeling that it would be advantageous to know who Miles was and why he wasn't around, because without that information she felt she was standing in the middle of a potential minefield. She took a sip of her coffee and nibbled her biscuit to cover her discomfort, but the rather awkward silence persisted.

'Would you like a walk around the garden?' offered Martin.

With relief Kate placed her cup back on the table and said that she thought it would be a lovely idea.

'Why don't you take Gemma with you?' said Barbara. 'She could do with some fresh air.'

Martin agreed and went to the big window. From behind the curtain he produced a ramp, which he fitted carefully over the sill.

'Come on, Gem,' he said cheerfully. 'Let's show Kate the pond.' The chair whirred again into life and Martin helped steady it as Gemma negotiated the narrow ramp. Kate followed as Gemma and her chair set off down the paving slabs that led from the patio and across the lawn.

'I'm sorry. You must think that I've played a mean trick on you,' apologised Martin once they were in the garden. Gemma's chair couldn't go very fast, so they were able to follow at a comfortable strolling speed.

'Sorry about what mean trick in particular?' asked Kate. She seemed to have been the recipient of quite a number recently.

'Springing my family on you like that. It was just that if you knew all the circumstances before you met them you would have had all sorts of preconceived ideas, and I wanted . . .' He paused. 'I suppose I wanted our circumstances to be a bit of a shock to you. I wanted to prove that drugs aren't just the problem of the Yardies or the kids from inner-city ghettos. They aren't just the province of drop-outs into New Age culture. They don't affect just the rebels, or rich kids who can afford an expensive habit, or rock-and-roll stars who think it's all part of the image. I wanted you to see that my background is about as far from the normal perception of drug culture as you can get and yet drugs have, in effect, wrecked everything for us.'

'Who is Miles?'

'My dad. The strain of everything was too much for him. He had a heart attack.'

'Oh, God! I'm so sorry.' Kate felt dreadful. 'I shouldn't have asked. It was just . . .'

'You weren't to know. It's not the sort of thing one introduces into everyday conversation. *Hello, my name is Martin, my sister is a vegetable and my dad is dead*. Anyway, it's all in the past now. What's happened has happened. But perhaps you can see why I am so committed to what I do.'

'I can.' The path had brought them to an old stone pond set in the middle of the garden. Pink and white water lilies floated on the surface and some large gold fish swam lazily around in the limpid water. 'But I have my own priorities too,' said Kate. 'I have a son. If anything happens to me there is no one else. His paternal grandmother lives alone in Spain and is pretty antique, and his father is dead. Of course there is my mother but she's not exactly an ideal substitute.'

384

'But we wouldn't let anything happen to you.'

Kate turned on him. 'You can't guarantee that. Turin was a cock-up. Have you any idea how scared I was? If something unpleasant had been planned, the first thing you lot would have known was when I arrived back in a zip-up bag.'

Martin looked suitably contrite, then turned and walked over to where Gemma had parked herself. He crouched down and tickled the surface of the water with his fingers and a group of fish shot over to see if the disturbance was indicative of the arrival of food. 'See, Gemma. The fish have come over to see how you are.'

Whether Gemma cared or not was difficult to tell but Kate felt incredibly touched by Martin's concern over his sister's welfare. He obviously adored her and Kate admired the way he cared for her, which was conscientious without being smothering.

'But you coped. The courier had no idea that you knew what was going on. It's exactly that sort of pluck we need. Without your help it will take us forever to nail Andreas, and if he is shifting anything like the amount of heroin we think he is, then this little scenario' – Martin gestured towards Gemma – 'could be repeated a thousand times.'

'Look,' Kate said, 'I can sympathise with how you feel. I am appalled by what has happened to Gemma, but this is your crusade, not mine. I despise what Andreas is mixed up with and I don't want any part of it, but until I find another job I've got to live. I've got a son to support and bills to pay. I know you asked me to agree to help you if you could prove to me that drugs can damage nice ordinary families, and you have proved that. But I just can't.' Kate felt a complete heel. 'I *have* to think of Edward. He has to come first.'

'I understand,' said Martin. 'And I understand just how much you love Edward. But how would you feel if something like this happened to him?' He looked at Kate with raised eyebrows.

Kate had opened her mouth to say that she wouldn't allow such a thing to happen to him when she realised that that was probably exactly the view that Barbara and Miles had held. She shut her mouth again and wandered around the other side of the pond. Martin was right: she couldn't just turn her back on the problem. Now that she knew precisely what Andreas was mixed up in, there was no way she could justify working for him unless . . . Unless she was also working against him. She turned back to Martin.

'Can you be sure that I'll be OK?'

Martin looked her directly in the eye. 'I can't guarantee it, but we'll do everything we can.'

'Well,' said Kate slowly, 'if that's your best offer, then I suppose it will have to do.'

Martin grinned broadly at her. 'That's my girl.'

Perhaps he wasn't such a bastard after all.

Chapter Thirty-Three

The temperature in Cyprus when Kate landed at Larnaca was reported to be eighty degrees, but a light sea breeze made conditions perfect. The sea, she had noticed on her approach to the airport, was almost a flat calm and the beaches, now the school holidays were nearly over, were relatively empty. Kate felt that under normal circumstances life could offer worse things than a couple of days at Ayia Napa with nothing much to do but relax with a book in the sun. Unfortunately, she didn't think she would be doing too much relaxing in the short time they would be on the island. Quite what she was supposed to find out in just two days she didn't know, but Martin and Clive had told her to keep her eyes and ears open and tell them everything on her return. She had explained that usually she had little involvement with Andreas once they had landed – they only met in the evenings when his day's work was done. In the past, of course, they had also shared a bed, but Kate had explained that she didn't think she could bring herself to sleep with him, not now she knew he was a criminal.

'But you've got to,' insisted Clive. 'You've got to behave absolutely naturally.'

Kate noticed that Martin wasn't adding his weight to the argument. She hoped that it might be because he found the idea of her sleeping with Andreas as repugnant as she now did.

Kate stopped thinking about the task she had to complete while she was on the island and thought instead about her return to England. The trip had worked out quite well, as they would return the day before Edward was due to start his first day at his new nursery school. Kate didn't want to miss that. She wondered how he would cope. He seemed so little to be going off on his own every morning, but he didn't seem worried by the prospect. In fact, thought Kate indulgently, he seemed to be thoroughly looking forward to it.

Andreas interrupted her thoughts by making a call on his mobile phone. He yammered away in Greek, and for all Kate knew he could have been getting the latest street value of a kilo of cocaine. It was all very well being told to keep her eyes and ears open, but if you couldn't understand the lingo . . . Kate wondered if she really was going to be any use to customs – at this rate she didn't think so. Andreas finished his call and returned to his papers.

As she stared from the limo at the parched and barren scrub that flanked the road, her thoughts turned to how Andreas had engineered their relationship. First he had been her champion against Magda; then there had been the flying lessons and the gifts. He had organised her training on the Citation and then he had seduced her. And all the time she had been so flattered by his attentions she had hardly bothered to look beyond the thrill of being wooed by a rich and powerful man to the possible motives. Hadn't she once said to Maria that men like Andreas didn't have relationships with girls like her? Hadn't she known in her heart of hearts that it couldn't be because of her irresistible charms? But Maria had convinced her she was wrong and, it had to be admitted, her ego had wanted Maria to be right. But how could she have been so stupid? Kate sighed. Just look where that stupidity had got her now.

'Something wrong, my dear?' asked Andreas.

'No,' said Kate guiltily. Thank God he wasn't a mind-reader. 'Nothing. I was just thinking it's a shame we're here for such a short time.' She hoped that the lie sounded convincing.

'I can't afford to pay you and to have you on holiday at my expense,' said Andreas. He smiled as he said it but Kate didn't trust his smiles any more.

'No, of course not.'

'So what are your plans?'

'Nothing much. I've got a couple of books I want to read. I

388

vaguely thought of doing some shopping in Nicosia but it depends on how I feel. I expect I'll just chill out on the beach.' She could hardly say that she wanted to find out what he was up to before she made any plans of her own.

'Ah. I suppose I'd better tell you . . .'

'Tell me what?' said Kate, her apprehension that he knew about her pact with customs causing her heart to thump alarmingly. She tried to sound calm but she wasn't sure she succeeded.

'It's just that a couple of things have cropped up and my business here may take a little longer than I had anticipated.'

'But it can't!' squeaked Kate. This was awful. She had felt she could cope with about forty-eight hours of deception and Andreas's company, but more? And Edward was due to start at St Bede's on Thursday and she'd promised him faithfully that she would be there to take him to school.

'Why, will this be a problem?' asked Andreas.

Kate used Edward as her excuse for her reaction.

'But surely your nanny can cope? Can't she take Edward to school for you?'

'Of course she can, but I'd promised.'

Andreas shrugged in reply. 'Don't worry, we won't stay longer than we have to.'

Don't worry? thought Kate. If only you knew. But then it was as well that he didn't.

They drove the rest of the journey in silence, Kate, preoccupied with thoughts of what she was involved in and with others regarding disappointing her son, and Andreas preoccupied with his documents.

When they arrived at the resort, Yannis bounded up to the car, delighted to see Andreas, and took charge of their welcome. He snapped his fingers at a junior porter and gave instructions in rapid Greek before opening the hotel doors and ushering them into the relative chill of the air-conditioned lobby. 'So pleased to see you again, Mrs Thomas. You are well?'

Kate was flattered that he had remembered her name.

'Thank you, Yannis. I'm fine. It's good to be back on your beautiful island again.' Yannis beamed as if Kate was offering him a personal fortune rather than an off-the-cuff compliment.

He was still beaming when the lift arrived at the penthouse floor and Kate and Andreas were shown into their suite of rooms.

'Shall I order lunch?' offered Andreas.

'Great,' said Kate, trying to sound enthusiastic. 'Do you mind if I just go and freshen up while you do?'

She opened the door into her bedroom and collapsed on to her bed. She put her hands over her face and groaned. This was going to be awful. How on earth was she going to be able to cope with pretending everything was just hunky-dory knowing what she did? The occasional meeting in his office, a few words exchanged on the plane was one thing, but he was going to want rather more than that now – probably a great deal more.

There was a discreet knock on the door between her room and the lobby.

'Come in,' she called. The junior porter appeared with her case. Kate indicated where he should put it and gave him a handful of small change. After he had gone, she took her mobile phone out of her bag and then looked at her watch; it would be just after midday in England. Julie should be around. Kate switched the phone on and wondered if she ought to call Julie to warn her that she might be stopping longer than she had planned. Perhaps not. It might not come to that. Here's hoping, thought Kate.

Another knock, this time on the door that led into the vast sitting room. Kate knew this would be Andreas. She replaced her phone in her bag and stood up.

'Just coming,' she called. She stood up and caught sight of herself in the mirror. Her hair was a mess and her face was glistening with a faint sheen of perspiration. No way did she look as though she had freshened up. The door opened.

'Oh, you're not ready yet. I thought you might like to join me for a drink before we have lunch.'

'Lovely,' said Kate, forcing a smile. 'Two minutes, OK?'

Andreas left and Kate rapidly dragged a comb though her curls, dabbed on a touch of powder and sprayed on some scent.

'Although God only knows why I am bothering,' she muttered to her reflection. 'He's the last person in the world I want to find me attractive.' Yet, she thought, less than a year ago she had spent an age pampering herself, doing her damnedest to make herself irresistible.

'Well, we all make mistakes,' she said to herself glumly.

Reluctantly she went through the interconnecting door to meet Andreas.

'You look nice,' he commented.

Liar, thought Kate. I look like something the cat dragged in. But she smiled sweetly and accepted a drink.

'This is lovely,' she said after she had taken a sip. She had to say something. It would have been too rude to remain silent.

'Sherry from a local vineyard. When it is dry like this I like to serve it chilled – like schnapps.'

Kate took another sip. She wasn't really a sherry drinker but this was delicious, despite it being Andreas's choice. She could get used to drinking this stuff.

'I have a meeting in Larnaca later on today,' said Andreas, 'but afterwards I thought we could meet for dinner. Would you like that?'

'Would this be just us or would your business friends be there too?'

'Just us,' said Andreas, smiling at her. 'I will have had enough of work by then.'

The last thing Kate wanted was a romantic dinner for two, but she could hardly tell Andreas that, actually, she would prefer it if there were a few hangers-on playing gooseberry. What could she do but accept?

'Yes, I'd love to.'

'I'll send the car for you. Half past seven?'

'I'll make sure I'm ready.'

Lunch appeared, wheeled in on a trolley covered in a crisp damask cloth: bread rolls, smoked trout pâté, salad and a bottle of a local white wine. Kate tucked in with gusto. There was no point in forgoing nice food, especially if Andreas was paying.

'You are hungry,' chuckled Andreas as he watched her demolish a third roll.

'I didn't bother with breakfast,' she said. The thought of what she was about to get embroiled in had been too much for her appetite early in the morning, but now, hunger had won out in the battle with her nerves.

'You should have had something. My mother used to say that breakfast was the most important meal of the day.' He looked at his watch. 'I must go soon or I'll be late for that meeting.' He stood up and brushed a few crumbs off his impeccable slacks. 'Don't forget, the car will come for you at seven thirty.' He kissed Kate on the cheek. She suppressed a shudder.

After Kate had eaten herself to a standstill, she changed into her swimming costume, grabbed a towel and her book and took herself down to the beach. There were still a few holidaymakers around, but with schools starting the autumn term later on that week the beach was almost empty. The sun was deliciously warm but the sea breeze made conditions idyllic. Kate settled herself down on a sun lounger and opened her book with relish. Hanging around at airports meant that she often had the time to read, but there was something especially indulgent in lazing on a Mediterranean beach with a steamy bonk-buster. Kate immersed herself in the pages of her paperback; thoughts of Andreas and his shady dealings consigned to oblivion.

Kate was suddenly aware that her arms and legs were beginning to throb. What a fool she was! She'd been so engrossed in her book she had forgotten the time and now she was done to a crisp. She looked in horror at her thighs and forearms. They were bright red and she knew that they were going to cause her a lot of misery in a few hours. Her wish to get out of dinner tonight with Andreas had been answered – although she would have preferred an excuse that wasn't going to involve so much discomfort. She was going to look like a lobster. She returned to her room and slapped some soothing after-sun lotion on to her fiery skin. How could she have been so stupid? She eased her tender arms into a loose-fitting blouse and slipped on a light cotton skirt, but even these clothes chafed painfully against her skin. Her punishment for being such a moron, she told herself. She took her mobile out of her handbag and called up Andreas's number, and explained what she had done.

'So I really don't feel like coming out – quite apart from the fact that I look like a freak. Would you mind terribly if I cried off and ordered something to be sent up here? My legs and arms are awfully sore.'

'No, if you are really feeling unwell. Of course.'

Kate thought he sounded as though he didn't really believe her. Perhaps she ought to sound more disappointed. 'I am *so* sorry. I have let you down and I was so looking forward to dinner.'

'It can't be helped.' There was a definite chill in his voice.

'Right, well, I won't disturb you any longer. Bye.' Tough if he didn't like it. He could hardly accuse her of faking it. He obviously wasn't best pleased but he couldn't deny that she had got herself badly burnt. There was one other terrific advantage to this too: there was no way she wanted to have anyone snuggling up against her sore skin tonight. Too bad that Clive wanted her to try and extract secrets via the tried and tested medium of pillow talk – there wasn't going to be any of that tonight.

Kate ordered a light snack and turned in. Lying on her back, which had escaped the ravages of the sun, was one of the few positions that didn't hurt. She hoped that by the morning she would feel a lot better, but she didn't think that sitting around in the sun would be an option for the remainder of her time on the island.

At about nine o'clock there was a gentle knock on her door. Kate feigned sleep. She heard the door to her room open, and then close again after a couple of seconds. Thank God for that, she thought. He had gone back to his own room. She opened her eyes.

'Andreas!' He was standing by the bed looking down at her. Damn those thick rugs on the floor. She hadn't heard him tiptoe across the room at all.

'I just came to see how you are. Is it very bad?'

'It is a bit.' Kate pulled the bed sheet off her legs and showed him her glowing thighs.

'What a silly girl you are.'

'I ought to know better at my age.'

'So, no more sunbathing for a while.'

'No.'

'Would you like me to rub in some lotion to help soothe it.'

Yuck. No, she didn't want his hands all over her body. 'I put some on before I came to bed.'

Andreas looked hesitant, almost unsure. He probably is after an invitation into bed, thought Kate. Well, he can whistle for it.

'Well, if you're sure there's nothing I can do for you . . .?'

'I'm fine. I'll feel much better after a good night's sleep.' He should get that hint – it's heavy enough, she thought.

'Right. I'll see you in the morning.'

As he left, Kate breathed an enormous sigh of relief and reflected on how odd it was that human feeling could shift from love to loathing in such a short time.

'How do you feel today?' asked Andreas over the top of the morning paper.

'Better, although my skin feels horribly tight. I expect this is how a caterpillar feels before it sheds its skin.' Kate sat down at the table and helped herself to orange juice.

'So what will you do to amuse yourself today?'

'Oh, I expect I'll sit in the shade and read. Take it easy. Sunbathing is out of the question.'

'How would you like to come to Nicosia with me? You said you'd thought about going. I have to attend a meeting there. You could do some shopping.'

'Oh?' Kate was taken by surprise. Usually Andreas didn't like her hanging around him during the day. But the offer suited her, quite apart from the fact that she might find out something of use to Clive. She thought it best not to sound too keen. 'Well . . .'

'It would keep you out of the sun.'

'I'd be in your way . . .'

'Hardly.' Kate breathed a sigh of relief. She hadn't wanted to appear too reluctant and have Andreas change his mind 'That's settled then. I've ordered the car for nine. We want to be there before it gets too hot.'

Kate looked at her watch. She'd better get a move on if she wasn't going-to keep him waiting.

The drive up to Nicosia was pleasant enough, if you ignored the company, as Andreas's car was air-conditioned and the last word in luxury. Kate remembered her first hot, sweaty journey across the island with Maria. She'd never imagined that one day she would be back here in a chauffeur-driven limo with a Greek hotel tycoon cum drug baron at her side. The whole notion, even now, seemed completely preposterous; the sort of thing that happened in the more fanciful and lurid women's magazines. She'd seen the shout lines on the covers – 'My Time as a Gangster's Moll', or 'I Loved Him, How Could I Betray Him?' – as women shared their horror stories of living with serial murderers or other dreadful criminals. Kate glanced sideways at Andreas from under her eyelashes. It was difficult to imagine that this pleasant-looking man was involved in a trade that brought so much misery into so many people's lives.

Andreas's chauffeur dropped Kate off in the main shopping street and drove away with Andreas to his meeting.

They were to meet for a late lunch before commencing the journey back. Kate wanted some new shoes and she didn't think it would be impossible to kill a few hours exploring the innumerable and cheap leather shops and possibly taking in an iced coffee somewhere as well. But she hadn't counted on the heat. The sea breeze didn't penetrate this far inland, and the sweltering temperatures, coupled with the traffic fumes, the bustle and the noise, plus the fact that her arms were very sore where her shirt rubbed against them, soon made Kate feel completely drained. She looked at her watch. It was ages before they were due to meet. Well, she would just have to make the best of it. She carried on dragging herself round the shops but with less and less exuberance and more and more dejection.

By the time the limousine drew up at their appointed rendezvous and Kate climbed gratefully into the cool of the air-conditioned interior, she was feeling headachy and thoroughly out of sorts. She hadn't found any shoes she liked, her feet ached, her eyes felt scratchy, her sunburn was painful and now she had to face lunch with a man she had come to despise. How she wished that she had stayed on the coast.

'Good time?' asked Andreas.

'Not specially,' grumped Kate.

'I'm sorry to hear that. Let's hope that you'll feel better after a nice lunch.'

I doubt it, thought Kate, determined not to be cheered.

The restaurant was exclusive, the food was delicious and the bill was, no doubt, horrendous. Andreas made small talk and Kate tried to maintain an act of being agreeable and interested, but because she wasn't feeling in tip-top condition she was aware that her façade kept slipping. She'd trained as a pilot, not an actress, and she found it very difficult to carry on pretending that she was enjoying Andreas's company. More than once her reply to an innocuous comment was terse or sharp, and more than once she caught him looking at her curiously. Kate kept her fingers crossed that he put her brusqueness down to her still very tender sunburn and nothing else. She forced a saccharine smile in his direction and made a promise to herself to try a bit harder.

'I have to make a final call on the way back to Ayia Napa,' announced Andreas as they finished. 'It shouldn't take long.'

'OK. Where?'

'A fruit packing factory.'

'But you aren't in the greengrocery business,' said Kate, hoping she sounded mildly interested rather than busting with curiosity. She remembered his past interest in oranges and smelt a rat.

'No, I'm not,' said Andreas, 'but I ship such perishable goods in my planes. There is always space in the cargo holds and we often carry such things for a variety of supermarkets. I'm just stopping to collect some paperwork.'

'Oh.' Kate thought this sounded unlikely. Didn't Andreas have dozens of minions who could have done this? The boss doing a clerk's job? Hardly! The rat was getting distinctly pongy.

A few miles outside Nicosia the chauffeur turned off in a small village and drove down a dusty road, little more than a track, to a large warehouse. The forecourt had an air of scruffy neglect. Scattered on the ground were squashed leaves and a few broken orange boxes; white cardboard cartons were stacked on pallets, but from their shabby air they had obviously been there for some time. There was a raised platform along one side of the building and at one end was a rusty and scratched elderly forklift truck. This was obviously the loading area. There was no sign of activity, but then this was siesta time. The warehouse had been built so that all the windows were on the north side while the south side was protected from the worst of the sun by a screen of trees. Unfortunately the small patch of shade that fell on to the unkempt parking area was completely occupied by half a dozen grubby, battered lorries of the same vintage as the forklift. This was not a business that was part of the tourist industry, that much was obvious. Any concern that was out to fleece the island's visitors made sure it was spotlessly clean; not a sign of litter, windows washed and gleaming and paintwork bright and glossy. This was patently a place that didn't anticipate a visit from anyone not involved in the movement of local produce.

As Kate looked about her, she thought that she had rarely come across a more down-at-heel and run-down commercial concern in her life. The thought that anyone might wish to buy produce that emanated from here seemed quite unlikely – even less likely that supermarkets or shippers were going to pay to air-freight it to its destination. The rat was becoming overpoweringly whiffy.

The chauffeur drew to a halt outside the large roll-down metal door beside the platform.

'Stay here,' ordered Andreas. He grabbed his briefcase, then hurried into the relative gloom of the large building. Kate watched him enter the shadows and then turned her gaze back to the unappealing surroundings of the loading bay. The heat shimmered off the ground, making optical illusions as objects changed shape and nonexistent puddles and ponds appeared and disappeared. In the relentless glare the temperature in the car began to rise sharply now the engine was off and the air-conditioning was no longer running. The chauffeur opened his door and got out. He wandered over to the small patch of shade, where he removed his cap and lit a cigarette. Then he stood an old fruit crate on its end and sat down, half turned away from the car.

Stuff staying here, thought Kate. She wanted a look inside the building. She didn't think the driver would notice her from where he sat, but she had her excuse at the ready if anyone saw her – that she had got caught short and was looking for a loo. Not wonderful, but it would have to do. She threw open the door and climbed out of the car. It was like opening the door of a blast furnace as the full force of the afternoon heat hit her. No time to worry about the discomfort, she thought as she headed swiftly across to the inviting shade of the door. Her heart was thudding. Please don't let anyone see me, she prayed under her breath.

Once in the darkness of the interior, Kate waited a moment or two to let her eyes grow accustomed. Slowly she was able to make out crates and crates of huge glossy green globes. Watermelons. Apart from the fruit, there wasn't a sign of any other form of life – vegetable or otherwise. She looked carefully to check she really was alone. Not a soul. Her heart rate dropped a fraction, although it was still thumping wildly. I'm not cut out for this sort of thing, she thought.

She wandered around desultorily, wondering what she ought to be looking for. Everything looked so normal. There had to be something. Perhaps there wasn't. Perhaps Andreas had been telling the truth about picking up paperwork. She sighed. All that angst for nothing. Damn. She was about to make her way back out to the car when she noticed piles of pink diamond-shaped gummed labels on the table. She went over to examine them. It seemed that each melon had to have a sticker announcing: 'Watermelon, Produce of Cyprus'. Obviously some poor drudge was destined stick one of these labels on to each piece of fruit. Kate looked at a second pile of stickers, seemingly identical apart from a spelling error. 'Watremelons', these ones said. Kate grinned to herself and then realised that she wouldn't have the first idea how to spell watermelon in Greek, so why should she expect the locals be expected to be so observant and fluent in someone else's language?

Kate walked along the crates of fruit, hoping to spot something secreted amongst the great green globes, but nothing. She picked up some of the melons and examined them to see it they had been split to allow something to be introduced inside them, but still nothing. Everything looked exactly as it ought to. She couldn't spot anything out of the ordinary. She noticed that some of the crates already had their slatted lids nailed down. These she examined more carefully, but she could still see nothing.

Somewhere at the far end of the warehouse Kate heard the thunk of a heavy door shutting. She turned and scuttled back to the car. The chauffeur was still sitting in the shade, puffing away, his cap beside him. Kate didn't think he had noticed her absence.

'As I suspected, I won't be able to return to England tonight,' Andreas announced that evening as they got into the lift to take them up to the penthouse. Kate felt a surge of annoyance. God, she'd really had enough of Andreas, Cyprus, playing at spies and the whole shebang. Besides which, she really did want to be back for Edward's first day at his new school.

'I'm sorry,' he continued, not sounding the least bit contrite, 'but I have some very important arrangements to make here in Cyprus and they just can't be put off any longer.'

There was nothing she could do about it. After all, she was only an employee when all was said and done. Why should she expect special consideration when there were mega-bucks at stake?

'I'll have to ring home. Let Julie know.'

'I'm sorry.' Andreas still sounded anything but apologetic. 'It really can't be helped.'

'It's OK.' The lift slowed to a halt and the doors slid open. Kate went into her bedroom and extracted her mobile from her handbag.

'I'm sorry. Will you let me have that?' asked Andreas from the door of her room.

'I beg your pardon,' exclaimed Kate, first dumbfounded and then, as an unpleasant realisation struck her, frightened. She stammered, 'I – I just want to ring Julie and let her know the change of arrangements.'

'I have already informed her,' said Andreas.

Kate felt icy with fear, but tried not to let it show. 'And I would like to speak to my son,' she said, mustering all her self-control, 'and wish him good luck for tomorrow.'

'I am sure he will know you are thinking of him.' Andreas's voice sounded frosty, but Kate ignored him and continued to dial. She had to pretend she didn't understand what he was getting at. But she was concentrating on her finger moving across the keypad, picking out the international dialling code, and she missed Andreas striding noiselessly over the thick rugs and across the room.

'I asked you not to,' he said, sounding extremely angry as he grabbed the phone off her. He removed the battery, pocketed it, then handed the rest of the mobile back to her. 'You may have it back tomorrow.'

'How dare you!' shouted Kate. She was really frightened now, but she had to continue to play the innocent. She had no choice. She had no idea how much he knew about her involvement with Clive's investigation. Her only recourse was to try to convince him he had got it all wrong. She felt sick with dread that he knew everything, but she had nothing to lose.

'I'm sorry,' he said again, although from his tone he patently wasn't. He turned to the door to the lobby, locked it and pocketed the key, and then left her room, leaving Kate trembling and feeling incredibly vulnerable. So much for bloody Clive and his empty promises, she thought. Fat lot of protection she was getting right now. She went and sat on her bed and immediately her gaze fell on the hotel phone. She lifted the receiver, more in hope than expectation. Dead. Not much of a surprise there. She replaced the receiver. Damn.

So what now? She couldn't sit trembling in her room waiting for the worst to happen. If she was going to try and bluff it out, then she had better carry on. If he was only acting on suspicion and she cowered in a corner, then she would just confirm things for him, but if she faced up to him, like she would if she was the injured party, then maybe . . . She strode across her room towards Andreas's suite.

'I want an explanation of what is going on, and I want one right now,' she yelled from the door.

Andreas turned round slowly. 'I can't say I like your tone of voice.'

'And I don't like how you are treating me. You cannot prevent me from contacting my family.'

'But I think you will find that I can. And from contacting anyone else, for that matter.' He was unnervingly calm and certain. Kate felt very frightened again. This wasn't how she had hoped this scene would be played out at all.

'Why?'

'You know why. I would have thought that as a result of

your very amateur detective work you would have guessed.'

Kate's stomach contracted with a truly alarming lurch. She suddenly felt very cold and clammy despite the warmth of the room. 'I d-d-don't understand,' she stuttered. It didn't help that her mouth seemed utterly devoid of moisture.

'Please don't patronise me, Kate. You know very well what I mean. You've been spying on me. You know about Magda. And I think you know some other things that I would rather you didn't.'

Kate exhaled slowly, trying to regain some sort of equilibrium, but she could feel her knees shaking, and although she was trying desperately to think of a way out of this awful hole, all her mind was doing was silently yelling for help.

'How did you find out?'

'For someone with your qualifications you can be remarkably stupid. Do you think an insurance company would let me hang a Kandinsky on the wall of my offices without some very clever security systems?'

'So?'

'So, everyone who enters or leaves that lobby – *by whichever lift* – is recorded on a hidden video camera. You discovered my personal and private lift. When that lift is used, a buzzer sounds in my office. Magda had left; I was curious to find out who else wanted to pay me a visit using that route. I was even more curious when whoever came up in the lift didn't call on me but returned immediately to the ground floor. So when I had time, I checked the tape. I can only surmise that you saw Magda leaving by the side door and wondered where she had come from. Then I thought back to the incident on the way to Turin. I had assumed that my belongings had been undisturbed, but I think you used the opportunity of my moments of unconsciousness to riffle through them. You found the packet of heroin in my briefcase, didn't you?' Kate didn't say anything. 'You did, didn't you? I could tell because your attitude towards me became quite odd.'

'Yes,' she mumbled.

'And you told someone about it.'

'No.'

'Come off it. You must think I was born yesterday.'

'I didn't.'

401

'And then?'

'And then nothing. I thought the stuff I found was your own stash. Nothing more. But then when I saw Magda go to your office I got worried. I couldn't understand why Magda was still seeing you when you told me you had sacked her, and then when you asked me to take a package to Italy, I got scared that there was something else involved. Perhaps I was overreacting, perhaps I read too much into everything, but I was scared you were using me as a mule. I was terrified that I might get stopped at Turin and that I would be the fall guy. I became worried you weren't being completely straight with me. That's why my attitude towards you has changed. It's because I'm frightened.' And that's no lie, she thought.

Andreas was watching her carefully. Then he said, 'So you went to customs to protect your back.'

'No. No, I didn't,' lied Kate desperately.

'And you expect me to believe that? You are very friendly with Martin Brayfield.'

'I took him flying because he had never been in a plane. I wanted to show him what he was missing.'

'Highly likely.'

'Believe what you like, I'm telling the truth.' Andreas looked at her long and hard. Kate's fear had subsided now the initial rush of adrenalin was no longer there to sustain it, and she felt more sullen than anything else. She stared back at him. What had she ever done that she deserved all this on top of everything else? Hadn't she been through enough in the last few years? How come she got all the hard knocks and duff deals? Life was so bloody unfair.

Andreas was staring at her. 'Yes, perhaps you *are* telling the truth.' But he didn't sound one hundred per cent convinced.

'I am,' protested Kate.

'Hmm,' said Andreas. Obviously the jury was still out.

Kate knew there was nothing she could, or should, add. She had said enough.

'And today?' asked Andreas.

'What about today?' asked Kate.

'You followed me into the warehouse.'

There was no point in using the fib about wanting the loo.

402

If Andreas had seen her in there he would have known she was lying through her teeth. Kate squared her shoulders and looked at him with as much defiance as she could muster.

'So? I was frying in the car. I went to get into the shade. I wouldn't have left a dog in the car on a day like today.'

Andreas stared back at her.

'Look,' said Kate. She was running out of ideas as to how to convince him. If this didn't work, she didn't know what to try. 'I don't know why you are so worried. I don't care what you do in your spare time or how you get your kicks. And if you want to use drugs; well, that's up to you. I just don't want to think that I might be carrying them around for you.'

When she'd finished, there was silence. Kate wasn't certain that Andreas believed her. But she'd find out soon enough, that *was* a certainty.

Chapter Thirty-Four

When Kate awoke from a fitful and restless sleep she wondered how much longer she was to be kept a prisoner in her room. Andreas had made no mention of how long her incarceration was to last.

'What will happen to me?' she had asked, her fear returning as he went about securing her bedroom with chilling thoroughness.

'Nothing,' he had replied. But Kate hadn't believed him, and after he had left she had gone into her bathroom and lost what remained of her lunch.

And now, finally, it was morning. It had seemed like the longest night she had ever passed. Although she had managed some sleep, it had been spasmodic; the slightest noise causing her to wake with a start, her heart thumping as she strained to hear what was going on. Was it Andreas next door? Was it just a door slamming somewhere outside? Or was it something more sinister, like someone trying to get into her room, that had disturbed her? But nothing had happened and each time Kate had shut her eyes again and tried to get a little rest until the next noise had caused her heart to miss a beat and make her sit bolt upright in bed, wide-eyed with terror.

She stretched stiffly, sat up in bed and looked out of the window. As she watched, the strength of the sunshine increased from a mother-of-pearl glow on the horizon to broad daylight, but she didn't enjoy the spectacle; she was too busy straining for sounds of activity in the rest of the suite. As far as she could make out there was total silence. Was that good or bad? Christ, she didn't know. Once again she tried the door between her room and the lobby. Still locked. She sat on her bed feeling anxious and dejected, but that was an improvement on the abject and paralysing terror that had engulfed her the previous evening. And she also felt hungry. She had thrown up her lunch, she'd had no supper and her stomach was making pathetic little rumbling noises as if it wasn't sure whether this was an appropriate time to remind Kate that some food would be nice. She wondered when Andreas would remember about her and organise something for her to eat.

For a short while Kate perched on her bed, staring at the view out of her window and contemplating what would happen if she tried to attract the attention of some of the other people in the hotel. She wondered, if she hurled something hard enough, whether she could break the glass on the sliding doors that led on to the balcony. But double-glazing was pretty tough stuff and Kate didn't fancy the idea that the object she hurled might bounce straight back and clobber her.

Her stomach rumbled again, this time quite loudly. It was a shame the minibar, with its supply of bags of nuts, was in the sitting room. Kate didn't really fancy peanuts for breakfast but it would be better than nothing.

Not really believing that she would have any luck, she got up and tried the door into the sitting room. It opened, and Kate let go of the handle and jumped back as if she expected something horrible to charge through it.

Pull yourself together, she told herself. But was it surprising she was a bag of nerves? Tentatively she pulled the door open a few inches and peered round. Nothing – well, nothing obvious anyway. Andreas wasn't in the room; at least that was something. Kate edged though the opening, her heart crashing about in her ribcage. Still nothing, and not a sound to be heard. That wasn't surprising, considering that it was still very early. Perhaps Andreas was asleep in his room. Kate forgot that she was actually on a quest to find some food and tiptoed as silently as she could across the floor, using the thick rugs like stepping-stones to get to Andreas's room. There was a gap of several feet between the last rug and the door to Andreas's bedroom. Kate slipped off her shoes and, holding her breath, trod gingerly on the polished boards, praying that they wouldn't creak. Soundlessly she reached her objective.

She pressed her ear against the door and, trying to ignore the thudding of her heart, listened as hard as she could for any sounds on the other side. She couldn't hear a thing, but that didn't signify particularly. The doors were solid and well fitting and anyway her pulse was pounding so hard it would be a wonder if she heard anything over the racket. Very gingerly she grasped the door handle and depressed it infinitesimally. There was the minutest of creaks and squeaks from the mechanism. Kate froze, gulped, and continued. Inch by inch she pushed open the door. The bed hadn't been slept in. Andreas was gone.

Kate felt almost deflated as she leaned weakly against the door jamb. She breathed deeply in and out a few times to steady herself, then looked at her hands; she was shaking like a leaf. Her stomach grumbled loudly again and she remembered the minibar. Peanuts washed down by orange juice – not the best breakfast in the world, but under the circumstances it would do very well. Still shovelling nuts into her mouth, Kate returned to Andreas's room. She swiftly checked the drawers and cupboards. All his possessions had been taken. He had done a bunk. So where did that leave her? She wasn't sure how deeply she might be implicated if the police were aware of Andreas' activities and arrived at the hotel. Goodness only knew how long she might be detained in Cyprus before Clive or Martin got them to believe that she was on their side. For all she knew it might take days before things got sorted out, and all the time she could be in some Cypriot nick and Edward would be without his mother. And what if the local police hadn't cottoned on to what Andreas was up to and she went to them of her own free will and told them all she knew? How long would they hang on to her getting evidence, taking statements and the like? It could be days again.

And then a worse thought struck her. Andreas might have gone, but he had plenty of employees around. Maybe he had something unpleasant planned for her so she couldn't go to the police. Just because nothing had happened last night didn't mean nothing could happen now.

Kate made a decision. She would have to get away and make her way home. Once there she would be safe; well, safer. She could tell Clive everything she knew, she could make her statements back in England, she might even get some sort of protection if it were deemed necessary. All she had to do now was get out of this room and away from the hotel.

Kate looked at the door out of the suite. It looked pretty solid but she thought that if she really tried she might be able to kick out one of the panels. Just before she let fly with her foot she tried the handle, not expecting anything but disappointment. It was unlocked. Apparently Kate was free to go.

Was this a trick? she wondered. The phrase *shot whilst trying to escape* muscled its way to the forefront of her mind. Don't be so bloody melodramatic, she told herself sternly. Even so, she peered cautiously up and down the corridor, checking to see if there was anyone there and who might not have her best interests at heart. No one. She shut the door again and ran back to her room, grabbed her bag and a couple of essential items and then, gingerly, opened the main door of the penthouse again and peered outside to make sure the coast was still clear. She was about to press the button to call the lift when she decided that it might be best not to. Instead she continued along the corridor to the fire exit. It was just possible that someone might notice that the lift had been called to the penthouse. She pushed open the door gently and peered into the gloomy concrete stairwell. She couldn't see anyone. Quickly and lightly she ran down seven flights of stairs and then pushed the crash bar of the fire door. It was locked. Bugger! For a second Kate panicked, then she turned and raced back up to the first floor. Swiftly she ran along the carpeted hallway to the lifts and pushed the button. One arrived almost instantly – no one would think twice about the lift being called to one of the lower floors where the ordinary punters stayed. Thirty seconds later Kate was in the lobby. Instead of turning to pass the reception desk, she nipped into the main bar and out of one of the big sliding doors that opened on to the pool area. From there it was just a short walk down to the beach and then access to the gardens and facilities of a dozen other hotels. As she ran to the next-door hotel Kate couldn't help glancing over her shoulder. She couldn't believe she had got away as easily as this. Perhaps Andreas had believed her innocence after all. Whatever his agenda was, Kate still didn't feel safe. She wasn't going to relax until she had got off this island. But first she had to tell someone she could trust about her situation. If anything did happen to her now, she wanted to be certain that they would know who to blame.

Kate wasn't sure if she would be able to get hold of Martin straight away, so she decided to ring Julie from a phone box. The nanny could then track him down and pass on all the details. He would know who to contact and he could vouch for her innocence in this affair. Kate checked her watch. Seven thirty, so only six thirty in the UK. Plenty of time to catch Julie before she left to take Edward to school. Kate began to calm down. Perhaps everything would be all right.

She found a phone in the hotel that took credit cards. She dialled the number and waited. A single continuous tone was all she heard. She tried again, this time really concentrating to make sure she didn't make a mistake. The same. Kate felt a surge of panic. Why was the phone not working? What was wrong? What had happened to Edward and Julie? What had Andreas and his horrible associates done? Was this why she was free, because they had a better hostage? Her mind raced over all sorts of dreadful and terrifying scenarios. She needed to call the police. How the hell did you get hold of the British police from Cyprus? What about the Consulate? Kate knew she wasn't thinking straight. Calm down. Think, think! Her mother. That was it.

With a shaking finger Kate dialled her mother's number. It rang. Thank God for that.

'Hello, hello,' said Honour's bemused voice.

'Mother, it's me, Kate.'

'Have you any idea what the time is?' said Honour suddenly sounding wide-awake and angry.

'Yes, I know.'

'It's half past six,' she continued as if Kate hadn't spoken. 'I was fast asleep.'

'Mother, I'm sorry.'

'You never have had any consideration for me.'

'Shut up and listen,' yelled Kate into the receiver. There was a stunned silence. 'Mother, I'm in Cyprus, I'm in a terrible fix and I think Edward and Julie might be in some sort of trouble.'

That got her mother's attention. She was suddenly brisk and

efficient. 'I'll get dressed and go round there right away.'

'No. You mustn't do that.'

'But if . . .'

Kate cut her off. 'Listen, Mother, please. This is really important. It's not that sort of trouble. I want you to get hold of the police.'

'The police? What on earth is going on?'

'I can't explain over the phone. But I want them to go round to the house and see what the matter is.'

'Kate, darling . . .'

'Mother, there isn't time to explain. Also I want you to ring this number. Have you got a pen and paper?'

'Wait a minute.' Kate could hear shuffling noises as her mother scrabbled round to find a writing implement. 'OK.'

Kate read out Martin's office number. 'You are to ask to speak to Martin Brayfield. If he's not there, ask the duty customs officer to get hold of him as a matter of urgency. Tell him I think that Andreas has done a bunk in Cyprus. He'll know what to do.'

'Andreas?' Honour sounded horrified.

'Mother please, just ring off and do what I've asked.'

'Right. Goodbye, darling.' For once her mother sounded quite brisk and efficient.

Now what? thought Kate. She could wait here for Martin to sort things out, but what if Andreas's mob was out looking for her? No, better if she could get right away. Please God, she thought, don't let Andreas have used his plane to get away. She rang the handling agent. It would sound odd if she asked if the plane was still there; after all, she was supposed to be its pilot. She kept her fingers crossed that it was still where she had parked it. Sound confident and perfectly normal, she told herself as the phone was answered.

'Hi, this is Kate Thomas speaking on behalf of Mr Andreas Spyrou. I want Golf Alpha Bravo Zulu Yankee refuelled and ready for take-off as soon as possible. Also would you file a flight plan to Farnborough in England for me?' she said to the agent.

'Sure thing, Mrs Thomas,' he replied.

Kate breathed a sigh of relief. The plane was still there and Andreas hadn't given instructions that it was to stay there.

409

Kate left the hotel to find a taxi. Despite the early hour there was bound to be one around somewhere, but it seemed ages before she tracked one down. In reality it was probably only a matter of twenty minutes or so but Kate was terrified that either the police or Andreas's staff would come looking for her and find her before she had time to get to the Citation.

'How much to Larnaca Airport?' she asked a tired-looking driver. He had an air of having been up all night.

The driver told her. Kate checked her cash. If she didn't worry about a tip she could just pay the fare.

'OK,' she said.

'No luggage?' he asked.

'No luggage,' Kate confirmed. Perhaps she could persuade the hotel to send it on one day.

When they reached the airport Kate directed the driver to the handling agent. On the concrete pan, shimmering in the early morning sun, was the Citation. Kate had never been more glad to see anything in her life. She thanked and paid the driver – who looked daggers when he realised he wasn't getting a tip – then scuttled into the office before he could shout at her. She'd had enough nastiness recently to last a very long time.

She was disappointed to find she couldn't take off for another half-hour. 'Damn.'

'Sorry, Mrs Thomas. There was no slot,' apologised the agent.

'It's not your fault.

'You going without Mr Spyrou?' he asked.

Kate's stomach lurched. Why was he asking? Then she realised that it was a perfectly innocent question. 'Yes, I've been sent back to England to collect some clients,' she lied. 'Look, I need to make a call. May I?'

'Of course.' He had a soft spot for the English lady pilot. He pushed the phone across the desk to her.

'I don't suppose I could make it from the other office?' she asked, giving him her best smile. 'It's a bit private.'

'Of course.'

Kate blew him a kiss and went next door. Quickly she dialled her mother's number. It rang and rang. No reply. Where was she? She tried Martin's number; nothing. He seemed to be out too. She tried her own number. The line was still out of order. Kate felt panic rising. She needed to know what was going on. This was hopeless. Damn Andreas for wrecking her mobile. At least if she'd had that her mother could have phoned her. Kate felt completely helpless. What the hell was happening, and was everyone all right?

She thanked her admirer for the use of the phone and went out to the aircraft to start her pre-flight checks. Despite her anxiety to get away and her fear that at any moment her disappearance from the hotel might be spotted, this was no time to cut corners. She had a good look at the outside, the tyres, the surfaces, before opening the cabin door and getting in. As she did this she realised that this might well be the last time she flew this little jet. Whatever Andreas was up to, if it involved drugs, she thought that his plane would probably end up being seized. Or did they have to catch him first? Well, either way, Kate reckoned she was out of a job. It was going to be interesting paying next month's bills.

She stopped wondering about her financial future and climbed into the cockpit. It wasn't that long till her slot. She put on her headset and called the tower to request permission to start engines.

'Roger Golf Alpha Bravo Zulu Yankee. Start approved. The temperature is twenty-six degrees.'

Thank God for that, she could get going. 'Zulu Yankee, roger,' she acknowledged. The sooner she got into the air the safer she would feel. She still wasn't too sure about the legality of her taking this aircraft. She didn't exactly have the owner's permission. Well, stuff that, she thought as she began the start-up sequence. She went through the checks quickly and efficiently. Everything was in full working order. She glanced at her watch. Her slot was coming up. She asked if she could taxi.

'Zulu Yankee, taxi to runway two-two. The QNH is one zero two zero.'

Kate set the figure, eased off the brake and began to head for runway two-two as directed. The Citation trundled along, the wingtips bouncing up and down fractionally each time the little plane crossed a join in the slabs of concrete. Kate began to feel quite relaxed as she completed her checklist. The de-icing boots worked, so did the brakes, and the instruments did what they should be doing as she changed direction. She was given her clearance and checked that she had copied it down correctly, then set her flaps for take-off; it was all hunky-dory. She reached the threshold.

'Larnaca tower, this is Golf Alpha Bravo Zulu Yankee, ready for departure.'

'Golf Alpha Bravo Zulu Yankee, clear take-off.' They gave her the wind speed and direction. She pushed against the throttle levers and the plane leapt forward.

Quite why she looked sideways at that particular moment Kate didn't know, but she felt a simultaneous feeling of shock and relief as she saw two police cars, lights flashing, screech to a halt outside the agent's offices. It might have been nothing, but Kate had a sneaking feeling they were after her or the plane. Either way they were too late. The plane raced along the runway, Kate pulled back fractionally on the stick and then it swooshed into the air. She was on her way home and she couldn't be stopped now.

There was a reception committee to meet her when she landed: Martin, naturally, Clive, the police and her mother. The first thing Kate noticed was that Edward wasn't there. As she climbed down the steps she was praying that it was because he was at school, but one look at her mother's face told her all was not well.

'Oh, Kate, darling,' Honour sobbed.

Kate, despite the fact that the sun was shining and the air was warm, felt every inch of her go cold.

'What is it?'

'It's Julie and Edward. We don't know where they are.'

Martin butted in. 'I'm sure there's a rational explanation.'

'I don't want a rational explanation. I want my son,' said Kate, feeling panic start to rise.

Chapter Thirty-Five

'Mrs Thomas,' said one of the uniformed officers, 'there was no sign of a struggle at your house and it looks as though your nanny and your son took a few things with them. It may be that they have gone to stay with a friend and forgot to tell you. I am sure that they will turn up safe and well very soon.'

How could this man be so sure? What did he know? If he was so fucking clairvoyant, why hadn't he found them? Kate thought angrily.

She looked around desperately. Why was everyone standing around here? Why weren't they out combing the country for her son?

'We need to go over recent events with you, Mrs Thomas,' he continued. 'You may know things that may lead to the arrest of Mr Spyrou and the safe recovery of your son.'

'Now?'

'I think the more you can tell us now, the quicker this can be resolved.'

Honour put her arm around her daughter. 'It'll be all right, darling,' she said.

'Oh Mummy,' sobbed Kate as her tension, fear and tiredness overwhelmed her. She flung herself into her mother's arms and buried her face in her shoulder.

Why me, she thought, why me? Not Edward as well as Eddie. Why doesn't God pick on someone else? she pleaded, and then she sobbed even louder as her own helplessness in this situation overwhelmed her. Honour patted her on the back soothingly and wished she could offer something more than mindless, banal platitudes.

Kate was still red-eyed and pale as she sat opposite Martin and the police officer and slowly and carefully went over the events of the last two days.

Finally, wearily, she said, 'And when I woke up he had gone.'

'And you had no idea that was what he was planning?' asked Martin.

'No. If you really want to know what I thought he had in mind, I thought he was planning to kill me.'

Martin smiled slightly. 'He's a criminal, that's for sure, but I don't think he's a murderer.'

Kate saw red. 'It's all right for you to sit there and say that,' she shouted. 'I'm the one who was there, remember. I was the one he locked in. I was the one who had found out what he was up to.'

'I'm sorry. I really am. You must have been terrified.'

Martin's kind words tipped the scales of Kate's precarious emotional equilibrium and she dissolved into tears again. She didn't notice him getting up from his chair and fumbling for a handkerchief.

'Here,' he said, pushing it into her hand. 'It's perfectly clean.'

'Thank you,' she snuffled, blowing her nose into it and trying to get control of herself. 'I'm sorry,' she apologised as her sobs subsided once more.

'Don't apologise,' said Martin. 'Not many young women could handle what you have just been through.' He placed a comforting hand on her shoulder and patted her in what he hoped was a reassuring manner. 'For the record, I think you have been quite remarkable throughout this awful business.' He sounded as though he genuinely meant it. Kate smiled wanly at him and her sniffs became less racking and more spasmodic. She was sorry she had shouted at him. It wasn't his fault that her son was missing.

'Right,' said Martin gently. 'If you are OK now can I just go over the details one last time?'

'If you must.'

Martin read from his notes. ' . . . and you say you don't know who he met in Nicosia as you went to do some private shopping. Then you met for lunch and finally drove back to Ayia Napa via the packing factory. Do you know where that was?'

'Not really. On the main road out of Nicosia.' She was able to say roughly where it was in relation to the road. 'And it must have been in either the first or the second village outside Nicosia itself.'

'Anything else? Any details, no matter how trivial.'

'I don't think the owner was too good at English,' she added flippantly. 'He hadn't noticed that some of the sticky labels that were being put on the fruit were misspelt.'

'How so?'

Kate explained.

'Thank you,' said Martin, leaving the room. 'I won't be long.'

'Can you find out if there is any news about my son?' Kate asked the policeman as the door shut behind Martin.

'I'll see what I can do, miss,' he said. He got out his mobile phone and rang a number.

'Don't you use radios any more?'

'Not if we want to talk to someone in particular. Sorry. Hello, yes. It's Constable Minors here. About Edward Thomas. OK, yes. Right, I'll tell her.' He ended the call. 'The boss says nothing yet. They'll tell you as soon as they know anything.'

'Thanks. Any idea how long that'll be?'

'No, sorry.'

He noticed Kate was staring at his mobile.

'Excuse me,' she said. 'Could I ask you a big favour? Could I borrow the battery from your phone for a minute, only I think it's the same make as mine.' The copper looked puzzled. 'Mr Spyrou took my battery away, to stop me making any calls. It's just possible Julie might have tried to ring me before the phone at my house went wrong.'

'It didn't go wrong, miss,' said the policeman. 'The wire to the house was cut.'

Kate had feared as much but it still came as a shock to be told as much. She breathed deeply a couple of times – she didn't want to fall apart again – then held her hand out for the battery. She clipped it in and keyed in her PIN. Blip-blip, went the phone. She called up her voice mail.

'*Kate, it's me, Julie. I'm scared. Something funny is happening. I'm taking Edward away. We'll be all right. Ring this number when you can.*' Kate heard Julie's voice detail a London number. She grabbed a pen and wrote it down. She listened again to check she had the number down correctly, and looked at the constable. 'Should I ring it?'

'I think we ought to find out the address of that number and send someone round. I'll get on to it.'

Martin returned from his errand. 'Come on, Kate, you look like you could do with a cup of tea.'

Kate suddenly realised that her last food had been what she had managed to raid from the minibar. Tea would be nice. He returned in a couple of minutes with a mug of hot sweet tea and Honour trailing in his wake.

'Kate, my darling,' she said, her voice full of sympathy, 'this is a perfectly ghastly situation but I do think the police are doing everything to help find Julie and little Edward.' She put her arm round Kate and gave her a hug.

It crossed Kate's mind that the only time her mother seemed to show her any real affection was when they were in the thick of a family crisis. She wondered how long it would be before she and her mother had another fall-out. No time at all if Horrible Henry was still on the scene. Kate couldn't resist asking.

'Does Henry mind you abandoning him like this?' She tried to sound innocent.

'Henry? What's he got to do with it?'

'But I thought . . .'

'Yes?'

'Nothing.'

'He was just a bit of company, but he got really very boring quite quickly. I haven't seen him in ages. If you had come round to apologise to me for the way you stormed out, I would have told you, but as it was . . .'

Some things would never change, thought Kate fondly. It was her fault for not apologising – her mother was, as always, the injured party.

Kate finished her tea, sipping at it nervously, wondering when she would get news of Edward. At last the door opened and the constable burst in, his face one enormous smile.

'We've got them. Right as ninepence. They're on the way down in an area car right now. Should be here in about forty minutes.' But Kate hardly heard the last bit, as she and Honour were both laughing and crying simultaneously. Martin was punching the air with his fist like someone who had scored the winning goal in an FA Cup Final, and yelling 'Yes!' and 'Brilliant!' alternately, and then, when Honour stopped hugging Kate, Martin grabbed her round the waist and spun her round. Now all her fears had gone, now everyone was safe and well, Kate allowed herself to enjoy Martin's attention. He was such a nice man – and so genuinely pleased for her that everything had worked out.

Edward, when he finally arrived, didn't seem to appreciate the enormous, enveloping hug his mother gave him and wriggled free at the first opportunity so he could tell anyone who would listen about his ride in a real police car with the siren going. In contrast Julie stood in the corner of the room looking white-faced and nervous.

'What's the matter?' asked Kate once the pandemonium had subsided a little.

'I didn't want to frighten you. I really didn't mean to. You must have been so worried when you found we had gone.'

'I was. Terrified. I thought Andreas had got hold of you somehow. I couldn't think what on earth for but I think he was quite desperate – desperate enough for him to want to disappear and desperate enough to do something terrible.'

'I didn't know what to do. I tried to ring you but I couldn't get through. There was this woman hanging around the house for about an hour and then she came to the door. She said she had a message from you and that there was a change of plan and because you were going to be in Cyprus for some time you wanted Edward to fly out to join you. She said you had asked her to escort him.'

'What did this woman look like?' asked Martin and Kate together.

'Short dark hair, very red lipstick, cross looking mouth.'

'Magda!'

'Who?' asked Julie.

'Someone who works for Andreas,' explained Kate.

'His cousin,' elaborated Martin. 'We got confirmation from

Interpol about her exact relationship with Andreas just after you took him off to Cyprus.'

'Ionescu isn't a Greek name, is it?' said Kate.

'It's her husband's. But Magda was born a Turkish Cypriot, like Andreas's mother. That's their connection with Turkey. That's why, when Andreas's family fled to the south they kept in contact with the north.'

'Anyway,' continued Julie, 'she didn't look very pleased when I wouldn't hand Edward over. I told her I was going to ring you to confirm it and shut the door. But I couldn't get through. The phone was out of order.' Julie stopped and looked sheepish. 'I know it sounds silly, but I felt she might have pulled the line out or something.'

'She had,' said Martin.

'You're joking?' Julie was open-mouthed. Martin shook his head.

'Carry on,' prompted Kate.

'Well, that's when I began to get scared. You hear about these weird people who try to take kids away under false pretences – pretending they're social workers or suchlike. I know I ought to have got hold of the police but what with the phone being out I suppose I just panicked. She was giving me the creeps, the way she was sat in her car watching the house, so I grabbed our toothbrushes and some clothes and took off to stay with a friend in London. I thought we'd be safer there.'

'Didn't she follow you?'

'Have you tried to follow someone in London?' asked Martin.

'That's what I thought,' said Julie. 'I knew she would lose us in all that traffic, and even if she didn't I would have been safer at Michelle's; her husband is six foot and once worked as a bouncer. When I got there, I tried to get hold of you but your phone was switched off. I left you that message in the hope that you would get it eventually. Edward and I were just about to come here to try and get hold of Martin when a socking great police car rolled up outside and they told us you had just landed.' Julie smiled at Kate. 'I've never been so pleased to hear anything in my life.'

'But why did Magda try to get hold of Edward?' asked Kate.

'My guess is that Andreas wanted you to fly him some-where and thought that if Magda had Edward in her clutches you would do exactly what he wanted,' said Martin. 'Or that Magda thought she could do with some sort of personal insur-ance of her own.'

'Scary thought. Thank God you were on the ball, Julie.' Julie smiled with relief that she had done the right thing. 'Where do you think Andreas and Magda are now, Martin?'

'Andreas is probably in northern Cyprus – most likely smuggled over the border along the same route the drugs came out. Does Black Knight checkpoint mean anything to you?'

'Isn't that the UN crossing point in the Eastern Sovereign Base Area?'

'Correct.'

Honour looked bemused. 'I'm afraid you've lost me, young man.'

'The British Sovereign Base area at the eastern end of Cyprus straddles the Green Line – that's the frontier that is manned by the UN – and both Turks and Greeks are employed on the base because they can both enter it without going through each other's territories. Andreas's Turkish contacts bring the stuff through on to the base and then hand it over to his Greek ones.'

'But aren't there checks?' asked Honour.

'Of course, but most of the people who work in the ESBA have done so for years. Because of the nature of the base most of them are trusted employees. They come and go every day. And of course once it's on the base there are no restrictions for getting out of there at all – hardly even a barrier. It would be a doddle for him to be smuggled northwards in a truck or car.'

'And Magda?' asked Kate.

'We don't know, but I expect she's already out of the country. I don't suppose she hung around once she realised things were going wrong for her.'

'Good riddance,' said Kate with feeling. 'Although I would have liked to have seen her arrested and charged.'

'We may get the pair of them back yet, although I wouldn't hold your breath if they've gone to ground in northern Cyprus.'

'Shame.'

*

The excitement was over and Kate was back home with Edward and Julie. Edward was pushing the remains of his supper round his plate and reliving his ride in the police car.

'The policeman said we were breaking the speed limit,' he said proudly. 'Does that mean we were going very fast?'

'I should think so,' said Kate, smiling indulgently.

'Can you break the speed limit, Mummy?'

'Well, it's not a good idea.'

'Why not?'

'Because it's not safe to go too fast.'

'So why did the policeman?'

'Because he was in a hurry.'

'What if you're in a hurry, Mummy?'

'Enough. I want you to finish you supper like a good boy. You've got school tomorrow, remember.'

'I missed today.'

'You did. But I'll explain to your teacher that it was a bit difficult.'

'Can I tell her about the police car?'

'Perhaps not on your first day.'

'Why?'

The obvious answer was that Kate would really rather that Edward's nice little nursery school didn't get to hear about her involvement with a crook. She looked at Julie, hoping for some inspiration.

'Because,' said Julie, 'it wouldn't do to make all the other little boys and girls jealous on your first day. They might not like you very much if you did and you wouldn't like that, would you?'

Edward was silent for a short time while he considered the pros and cons from the point of view of a three-year-old. Unpopularity versus the cachet of having had a high-speed ride in a police car – tricky. 'Can I tell them another day?'

'We'll see,' said Kate. She took his fork out of his hand, expertly mopped up the last few morsels and popped them in his mouth. 'Bath time,' she announced. Edward clambered off his seat and followed her upstairs, while Julie washed up the few bits and pieces and tidied the kitchen.

Kate returned half an hour later. Edward, exhausted by the events of the day, had fallen asleep long before Kate had got to the end of his story. She had tucked him up in bed, dropping a kiss on the end of his button nose and offering up a silent prayer of thanks that he was safe and well. She couldn't imagine how she would have coped if she had lost Edward too. It was an unimaginable horror. It had been terrible picking up the pieces after Eddie had died, but she had been able to mourn; she had known what had happened, she had known he had died instantly, that he hadn't suffered in any way. And cold comfort that that had been, it had helped her to come to terms with it all – eventually. But as she gazed down at the dark gold sweep of Edward's lashes on his pink cheeks, his fist clutching a teddy, his mouth sucking imperceptibly at an imaginary thumb, Kate wondered how the mothers of children who simply disappeared didn't go completely mad. How would anyone manage to get through even a minute of their lives without wondering what had happened? Was the child alive or dead; suffering; in pain? It was beyond horror to even contemplate it. Thank God Julie had been so sensible.

Kate smoothed the sheet down and tucked it in more firmly before blowing Edward a final kiss. She owed Julie so much – how was she going to break it to her that she would have to go? Kate sighed and steeled herself.

Chapter Thirty-Six

'Join me in a glass of wine,' Kate offered Julie as she walked into the kitchen. After the recent awful events life was returning to reassuring normality.

'Are you sure?'

'I wouldn't be offering if I wasn't.'

'That'd be great, thanks.'

Kate uncorked a bottle of supermarket red and glugged out two glasses.

'Cheers,' she said, raising her glass to Julie. 'And you know, I don't think I have thanked you properly yet for being so switched on when Magda came round last week.'

'It was nothing.'

'Hardly. It still makes me go cold when I think about it. Goodness knows what she wanted with him, some sort of insurance I suppose in case the police caught up with her.'

'Horrible thought. Have you heard if they have found her yet?'

'No. If I were her I would have scarpered back to Turkey.'

'Well, they're welcome to her.'

'I'll drink to that,' said Kate taking a sip of her wine. Julie followed suit. 'Julie,' continued Kate rather hesitantly, 'I don't just want to talk about how brilliant you were the other day. There's something else.'

'Yes?' said Julie.

'This business with Andreas buggering off.' Julie looked puzzled. 'It means, I'm afraid, that I'm out of a job.'

'Ahh.'

'And I won't have any money coming in.'

'Umm.'

'And I'm going to have to make some economies.'

'Yes. I was afraid it was going to come to this. I've got to be one of the economies.'

Kate twiddled the stem of her glass and nodded sadly.

'But can't you look for something else? I mean, surely there's something you could do?'

Kate took a big gulp of her wine. 'Don't you think I haven't been? Ever since I found out what Andreas was up to, I've been scouring the situations vacant for another post, but there isn't anything – nothing in flying and all the other jobs that I might be able to do just don't pay enough. I haven't got the experience in anything outside aviation to command any sort of decent salary. Things are already tight and it doesn't help that I don't suppose I'm going to see a pay cheque at the end of the month. If the news is halfway right, all Andreas's accounts are frozen while the fraud squad, the drugs squad and half the Metropolitan police force try to find out what he was up to. Martin says that it looks as though Andreas's business was on the verge of bankruptcy, which is another reason why he fled. It seems that their suspicions that he was trying to rescue it by expanding were right, and he was funding that with his dodgy dope deals. It seems as though it didn't work. So you see, if he has just gone bust then there'll be a lot more people out there who have a bigger reason to get a share of the leavings than I have. I'm sorry, Julie, but I simply can't afford to pay you any more.'

'How soon do you want me to go?' There was a hint of moisture in Julie's eyes.

'I don't want you to go at all but it's not fair on you. You can stay here as long as you like till you find something else. But apart from board and lodging I won't be able to offer you any sort of money. In fact, if I don't find the money for my mortgage, I don't even know how long I'll be able to offer you a roof over your head.' What with one thing and another Kate felt very close to tears herself.

'I don't want to go. It's been so lovely working for you. And I love Edward so much. I'll stay on for nothing as long as I can.' Julie sniffed, and two large tears rolled slowly down her cheeks.

'Don't, you'll set me off,' snuffled Kate, her tears spilling over too.

'But I mean it,' wailed Julie.

The doorbell rang.

'Who can that be?' said Kate, sniffing and rummaging up her sleeve for a hanky. She failed to find one so she grabbed a length of kitchen towel to blow her nose on.

'Coming,' she called as the bell rang again. Still sniffing slightly, she opened the door. 'Martin!'

He stood there looking faintly sheepish, then noticed Kate's still-damp face. 'I'm sorry, is this a bad time?'

'No, no, not really. Julie and I were just getting a bit maudlin over a bottle of red wine. Would you like to join us?'

'In the wine or the tears?' he asked with a grin.

'The wine, stupid,' said Kate.

'In that case, yes please.'

Kate led the way into the kitchen and got a third glass out of the cupboard.

'What brings you here?' she asked as she poured him some claret.

'I just came to check that you are OK,' he said, producing a big bunch of flowers from behind his back.

'I'm fine. What on earth are these for?'

'A present for the bravest person I've met in a long time.'

'Oh, for heaven's sake. Don't be so cheesy,' said Kate, embarrassed.

'I mean it. What you did was incredibly plucky. We had no right to ask you to do it and you ended up in a very dodgy situation. I'm sorry.'

'It wasn't entirely your fault. I could have bailed out, you know. I had a pretty good idea what Andreas was doing before I came to you, but I was so scared of not having an income, I tried to ignore it. Anyway, all's well that ends well. But thanks for the flowers. They're beautiful.'

'But you are OK?'

'I said, I'm fine.'

Martin's eyebrows shot skywards. 'Oh yes? And so why the tears when I arrived?'

'It's me,' said Julie. 'Kate can't afford to keep me on now she's out of a job. And I got all weepy – set her off.'

'Oh.' Martin didn't know what else to say. He took a drink of his wine.

'On a scale of one to ten it's not the end of the world,' said Kate, 'but we're both pretty miserable about it.'

'I'm not surprised. And what does Edward think of it?'

'I haven't told him yet. He needs to get over the last week's excitement before we tackle another obstacle.' Kate topped up their glasses.

'Not for me,' said Martin, putting his hand over the top of his. 'I'm driving.'

'Oh, come on. Take a taxi.'

'To Wiltshire?'

'You going to see your family, then?' said Kate.

'Not really. I mean, I am, but . . .'

'But what?'

'It always sound so ridiculous coming from someone of my age.'

'Uh?' said Kate and Julie together, neither of them understanding what Martin was getting at.

'I still live at home.'

'Is that all?' said Kate, suppressing a laugh. 'I did until recently.'

'I know, but it was different for you.'

'Hardly. And I bet your mother couldn't manage Gemma on her own.'

'True. But it's really just idleness that has stopped me looking for my own place. Mother, to put it bluntly, is loaded and could easily afford to employ a full-time carer for Gemma, and I could afford a place of my own, but I've never got off my backside to look for somewhere.'

'Well, if you hang around, you can buy this place. I'll have to put it on the market if I don't win the lottery in the next couple of draws. And then it'll mean *me* living with *my* mother again.'

'You'll find something.'

'Huh.' Kate was far from convinced. 'But all the way to Wiltshire! It's a hell of a journey you do every day.'

'It's not too bad, but it probably costs me as much in petrol as renting a room would, and I must admit that when I'm on the late turn or there's a flap on, I could do with having somewhere local to kip. It's my own fault. I'm just idle.'

Julie looked at her watch. 'Um, Kate?'

'Yes?'

'I don't want to break up the party or anything, but . . .' She began to hum, 'Da-da-da-da-daa-di-daa,' the rising and falling theme of a soap opera.

'Oh, go and watch it, philistine.'

Julie gathered up her glass and skipped off to the sitting room.

'She doesn't really watch that rubbish, does she?' asked Martin.

'Total addict.'

'And I thought my mother was bad.'

'She doesn't watch them too, does she?'

'You'd better believe it.'

'I liked your mother.'

'She liked you.'

'She hardly got to know me.'

'It was enough. She's a good judge of character.' Kate shrugged, feeling slightly uneasy with the compliment. 'And I like you too,' added Martin. Kate blushed. 'I was wondering, would you let me take you out to dinner? I feel I owe you more than a bunch of flowers.'

'Don't be ridiculous,' snorted Kate to cover her discomfiture. 'The flowers were more than enough.'

'Please. Couldn't Julie baby-sit?'

'It's a bit of a cheek – I've just told her she's out of a job.'

'Please.'

Kate gave in. Martin was rather nice, when all was said and done, and she deserved something nice to happen after the string of rotten events. Dinner would be more than acceptable and it would come as no hardship to get to know Martin better. She had a feeling that the more she knew about him the more she would like him – and to be honest, she liked him pretty well already. 'I'll ask, but don't bank on it.' She went into the sitting room where Martin could hear the murmur of her voice over the sound of the TV.

'I mean it.' Julie's voice came loud and clear. 'And don't you dare hurry back. I'm going to have an early night so I won't be here to play gooseberry later.'

426

'Sssh,' Martin heard Kate say.

She returned to the kitchen seconds later trying to look nonchalant.

'Well?' he asked, innocently.

'She didn't seem to mind too much. Best we aren't too late, though. It wouldn't be fair.'

'No,' said Martin, hiding a smile.

Dinner was more supper-at-the-local-pub than a romantic tryst in some swanky joint, but it was exactly what they both fancied. Kate had hardly eaten all day and wolfed down steak, chips and all the trimmings followed by banoffee pie and cream. Martin had the same but couldn't match the speed at which she cleared her plate. Kate managed to talk at the same time as eating and quizzed Martin relentlessly about his work, his background, his family and his travels. Good-naturedly, Martin didn't seem to mind the inquisition and even seemed flattered by her interest.

'And what about you?' he said at one stage.

'I can't think that there's much you don't already know, judging by the way you had me investigated when you thought I was working for Andreas.'

Martin had the grace to look a bit uncomfortable at this, until he saw the expression of wicked glee on Kate's face. They both laughed, and as Kate scooped up the last of her pudding and closed her eyes in bliss at its sticky sweetness, she regarded Martin from under her eyelashes. He's rather nice, she thought. In fact, she thought, he's nice enough to kiss. And as she thought this, she felt a thrill of excitement and anticipation.

'I'm impressed,' Martin said as he watched Kate lay down her spoon on an almost perfectly clean plate.

'Why?'

'There just seems to be no end to your talents.'

Kate pulled a face, thoughts of kissing banished. 'Get a life.'

'I mean it. You fly, you look like a fashion plate, you're a single mother, you can eat for England . . . Need I go on?'

'No,' she said, with a big grin, 'but you can if you like. I'm enjoying it.'

427

'Minx,' said Martin. 'Come on, I'll pay the bill and take you home. You can demonstrate to me that you can make coffee as well.'

'You're assuming a lot.'

'Why?'

'I may not want to ask you in.'

'Oh.' Martin looked completely crestfallen.

'Don't be silly, of course you can come in for coffee.' Actually, thought Kate, you can come in for almost anything you want, but she kept this rather naughty little idea to herself. Martin bounced off to pay the bill and then escorted Kate to the car.

When they arrived back, the house was in darkness.

'Has Julie gone to bed already?' asked Martin innocently as Kate let them both in.

'Apparently so,' said Kate, half wishing that the nanny hadn't been quite so good as her word and half grateful that she had. Part of her wanted an opportunity to be alone with Martin and yet another part of her felt wildly apprehensive. Supposing he didn't feel the same way, supposing he gave her the brush-off, supposing . . . Oh, never mind, they were here now. Let whatever was going to happen, happen. She opened the door wide to let Martin past as she extracted her key from the lock, and was acutely aware of his faint musky yet clean smell as he squeezed past. Kate was reminded that she liked men who smelt of being a man, rather than men who smelt of expensive lotions. Yum, she thought, then gave herself a shake.

'Now, coffee,' she said, switching on a couple of lights and bustling into the kitchen, deliberately ignoring where her thoughts were trying to lead her.

Martin followed her. Kate had had a glass or two of wine – well, rather more than that if she was completely honest – but even her rather dulled senses could tell that he was staying awfully close to her though there really was plenty of room. She tried to ignore it, pretend she was imagining it, that it was just wishful thinking – wishful thinking? Good heavens, no! – but as she finished filling the kettle and turned round to plug it in, she found herself staring at one of his shirt buttons, only half an inch from her nose.

'Oh,' she said with a squeak, but then she let her gaze move upwards. Martin was staring down at her, smiling. The kettle suddenly felt dreadfully heavy and Kate was aware that her knees didn't seem to be working quite as they should. She leant against him for support. Martin removed the kettle from her hand, wrapped his arms around her and nuzzled his cheek against her hair.

'I've been wanting to do this ever since that day at Farnborough when you cried on my shoulder about your mother.'

'Have you?' Kate tentatively linked her arms around his waist and snuggled her head more comfortably against his chest, breathing in his delicious smell.

'But there was the suspicion of your involvement with Andreas at the time.'

'So it was business before pleasure, then, was it?'

'I didn't mean it like . . .' started Martin defensively but stopped when he saw Kate look up at him, a broad smile on her face. He held her gaze and her smile slowly faded as she closed her eyes and edged upwards on to her tiptoes – or did he bend down slightly? Neither seemed to be aware of moving and yet they were drawn towards each other as inexorably as the tides are drawn to the moon. Their lips met, softly at first, and then with sudden ardour and passion.

'Stay the night,' said Kate, throaty with desire as they pulled apart after several minutes.

'I shouldn't,' murmured Martin. 'Mother . . .'

'With respect,' said Kate quietly and deliberately, taking his hand and kissing each of his fingers in turn, 'stuff your mother.'

'That's incestuous,' he retorted in whispered mock indignation.

'Then stuff me.'

'Were you this romantic with your husband?' asked Martin, laughing softly.

'All the time,' said Kate. And she thought about Eddie and realised that she didn't feel any of the guilt about wanting Martin that she had felt about Andreas. Was it because it was right, was it because somehow Eddie approved? She didn't know and she wasn't going to try and analyse it now as she

429

took Martin by the hand and led him upstairs.

Kate was surprised to find a little yellow note attached to her pillow when she switched on her bedroom light.

Dear Martin, it read. *Had an idea. Don't go till I talk to you in the morning. Love Julie. X.*

Kate sat on the bed giggling slightly tipsily. 'Was it that obvious that we fancied each other?' she asked, handing it to Martin to read.

'Lucky guess on Julie's part.' Then he sat on the bed beside Kate and took her in his arms again. 'Seriously, I've fancied you for ages but I always thought you were completely unattainable.' He began to undo the buttons of her blouse. 'You seemed to have so much – everything, in fact.' He slid his hand inside her top and began to caress her nipple. Kate moaned softly despite herself. This was more like it, she thought. When Andreas had made love to her it had been satisfactory, but that was the highest accolade she could have given it. He had been too wrapped up in his own pleasure, too selfish to notice Kate's desires and needs. She dismissed Andreas from her thoughts and turned towards Martin as together they rolled sideways on to the bed to lie in each other's arms and really begin to get to know each other.

'Mummy, Mummy, wake up,' insisted a small voice by Kate's ear. 'Is it time for school yet?'

Kate opened one eye groggily and focused on her watch – six thirty! 'No it isn't,' she said, trying not to sound too cross.

'Is that Daddy?' said Edward.

Daddy! Kate was suddenly wide awake. One glance made her understand the reason for Edward's fascinated stare. Swiftly she tugged at the duvet to cover as much of her and Martin's exposed flesh as was possible. 'No,' she said trying to sound casual. 'Just a friend.'

'Is it Martin?'

'Yes, yes it is.'

Martin was beginning to stir, disturbed by the hushed conversation beside him. 'Huh, huh?' His hand slithered over Kate's shoulder and tried to find her breast again.

'Back to bed, Edward,' said Kate loudly, hoping Martin would get the hint, but he just grunted and nuzzled closer.

Kate heard Julie get out of bed. So did Edward.

'Julie,' shouted Edward. 'Mummy's got a friend staying.'

That did it. That woke Martin up. 'Hiya, old friend,' he said, completely unfazed by the situation. Kate was impressed. It wasn't every red-blooded male who would accept, with equanimity, being caught stark naked and *in flagrante delicto* – or as near as made no difference – by a three-year-old boy.

Julie, yawning in her dressing gown and slippers, shuffled past the door left open by Edward. 'Morning, you two,' she said, rubbing the sleep out of her eyes. 'Tea?' Edward leapt off the bed to follow Julie downstairs.

'God, it's like Clapham Junction,' murmured Kate, still trying to rearrange the duvet to provide at least a modicum of decency.

'Was that a yes?' asked Julie.

'Yes,' said Kate. She lay back in bed, recalling the night before, aware that she didn't feel the least bit worried that both her son and her nanny had caught her in bed with Martin. She realised that she would have been devastated if they had found out about Andreas – looking back, it wasn't an affair to be proud of – but Martin was somehow different. She felt – she paused to check her feelings – yes, she did feel proud, and glad and happy. Was this love? It certainly wasn't exactly how she had felt about Eddie and it certainly wasn't the lust and the attraction of money and power that she had felt for Andreas. This was like putting on an old pair of slippers: comfortable, right, familiar. Downstairs she could hear Julie clattering about in the kitchen and Edward clamouring for a video. Kate rolled over and cuddled Martin.

'Morning, hunk,' she said giving him a squeeze.

'Morning, gorgeous,' he said, planting a kiss on her nose.

Julie tottered into the room carrying three mugs of tea. She placed one beside Martin and one on Kate's bedside table, then plonked herself down at the foot of the bed.

'Budge up,' she demanded. Kate, too surprised to protest, rolled away from Martin again and shifted her feet to give Julie more room.

Julie slurped her tea noisily. 'Did you get my note?' she asked.

'I did,' said Kate.

'It was for Martin,' said Julie with a smirk.

'OK, clever clogs, we noticed. So what was your big idea?'

'Well, tell me if it's none of my business but it seems to me the solution to everyone's problems is simple.'

'How?' asked Kate and Martin.

'Martin and I should swap places.'

'I beg your pardon,' said Martin, shaking his head disbelievingly, 'but what do you know about being a customs officer?'

'And, come to that, what does Martin know about child care?' added Kate.

'Probably a damn sight more than Julie does about Customs and Excise,' muttered Martin.

'I don't mean like that. Listen, you want to move nearer Farnborough, don't you?' Martin nodded. 'But if you do, there's no one to help your mother with your sister, correct?' More nods. 'And I'm out of a job.' She checked for nods so she knew they were still with her. 'So if I help your mother with Gemma, I get a job and Kate has a spare room she can rent – to you, Martin.' Blank looks. Julie went over her plan again as if she was explaining it to a group of pre-school children. 'You pay Kate rent, and that, coupled with the fact that she no longer has to pay my wages, means she can afford her mortgage. Meanwhile, your mum gets help and I get a job.'

'Well,' said Kate sounding doubtful.

'I don't know,' said Martin dubiously, picking up what he thought were Kate's reservations.

'You don't like it. Oh well, it was just an idea. I'll leave you in peace.' She got up to go.

'It's not that,' said Kate hastily. 'It's just a lot to take in this early in the morning. I need to think about it. I mean, what happens when I do get a job and I need someone to look after Edward?'

'You don't need a live-in nanny if you go for something that doesn't involve daft hours.'

Julie had a point, conceded Kate to herself. Out loud she said, 'But supposing Martin doesn't want to move in.'

'As if,' said Julie, rolling her eyes and raising her eyebrows.

432

'There's a difference between staying the night and moving in,' responded Kate a little tartly. 'And supposing Mrs Brayfield doesn't feel you are suitable to help with Gemma,' she continued.

Again Julie looked incredulous. '*Moi?*'

'Precisely. Look, it's fine in theory but just give us an hour or two to get used to it, please?'

'I can allow you that much time, I suppose,' she said with fake huffiness. 'But don't take too long. I may change my mind about my offer to move.' Julie took her tea and returned to her room.

'I'm sorry, what can I say?' apologised Kate.

'Don't. It's a brilliant idea.'

'But surely . . .?'

'But nothing. Julie's right. She would be great with Gemma, and it would suit me down to the ground to live round here.'

'But what about your mother? Supposing she and Julie don't get on?'

'Not get on with Julie? Do me a favour. Besides, it would suit Mum. I don't work regular hours so I'm not always around when she needs me. Anyway, the house is plenty big enough for Julie to have her own bit of it, so she and my mother don't have to live in each other's pockets. And it would be good for Gemma to have a girl of her own age around.'

'There is one problem that won't be easy to overcome.'

'What's that?'

'My mother. Can you imagine her reaction when I tell her I'm taking in a male lodger?'

'She won't approve?'

'Good God, no. She thinks taking in a lodger is only one step up from taking in washing.'

Chapter Thirty-Seven

'A customs officer?' exclaimed Honour. Kate thought that her mother couldn't have sounded any more horrified if she had announced that she was giving a pimp a room to operate from.

'But Martin's perfectly respectable,' protested Kate.

'If you say so, dear, said Honour, completely unconvinced. 'But I don't see why you want to keep that house on. You know you are welcome back home any time. I miss Edward,' she added a little sadly.

'But Edward goes to school here now. He has friends around here; I don't want to disrupt that. We don't live far away, and you're welcome to visit.'

'It's not the same. But a lodger!' Honour rolled her eyes at the thought.

'He's lovely. Anyway, you've met him. You met him the day Andreas did a flit and we were so worried about Julie and Edward.'

'Did I? I don't remember. I was more concerned about other matters that day than wondering what sort of tradesman my daughter was planning to invite to live with her.'

'You'll like him,' said Kate ignoring her mother's deprecating comment.

Honour gave her daughter the sort of look she might have used if Kate had tried to convince her that she would like tripe and onions if only she would try it.

'So when do I get to meet him properly?'

'I thought I could take you to see him next weekend. It's the Michaelmas fête in his mother's village and it's being held in the grounds of their house. He was telling me about it and it

434

sounds so much fun. It's a proper old-fashioned one, with pony rides and a coconut shy, a roundabout and swing boats. I'm sure Edward would love it. Why don't you come with us?' Besides, thought Kate knowing her mother only too well, when you clap eyes on the house you will instantly approve of Martin. Quite why her mother's approval mattered she didn't ask herself, but it did.

'Very nice,' said Honour, as they walked up the drive, having been requested to park their car on the village green. The chestnuts were turning and every now and again there was a soft rustly plop as another fat conker landed amongst the vegetation. Ahead of them was the Brayfields' beautiful house, looking magnificent in its frame of golden chestnut leaves

As they walked round the side of the house, Kate could see her mother taking in all the details: the pretty curtains at the windows, the carefully raked gravel, the stone urns still vibrant with colour despite it being late in the season, the beautiful gardens, and in particular the air of unassuming but considerable wealth required to produce the overall effect.

'Kate,' a voice shrieked. Kate spun round, recognising it.

'Julie!'

Julie flung herself at Kate like a Labrador welcoming its master home after a long absence.

'It's so good to see you. How are you?' yelled Kate in happiness.

'I didn't know you were coming. Martin said he had a surprise for me today but he didn't say what it was.' They were both talking at once, hardly listening to the other in the excitement of the reunion after a month of separation. Edward was jumping up and down trying to get his share of the attention, and for several minutes there was complete bedlam on the Brayfields' drive. Honour looked on with disdain at the sight of the young people making such an exhibition of themselves, while other villagers arriving for the fête smiled indulgently at the exuberant display of high spirits.

'Where is Martin?' asked Kate, finally.

'In the marquee. I'll take you there. Would you like to come along too, Mrs Hayleigh-Ffoulkes?'

'I'll follow in a minute,' she said.

435

'She wants to have a good nose-round while no one is looking,' Kate whispered to Julie as they set off along the front of the house together, Edward trotting happily alongside Julie, clutching her hand firmly as if he was never going to let her go again.

'So where is Gemma?' asked Kate.

'She's in her room. She doesn't like the crowds here and she's happier on her own. I'll have to go and check she's all right in a minute, but I'll show you where Martin is first.'

'And are you still enjoying it here?'

'It's wonderful. I love it. Gemma's a sweetie and Barbara is so nice to me. Talk about falling on your feet.'

'Well, it was all your idea. You planned this – I'm glad it's working out so well.'

They scrunched slowly along the gravel path towards the back of the house.

'And what's it like living with Martin?' asked Julie cheekily.

'He's the perfect lodger,' said Kate with feeling. And so far he had been, she thought. He was tidy, he could cook, he was great with Edward, he paid his rent on time and he was a knockout in bed. Not that Kate thought that lovemaking was the sort of attribute most landladies got to check out. She smiled at the idea.

Julie saw Kate's smirk. 'Is he now?' she said archly.

As Julie had predicted, Martin was in the marquee, helping to judge the homemade chutney competition.

'I don't think you can disturb him till the judging is finished,' said Julie. 'Everyone seems to take this all frightfully seriously.'

'They do,' agreed Mrs Brayfield from behind them. 'How nice to see you again, Kate. Martin told me about last month's excitement. I was so horrified to hear about it all.'

'Hello, Barbara,' said Kate with enthusiasm, thinking how much she would like her own mother to be like Martin's: practical, kindly, un-snobby. 'It was a bit scary at the time but it's all over now. Edward and I have nearly forgotten all about it, haven't we, Edward?'

'Forgotten about what?' asked Edward, who was riveted by the display of Victoria sponges and had been wondering if anyone would notice if he had a bit of one of them.

'I rest my case,' said Kate with a smile. She saw her mother come through the entrance to the marquee and waved to her to attract her attention. Julie used the moment to slip away to check on her charge. Honour came over looking much happier than she had for some time.

'Kate,' she said, ignoring the fact that her daughter was already in the company of a stranger, 'Kate, this house is to die for. You didn't tell me that Martin came from such a lovely family. You let me think he was some grubby little blue-collar worker's son.'

'Mother,' hissed Kate, mortified at her mother's dreadful exaggeration and knowing she had done no such thing. 'Mother, let me introduce you to Martin's mother. Mother, this is Barbara Brayfield. Barbara, this is my mother, Honour Hayleigh-Ffoulkes.' Unusually, Honour looked momentarily discomfited, but she quickly regained her composure.

'I was just admiring your house,' she said smoothly.

'So I gather,' said Barbara wryly. 'Look, the judging is finished and here comes Martin.'

'Hello, Kate,' said Martin, giving her a hug and a peck on the cheek. 'Hello, Mrs Hayleigh-Ffoulkes.'

'Call me Honour, please.'

Kate could barely suppress a giggle. He mother was *so* predictable. Always the snob. Kate had been almost married to Eddie before he'd been allowed to call her Honour, but then his family hadn't been able to boast a house like this.

'Why don't we leave Kate and Martin to entertain Edward and I'll show you round the house?' Barbara said to Honour.

'That would be lovely.'

Kate and Martin watched the two women walk off. 'Your mother didn't seem to be fazed by mine at all,' said Kate.

'Well, I have to admit to warning her a little bit.'

'Thank goodness for that.'

'I think it's important that they like each other, don't you?'

Kate was distracted from thinking too closely about what Martin might mean by such a statement by Edward pulling impatiently on her hand. 'Come on, Martin. If we don't give this one something to do soon, he'll take my arm out of its socket.'

'Then let's go to the merry-go-round,' offered Martin. They made their way out of the giant tent and down the garden to the carousel. Edward chose a wonderful horse called Valentine to ride, and hung on tightly to the gold post that held the horse in mid-air.

'He'll be OK on his own,' Martin assured Kate. 'This is a very gentle ride, it doesn't go too fast.'

The brassy organ music started, and Edward bravely removed one hand long enough for a perfunctory wave before clasping the post again as the ride began to revolve.

Kate remembered what Martin had said before Edward had distracted her. 'Why do you think it's important for our mothers to get on? It's not as if they need to see much of each other in the future.'

'Don't you think so?' said Martin, taking her in his arms. Beside them Edward whirled in and out of sight, shrieking with delight, but Kate, for once, had no eyes for him. She was gazing at Martin. 'I think they'll probably be seeing each other quite frequently, don't you?'

'Why?' Her heart was thudding like a steam hammer. Was she reading things right?

'Can't you guess?' said Martin. He bent down to kiss her, and then took a small square box from his pocket. Kate looked at the box and then at Martin, and suddenly felt incredibly foolish as she became aware of a couple of big fat tears rolling down her face.

'I'm sorry,' said Martin. 'I thought you felt the same way about me as I feel about you.'

'But I do, I do,' sobbed Kate.

'Then why the tears?'

'Because I can't remember the last time I felt this happy,' wept Kate, flinging herself against him and hanging on to him as if everything depended on the strength of her grip.

From the drawing room window the two mothers looked on and nodded in approval.

Sisters in Arms
Catherine Jones

If you can't take the flak, get out of the firing line!

The three of them couldn't have been more different. Red-headed Edwina, bursting with energy, attitude and Northern outspokenness. Lizzie, kind and tactful. The Right Sort. And Amanda, cool, logical, focused and deeply private.

From their first day at Sandhurst they had become friends, supporting one another against their common enemy – their sadistic platoon commander. Only now they have to go their separate ways to their first assignments and stand on their own...

Through the good times and bad, Edwina, Lizzie and Amanda are there for each other. But when a long-hidden secret emerges it shatters their friendship, seemingly beyond repair. Until they are forced to unite once more to face a threat from their old adversary...

A shrewd, unsparing, totally honest look at life for women in the modern army from the author who knows the truth from the inside...

Praise for *Army Wives*:

'A sexy romp'   *The Bookseller*

'If you like *Soldier, Soldier*, you'll love *Army Wives*'
                                                      Evening Express

'A sparkling combination of wit and insight'
                                        Cumberland Evening News & Star

Bouncing Back
Zoë Barnes

The new novel from the bestselling author of *Bumps*,
Hitched and *Hot Property*

Everyone has one really bad day in their life. For Cally
Storm it's the day she loses her job, her marriage and her
home. While everyone around her seems to be settling down
with Mr Right and 2.4 children, Cally is back living with her
mother. Still when you've hit rock bottom the only way is
up...

Everyone's got an opinion on what will turn her life
around: a new man, a new career... But the only job she can
get is at a local wildlife park. And as for romance – well, if
good men are so hard to find, frankly she'd rather not bother.
Only she's reckoned without the collective matchmaking
efforts of her friends and a strange – almost animal – attraction
to her unconventional colleague, Will. Can this wrongest of
Mr Wrongs ever turn out to be Mr Right?

The very best of Piatkus fiction is now available in paperback as well as hardcover. Piatkus paperbacks, where *every* book is special.

☐	0 7499 3088 8	Sisters in Arms	Catherine Jones	£5.99
☐	0 7499 3189 2	Bouncing Back	Zoë Barnes	£5.99
☐	0 7499 3212 0	Mad About the Girls	Francesca Clementis	£5.99
☐	0 7499 3193 0	Moving On	Emma Lee-Potter	£5.99
☐	0 7499 3182 5	Good Husband Material	Trisha Ashley	£5.99
☐	0 7499 3188 4	Mother Love	Martine Oborne	£5.99
☐	0 7499 3152 3	Pride, Prejudice & Jasmin Field	Melissa Nathan	£5.99

The prices shown above were correct at the time of going to press. However, Piatkus Books reserve the right to show new retail prices on covers which may differ from those previously advertised in the text or elsewhere.

Piatkus Books will be available from your bookshop or newsagent, or can be ordered from the following address:
Piatkus Paperbacks, PO Box 11, Falmouth, TR10 9EN
Alternatively you can fax your order to this address on 01326 374 888 or e-mail us at books@barni.avel.co.uk

Payments can be made as follows: Sterling cheque, Eurocheque, postal order (payable to Piatkus Books) or by credit card, Visa/Mastercard. Do not send cash or currency. UK and B.F.P.O. customers should allow £1.00 postage and packing for the first book, 50p for the second and 30p for each additional book ordered to a maximum of £3.00 (7 books plus).

Overseas customers, including Eire, allow £2.00 for postage and packing for the first book, plus £1.00 for the second and 50p for each subsequent title ordered.

NAME (block letters) _____

ADDRESS_____

_____

I enclose my remittance for £ _____

I wish to pay by Visa/Mastercard   Expiry Date:_____
